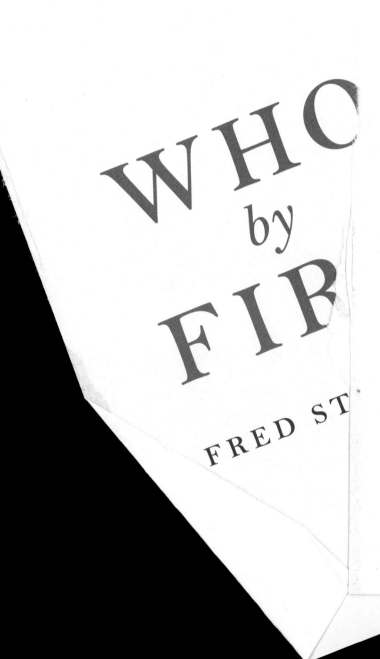

PRAISE FOR

WHO *by* FIRE

"On the page Stenson is like Frank Sinatra in a stetson—smooth and pitch perfect. And if details give literature its staying power, Stenson is writing for the ages."

—Caroline Adderson, *The Globe and Mail*

"Intriguing, fast-paced and a delight. . . . *Who by Fire* is the biography of Alberta. The story we all live today."

—*Calgary Herald*

"A novel that will stir inner emotions in the reader. . . . This is a must read for any Western Canadian."

—*Cochrane Times*

"*Who by Fire* reads like the work of someone who knows Alberta intimately—its booms, busts and echoes. It's a generational tale grounded in social critique, tragic and uncompromising, and [Stenson's] most powerful yet."

—*FFWD* (Calgary)

"An emotionally resonant, highly readable novel. . . . A well-researched and compelling narrative about the price paid in our complex relationship with an industry on which we are now dependent." —*The Globe and Mail*

"Alberta's Fred Stenson . . . has done Canadian literature a service by producing the long-awaited oil sands novel. . . . He portrays a corporate world in which oil companies have become better at speaking in soothing tones and issuing mild mea culpas, all the while speeding up their efforts to pump every last drop. And though he holds out some hope for personal healing from psychological wounds, he's clear that neither the oil companies nor the Alberta government are likely to change course."

—*Winnipeg Free Press*

ALSO BY FRED STENSON

FICTION

The Great Karoo
Lightning
The Trade
Teeth
Working Without a Laug
Last One Hom
Lonesome He

NON-FICT

Thing Feigned
The La
RCMP: T
Stor
Wo
Rock

Library and Archives Canada Cataloguing in Publication data is available upon request.

ISBN 978-0-385-66881-1

Who by Fire is a work of fiction. Names, characters, places and incidents are products of the author's imagination or are used fictitiously. Any resemblance to actual events or locales or persons, living or dead, is entirely coincidental.

Book design: Leah Springate
Cover image: Cover images: (landscape) Shahriar Erfanian, 41 Stories/Getty Images; (scratches) © Milosluz | Dreamstime.com
Printed and bound in the USA

Published in Canada by Anchor Canada,
a division of Random House of Canada Limited,
a Penguin Random House company

www.penguinrandomhouse.ca

10 9 8 7 6 5 4 3 2 1

Penguin
Random House
ANCHOR CANADA

To my sisters, Marie Gray and Lois Johnston,
and in memory of our parents, Ida and Ted Stenson

who will die at his predestined time and who before his time;
who by water and who by fire

Unetaneh Tokef, from the liturgy of the Days of Awe

PART ONE

So bright was the light outside his window that the frost on the stippled wall was glinting. This he saw as he came awake. A deep rumble from outside had woken him, and a humming in his bedspring. He reached above his head and touched a metal flower in the bedstead. It buzzed against his finger.

He slid from under the heavy tick. His feet found the hooked rug. Through his window he could see along the snow to the top of the church hill, could see the cross on the steeple that his mother's father had placed there on a windy day long ago. He wondered what could make a light at night brighter than a moon, and a sound that made a house shake. God, he supposed.

The boy heard voices. The younger of his sisters was crying and the older one scolding from their bedroom across the hall. Between his and their room was a grate in the floor to bring up heat. His father's growl and his mother's higher voice rose through it.

He went to the stairs and crept down. Through the doorframe at the foot, he saw the shadow of his father cross the window. His father was wearing winter underwear, and the boy could see the comical lump at the back: the poop-flap hanging by its button.

He did not announce himself but followed. He stopped in the kitchen while his father shoved his feet into gumboots in the porch. With no more clothes than that, his father opened the door and stepped into the freezing night.

The boy copied his father exactly. Bare feet into cold boots. He left the house and went down the shovelled cut to where the trucks were parked and beyond to where his father stood, his face a moving yellow.

Above the driveway hill, a fire leapt and twisted, like the fire in the Bible that burns without wood, or the fire that comes out of the rubbed lantern in Illustrated Folk Tales of the World. *A genie set free after a thousand years. The boy could smell hard-boiled eggs. His eyes stung. His stomach filled with pressure.*

His father set his big hand like a collar on the boy's neck, turned him, and pushed him toward the house. The boy ran ahead to where the door was open and his mother's nightgown glowed. She took him and held him to her hot flannel shape. When the door closed behind them, she asked, "What?"

"Sulphur plant," his father said. "Goddamn thing's upset again."

Teacups rattled in their saucers in his mother's china cabinet. The linoleum floor sizzled through his socks. A wall cracked.

The boy was embarrassed that his father's words for this were so small. The roaring genie eating the darkness needed more. The boy could not say it either, but someone should.

1

RUMOUR HAD IT there was going to be a gas plant, what some called a sulphur plant. The story had been around since the first crews came five years earlier, shooting seismic lines and drilling wildcat wells in the foothills. Ella first heard of the gas plant's actual location on a supply trip to town in summer. While Mildred rang up Ella's groceries at the Co-op, she asked, "Is it true the gas plant is going to be by your place?"

Ella said she had not heard anything like that.

"I did," Mildred said. "Near Ryders' and Bauers'. That's what I heard."

On the drive home, their youngest, Billy, sat in his usual spot on the front seat, tucked against his mother's side. The girls, Jeannie and Donna, were in the back, taking turns with a movie magazine they had pooled their allowances to buy. Billy had a *Classics Illustrated Robinson Crusoe* comic, but Ella could tell by the way he was leafing back and forth that he was losing interest. He would soon regret not having bought the one about Mickey Mouse and Donald Duck in Hawaii, and then he would cry. He was only five.

In fact, Ella started crying before her son did. The car was leaving the flat that contained the town of Haultain when the tears came.

"It's only a garage door," Tom said. She knew what he was thinking: that she was crying because of what had happened at her parents' place. They had stopped there for a minute to drop off groceries and Ella's parents insisted everyone come in for coffee and cake. Billy stayed outside and nobody noticed him climb into the car. He liked to sit behind the wheel pretending to drive. His father had told him to *never* touch the green button under the dash. Billy pushed the button, and the car had lurched into the garage door.

The car only went a foot before the transmission held. Still, it hit the door hard enough to crack it. Tom went racing out, and Ella followed. She could already see that Billy was fine, but she did not trust Tom's temper. Before she could stop him, he had grabbed Billy's arm and pulled him from the car. Ella caught her husband's sleeve and told him to let go. She had read that it was possible to pull a child's arm right out of the shoulder socket.

Tom dropped Billy's arm like a live coal and gave the boy a scolding.

"It's not the garage door," Ella said now. "It's the gas plant."

"Oh, hell," said Tom. "That Mildred likes to pass on bad news. She makes up half of it. How the hell would she know where the plant's going to be?"

"Those girls hear things. They hear everything."

"That doesn't mean what they hear is true."

"The way she put it. Ryders' and Bauers'. If she'd said it was near Ryders' place, that could mean farther away, but Ryders' and Bauers' means right at our place."

"Oh, for chrissake." Tom turned toward her and was not even looking at the road. As always he had a roll-your-own in the corner of his mouth. Ash fell and Ella grabbed at it. Billy flinched away.

"That company's not stupid. It's not going to set a plant on top of two families."

"You don't *know* that, Tom."

"Okay, I don't. But there's no sense crying about what you don't know either."

But the gas plant site was at Ryders' and Bauers'. Three weeks after that day at the Co-op, a stream of caterpillar tractors entered the field across from Ryders' driveway, followed by dirt haulers that Tom called yukes. The cats and yukes scraped off a big area—down to the clay—in the middle of Bauers' hayfield. Ella had been born in this house, had looked at that field all her life, and now it was nothing but a black and tan surface around which yellow machines crawled, carving and filling.

"That's less than a half mile from our house," Tom said as they stood watching. His voice was strained and peculiar. The whole family had walked to the top of the driveway hill, the wind in their faces.

"The stuff from the plant will blow right at us," said Ella, and Tom's look suggested he would like to argue but couldn't.

Not long after the machines showed up, Dora and Curt came over to the Ryders' house. They were good friends, had been neighbours forever. Both families had three children, almost matched in age and sex. When Billy saw the Bauers' car, he expected Petey to be in it. When Petey was not there, Billy went into a sulk, and Ella sent him outside to play with the dog.

Curt and Tom went to the living room, while Dora and Ella sat at the kitchen table. The women could hear the men, and the first thing Curt said was, "I should have told you before I signed."

Dora turned to face Ella. "The company man who came to the house said the site was on our land. We thought we could say no if we wanted, but that's not true. Since the government owns the mineral rights, they'd already approved it. We didn't really have a choice, except to sell part of the land or all of it." Dora paused, sat up straighter. "And you know, Ella, their offer was better than what land goes for around here. I can't speak for Curt, but I think we might have argued harder if it had been a normal price."

Then she started to cry. "Curt asked me to come outside with him. We stood there looking at our field. The man from the company had pointed at the spot and asked us to imagine a gas plant there. He asked us to think what it would be like to live so close. Curt said he thought we shouldn't dicker. We should take their price now, in case it went down."

Ella was imagining herself in Dora's shoes. She knew that she wouldn't have had the same thoughts. Dora wasn't born and raised on their farm. Ella didn't think Dora's decision had been easy, just different than her own would have been.

Tom came into the kitchen, talking back over his shoulder. "Oh hell, Curt, don't worry about it. Wouldn't have changed anything if we'd talked." He was on his way into the pantry to get the whisky bottle. Ella went to her china cupboard for the little glasses.

"I imagine we'll move closer to town," Curt said as Tom poured the whisky.

Dora said, "I thought we might as well move closer if we're moving."

"Closer's good, especially in winter," Ella said, though she didn't believe it. She preferred this distance.

The men went back to the living room, and somehow that was a signal to the women. Dora rose. They hugged each other, weeping freely.

"Whatever will I do without you, Ella?"

"Let's not worry" was all Ella could think to say.

———

The Bauers moved on the Dominion Day long weekend. The Ryders and their Dutch hired man, Kees, helped empty the rooms and fill the two grain trucks. Every time a piece of furniture was taken out, the space it left held some lonesome fact, but the work was hard and kept everyone on the dry side of grief—until Dora and Ella moved the old crib. Now that Petey was a boy, the crib did nothing but hold Dora's ironing. Still, picking it up made the two of them cry so hard they had to set it down again. How were they *not* to think about their time together, their lives as women led so amazingly in tandem? Sixteen years ago, their husbands had taken them to the Haultain hospital on the same day. Within hours of one another, they had given birth to their first children, both girls. They were not the kind of women who liked to talk about such things, but Ella knew from various signs that they had their monthlies at the same time, were simply joined together in that way.

By mid-afternoon the Bauer household was mostly loaded into the trucks. It had been agreed that only Tom and Kees would drive over and unload at the other end. The two sets of children stared at each other in numb confusion. "We'll get together all the time," Dora said, with her arms across her daughter's shoulders.

"You children can use the phone to talk," Ella added. But all six kids stood like stones.

Ella stayed with her children in Bauers' yard until there was nothing to see but dust hanging over the road. Then Jeannie, the eldest, said, "This is stupid," and started walking home. Ella, the girls, Billy—they all fanned out, wanting to be alone.

Two weeks later, at the end of a blistering day, Ella took Billy upstairs to bed. She noticed that Jeannie and Donna's bedroom door was closed. She thought it must be terribly hot in there, and she was on the verge of throwing the door open to allow a breeze, when she stopped herself. The closed door meant Jeannie was having, or about to have, a cigarette. She kept them in a little cedar box that had belonged to Ella's mother. Ella checked the box when she cleaned, and some dry crinkly specimen of a cigarette was usually there, on a bed of Jeannie's cheap jewellery.

As long as Ella did not let on that she knew about Jeannie's smoking, she did not have to have a fight with her headstrong eldest daughter. She would rather Jeannie did not smoke, but a lot of girls did. What ladylike meant was being reshaped by the movies, and who could control that? If she thought Donna was also smoking, Ella would have intervened, but somehow she knew Jeannie would not offer and her sister would not ask. Likely, Donna would be disgusted but would pretend otherwise. Donna was thirteen and only beginning to question her sister's authority.

Ella started down the creaky steps, Jeannie's cue to light up. She imagined her daughter hunched in front of the metal screen set in the summer window; imagined her blowing smoke through the wire.

Downstairs, instead of returning to the kitchen, Ella went into her own bedroom. She opened the closet door and pressed back the hangers. One of the oddities of the old house was that you could hear the girls' room perfectly from inside that closet.

"Rhonda and I went to the barn and had a smoke on their moving day," Jeannie was saying. "She told me the barn was going to be knocked down and burned. The house too. Burned to the ground. The plant people don't want anyone to live there, not ever again."

There was no sound from Donna. Jeannie must have thought she wasn't getting through to her sister, because she said again, quite loud, "Burn down the house!"

After some smoking time, Jeannie started in again. "You know, if the house you've lived in all your life is burned, your whole life goes with it. You can't go to the places where things happened, and that makes it like nothing ever did happen. Rhonda'll be a zombie."

This time Donna did say something. Her voice was smaller, and Ella had to strain to make it out. "The people who live at the plant aren't." During the last two weeks, crew shacks had popped up beside the plant site: flat-roofed affairs, each one containing four living spaces. Donna perhaps meant that those people moved all the time, but they still had memories.

"Take Mom, though," Jeannie said. "She's lived her whole life in this house. She was born in it. Her father built it. It's a good thing we're not selling out or she'd be a vegetable too."

"Maybe we will."

"Be vegetables?"

"Sell out and move."

"Don't be stupid. Mom would never. And Dad knows better than to try."

"What if we had to?"

"You don't know what you're talking about."

There was some noise Ella could not decipher.

"Oh my God, Donna! Quick!"

Ella imagined the two girls fanning smoke toward the screen.

When summer ended, Jeannie and Donna took the bus to St. Theresa's Roman Catholic school in Haultain. It was Jeannie's third year of going to town school and Donna's first. At the end of June, the one-room school east of the farm had closed.

All five days of that first school week, Billy walked his sisters up the driveway to the bus and came back with a big lip. Keeping him amused was going to be hard.

By then, many of the steel structures at the sulphur plant had been erected, including a flare stack that, on some days, held a meagre flame. Tom and Ella had learned the term "flare stack" from Don Harbeg, a bachelor farmer who lived south of the river. Don's farm was only a quarter section, and he had always worked other jobs to support it. Before the plant had even advertised for help, Don went to the trailer office and asked if he could work. They gave him a job, just like that. Pleased to be the centre of attention, Don gave the community weekly reports, on the steps of St. Bruno's after mass.

During summer, a few phone calls came to the Ryder house from representatives of Aladdin Oil and Gas. Ella always answered; she was in the house more and Tom hated telephones. Ella was used to American accents, because most everyone across the river to the east were Utah Mormons. But these accents on the phone were different. Some were so drawly she had to cover the mouthpiece in case she laughed.

The last caller said that somebody from the company was going to pay them a visit, but no date was mentioned. Mr. Clint Comstock was the visitor's name, and he intended to visit all the local families. Mr. Clint Comstock was a busy man, and it was not easy to find time for them in his schedule.

"Of course we're up here sitting on our hands," Tom said.

The visit happened toward the end of September.

"Clint Comstock and his assistant will be at your house in an hour," a fellow said on the phone.

Ella ran to her car and raced to the Lower Place. She found Tom and Kees in a field of wheat, rubbing kernels into their palms and chewing them. Tom looked up, saw her, started over.

"Goddamn him," Tom said when she'd told him. "He should've given us more notice."

"I don't even have time to bake."

"Give him last week's scone same as you give me. Don't bend over backwards."

She waved him off—not his business. She jumped in the car, U-turned, and returned up the road.

Ella was barely back home when the white car pulled into the yard. She answered the door and invited the two men in. She said for them to sit at the table, and Mr. Comstock sat in Tom's place. It seemed rude to ask him to move so she didn't. She had a fire in the stove and a pot of coffee ready to perk. She set out small plates, knives and butter, along with the plate of dry scones.

Clint Comstock was tall and broad shouldered, possibly less broad shouldered than his western jacket pretended. Under it was a bone-coloured shirt. He had on blue jeans with a razor-sharp crease. He wore his blond hair brushed back same as Tom, but the Texan controlled his hair with pomade, a sickening smell like the beginning of rot. He was so red across the cheekbones, like he had gone at himself with a wire brush.

That Mr. Comstock was sitting in Tom's place seemed not to matter until Tom arrived. After introductions, Tom had to sit on the children's side, and Ella could see it made him ill at ease. She had the odd thought that someone who did not know them, coming into the house, might assume it was Comstock's home, that she was Comstock's wife. Tom would look like a shy visitor, maybe a vagrant looking for a job.

As soon as Ella poured the coffee, the Texan pushed the cup forward on the table and set his hands behind it, fingers laced. He spread his elbows wide so they almost went to the table's corners. He had by now taken a scone. He'd broken it in two and buttered it, but had put the pieces back on his plate without taking a bite.

The younger man had a brush cut, so close you could see the middle bone of his head. Comstock introduced him, but Ella promptly forgot the name. She felt she was supposed to forget. This one rustled around in a briefcase and set out writing pad and pen.

From the start, Ella could see that Clint Comstock was a mixture of politeness and pushiness. In the introductions he'd called them Mr. and Mrs. Ryder, but abruptly switched to Tom and Ella without being asked. Now, he looked Tom in the eye and pushed himself forward so his chest was tight to the table. This caused Tom to slide his chair back, cross his legs, and start rolling a cigarette. When Comstock spoke, he mostly addressed Tom, but swung around every few sentences to toss a few words at Ella. This part was just small talk. He adjusted himself to indicate when he was moving on to business.

"I wanted to say hello to our nearest neighbours. It's nice of you folks to make time for me."

Without looking, he reached to his assistant, who put a sheet of paper in his hand. Comstock set it on the table and twisted it around so the print was right side up for Tom.

"You can keep this. It includes what we call plant specifications. A copy of it was filed with your government in Edmonton. Your health minister and the minister of mines and minerals signed it. So did your premier, Mr. Manning. Yours is a farmers' government, isn't it."

"Started that way," said Tom, showing a bit of his real self. "Sometimes they forget."

Comstock pointed at one of the numbers. "When we're up and running, we'll be processing hundreds of thousands of cubic feet of gas a day. That's to start with."

"You mean it'll get bigger?" Tom said.

"That's right. In a year or two, we'll move to the second phase."

"How much bigger?"

"Several times bigger. Millions of cubic feet."

Tom's cigarette had gone out. He felt his trouser pocket for his lighter. He pushed it up with his fingers until the metal head showed.

He flipped the lid and thumbed the wheel, he closed the eye nearest the flame.

Tom pushed his tobacco pouch toward Comstock, but the other man held up his hand. He probably thought it a primitive way to smoke.

Tom breathed out a cloud and said, "Maybe you better tell us how this plant will be to live beside."

"You know what I mean when I say it's a sour gas plant, right?" Comstock said.

What they knew came from Don Harbeg and a piece in the *Haultain Herald*. Tom said he wanted Comstock to explain from scratch. This was smart, Ella thought. Better than trying to show off and getting confused. She wasn't sure yet how she knew, but she felt Comstock wanted Tom to make mistakes that he could correct.

"Sour means natural gas containing hydrogen sulphide," Comstock said. "The gas here's about eleven per cent hydrogen sulphide, and there's also six per cent carbon dioxide. The second field we're testing for this plant is over twenty per cent hydrogen sulphide. The plant will run at fifteen hundred pounds per square inch. Trust me, that's a lot of pressure." Clint Comstock leaned back in his chair.

Ella felt a weight or a pressure lift from her and imagined Tom feeling the same thing.

"I'm not going to pussyfoot with you, Tom, Ella. This hydrogen sulphide is poisonous stuff. In certain circumstances, it can kill a person."

Ella felt a new pressure come on. She understood then that this was something Comstock was doing on purpose.

"Nor am I here to scare you. That plant we're building in your neighbour's field has several functions, but the main one is to change that dangerous gas into something safer. I see you've got a good old wood stove there. I grew up with one just like it. I'll bet you five dollars that within five years you'll have a propane tank outside. In ten years, you might have a natural gas line right to your house. Those fuels are products we'll make at our plant."

He broke off a tiny piece of his scone, lifted it toward his mouth, then set it down again. He reached toward the assistant, and this time the young man placed a little yellow brick on his palm. Comstock held the brick out to Tom.

"Go ahead, take it. The plant's main by-product is this, sulphur, which might wind up in the fertilizer you spread on your grain field. It's dark orange in its liquid form. When it solidifies, it turns this nice lemon yellow. You can keep that."

Tom weighed the brick in his palm, then handed it to Ella. It was heavier than it looked. She held it to her nose and it had a nasty but familiar odour. The smell of a lit match.

"How do you get the sulphur out?" asked Tom. He was becoming more confident.

"It's complicated, but, to put it simply, you heat the raw gas very hot. You add oxygen. There's a chemical reaction. You get liquid sulphur out one end and sulphur dioxide out the other."

"Does all of the poison get changed?"

Comstock favoured Tom with a wink. "You're an astute man, Tom. Nope. Chemical reactions never react a hundred per cent. Our plant is built to recover ninety-three per cent. That's state-of-the-art."

"That other seven per cent must be dangerous."

"Right again. It could kill you."

Comstock said this and held a sombre impression. Then he let his lips spring apart over his big white teeth. He laughed and slapped his leg.

"But *that's* not all we do with the hydrogen sulphide. We're just now completing the sulphur stack. It's got an incinerator at the bottom, one that will burn at one thousand degrees Fahrenheit. In that incinerator, we'll burn the residual H_2S—that's what we call hydrogen sulphide, H_2S. We'll send what comes off that fire up the sulphur stack. That cement stack will be eighty feet high for two reasons: so the gases cool before they exit, and so they go high in the air, where the wind can take them away."

Comstock made an upward motion with both hands—gas shooting out the stack. Then he nodded at the window. "It's blowing pretty good out there today. I gather that's typical."

Ella and Tom started talking at once. Ella gestured for Tom to say it.

"This is a calm day. Wind here can blow hundred mile an hour."

"Well, there you go," said Comstock. "That's going to help a lot. Dispersion. We'll also be pumping out some sulphur dioxide, and some people ask me if that's dangerous. What I say is, if you had to sit with your head in a bag of sulphur dioxide, it would be an uncomfortable experience. But once it's shot out that big stack, blown all over the place by this wind, it won't be anything at all."

The assistant started packing things into his briefcase. Ella was struck by how much this was like a recent visit from a vacuum cleaner salesman. Spiel, demonstration, pack up, go. A formula. But then Clint held out his hand to stop the secretary.

"Hold on. Let's let these folks ask their questions."

The secretary looked at his watch.

"Never mind that. What about it? Ella? Tom?"

Both were flustered. They should have had questions but none came to mind.

"It's going to smell, isn't it?" said Tom finally.

"Yes, it will smell. Tom, let me be blunt. Some people dislike living near these plants so much they prefer to move away. I understand you and the Bauers are friends. As you know, we offered them a chance to sell out and move, and they took it. I can't say for sure, but my feeling is that Aladdin Oil and Gas would make you a similar offer if you want to go."

Ella knew he was going to say this as soon as he'd mentioned the Bauers, but when he got to the words "want to go," tears jumped into her eyes. She put her hand to her brow to hide it, but Comstock noticed.

"I'm sorry, Ella. I've upset you."

She shook her head.

"Ella was born here," said Tom. "It's her parents' homestead." From beside her fingers, Ella saw her husband raise and lower his shoulders at Comstock.

She wiped her eyes on her apron. "I cry easily. People who know me don't pay any attention."

She felt angry was what she felt, at both of them. It was the feeling that everything in the last hour, even her crying, had been made to happen by Clint Comstock, and that Tom was being duped. She could not help feeling angry at herself too. If it wasn't for her feelings about this farm, leaving would be an option: the possibility of putting their backs to these Texans and their stinking plant.

"I understand, Ella. I'll also admit it's not the best of luck that the preferred engineering location for our plant happens to be so close to your farm. Upwind, to boot. Thank you for the coffee and the delicious scone. I'm sorry I left some. I just had lunch. Thanks for being honest with me. I hope I was honest back."

There was his big white smile, his hand demanding to be shaken.

After the assistant had piloted the white car from the yard, Tom stayed sitting at the table, smoking. Ella gathered the cups and plates. She put Comstock's scone, of which he had not eaten one crumb, into the swill pail in the porch.

"I like him," Tom said when she came back.

"I don't." Ella went to their bedroom to lie down.

Clint Comstock phoned from Houston in December and told Ella to expect the plant to go into action during the first week of the new year. It now had a name: Aladdin Hatfield.

On every Sunday leading up to that day, the talk on the steps of St. Bruno's was what would happen next. As much as people could tell from the outside, construction was complete. The tallest, fattest tower, a giant concrete tree, stood alone, while shorter silver towers pierced through metal roofs and shone and sparked in the sun. Ladders wrapped these towers, giving them a fairy-tale appearance. At night, when he was trying to sleep, Tom, who had a fear of heights, yielded to sick imaginings of climbing them. During the day he made fun of it all. It was he who had come up with the name "Sulphur City."

Don Harbeg had been working full time on the plant's construction since harvest, and at church he drew crowds with his explanations. He said it was inside the silver towers that the fuels would be split out: propane, butane, and the mixture that made car and truck gasoline. "North of the cement stack is the sulphur building. Big vessels in there extract and condense the sulphur." He flung around words like "condense" and "extract" as though he had always known them.

Besides the new words, Tom had noticed that, if someone said something about the plant that wasn't favourable, such as that it would stink more than anyone was admitting, Don would say he doubted it, that the plant was going to be all right. Tom suspected that Clint Comstock had hired Don Harbeg so he could play this part. If you worked on something, it was natural to stick up for it. The Texan's strategy was that of a cutting horse: get one out, then try to get another from the herd to join it.

———

The time for the plant to start operating came marching toward them. It was like the plant was filling with pressure and they could feel it in their own bodies. As Christmas neared, the normal good feelings that came with the season were replaced by an anxious mood. There were arguments about things that had never been argued about before.

Part of the Ryders' Christmas tradition was a buying trip to Lethbridge. Some neighbours went farther, to Calgary, but Tom found Calgary an unnerving place to drive. Lethbridge had wide streets and a few street lights that changed colour on a leisurely schedule: a farmer's city.

When the Ryders crossed the Old Man River Valley into Lethbridge, they ducked under the railway bridge and passed the brewery garden with its Christmas display. They parked in their usual place a block from the biggest stores and walked downtown together. At that point, they divided up so they could buy each other presents. Ella made the girls take Billy, and they groaned their disappointment. Billy was too excited to take offence.

Tom went to Woolworth's and walked back and forth along the jewellery counter. A salesgirl with a Christmas corsage on her white blouse homed in on him, but he turned his back. He did not want help so much as time to think. Ever since the construction machines came and the Bauers left, he and Ella had been bickering. It was a kind of irritation more than actual fighting, but it was getting worse. Ella claimed he was angry every time he came in the house. He thought he was no different than he'd ever been. There was just more to be angry about.

Tom wanted to give Ella a present that showed he had put some thought into it. But he could not spend any more than he usually did. Ella did not like extravagance and would take it back if he over-spent. He stared at every object in the glass case, then at its price tag. He would only submit to the salesgirl if time ran out.

Then it caught his eye: a silver brooch a couple of inches high that was one of the symbols on a sheet of music. Ella's parents had been short of money all their life but had sprung for an upright when the Heintzman man came around. Ella had taken lessons as a girl and nowadays played the organ at St. Bruno's. During the summer of their courtship, Tom had groomed and saddled his horse and ridden across the hills to visit her. Sometimes they went riding; other times they sat in her parents' living room, and Ella played for him.

The brooch was the perfect thing, and now he was nervous lest it get away.

"What's this called?" he asked the girl as she came up behind the glass cabinet. "It's got to do with music."

She looked like the kind of girl who would have had music lessons.

"Treble clef," she said. "The other one's the bass clef, but we don't have a brooch for that."

"Treble clef," Tom repeated, and asked her the price. She reached inside the cabinet and flipped the tag, and he felt a thrill of relief. It was high but in the range Ella would accept. He paid the extra to have it gift-wrapped.

Tom now had time to kill. He went to the lunch counter at Kresge's and treated himself to a chocolate milkshake. It took a while to notice that Ormond Cardwell was three stools down, having a bottle of orange pop and a piece of pie with ice cream.

Ormond and Tom had known each other since childhood. Ormond's family lived close to the Kootenay River on the Mormon side, while the Ryder place was two miles away on the west side. On hot summer days, the Mormon and non-Mormon children had gravitated to the same swimming hole. Between swims, they played baseball on the river bench, Mormons against the rest. Nowadays, Ormond was a member of the Alberta legislature.

When Tom waved and got the MLA's attention, Ormond said, "Well, for heaven's sake, Tom. Will you join me?"

Tom left his emptied milkshake can and moved to the stool beside Ormond. He felt compelled to make his first question about the government, to which Ormond gave a joking response. "We're stealing your money as usual."

Tom wanted to bring up the gas plant, but Ormond did it for him.

"How do you feel about that plant?" he asked. "Having it so close?"

"I don't understand why they had to put it on our doorstep. Why were they allowed?"

"Thing is, Tom," and Ormond twisted on his stool to face him, "our government doesn't know a heck of a lot about oil and gas. We have a conservation board, and that was a good thing to create, but mainly it's those conservation board engineers talking their mumbo-jumbo to the same types on the oil side. When they're done, they make recommendations and usually we accept them. Frankly, we always do. They said Curtis Bauer's farm was the best place for the plant, based on gravity flow or something, and we said okay. Our health man, Dr. Onge, is well educated, and he badgered them pretty good on air and water. Anyway, I'm sorry it landed on you."

Tom looked away. He didn't like the answer but was grateful for Ormond's seeming honesty. "I guess these things bring in money," he said.

Ormond smiled wide. His teeth were full of lead but they were his. "Oh, do they ever. When I think of how it was for us? One ball glove per family. Old broken bat held together with nails. It's going to be a lot different for our kids."

"They probably won't be farmers, though."

"That could be a good thing."

Ormond and Tom were thinking about different kinds of families. Ormond had big Mormon ones in mind, where not all the kids who wanted to farm could. Tom had three kids and only one son. If his son moved on, and his daughters didn't marry farmers, Ella and Tom's farm might not last beyond this generation.

"And Ella, how's she dealing with it? She grew up on your farm, didn't she?"

"She did, and it upsets her to see it changed. None of us really likes it or knows what it will be."

Ormond had a pen and pad beside him. He wrote his government address and phone number, tore out the sheet, and handed it to Tom. "I'm not the most powerful guy up there, but if things happen that are bothering you, let me know. Right now, I best go find my wife before she spends the whole paycheque."

They stood up and shook hands. Wished one another Merry Christmas.

The offer seemed genuine, and kind given that Tom did not live in Ormond's riding. Tom put the slip of paper in his shirt pocket, and the two men shook hands a second time.

Around noon on January seventh, 1961, the plant's flare lit with a crack that ricocheted like a rifle shot off the Ryders' barn. The flare grew, and grew again, against the western sky. The plant ripped and snorted all that day and the next.

Around midnight on the third night, the rotten egg smell began coming into the house, thick and continuous. Everyone in the family had headaches, sore throats, were sick to their stomachs. Billy said he could feel something swelling inside him. He kept talking about it until he threw up. Wiping his face, he said, "It broke," which made everyone laugh. He was right too about the sensation the gas caused. It was different than normal nausea. Just like Billy said, it was like something swelling slowly inside you.

The following afternoon, the girls came home on the school bus and said they'd felt better the moment they left, had felt good all day at school. Tom, Ella, and Billy had been sick all day. This proved it wasn't the flu.

When Tom stared at Sulphur City, he boiled with frustration. The plant never looked any different, just buildings and towers, and the flare and steam rising in the blue cold air. You wanted to see some putrid yellow or purple smoke, or an explosion, something you could point at and say, "There it is. There's the bastard that's making me sick."

In the late afternoon of the fifth day, black smoke billowed from the ground on the plant's nearest edge. Whatever was in that smoke entered their throats like a rasp. Billy started coughing and could not stop.

In the night, the boy woke crying. Ella got up from beside Tom and ran up the stairs. She shrieked and then Billy did too. When Tom got there, Ella was sitting on the edge of the bed, holding their son and rocking him. In the light from the bed lamp, one shoulder of the boy's pyjamas was wet and black, and so were the pillowcase and sheet. Ella had the corners of a handkerchief wound into his nose.

"I lost all my blood," Billy whimpered to his father.

"It's almost stopped," his mother said. "I told you your body makes blood, remember? It's making blood right now to replace what you lost."

Tom had been told by the plant to call if anything serious happened. Ella was still busy with Billy, so he went down and cranked the hated phone himself. He was surprised the operator came on right away. He had never made a call at night and thought he'd have to wait. When she rang the plant, someone young answered.

"This is Tom Ryder. I'm at the farm east of you. What the hell's going on?" Tom thought he was sounding too calm, too reasonable. "It stinks like hell down here. My son's bled from his nose all over his bed."

Sounding harried, the young fellow said he was sorry. He said he wasn't the right person to talk to. Then the phone was taken from his hand.

"Alf Dietz. How can I help you?"

An older, rougher voice. Ill humoured too. Tom said his piece again.

"Yeah, well, we got problems galore. Too much sulphur. It's overloading our incinerator. But that shouldn't cause a problem for you. It should be going over top of you."

"The hell it is. It's in my house."

"Must be the waste oil pit, then. We set a fire to kill the H_2s. Look, Mr. Ryder, if it gets worse, call me again. I'll check on you in the morning. All right?"

Tom didn't know what else to say. It was bad now. What would worse look like?

"These plants are complicated," Dietz continued. "Take a new piece of farm machinery and multiply that by ten thousand. It's going to take a while to get this place running right."

"How long?"

"I don't know."

Ella had put clean sheets on the boy's bed but, since Billy was still upset, she brought him down and let him lie down between them. He was soon asleep. Then Tom remembered. "Ah shit."

"What is it?"

"I didn't check on Kees."

"Well, you had better."

As he crossed the yard, Tom could see by the plant's flare that the chimney on the hired man's shack was smoking. He banged on the door. Kees did not open up, so Tom turned the knob and pushed inside.

First thing he noticed, as he always did, was the smell. However bad it smelled outside, Kees's bunkhouse was a match for it. The Dutchman was a hard worker but not a bather, no matter how often Ella offered to heat water for him. Now vomit was part of the stench.

"You're sick, Kees."

"Ja, Tom. I'm bad." Some of the flare light poked between curtains Ella had sewn for the tiny west window. By it Tom could see the white of an enamel basin on the bed.

"You been throwing up?"

"Ja, Tom. Puking."

Tom threw the basin's contents out the door. He knelt in the frame and scooped up snow, rubbed it around the basin.

"We die from that plant," Kees said from the bed.

"Damn well hope not." The water bucket was on the floor. Tom felt around the rim for the ladle. "You better drink some water."

Tom held the ladle and Kees took his drink.

"I like you Ryders, but I'm not staying."

Much of the next day was shot on the telephone. Everybody for miles had the same complaints: headaches, nausea, nosebleeds, sore throats, sore eyes. Johnny Court just over the church hill had packed up his wife and new baby in the night and taken them to her relatives in town.

Bertha Kenhardt, a retired schoolteacher and widow who lived to the northeast, phoned around and suggested people start writing down what was happening. A diary of plant events: date, smell, how they felt, where the wind was coming from. Tom borrowed a couple of pages of ring-hole paper from Jeannie and started.

As promised, Alf Dietz visited the Ryders. Though he called himself a plant superintendent, he was reassuringly ordinary. It was easy for him to step out of his boots in their porch because he didn't tie them, just pushed the laces inside the open tops. He wore a plaid flannel shirt, half tucked. When he stripped off his greasy cap, he was mostly bald, a few grey tufts sticking up.

Sitting in front of his cup of tea, Dietz stared solemnly at the table. He listened to their story in silence. When they'd finished, he said, "I don't know much more than I said on the phone. I'm adjusting everything I can adjust. If it doesn't work, I'm not sure what next."

"Why not shut the plant down?" Ella said. It had not occurred to Tom.

"That would be the very last resort, Mrs. Ryder. Put us back a month or more if we do that. We'll work at it."

Dietz stayed longer because Ella got him talking about himself. He wasn't American, though he sounded like it. He'd grown up in the West Kootenays, in B.C. His family had started out as farmers, but when that went poorly, his father took a job at the Trail lead and zinc smelter. When Dietz was old enough, he worked there too. Somehow that led to a sour gas plant job in a mountain state in the U.S. Because he was a Canadian with sour gas experience, Aladdin had offered him the job of running its Hatfield plant.

Ella was good at this, drawing people out, and Tom watched as Dietz told more than was probably normal for him. Suddenly aware of it, he slapped on his cap and said he had to go.

It was a week after Dietz came to the house that the flare shot to twice the height of its stack. The Ryders' house shook on its foundation. Tom was barely awake when he walked through the rooms to the porch in his underwear. The linoleum quivered under his feet;

the windows were bright. He pulled on his gumboots and walked into the frozen night.

The flare was a hard thing to stand before, like a grizzly bear roaring in your face. Tom didn't notice the boy until he was by his side, in his pyjamas and little gumboots, imitating Dad. What funny things children were. A week ago, the boy had been terrified by a nosebleed. Now he stood staring at something like hell released and was calm as a stone.

Tom placed his hand on the back of the boy's neck and the slimness of it shocked and rebuked him. Here was his family in danger, and he had no idea what to do.

2

Waddens Lake, Athabasca Oil Sands

THE BANK OF WINDOWS framed it nicely. A flare as still as a candle in an airtight room, except that every once in a while, some burp in the system caused the flame to surge.

The flare was not dangerous, its height was within the provincially regulated limits, but, not quite believing these lenient rules could last, Bill's company had recently imposed its own clean-air regimen. That was what Bill's flare was exceeding. If anyone in the computing heart of the upgrader was reviewing all systems—or chanced to walk or drive past Bill's flare—there would be hell to pay and bosses to appease.

In front of the control room's arc of windows stood an extended desk, where Bill's crew sat staring at screens and poking keyboards. Each man and woman was trying to find the cause of the errant flare, but the only one capable of doing so was Bill's junior engineer, Henry Shields. Still, Bill felt it important the others try. Extended periods of non-emergency bred overconfidence and made his crew feel they were responsible for the peace and equilibrium. Today's problem and their failure to solve it would tamp down the size of their heads.

The person having the most trouble sticking with the task was Bill himself. As he sat at one of the computers, jabbing keys, he could feel his scalp bunching under his hair. His arms were zooming. Little workmen with tiny powerful wrenches were tightening a collar on his neck.

"Frig this," he muttered. He boosted to his feet with a violence that caused his chair to jump and its wheels to jangle. The crew stared—except for Henry, who was too deep in the cascade of numerals, the fractal art, to notice.

"You mean you want us to stop?" one of the crew said hopefully. It was Dennis Whitcomb, his plastic-looking eyelashes fluttering. He would think that, the lazy whale.

The thermometer out the window read thirty below. Bill pulled on his snowmobile suit, steel-toed winter boots, and hard hat. He drew the flaps of the hat's winter liner together and snapped them under his chin, donned his mitts.

He stepped outside into the upgrader's corral of hulks. All along the tall walls, pipes came out to cool and dove back in for heat. Shit streams raced to their confluence with other shit streams, heat and pressure making the molecules jig and mate. Atomic plumes of steam and ice fog billowed above the highest catwalks. For all they were doing to it, the sky above was blue.

At ground level, Bill stood at a three-way intersection of salted sidewalks. On his left, a stack of horizontal pipes flew to their vanishing point. A deep thrum battered his eardrums. The only thing he could think to do was to walk out of the cubic forest and stand beneath the flares. If he stood at the foot of the stack and listened, maybe timed the eruptions, he might find something. A rhythm. A meaningful pattern.

Ahead, something in a down parka made a robotic turn and came toward him. Dark blue balaclava pulled over the head. Frozen breath puffing out the blowhole. It spoke Bill's name and asked him where he was off to.

Clayton Brock. He remembered now sending Clayton off to do air tests at last week's maintenance sites.

"What did you find, Clayton?"

"Clean as a whistle."

Ironic tone. Synchronized pig roll of the eyes. It tired Bill, this business of having to tell young operators and junior engineers that the nature of precaution is to find nothing most of the time—and to be on it early when something does go wrong.

In the olden days, engineers had their office building upwind of the plant, while operators like Clayton worked near its stinking heart. Now they shared a control room. A work dynamics expert dropped by weekly with a box of doughnuts, from which they fed like a peewee hockey team.

Farther along the service road, Bill came to a silver pickup, diesel engine drumming. On the opposite side of the sidewalk, two men on ladders were removing tin from a horizontal pipe. Batts of yellow insulation curled on the ground below.

"Billy Ryder."

Rime on Bill's eyelashes made a blur of the ladder man. He brushed it away and squinted. A brown face; frost in a ragged moustache. No one called him Billy except his sisters.

"You don't know me, do you." Native guy.

A bubble of memory rose. "Johnny Bertram?"

"Ha!" The man punched the ladder rung with his mitt and started down. "Get in," he ordered.

Inside the truck, Bill asked Johnny how he'd recognized him. "I mean, in all this gear."

"No trick, really," Johnny said. "Remember my sister Shirley, who you once loved dearly? She's a friend of a friend of an old girlfriend of yours who told her you'd moved to the tar sands. When I started my company and got work up here, I Googled around and saw you were at Aladdin. We got a contract." Johnny pointed at the ladders. The rest was obvious.

Before he'd climbed in the truck, Bill had read the print on its door. *Black Hole Insulation*. He caught up to the joke.

"This is your company?"

"One hundred per cent."

"Black Hole?"

Johnny smiled. "A guy in Gleichen told me he didn't believe companies in the tar sands hired Indians as much as they say they do. I bet him I could call my company Black Hole Insulation and still get hired."

"I thought you were a cowboy."

"A man can be more than one thing, Billy."

Johnny pointed his mitt at the spidery youth still up the ladder, wrestling tin. "That's Elmer. We call him Elmo. He's Shirley's youngest. He thinks he's a cowboy too."

Bill had a country hall in his head. A beautiful girl stepping into his arms to dance.

"You got a few minutes? To drive me somewhere?" Bill asked.

The roll of tin Elmo was trying to handle got away on him and fell to the ground. He jumped from the ladder and landed crookedly. He threw his mitts down and hopped on one leg. "As you can see," Johnny said, "we're not really doing anything."

He got out and ran up the ladder with one end of the fallen span of tin. Elmo limped up his ladder with the other end. They pushed it over the new batting and Johnny shot in some screws. He gestured for Elmo to finish on his own.

They drove with Bill giving directions until they were among the flare stacks. When the exhaust cloud cleared, Bill saw that the flame on his stack was normal. He counted to one hundred and twenty and it stayed that way.

"Okay. That's all I need."

"Tough job, Billy. You ever go up a ladder anymore?"

"If my eavestrough is plugged."

"Do *you* have a minute?"

"Of course."

Johnny drove them to the tailings pond, where the fouled water from the separation plant went and never returned. He drove the service road to the pond's dyke.

"I want to climb up and look. You?"

"It's frozen. Nothing to see."

"I don't believe the shit they put in there can freeze. I want to look."

They scrambled up the gravel face. At the top, the wind was stronger and viciously cold. Johnny squinted at the slab of ice. The only wet was where the new tailings coughed out.

"So what interests you?" asked Bill.

"This isn't the one where the sixteen hundred ducks died, is it?"

"Nope."

"Would ducks die in this one?"

"If it was thawed out, yeah. See those things sticking up?" Bill gestured at armatures dressed in yellow rain jackets, one arm pointing skyward.

"Scarecrows?" Johnny said.

"We call them bitu-men."

"Witty. They look like John Travolta on the old *Saturday Night Fever* poster."

"When the ice goes and ducks come around, we'll have cannons firing."

"How big is this thing?"

"Four square kilometres. It'll be bigger when the second phase kicks in."

"You got to be some kind of spin doctor to call that a pond."

Bill laughed.

"Walden Pond," said Johnny.

Bill laughed harder. Long-dormant muscles in his face were paining.

When they were back inside the upgrader's quadrangle, Elmo had finished his chore and the ladders and tools were lined out in good order beside the service road.

"You seem more serious now than you used to be, Billy."

"Maybe life got less funny."

"Black Hole," Johnny said.

At the end of the workday and work week, Bill walked to his parking spot. Ice crystals floated down through the orange light. He pulled the block heater plug and battled the extension cord into roundish loops that he left hanging. The engine kicked off easily but he sat for a while in sympathy for the engine parts, beating in their taffy.

The big engine loosened and began to roar. There was nothing sporty about this sport utility vehicle. It had a truck chassis and weighed a ton, drank gas with abandon through six steel throats. He'd bought it to impress a woman and to give a sign to his daughter and son that their dad was solvent. The woman, the only one he'd dated in Fort McMurray, hated the stiff ride and eventually would not travel in it. His children could not believe their father had invested fifty thousand in something so literally square.

Bill joined the line to the gate. The vehicles ahead were mostly new pickups. Every driver had his foot on the gas, goosing away. Under the accumulated cloud of exhaust fog, some would be drinking, toking, snorting—and all would shortly be entering the river of oil sands traffic that rallied south to Fort Mac. The main drag through the oil sands, Highway 63, was Canada's most dangerous highway. It had many nicknames that sounded like heavy metal bands—Highway of Death, Suicide 63.

The lineup was mostly stopped. The drivers were on their horns. "What the fuck?" roared the guy ahead, hanging out his window.

In fact, Bill knew what the fuck. The folks running the gate had been told to check each vehicle for contraband. By that they did not mean booze and dope but stolen things like tools and copper. As the cause for the stoppage worked its way back, the horn chorus grew. It was possible upper management did not understand that workers accused of being thieves were more likely to steal; that, if there was stolen gear in these trucks, it would not be where a gatekeeper with a flashlight could find it.

The chaos made Bill think of his own crew. They were in this lineup somewhere and had invited him to come for beers at The Pit in town. The Pit was a bad bar, but Bill had been there many times without incurring blunt force trauma. He'd told them he would think about it.

A shift bus roared past the line. The gatekeeper swung the gate to let the bus through. Four trucks jumped out of line and tried to follow. The keeper ran the gate back and slammed in the post.

Among the odd things about Fort McMurray was how every day was part of someone's weekend, and, by extension, every night was Friday or Saturday night. Though he felt a hermit's sadness about entering this frolic, Bill had made up his mind to go to The Pit. The boys, and Marion if she'd been invited, thought of him as a humorous old elf, despite his occasional grumpiness. Going for drinks was a way of assuring them he was still their good boss, someone they could like.

Parting his way through the crowd, Bill met a chesty waitress with a small barbell through her lower lip. She had a tray of drinks balanced on an upturned hand and still managed to throw a hip into him as he squeezed by. "Sit down, grandpa. Before you fall down."

Bill plunked into a captain's chair that Henry had swung out for him. Clayton was pouring him a beer from a pitcher. Henry's mouth was moving but Bill couldn't hear. Behind the bar, a guy with a face like an open wrench was yelling. A nearby table cheered, and a muscular joker jumped up, fought clear, and duck-walked to the front. He held his paycheque in front of his face, kissing it repeatedly.

This was the normal run of things at The Pit but it felt suddenly false, as if they were in a rehearsal for a Broadway musical. *Fort McMurray: The Early Years.*

"Where did you park?"

Henry's voice got through this time. It seemed an irrelevant question, except that Henry never spoke without purpose. He could care less where Bill parked but wanted to know, early on, if he needed to worry about his boss driving home drunk.

"Two blocks east," Bill told him, and it was a lie. He had taken his truck home and ridden down here in Mr. Khalid's cab. He was lying to Henry to give himself an excuse for leaving early.

"Be even louder in here soon," Clayton told Bill. "Band tonight."

There was a band every night. Bill raised his pint. "Here's to Friday."

The golden mugs clashed, some beer fell.

Clayton said, "Sorry, chief, it's Wednesday."

"No such thing," Bill said, and Henry laughed.

The talk turned to Dennis Whitcomb: a top-ten of his screw-ups of the week. Dennis had been hired during the last big boom, then laid off in the 2008–09 bust. Recently, when the oil economy was showing signs of revival, he had been rehired. No one could figure out why he was back, since they regarded him as too dumb to operate. Clayton tried to hang it on Bill.

"I don't hire people, Clayton. Consultants hire people."

"That's fucked," Clayton offered.

"Was Dion Elliott around this week?" Bill asked, pushing the topic elsewhere.

Everyone agreed they had not seen him.

"Then it *was* a good week," Bill said.

Too late, he saw a look of grievance spreading across Huge Boschuk's face.

"I like Dion," Huge said. Boschuk always looked to Bill as though he was about to cry. His face was fleshy and immature—the face of a giant baby.

"Dion's fine," said Bill. "Just seems to signify trouble when he's around."

"You call him a PR man. He doesn't like that."

"I have trouble keeping track of current lingo."

"The work he does in the community is important."

The other two were staring at Huge, a seldom-talker. By Boschuk's standards, this was more than rebellion; it was mutiny with bloodshed.

Bill looked into the sorrowful eyes. "I'm sorry, Huge. I tell you what. I'll stop complaining about Dion if you—all of you—give Dennis a rest."

After a couple of beers, Bill lost interest in what his crew was saying. He tuned in conversations from other tables. The talk was about money and the courses needed to make more money.

"Ten grand clear, a guy told me."

"Yeah, but that's with your B Pressure."

"First Aid, H_2s, CPR."

"To be a lease-hand?"

"PST, CSE . . ."

"Fuck's that?"

"Confined Space Entry."

From another table came a yarn about a guy who'd bought a '70s hearse, brought it up to McMurray, and was now renting it to people as accommodation. Making two grand a week.

"I can't believe those fucking tree-huggers. I'd like to see those assholes do my job."

This came from closer at hand: from Clayton. He was drinking like a pig and had turned bright red. Already his eyelids were lined with tiny sandbags. No one seemed to agree or disagree with him. Henry was looking at something under the table.

"I'm telling you, if one of those pricks was here right now, I'd cold-cock the sucker. I heard a guy on radio saying Indians are getting screwed up here. They should go down to the casino and see those dumb fucks playing machines. Can't piss it away fast enough. My fault, I suppose."

Bill began to plan his escape.

Clayton continued to rail. "Fucking casino. Might as well take your money and burn it. I'm glad I wasn't born stupid."

Bill rested his eyes on Henry. While appearing to do nothing, Henry would be assessing the distance to each Native in the room. He would have also considered how the casino comments were going down with the people slugging money into VLTs beyond the bar.

But the one who got between Clayton and his rant this time was Huge. Without anyone's noticing, Huge had acquired the bill. The waitress was pushing the chip end of his credit card into the machine.

"What doing, Huge?" said Henry.

"It's done."

"We'll give you money."

"Pay at the next place."

"I'm not going on," said Bill. "You better take mine now."

"What's the matter, Bill? You don't like our company?"

"First rule, Clayton. Don't run with the young bucks."

"But what are you going to do, Bill?" Huge asked, from his sad concerned face.

"Tie a dry fly. Listen to some Pavarotti. Read an existential novel."

On the street outside, the air was so cold it breathed like metal. They said their farewells and walked in opposite directions. The block was surrounded by trucks going nowhere. The frozen air was thick with exhaust. Out of sight of the others, Bill stopped.

Four hours later, Mr. Khalid's cab pulled into the pool of street light outside the condo complex. Bill's fingers shook when he tried to navigate his wallet. He was having trouble distinguishing the colours. Mr. Khalid showed no impatience, just stared through his prayer beads at the windshield.

When at last Bill had himself sorted, Mr. Khalid took the money with slim fingers, doubled it, and slid it inside his jacket. "Thank you," he said with a nod. Bill nodded back. Old-timers in a town of wild kids, silent commiserators. It was also possible that Mr. Khalid found Bill disgusting, an older man who drank alcohol and stayed out half the night. Mr. Khalid was excellent at concealing his feelings, which was another reason for calling him.

The building's entrance had two doors for weather and security. In the chamber between, Bill dug under his parka for keys. A cardboard box, swathed in tape, was pushed against the wall below the intercom. He got the door open, held it with his foot, and contorted himself until he could see the writing on the box. His name. His sister's large, emphatic printing.

After more buttons, keys, and struggles, he was inside his condo and able to drop the box on the floor. What passed for silence ticked and hummed through the apartment. In the dark living room, the message light on the phone was blinking red. He went to the light in fear. That he'd been out all night doing foolish things provoked a sense that something awful must have happened, to one of his children, to one of his sisters.

The first message was too garbled to understand. It sounded like Lance Evert's voice, but was so broken up he could not tell for sure, though he rolled it back and listened several times. This bothered him because he almost never heard from Lance; also because Lance was extra precise, even for an engineer. Not the kind of guy to make a mess of leaving a message.

The only other message was from his sister Jeannie.

"I sent you something. The courier said it would be there today. It belonged to Dad and I think you should have it. Call me."

He sat down at the kitchen table and tried to slow his breathing. He closed his eyes but it was worse in there: a robotic dance of things rolling and falling into place. He stood, and when he had his balance, went around flicking on the lights.

Something belonging to his father. Something he should have.

But why should he have it? And why would Lance, if he screwed up the first message, not call again?

He reached for the TV remote but paused and considered the time of night. Beast heads bursting from people's chests. Serial killers in goalie masks. And creepier still: Texas Hold'em tournaments.

He had an urge to throw up, but understood that it had nothing to do with food or drink or illness. What he wanted to throw up was the experience of the last few hours. Before he knew it, he had been to the kitchen and returned with the butcher knife. He jerked the blinds closed and chopped at the endless tape Jeannie had wound around the box. Inside was a filling of newspaper balls into which he plunged his hands.

What came out was a binder: cloth cover, red-and-black checks.

The plastic along the spine was crumbling. The zipper tab was spotted with orange. The whole thing emanated an attic smell. He kicked the paper balls and box aside and set the binder softly on the coffee table. It was as fat as a seal and he knew what it was; had an image of his father sitting at his desk, taking things out of it and putting things back in. For a second he had his fingers on the pull-tab, but he made them spring apart.

"No," he said. "Not so easy."

3

Ryder Farm, 1961

TO GET TO THE MEETING at Hatfield Hall, Tom had taken the Callaghan valley road. A slip of paper stuck in their door jamb had told them to come to the hall for seven that night. Ella had read it out to Tom: "Mr. Clint Comstock of Aladdin Oil and Gas will host the evening. He will welcome your questions about the first weeks of operation at the Aladdin Hatfield gas processing plant."

It was strange wording for a meeting that was happening because the plant threw a fit every second day; because, when it was upset—their word—it stank and made everyone sick. Even the idea of Comstock *hosting* them in the Hatfield Hall was ridiculous. A man from Houston, Texas, hosting them in their own community hall.

By now, Ella had won Tom over to her view of Clint Comstock. But Tom still believed it was better to hear from someone higher up in the organization than the men who ran the plant. Even on this point, he and Ella argued. "Why look down on Mr. Dietz?" she'd said, while they changed their clothes. "He's trying to fix things, at least. I doubt Mr. Comstock is bringing a magic wand."

"Goddamnit, I am not looking down on Dietz. Or up to Comstock."

The sun had set an hour ago and the valley was full of shadows and half-seen things. Ella pointed when a deer stepped from a bluff of aspens. Tom had seen it too and was slowing down. He stopped the truck and waited until another half-dozen does crept from the bush. They skittered across the road, white tails wagging, bounced over the fence into some spruce along the frozen river.

"Deer," said Billy.

"We're going to be late," Ella said to Tom.

"Cutting it a little fine," he admitted. "They'll probably start late."

By the time they made the highway turn, the darkness had deepened. A mile more and he could see the lights in the hall windows blooming in the distance. He found a spot in the row of trucks facing its north wall.

Ella had predicted the building would be cold, that whoever was in charge of lighting the furnace would have come too late. She was right; the place wasn't much warmer than outside, though the furnace rumbled away under the floor. The benches from the side walls had been pulled into rows.

People were leaving their boots on and Tom, Ella, and Billy did the same. Billy tried to pull off his hat but Ella caught his wrist and whispered to leave it.

"I won't hear," he said.

"Yes, you will."

Tom found this funny, this concern of Billy's that he might miss something. He had told the boy tonight's meeting would be dry stuff, but that made no difference to Billy. He sensed from his parents that it was important and insisted he be there.

Everybody in the hall was familiar. Most wives had come with their husbands. Everyone who had kids big enough to look after the little ones had left their children at home. Alice Court was there with her baby, and Tom saw Ella frown at this. Ella had heard the child was sick, an illness caused by the plant. They'd probably brought the sick baby as proof.

Tom was looking for Comstock or Dietz when the two came in at the back. Comstock kicked his boots noisily in the porch, then bowed deeply under the door frame between the boot room and the main hall. He was tall but not tall enough to crack his head. He exaggerated everything.

Dietz came along behind him, and was just the opposite: shambling and dressed in his flannel shirt with the snoose can making a circle in his breast pocket. Tom and Ella had been expecting only these two but a third man came in after them: dark hair slicked back, skinny; not much more than twenty. He held his body like a soldier on guard duty.

As soon as Comstock was in the hall, he made a show of taking charge. He ordered the younger man to put leaflets on a side table, then went to the front and stood there tapping his long chin with one finger. "I think I'll speak from the floor," he announced to Alf Dietz, but loud enough for everyone to hear. The stage behind him was used for Christmas plays and dance bands. He would look like a fool talking to them from up there.

Comstock began marching back and forth at the front, while the audience went to the benches and sat. Dietz and the young fellow sat in the first row. Ella led Billy and Tom to a bench two rows back.

Tom studied the American while the rest of the people found places. Comstock was pretending to be comfortable in the cold room in just a sports jacket. The jacket was the colour of a tanned deerskin and matched his cowboy boots. He had the fingers of both hands poked in the pockets of his jeans. The western get-up was meant to make them comfortable, Tom supposed. But no local man wore clothes like that.

Comstock started to talk.

"Aladdin has been producing gas for fifty-three years—in all parts of America where petroleum is found. Based on that knowledge and experience, we built this plant. There are new factors here, things we must respond to as they show themselves. That's how the history of this business is written: you apply what has done well for you in the past. You adjust to the conditions of the present. That's how we get to the future."

The Court baby started to cough. A ripping sound for a creature so small. Alice stood up with the baby tucked inside the opening of her parka and bounced. Then she went behind the last row and walked with a jogging step.

"In visits with you—and my apologies to any I missed—I explained sour gas, explained how we take this very poisonous gas and render it mostly harmless by removing the elemental sulphur. That is happening at the plant today and every day. To start up this plant we hired the very best men we could find." He opened a hand toward the front bench. "Mr. Alf Dietz, one of the most experienced men in sour gas processing in North America. To Mr. Dietz's right, Lance Evert, a sharp young engineer from Saskatchewan. Lance graduated top of his class from your University of Alberta."

Comstock made himself more solemn. "I am aware there have been difficulties here. Plant start-ups are difficult. Such problems are regrettable but not unusual. And yes, some of these are different problems than we normally see—the kinds of things you can't turn a valve or two and fix. Now, I think that's enough of an introduction. I want to hear from you. Let's hear your questions."

For a while it seemed no one had a question, and Tom could feel Ella grow tense beside him. They could see other wives looking at their husbands, some whispering at them to speak up. Ella was not urging Tom. His cursing embarrassed her, and it was true he probably could not get through a question about the plant without some bad language.

Finally it was Ernie Dewart who rose, and Tom was glad. Ernie had fought in the war, and Tom hoped he'd mention that. *I fought for this country in France and Germany. I didn't go there to come home and have a gas plant drive me off my place.* That would be good.

Ernie fiddled briefly with the knot on his cowboy scarf. "My family live a couple miles east of the plant," he said. "We can't see it because of the hill, but we're getting plenty of gas. Every one of us has been sick. What I want to know is how much longer it's going to continue." He sat down.

Clint Comstock thanked Ernie. Then he paused as if in thought. Standing straighter and looking over their heads, he said, "Twenty-five years."

Chairs scraped. People made various kinds of noises. A few even laughed.

"Nope, I'm absolutely serious," said Comstock. "Twenty-five years is the answer. The life expectancy of the gas plant. I didn't come all the way from Texas to lie to you. For as long as it's a sulphur plant, Aladdin Hatfield will smell like a sulphur plant. However, the intent of this gentleman's question is, I believe, how long will the odour be a problem. The answer to that is different. Ladies and gentlemen, I would like to turn this over to Alf Dietz, the plant superintendent, who can speak to the details."

Dietz rose slowly. He looked dead tired. He had a cornered look on his riven face, like a live-trapped animal.

"There's smell and then there's smell," he said sadly. "I think that's what Mr. Comstock means." He wrestled in search of something and did not find it. "Keep calling me. I'll keep working with the plant and trying to get a handle on things, on the wind and inversions and whatnot."

He returned to his chair heavily. He looked at the south window, though it was just a frame full of darkness.

Comstock started up again and now he had a bunch of energy and all the answers. Showing off, Tom thought, pumping himself up at the expense of Dietz. It was poor strategy because it would be Dietz, not Comstock, who'd have to deal with their problems—like Ella said.

Tom looked down at his son. Billy's interest had faded. He'd been looking over his shoulder at the crying baby, and now he turned all the way around on the bench so he could see more easily. Ella twisted him back and spoke to him sternly. Soon he was kicking his boots so the heels hit the board.

Tom returned his attention to the front. Comstock was spouting statistics: all to do with how much gas the plant would produce after the expansion, how much sulphur that would translate into. Tom's eyes had started to itch. He had been up since before six, had worked hard all day, and now sleep was coming for him.

He turned to Ella to see how she was faring and saw that she was looking forward but not at Comstock. Her black eyes were sparking. He followed the line of her eyes to the young man who had come in with Comstock and Dietz. He was turned halfway and looking back at them. Just as Tom was trying to make sense of this, the fellow turned away and watched Comstock.

Tom nudged Ella. "What?" he said. She shook her head.

Comstock asked for more questions and there were two more not very good ones. The steam had gone out of the meeting. The "twenty-five years" statement hung above their heads, and nothing else could match it. People were tired and thinking about their kids at home or some chore that needed doing before bed.

Comstock got the point and thanked them for coming. The women with children got them ready for the out-of-doors. Tom went directly to Comstock.

"Evening, Tom," the Texan said. "Glad to see you in the crowd."

He was playing up the host business again, and Tom had an urge to say, "You're the stranger here, not me." But he had something to ask.

"I been thinking about pig litters and calves. In your experience, what will happen when piglets and calves have to breathe the stuff from your plant?"

"That's a bit like asking how big a fish is."

"Then how big is the fish?"

"How about this? If I was representing a train company, and I said there were sparks from trains and sometimes those sparks caught grass on fire, would you ask me if that train could burn your house down?"

"In other words, the young pigs and calves could die."

"I didn't say that, but I've told you that hydrogen sulphide can kill. Then again, if our men can work inside the plant and stay alive, the creatures that live downwind should be able to handle it."

None of this was satisfying. Comstock said something about the long drive to Calgary and an airplane to Houston in the morning. Tom turned to look for Ella and found her talking to the young man from the plant. The fellow was playing a game with Billy. The boy would dodge behind his mother's coat then stick his head out. The plant man would jump as if surprised.

Tom came up. Ella introduced them. Tom shook Lance Evert's hand.

"Should I warm up the truck?"

"Let's just go," she said.

They travelled in silence until the engine warmed enough to get the heater working. "You had quite the face on you during Comstock's talk."

"I don't know what you're talking about."

"You were looking at that Lance like you do at me when you're good and mad."

"He was staring at me. I suppose he was just lost in thought but it made me mad. Gaping like that."

"You were chummy afterwards."

"He came to apologize. He seemed all right. Young and awkward. Billy liked him."

"He's not the one I'd worry about, that's for sure."

"What?"

"Out of those three. Evert's not the one that concerns me. Comstock's the problem, just like you said." Tom glanced sideways, and, though Ella gave no sign of being interested, he spoke more. "I didn't learn one goddamn useful thing tonight. He didn't say whether the stink would get better or worse. No instructions about what to do when the gas gets bad. And as far as when the plant gets bigger, he didn't say if the stink would be over by then or would be worse. Jesus Christ. If the bastard gets us all out on a winter night, he should have something to say."

"You should have asked those questions when you had the chance." Ella's voice was drowsy and irritated. She hadn't asked any questions either, but he kept himself from saying that. He wanted to tell her about his talk with Comstock about piglets and calves, but he didn't say that either.

"Lance Evert," she said, near sleep.

"What?"

"That's his name."

Then she was asleep, and Billy was asleep, and so almost was Tom as he climbed up the hill out of the Callaghan. When the road fell level, the lights and fires of the plant rose into view, more lights than a town, and so much smoke and steam. The smell was there too, the spunky fume from the deeps, the stuff that knocks birds off the perch at a coal face.

Though it had been Tom who started the note-taking, Ella took charge soon after. This morning, after breakfast, she wrote: "February 10: Gas strong in the night. Billy sick again. Nosebleed. Vomited once. Hired man, Kees, with us for 18 months, quit this morning."

As if poor Billy wasn't feeling bad enough, she had to wake him to say goodbye. The hired man had always been like a big brother. Billy cried, and Kees stood beside the bed strangling his cap in his big hands. He had no idea how to console Billy, so, instead, he started bawling too.

Tom had been out in the truck, waiting. When he stormed in to tell Kees to hurry up, that's what he saw: Billy, Kees, and Ella, all with wet faces. Tom was impatient with Kees, saying the trip to the Greyhound bus in town was lost time he could not afford. It was Tom's way when hurt to become angry. As far as Ella was concerned, Kees was the only one of them not tied to the farm. Leaving was the smart thing to do.

After Tom and Kees had been gone an hour, Billy was still in bed—or was back in bed, having tried once to get up. Ella was brimming with anger when she finally went to the phone. To the woman who answered, she said, "I want Mr. Dietz to come to our house right away. It's Mrs. Ryder. He knows where we live and so should you. We're your closest neighbours."

A half-hour later, it was not Dietz's half-ton that came into the yard but a little car with rusted fenders. Lance Evert climbed out.

"I was expecting Mr. Dietz," Ella said when she pulled back the door.

He was so cast down she almost laughed. But she would not let him off.

"Come in, but I'm telling you, Lance, if Mr. Dietz has the idea he can send you instead of coming himself and that will calm me down, he doesn't know me. I'm very angry with him, with you, and with your plant. You're going to hear about it."

Like a struck puppy he entered, shed his boots in the porch, hung his coat on a hook, shuffled forward into the kitchen in his socks. She pointed at the children's side of the table, and he sat there. He had yet to say a word. The coffee was low in the perk, but she poured it anyway. Let him get some lukewarm grit in his pretty teeth.

"The crew foreman told me it was a bad night. I'm sorry."

"Don't bother being sorry. I'm not interested in sorry. It was a *very* bad night. Our hired man has quit. But the worst thing is that Billy's been sick all night again. He's had to go back to bed. It is not fair, you know, that a small child should suffer so you people can make gas and sulphur. If you had any decency, you'd understand that letting your plant go on pumping out its sickening stuff is no better than if you came down here and beat that boy with a stick."

Lance lost the last of his colour. It seemed fair that she had made him look sick, the way Billy always looked. He had the sense to say nothing, could probably tell from her tone that she would leap all over any excuse he made. Head down, he waited for more.

"You're letting your coffee get cold." Which was a laugh since it hadn't been warm to begin with. She would have liked him less if he had taken a drink in response. He did not move at all.

"I suppose if you could do anything with your plant to make it stop stinking, you would."

He nodded.

An odd idea came over her: that she had power over this boy. She was remembering how he had gawked at her in the community hall, seeming helpless not to. And the way he looked now, punished and sad. She wondered for a second if she'd ever had as much effect on Tom and supposed that the real answer was that she hadn't wanted or needed it.

She wondered what might happen if she asked, "What would you do to make me happy right now?" She was almost certain his answer would be: "Anything."

These thoughts calmed her. Having wanted to chew his ears off, she now felt something like gratitude.

"Did you eat anything this morning?"

"I had breakfast at the motel."

"Then I know where you live, since there's only one motel in Haultain that has a restaurant. I've heard the food there is terrible."

"Bacon and eggs. Most places get that right."

Now he was smiling, which made her focus on his mouth. His lips were so youthful, as if they had never cracked in the weather. But he had grown up in this climate, according to what Comstock said.

"Mr. Comstock said you're from Saskatchewan."

"Saskatoon. I started university there but thought the University of Alberta would have more about oil and gas in its engineering program."

"And did it?"

"No. But it's a good university. I had good professors."

"And you did well, I understand."

He had been looking at her. At her mention of his doing well at university, his eyes shot down.

"It's not a crime to do well. I did."

"You went to university?"

"To normal school. I was hoping to become a teacher but my father got ill. This is their house, Mom and Dad's. I'm their only child. Dad became asthmatic in middle age and certain kinds of farm chores were impossible for him. Chopping grain, shovelling chop. So I came home."

She watched the play of emotions on his face, his trying to decide on a best response. How odd to be around someone constantly wanting to say what you wanted to hear. It made her wonder what she looked like to him. Her hair was still black. She knew she was pretty, black eyes and a curve in her smile that people had always commented on. Her facial lines hadn't deepened enough to take that away.

Normally, she followed up the story of her interrupted education with the fact that Tom had come home from the coal mines about the same time. His own father's health had gone bad, a thing in common between them when they met at dances. When it was a romance, Tom had helped Ella and her father with the fieldwork. But she did not say any of that to Lance Evert.

"What's going on at the plant, Lance? Is it supposed to be like this?"

"It sure isn't. The mixture of hydrogen sulphide and carbon dioxide, at this pressure, is new to even Mr. Dietz. I wasn't taught anything about it at university."

"So you're unprepared for the problems, is what you're saying."

"I guess so. They built the plant out of expensive high-grade steel and that was supposed to take care of unknowns. But this gas gets right inside the steel and cracks it. Dietz has seen it before and says it's the hydrogen does that. But it's happening way faster in this plant for some reason he doesn't know."

"If it cracks steel, gas must get out."

"That's right. What Dietz has our men doing is puncturing the blisters on the vessels, flattening them with hammers, and covering them with gunnite."

"What's that?"

"Thick grey goo that dries hard."

She put scones on the table, and he automatically took one and bit into it. She had given him butter and a knife but he didn't use them.

"I phoned my professor in Edmonton. He says it's called hydrogen embrittlement. The hydrogen ion gets loose and invades the steel. When I told him about the good steel they used to build the plant, he said it's probably too good, that the molecules are too lined up. Dietz was interested in that, and we've started substituting old bolts for the fancy ones that fail."

Ella was concentrating hard. She would have made notes but had a feeling that Lance would wake up if she did, would realize he was spilling the beans. She would put what she could remember in the binder later. But then she decided to push him a little more. She mustn't be too polite.

"Is that the worst of it, then? The hydrogen business?"

He said there was something else, but then he was talking a language that made no sense to her. Foaming amine tower. Catalyst smothered in hydrocarbon overflow. She didn't bother trying to commit this to memory, as it wouldn't mean anything to Tom either. She drew Lance back out of his trance.

"Are there many in your family?"

"Only child."

At once, Ella imagined an easy life, which was probably unfair. Farmers too often thought of city people as well off.

"Why did Mr. Dietz send you down here, Lance?"

This question caused his face to lose its handsomeness. It was more the boy he had recently been that came visible.

"He didn't say why, but he's been sending me on all the complaint calls."

This was so easy to understand it was hard to believe Lance

didn't know. Dietz was gruff and stone faced. Lance was young and nice looking; much harder to be mad at.

"I wish he wouldn't." Lance blushed. "I don't mean I don't want to be here. It's nice here."

"What do you mean?"

He huffed out a breath, a burden. "I've been to the Gerstens' a few times. I'm not used to places like that."

Ella tried not to smile at this but did. A city boy with no siblings going into Paul and Gertie's explained itself. Sometimes, when Ella had been to visit, the smell in that house would have offended a dog. Poor Gertie had three children in diapers, and between feeding all those babies and the rest of it, she never caught up with her laundry. Paul had bought a wringer-washer second-hand but of course it was on sale for a reason. Last time Ella visited, it was standing lopsided outside the door. It could not be fun for a young engineer to go house to house listening to complaints, getting blamed.

"I guess it's time we both went back to work," she said.

He got up reluctantly. She could barely remember if she'd scolded him or not.

When he had his coat on, he said, "I hope Billy's better soon."

"I'm letting him sleep."

"That's good."

"You can come again," she told him, watching his mouth. "You don't have to wait for me to be mad."

The lips smiled. "We'll keep trying to fix things. I'll let you know how it's going."

When he was gone and she returned to the kitchen, Billy was there in his flannel pyjamas. The bottoms were twisted at the waist. She slid her fingers in and straightened them. He was pale but he wasn't green. "Who was that?" he asked.

"Mr. Evert. The man you met at the meeting."

Suddenly the boy had energy. He pulled a chair to the window and climbed on, caught the last of Lance's little car circling the yard and entering the driveway. "I remember," he said. "I like him."

"I like him too," said Ella. "Do you feel like eating?"

He was still watching out the window. He shook his head.

"You have to eat, you know."

"But not now."

When Tom got back home, Ella had a cold lunch waiting for him. Billy was asleep on the couch.

"He's always pale," Ella said. "I'm going to take him to the doctor."

Tom had an urge to argue and did not know why.

"I'll wait a week, then," she said, as if he had spoken against her.

He quickly finished the sandwich and drank off the last of the tea. When he took his dishes to the sink, he saw cups and bread plates already there.

"You had company."

"Lance Evert from the plant. I phoned and asked for Alf Dietz but he sent Lance."

"Did he have anything to say?"

"Not really. Just that they were trying this and that."

"That's helpful."

"You can phone them yourself. Be as forceful as you please."

Tom put on his coveralls, parka, moccasins, and overalls. When the stinging air hit him, he was glad, even though it tasted of the burning pit. Lately every conversation with Ella went like that: shooting off into sourness over nothing. He could say it was not her fault, when she'd been up half the night with a sick boy, but why was it never anyone else's head she bit off? She had patience with the kids but none for him.

He started across to the one-ton, and King, the black Lab, came trotting from his doghouse. Together they would go to the bale pile. King would dive under every bale Tom lifted, hoping for a mouse. When the load was on, they would head for the sweeter air of the Lower Place, where the cows would be crowded in the nearest corner bawling for relief.

Weeks later, Tom and Ella were outside doing chores in the morning dark. There had been stink again, and Billy woke up twice during the night. Tom's usual chores were to water and feed the pigs, but today he grabbed a bucket and followed Ella to the barn. They sat on their three-legged stools, heads in the flanks of the cows, and roared milk against the metal until both buckets had a halo of froth. The cow-smelling warmth was comfort, and, though they did not speak—or because they did not—there was a feeling of well-being between them. This was what it had been like, Tom remembered, before the plant came. They had been living with the plant for so short a time but it had changed everything.

The light before dawn came while they were in the barn. Ella said there was something funny about the hired man's shack, something about the walls, but he could not see it and thought she must be wrong. Later, when she was making pancakes, Tom scratched ice off the window so he could look at the shack again. Just then, the first ray of sunlight shot across the yard, and he saw it clearly. The walls, which Kees had painted white last summer, were streaked yellow and green. With the leftover paint, Kees had done the trim on the chophouse, and every length of trim was the same mess. As Ella came toward Tom, drying her hands on the tea towel, he said, "Look at this, for Jesus sake."

"Tom, I've asked you to stop that."

"Well look for yourself."

Ella stared for a while, then said, "I'll phone later."

"Eat your breakfast first."

"I said later, didn't I?"

Then Jeannie and Billy were in the room, and went to look out where Tom had scratched off the frost. Jeannie started to cry, which she almost never did, and that touched off Billy, who didn't even know what he was looking at. Tom shouted, "Stop crying! Both of you!" and the way they looked at him, and Ella looked at him, filled him with such shame he left the house. He went to his shop and sat in the banded light from the cracked windows, smoking away the hunger that gnawed in his stomach.

For Ella the week was a nightmare from which she could not wake. Billy simply would not get well. For two nights after the night the paint had discoloured, he slept through but was so tired in the morning she had to pick him up and carry him to breakfast. Then he fell back asleep over his cereal, the spoon falling out of his limp hand to the linoleum.

Ella did not phone about the paint for several days. She wanted Lance Evert in her kitchen again, but was afraid that, if he came, she would break into sobs before him. Finally she admitted to Tom that she hadn't made the call, and he surprised her by going straight to the wall and making it himself. He seemed to be talking to Dietz and said something about replacement paint. The idea that it would probably be Lance who brought the paint lifted her up higher than she'd been in days.

But Lance's car did not come into the yard that day. It was another bad morning when he did appear. She opened the door before he knocked. He had two one-gallon paint cans by their wire handles. King wasn't barking which meant Tom and he were off somewhere with the old truck. Lance asked where he should put the cans.

"How about on that building?" She pointed to Kees's shack. Lance stood round shouldered. "I'm joking. Bring them in and set them in the porch."

"The paint that's on there is lead based. That's why it discoloured. This paint has no lead. It should be fine."

She had made herself a pot of tea and it was steeped on the table. She poured him a cup and offered cream, which he took. She sat on the edge of her chair, her hands in the apron over her lap. She knew she looked like hell, probably had a cinch of worry in between her eyebrows. Hadn't even looked in a mirror this morning.

Lance asked where Billy was, and she said he was lying down in the living room.

"Have you taken him to the doctor?"

"Yes, we went yesterday. They took blood. The doctor thinks it's a problem with his blood but won't say until the test comes back."

A silence spread.

"I'm afraid they won't find anything, and this will go on and on." She raked a hand back through her hair, and that made her think again about what Lance was seeing. Her hair had not been washed for a week. Her hands were sore and red from the cold and the morning's milking. "Can't you stop it? This stink?"

"Is it still as bad? We've found a couple of sources and dealt with them."

"When Mr. Dietz came here the first time, I asked him why he didn't shut the plant down—if it doesn't work properly. He said it would take a long time to start up again. I want you to tell Mr. Dietz, and Mr. Comstock—and yourself—that I don't care how long it takes your plant to start up again or what it costs you in time and money. I don't think it's a good enough reason to take a child who was perfectly healthy and make him sick."

"I'll tell them," said Lance.

She realized she had no more to say, that she had been hoping he would have a solution, or some encouragement at least. But now she felt this empty silence was all there would ever be between them. She had wanted badly for him to come, but now she wanted him gone.

"That's all I have to say."

"I don't like that I have nothing to tell you," said Lance. "I hate that this is so hard on you and Billy. And your daughters."

"The girls are the lucky ones. They go off to school and breathe clean air."

Billy appeared beside Ella's chair. He was ghost pale, but smiled when Lance looked at him.

Lance reached and touched Billy's shoulder with a fingertip. The boy ran off. He had his red hand-knitted slippers on. He ran a couple of steps and slid. His feet hit the wood sill of the door into the next room. He pretended to stumble.

"I want you to know that I care about you and your family," Lance said, staring after the boy. "I'm not just pretending. If there's anything I can do to help, I will."

Ella could not stop looking at Lance, until Billy came back again. He was carrying the little blue box, and he raised it toward Lance's face and lifted off the lid at the last moment. Inside on the bed of cotton were half a dozen birds' eggs, holes poked in the ends, blown empty.

"Nice, Billy. Did you find these yourself?"

He shook his head.

"It's his father's collection, from when he was a boy." Ella slipped an arm around Billy's slender waist, drew him to her. Billy put the lid back on, ducked out of Ella's arm, and ran and slid away.

Because she felt so tired and empty, Ella let herself stare more at the pretty clean-shaven face before her. Finally, he was embarrassed and looked away.

"I'll go, then," he said and rose. It took every bit of resistance she had not to ask him to have another cup of tea, another scone. She would not let herself get up from her chair until the rustle and thump of parka and boots had stopped and the outside door had squeezed closed. Then she watched him get in his car, start the motor, and leave.

Bertha Kenhardt had called the meeting. Tom and two other local men sat in her varnish-smelling living room, a place heavy with antiques that her dead husband had bought at auctions. Vic Sebald and Johnny Court were on the couch, Tom in the armchair. Bertha perched on a spool-back chair that she'd dragged from the kitchen. Her legs, in stockings the colour of calamine lotion, were folded underneath.

Back when Bertha had asked them to keep journals about the gas, Tom had thought she lived too far away to be getting much of it. Now he knew better. The rotten-egg smell was strong, and his eyes stung.

"Did you men bring your journals?"

Vic and Johnny held up scribblers. Tom just had loose sheets in his lap. Bertha's own document was in a three-ring binder. She flopped it open.

"What I'll do is pick a date when I had a problem here at home. Then I would like you men to read what you have written for that date.

"February twenty-third," she began. "I woke up in the night because I had a severe headache. The smell of rotten egg was very strong, and I was frightened. I went outside and checked my dogs and cats. I could not see that they were affected. Also the gas outside seemed to be dissipating better than it did in the house. I opened my windows, even though it was very cold, and that seemed to help."

Johnny read next. Alice had woken him up that night to tell him the baby was hot and sick. He drove them to her mother's place in town.

Vic said he had nothing written down, so they must have been okay that night.

What Tom had to read was that Kees had been sick and came pounding on the house door.

"Are you saying the hired man had a problem but you did not?" Bertha asked.

"The hired man's shack is pretty breezy. Whatever is outside gets inside. Our house is a little tighter."

"Maybe that's it," said Bertha. "Maybe I need to have someone putty my windows."

Tom was feeling impatient. Did Bertha mean for them to go through every day of their diaries? "Bertha," he said, "I was hoping we'd discuss what we're going to do."

She arched an eyebrow. "Tell us what you think, Tom. You clearly have an opinion."

"I think we need to work on a letter to the government. I was hoping you might write it and we could sign it."

"If there is to be a letter, it would be best if I wrote it."

"I'm not getting this," Vic said. "A letter to who about what?"

Tom had thought this through. "A letter in which we describe the trouble we're having and how it connects to the plant. I don't think our MLA will help. He's too concerned with staying in good with the premier. I was thinking we could send it to Ormond Cardwell."

"You can't complain to someone else's MLA, can you?" said Johnny. "Why not send it to Manning? Go to the top."

"Clearly," said Bertha, "it should go to the health minister. That's Mr. Onge. I'll make a carbon copy and send that to Mr. Sturgeous, the MLA for Haultain."

"We should pass the letter around to everyone who's affected here," said Vic. "More signatures, the better."

"Paul Gersten should sign, that's for sure," said Tom. "He gets more gas than we do. And Hughie McGrady. I can take the letter to those two."

"*Gertie* Gersten," said Bertha, staring coldly at Tom. "All the wives should sign. Your Ella should certainly sign."

"What about Don Harbeg?" asked Vic.

"I don't know," said Tom.

"Why not?"

"He works at the plant."

"So you don't trust him."

"Oh hell. Ask him, then. If he doesn't want to sign, he doesn't have to. But as soon as he hears about it, the plant will know."

"Can we get started on the letter?" said Bertha.

Each man stated his family's complaints. Bertha translated aloud while she wrote. It was amazing how she could take what each of them said and turn it into her kind of language on the fly. It was better the way she said things.

As Tom was getting ready to go, Bertha said to him, "I assumed Ella would be coming today."

"Ella doesn't like to leave Billy right now. He's been sick."

"Because of the plant?"

"They're testing his blood."

"She could have brought him too."

"He's sicker than that."

"You take this to her." Bertha gave him a pie covered in wax paper.

Sitting with his truck running, Tom pulled out his makings bag and rolled a smoke. He had not been allowed to smoke in Bertha's house. Vic and Johnny idled their trucks for a minute and left, each man waving, but Tom sat rooted. *Why have you kept Ella from coming? Make sure you let Ella sign the letter.*

For a few seconds, Tom thought of going back inside. He imagined telling Bertha Kenhardt, straight out, that he was not a tyrant in his marriage. If she didn't believe him about Ella and Billy, she should phone Ella and ask. Then he heard in his mind what that would sound like, and was glad to have said nothing.

It was Friday, Billy's most frustrating day. Though the girls likely did not miss him at all, Billy missed them badly when they were at school. It became worse as Monday marched toward Friday.

By afternoon, Ella could no longer placate him with games of fish. He had been harping about one of the barn cats that had recently had kittens, so she dressed him in his antique snowsuit (his father's when he was a boy) and led him to the barn. She would not let him climb to the hayloft but went up herself. She walked around heavily so Billy would hear the creaking and believe she had done a proper search. But while she was up there, Billy called that he'd found the cat family in a manger. The kittens were old enough to run away but did not. They were in a daze of kneading and suckling.

Then came a loud noise in the north end of the barn, and the cat ran with a kitten in her mouth. In half a minute they were all gone from the pocket of straw.

Billy slammed his hands on the polished rail just as Lance Evert's head appeared over the box-stall gate. Billy plunged out the small door in the gate's bottom, pushing Lance's legs out of the way. Lance looked after him, confused.

"Never mind," Ella said. "You scared some kittens."

But there was more on Lance's face than that.

"Oh, Lord, what now?"

"We've had an accident at the plant, caused by a bad leak. Alf Dietz says you should evacuate."

Ella pulled off her glove and wrapped the bare hand around the back of her neck. She was so angry suddenly she could hardly look at him. At the same time, she felt herself begin to cry. He opened the gate and entered the stall; stepped toward her with his hand raised, wanting to console. She lifted her own hand like a stop sign.

"I don't know how much more of this I can stand," she said.

"I'm sorry."

"Of course you are. But you can't do anything. What do you mean by accident?"

"There are valves where the pipeline from the field enters the plant. A side-pipe to a pressure gauge there must have cracked. The gauge blew off."

"What's that got to do with us?"

"One of our men went in the shack when he heard liquid hitting the roof. He tried to pinch the pipe shut and he was gassed."

"He's dead?"

"Our safety man got him going again. I was there."

"You're saying the gas could be coming here."

"You should get out."

"Have you been to Gerstens'?"

"I'll go there next."

"Don't stare at me. Go!"

He turned to leave, but she grabbed his arm, pulled him back around, and kissed his mouth. Then she pushed him hard away.

Billy was on his way back as Lance ran past him. "Why is Mr. Evert running?"

"He has to tell Mrs. Gersten something. And we need to go to town, right now."

"Why are you laughing?"

"I'm not laughing, honey. Let's go."

4

Ryder Farm, 1961

TWO DAYS AND NIGHTS in her mother's house, with crucifixes above each doorway and statues of Mary and Joseph in front of the dresser mirror where she slept, pulled Ella back from the reckless feeling. It reminded her that what she had done was a sin. In her mother's house, swathed and almost smothered in the smells of her childhood, she could not imagine doing any such thing again. A moment of madness brought on by fear and sorrow. That was all.

It was two more days until Tom felt the stink had tapered off enough that it made sense for Ella and the children to return home. They had been back only one day and a night when a blizzard tore into the farm from the north. The windbreaks on that side were younger, and the wind and snow poured through and tossed up drifts around the house almost to the eaves. The municipality did not send any ploughs before the storm stopped, and by then the girls had not been to school for three days. Tom was having to feed his feedlot calves black hay from the roof of their bedding shed. His mood was just as black as the hay when he described how it made them cough. Like big dogs barking.

It was when the roads were finally cleared that Lance Evert called. Ella was playing cowboys and Indians with Billy, using a bunched-up rug for hills around the fort. Lance was awkward on the phone and could not seem to come to the point. He was bursting with whatever it was he could not say. It sounded like he had something to give her, and Ella was made nervous thinking what that might be.

"Is there something wrong at the plant?" she asked.

"Not now, no."

"I have food on the stove," she lied.

"I have some news. Something's going to happen in a few weeks that I'd like to tell you about. I was wondering if I could come down."

"Tom's the one you should talk to, and he's at our Lower Place. If it's important, I'll give you directions."

Lance gave false-sounding excuses why he could not look for Tom but had time to come to the house right now. That he wanted to see her badly enough to lie and cavil touched her hard, like a finger jabbing the bone at her collar.

"Come, then." When she hung the earpiece in its cradle, she was out of breath.

Billy had long ago tired of waiting for her. He had switched to cards and had them laid out all over the hooked rug. Ella did not ask why. She went into the bathroom and, behind the closed door, looked at herself in the mirror and primped her hair. She wanted to tell herself that she had no intention of leading the young man on—but she had already kissed him. In the mirror, she saw her face redden. "Kissed him," she said aloud, so she could watch her mouth make the words. She brushed the red spot on her cheek. Her hand, veined and corded, looked like her mother's.

She smoothed her dress tight over her breasts. She told herself she was doing something for her family that Tom could not do. Right now, Lance was on his way with information they probably needed. The fact that she had not written anything in the binder or told Tom what Lance had already said was something she batted away like a fat old fly. She could still do it. She would when she was ready.

Minutes later, Lance sat at her table. He was having his usual problem raising his eyes. They were focused into the orange tea in his cup. His nose was slim and precisely made, unlike any nose she had seen on a man. She suspected he would have preferred coffee but they were running low. She could have served Lance water stirred with ashes and he would have thanked her very much.

He asked about Billy. "You said you were taking him to the doctor."

"They phoned during the snowstorm. The tests show that he has anemia."

Lance winced. "Did they give him something?"

"Iron pills. I haven't picked them up yet because of the storm. They want him to eat liver. What's this about, Lance?"

He looked into his tea. His ears were red. "There's going to be testing. The air will be tested, to see if it's safe."

"Because of your accident at the plant?"

"It's more because of complaints from the community."

Ella had signed the letter, while telling Tom that she sincerely doubted that a letter from a few farmers and their wives was going to change anything. She was having as much trouble imagining it now, but where else could the complaints Lance was talking about have come from?

"Who will be doing it? The testing. You people?"

"Someone else. His name is Dr. Hemmel."

"Who is he?"

"An independent expert, a scientist from a university down east. He's an expert in industrial fogs and acid in rain."

"When will this happen?"

"Sometime next week."

Everything Ella could think to say was critical. The tests would be faked or fixed. They would not lead to the closure of the plant no matter how bad the results were. Lance had probably come here imagining the news would fill her with delight—and that the delight would spill over onto him.

"You'll hear this again, officially," he said. "I just wanted to tell you as soon as possible."

"I wish Tom was here. He would have questions. How does a scientist test air?"

"He'll bring vacuum bottles, bottles with the air sucked out. When he's in a place he wants to test, he breaks the vacuum and lets the bottle fill."

"And will he test our farm?"

"I'm sure of it. Probably right here in your yard."

She took slow breaths. She got up and put scones on a plate, brought butter and a pot of jam. As he scooped both onto the scone, it occurred to her that he must not be eating properly.

"If you were in our shoes, would you trust these tests?"

"I'd trust Dr. Hemmel. I mean I do trust him. I phoned one of my professors in Edmonton when I heard. He couldn't believe Dr. Hemmel was coming here. He said he's a world authority."

"And is Aladdin paying him?"

"I'm not sure. Aladdin or the government. Or both." After a moment, Lance spoke again. "I know how that sounds but I doubt a man of his standing would risk his reputation to please an oil company—or a government, for that matter."

It was time to get him out of her kitchen. She did not want him here when Tom came home for lunch. But she had another question.

"Why are you excited about this? What if they find the gas is bad and shut your plant down?"

"I want things to be safe. If it isn't, we should shut down. Like you said."

Watching him dab crumbs from the plate with the pad of his finger, she asked, "Are you still at the motel?"

"I'm renting a house with someone now."

"Who?"

"A mechanic from the Crowsnest Pass. A guy named Andy."

"A friend."

"Yeah. He's a friend."

"The two of you could save to buy your own houses if you cooked your own meals. Men can cook, you know."

"It's good advice."

"Take a couple of scones. One for Andy. I need to finish them up before I bake again."

She was careful not to touch him, to stay far back so he wouldn't be tempted to touch her either. All the same, she was sure she had sent him away happy and didn't mind that she had.

Tom was having supper, and his girls were arguing over who could sing better, Bobby Vinton or Bobby Curtola. Tom had heard of neither of them. Billy was doing everything with his liver but eat it. Then Ella said that Lance Evert had been around again, to talk about air testing.

"They'll be doing it next week."

Tom cut a little piece of liver and waggled it on his fork until he had Billy's attention. Tom put the liver in his own mouth and chewed slowly, smiling. "Good stuff, eh, Billy?"

Billy scowled.

When Ella told Tom about the anemia and that Billy should eat liver, she'd said, "We will all eat liver—and like it." There were bits of chewed grey at the edges of each plate. The piece in front of Tom looked like the sole of a hobo's boot.

"Can I go now?" Jeannie asked.

"Not yet, dear. Finish your meat."

"What else did he say? Lance."

Ella rattled off a few things about an expert from down east. "I have to admit, I think it was your letter that caused it," she said.

"Did Evert say that?"

"Not in so many words. He said it was about the complaints, and that's the impression I got."

"You should've asked him."

At once, she was angry. "I told him he should talk to you. I told him to find you at the Lower Place. But he wanted to come here." She jumped up and started scraping liver from all the plates onto one. "If you're not satisfied with how I handle things, you can go to the plant and talk to Dietz or Lance Evert yourself. I suspect Lance was telling us before Dietz was planning to. A favour, in other words."

"Why would he do us a favour?"

"You kids can go now," she said, but she was glaring at Tom.

"When will they do these tests?"

"I already told you. Next week."

"Will they come here? To the farm?"

"Where else would they go?"

The kids were gone. Tom pulled his tobacco can toward him, unscrewed the lid, began rolling a smoke.

"I can't stuff the liver into him, now, can I?" Ella said.

Tom snapped the lighter wheel, sucked in deeply, coached himself to keep quiet.

Ella needed a friend. Though they hadn't talked in a while, she phoned Dora Bauer and asked if she wanted a visitor. Dora sounded hesitant. "When?"

"I was thinking of today, but it could be another day. The plant has been so smelly, and Billy gets quite sick with it. I was thinking of going to town with him to shop, but then I thought how long it's been since he's seen Petey."

"We call him Pete now. He insists on it."

"It sounds like I've picked a bad day."

"No, no. You come. You and Billy."

When they got to Bauers' new place, about halfway to town on the gravel roads, Dora was in the yard to greet them. She had on a thick grey sweater, the kind Indians make on the coast. Pete came from around the corner of their house. He had grown, but what was more pronounced was a change in his manner. He was less giddy; stern and a bit suspicious.

Billy must have seen it too, for he stood back as if waiting for an introduction. The Bauer dog stood at a distance, barking. The fool. Ella had known that dog since it was a puppy.

"Go to your house, you blasted thing!" roared Dora. Then she hooked Ella's arm and said, "Come to the barn." She led for a few steps, then stopped. "Billy, I didn't even say hello. Come closer, Pete, for heaven's sake. It's your friend Billy."

The two boys came side by side and walked together, but, continuing to the barn, Ella could not hear any talk between them.

Dora went ahead through the gloom. It was very clean for a barn, and the light bulbs were high up and cast little light. Over the wall of a box stall, a horse of incredible height shoved its head and murmured. Dora drew a carrot from her sweater pocket and fed it into the horse's teeth. The crunch was loud and made them laugh. The boys laughed too.

"What is he?"

"Purebred Tennessee Walker. A stallion. I've always wanted one."

"Do you ride him?"

"Of course! And what a stride, Ella. Like a rocking chair, and very fast. I haven't seen a horse that can outwalk him."

"But how do you get on?"

"I need a fence or a stool. I don't mind. He's quite patient as long as I keep the oats and carrots coming."

After the horse, Dora showed them a few fancy chickens she'd gone to great lengths to buy. Finally, they were in the house. Pete invited Billy down a hallway to his room to show him sports cards. Dora seated Ella at the dining room table while she went into her big kitchen to make tea. She kept talking in a loud voice, though there was no partition between them. Ella kept noticing things about Dora that she thought were new, but was it possible she had forgotten what her friend was like? Or wanted to believe that she had changed?

"We haven't gone to the old place much. I find it easier to accept if I don't go. The sacrifice is that I don't see you. But I do like this house. I do think it's better."

She was begging confirmation of her choices, and Ella gave it. But while she praised the house, she was finding flaws. The dining room being part of the living room was a big space to heat. Long after she heard the propane furnace cutting in, she was chilled.

When they got down to visiting, Ella realized she did not want the conversation they were having. It could not go where she needed it to. Maybe if Dora had never moved, they could have taken one of their long walks, and Ella could have said something about the young man at the plant. "He has a crush on me, odd as that might sound." But here in this strange house, with this strange Dora, who would rather talk about her Tennessee Walking Horse than any-thing else, it was not possible to say even that little bit, let alone the absurd truth that she had kissed the young man.

Dora's company was only making her feel lonelier, and she longed to leave even before the tea and squares were on the table.

She considered hopping up and saying, "Oh my goodness, Dora, look at the time. We have a doctor's appointment." But she sat slack shouldered, dazed, and let Dora account for the time that had passed.

"You're very quiet, Ella. I thought you'd be full of news."

"I don't have any, really. I'm just thinking what a mistake we've made to stay. We would have been better off selling like you and Curt did. Maybe we'd still be neighbours if we'd sold at the same time."

"I'm amazed to hear you say that! I can't imagine you anywhere except on your home place. I've often told Curt that's what made it easier for us."

"You're right," Ella said. "It would break my heart to leave. But it might wind up breaking my heart anyway."

"Oh, dear. I hear that the gas has been awful."

Maybe Ella imagined it, but she thought Dora brightened a little as she said it.

Ella finished her tea and one small square. She told Dora it had been a great pleasure to see her. Dora asked her to stay longer, let the boys get reacquainted, but Ella rose, said they were out of time. She had much to do in town and was needed back home for chores. Billy was back with her by then, and perked up at the word "town." He had twenty-five cents burning in his pocket.

When they were in the car, Ella turned for home.

"You said town!"

"We have no time for town."

"Mom!"

"We'll go tomorrow. You'll get two trips in two days."

"I want to go now!"

"You're being childish," she said, and he began to cry.

"You lied to Mrs. Bauer."

She took a shortcut over seldom-used roads, having to bash her way through drifts. She hoped that would catch the boy's attention, but he preferred to cry. She felt her own tears welling, and what she kept seeing in her mind was the sweet treble clef brooch that Tom had surprised her with at Christmas. Why had that not worked? she asked herself. Why had they started bickering again so soon afterwards?

The kiss with Lance would not fade away. She would have to confess it to the priest if she was ever going to be rid of it, and her faced burned at the thought of saying the words through the confessional screen. And there was absolutely no sense confessing a sin you were likely to commit again.

Another night of smell, of Billy thrashing in his bed. Another flat discussion in Tom and Ella's bed about whether to get the kids up and take them to town.

Tom asked Ella to phone the plant, thinking she would rage less and get more out of them. But she was practically shouting herself when she asked for Dietz. After a while, in a quieter voice she asked for Mr. Evert. But he wasn't there either. She asked that Dietz call her first thing in the morning. Tom thought the conversation was over when Ella said, "I know we can leave. We've left often enough. You should try living like that, picking up in the night like people in a war."

In the end they let the kids sleep as long as they could. They checked on Billy a few times and hardly slept themselves. When they got up, it was still in the solid dark, and Ella said she would take Billy to her parents after chores were done. She had shopping to do: more bloody liver.

Tom told her to leave straight away and take the girls. It would give them a break from the school bus.

"What about the cows?"

"I'll milk them."

"How will Mr. Snow know not to wait?"

"You'll see him on the road. Flag him down and tell him." He could see she was working up other complications. "Just go."

Tom got the buckets and was headed for the barn. The two Holsteins waited at the half door with their tight bags. One groaned at the sight of him. Then Lance Evert's car tumbled down the hill from the plant, looking like a toy. Tom stood with the buckets, expecting a blue roof to crest the top of their driveway. Instead the car appeared farther along, headed north toward Gerstens'. He dropped the buckets, jumped in his one-ton, and drove as fast as it would go. Paul had pigs of all ages, and Tom wanted to know if they could live in this gas, wanted to know too what Evert would say if Paul's pigs weren't doing well. That's where he was headed.

Evert did make the turn into Gerstens', and when Tom got there he edged his truck up tight to Evert's rear bumper, so he had the little car trapped against a row of caraganas.

He walked the footpath to the top where he could see Paul's hatless head, then the whole of his lank body crossing his yard to the pigpens. He had full slop buckets weighing his long arms. Luke, his twelve-year-old, was close behind, dragging a straw bale on a hook. Lance Evert came last, his hands plugged in the pockets of his jacket. As always, he looked out of place. Tom's girls used to cut the people out of the Eaton's catalogue and glue them into their colouring books. That's what neat, clean, slender Lance Evert looked like walking behind Paul and Luke Gersten: like a cut-out from an eastern catalogue.

Already Tom was dizzy from gas. Whatever it was at home, this was worse. Paul reached one end of his line of pigpens and leaned a bucket on the first trough. He spilled slop as he moved along, changed buckets and continued down the line. Luke had broken the straw bale. He climbed the fence with an armload of flakes and landed in the muck, a sow grunting at his legs.

"C'mere," Paul called to Evert when the second pail was drained. He led the engineer to a larger enclosure thick with weaner pigs.

Tom was quite close now, but neither Lance nor Paul had seen him. Lance was staring into the pen blankly, the way town people always look at farm animals. Then one of the weaners fell on its side, and the others stampeded over it. Paul leaned in and knocked them away. The downed pig got woozily to its feet.

"It's like they're drunk," he said to Lance. "I bet they die."

Turning away from this pronouncement was when Lance saw Tom. There was a second before his blank face broke into a smile.

Paul said, "Hello there, Tommy." His long wrists hung slack over the bristled fence. "You got pigs yet?"

"Two sows are due any time."

"Hope you have better luck than me. Mine are dying and walking into walls."

"What do you make of it?" Tom asked Lance, who was rummaging in his coat pocket.

"I don't know much about pigs," he said.

"You can see they're sick, can't you?"

"I see that."

This got a lazy laugh out of Luke.

"We did some work on the amine tower," said Lance. The thing he had pulled out of his pocket looked like a thermometer. He broke the tip off and brought the tube close to his eyes. "The tower's been overflowing and we've almost fixed that. It should have reduced the gas loss."

"I don't know what any of that means," said Paul, "but either it didn't work or the gas came out somewhere else."

"What about that?" Tom asked, pointing. Black smoke rolled at them from the burning pit.

"Yeah," said Paul, "that stuff stinks like hell and hurts your throat too."

Lance stared at the glass tube.

"Are your kids okay?" Tom asked Paul.

"They're not. I'd take them out of here but my truck's broke down."

Lance put the glass thing back in his pocket, then reached and scratched the back of his head. "I'll take them."

"That would help."

"You should probably go too. You and your son." Lance nodded at Luke.

"Can't be done, not in that little car of yours."

"You can come to my place if you want," said Tom. "It stinks there too but it's not this bad."

"Luke and me better stay with our pigs."

It made no sense but Tom didn't argue. Evert and Paul discussed where Gertie and the kids should go. Luke was sent to the house to get things moving. Tom followed Lance to his car. The look of Lance's tiny car sandwiched between the caragana row and the rusted grille of the truck pleased Tom, made him swagger a bit. Lance stood by his car door, hand on the handle.

"Something else you wanted to say?" he asked.

"I've got two sows about to farrow. We're not in the pig business for fun."

"I understand that."

"I doubt it. Do you know what Paul's truck is broken down from? No gas in the tank or money to buy any. Pigs and a bit of cream are his only sources of income."

"Is your family all right?"

"You know they're not because Ella phoned last night. Ella's taken Billy to town, so don't bother going to our place."

There was no sign of Gertie and the Gersten kids yet. Tom leaned on the tall fender of his grain truck and rolled a smoke. He held out his makings to Lance but the young man shook his head.

"I'm sorry about last night," Lance said.

"They blood-tested Billy," Tom said. "Doc says he's got anemia. Said we should feed him liver. He hates liver, and so do I. Even the dog will only eat it raw."

Tom waited, expecting Evert to say he was sorry again, but the young fellow seemed to understand how weak and unhelpful that was to hear.

Tom continued. "I could say the plant caused Billy's sickness. You could say it didn't. But I'll tell you one thing. Ella and I grew up around here, eating what our kids eat. Our families' beef, pork, eggs, milk, butter. Lived out of our gardens in summer and ate our own canned stuff in winter. Now suddenly our boy can't make good blood."

"We're starting a new round of maintenance. We'll change out filters and solutions."

"Why don't you just admit you don't know what to do?"

The two of them stood looking at each other until Lance turned sideways and stared at the plant.

"This is an important time of year on a farm," Tom said. "Besides the sows, the cows will start calving soon. My neighbours say I should take the whole works to our Lower Place, but I don't have electricity or buildings there for pigs. Or enough shelter for calving."

A deep rumble came from the plant. Tom nodded toward it.

"I can't even imagine what it's going to be like when that sonofabitch is bigger."

Then Gertie Gersten came, carrying two kids and bunting two more along the path with her knees. A fat cloth bag dangled from the crook of her arm. Lance ran to help. Tom remembered Ella's milk cows. He tipped his cap to Gertie and got into his truck.

Ella's car came into the yard earlier than Tom expected. He had finished feeding his cows and was unspooling straw bales, making a clean bed in the A-pens that held the heavy sows. He kept expecting Billy to come, to peek through the rails and make some funny comment about the sows and their peggy teats. But Billy did not show, and when Tom went inside for lunch, Billy wasn't there either. Ella explained that she had left him in town.

"Is he sicker?" Tom asked.

"Mom wanted him for a while." After a pause, she said, "I wanted to see if a week in town would help, if it would make his colour better."

"A *week*?"

"A day or two wouldn't prove anything."

"What if he gets a lot better?"

"I don't know," she said. "I haven't thought that far."

He tried to tell her about the situation at Gerstens', how it had left him worrying about the litters inside their own sows. But Ella hurried away on an errand he suspected was imaginary.

Tom's pattern was to have a second cup of tea and a smoke before he returned to work, but now he went outside and did his smoking by the pigpens, studying the sows. They lay inside on the fresh straw with their snouts into the fresh air, their ears forward over their tiny eyes. He also thought about how Ella had not looked at him the whole time they ate lunch.

Then came a new thought. In all the time since they met and were married, things had gone along, if not always well, then much as he had expected. They were both creatures with tempers and had occasionally had fights that shocked them both, rocked them back on their heels. But after it was over, what they wanted most was to mend the tear. That had always been possible before.

When the time in his life came to be a husband, a father, Tom had felt he was up to it. As long as things in their lives and the children's resembled what had gone before, he was able to do it all, even easily, and mostly without thought. But now, this thing, this plant, was testing him in undreamt ways. Daily he felt too ignorant and weak to solve their problems. He guessed that Ella felt the same way—that she was living in a life too foreign to predict. But knowing that was not a solution either.

The plant made a crack and then a huge shifting noise behind his back. He looked and there came the black smoke from the pit. The wind had moved, and the smoke coiled toward him. He saw the house door open and Ella come out in her town clothes with a suit-case. This she slid onto the back seat. She did not beckon him but stood beside the car waiting.

"What now?" he asked.

"I didn't have Billy's iron pills with me this morning. I have to go back. I might as well stay the night. He doesn't want to be there and he's probably upset."

"He never has liked their place much."

Tom was thinking of the odd smell, medicine, brandy, pipe smoke. The old man rocking in his leather chair with a three-foot-long pipe-stem in his teeth, the bowl on the floor, and a taper for relighting it.

"I wouldn't say he doesn't like it," Ella said.

Then don't say it, thought Tom.

"He prefers home, that's all," she added.

"Like you."

"Like anybody."

"You'd better go, then."

She studied him, her black eyes dancing around his face. She'd explained what she was doing clearly enough, but he felt left out anyway. He turned and went back to the pens. He heard the car door slam and the motor start. The tires spun in a pocket of mud. He was glad not to be watching.

———

Ella drove north and then west, but at the next intersection, she turned south for a mile, then east. She had made three sides of a square back in the direction of home and stopped in the blazed place that used to be Bauers' yard. A crew working for Aladdin had burned the house down and pushed the charred remains into the cellar hole. Then they bulldozed it flat. She parked atop where the cellar had been and waited. Soon Lance's car came around the corner of the windbreak. He pulled in between the caragana rows that had been the sides of Curt and Dora's garden. That was smart: to ensure the two vehicles were not seen together.

She followed his tire marks into the garden space. Lance jumped from his car as if levered by a spring. Then it was just the two of them, with the sixty-year-old poplars towering and the melting drifts leaking wet around their boots. She saw no need to be coy and took his hand and held it. They kissed. It lasted, and they held each other close afterwards. She got that far before being swamped by dread. She broke free and stood with her back to him, feeling the wind, a warm chinook, stroking through the trees.

Five minutes passed like this. It was odd how they did not talk, how it was like they lacked a language to do it in. Except for her everyday desire to see him and kiss him more, she had no list of wants, nothing on earth to ask or give.

"Did I do something wrong?" he asked, shy as a boy.

"No." She turned and took his hand again. Smooth, cool, young hand. It must disgust him a little, inside all his foolish love, to feel the rough splits on her fingers.

"Things like this don't happen," she said. "Not here. You must know that."

"But here we are."

"I honestly don't know what I'm doing." She laughed. When she heard the songbird sound of this, it was shockingly like a stranger's voice. "I don't want any of the outcomes this leads to. It's like the gas from your plant has made me crazy."

"You're not crazy."

"Then you must be."

When she had phoned him and asked him to come here at this time, she had indeed meant to touch him and kiss him. But what was supposed to follow was that she would tell him it was over before it started, this whatever-it-was, and that she would never meet him again. From this moment onward, he must treat her like any other local woman. She had planned that speech and was not saying any of it.

"You probably think I hate my husband to do this."

"I don't know about that."

"That's what I would think, if I were you, but it isn't true."

"I guess I don't know anything about being married."

"I thought I did. Back before the plant, I thought I was an expert. I looked down on people whose marriages went wrong."

"Is it the plant that changed things?"

"Of course, but I don't know what that means. Didn't there have to be something wrong in the first place?"

"It wasn't me that changed things, then." He was looking down at the ground between them. She couldn't tell if he wanted to be the reason or not.

"You're just a nice young fellow who came along."

"Is that all?"

"No. It's not all."

She kissed him again, and he was eager to continue. "I have to go," she said. "Billy's in town. He's expecting me."

"Can we meet again? Here?" he said, and she knew how it was for him, how he was blindly driven to do this and then push it further and further. The flattering, maddening thing that women always deal with when they deal with men.

"I just don't know."

Then he was different. She saw the change. Someone else emerged, maybe the person he was at work.

"Could you meet me here on Monday? At the same time, if it suits you?"

She looked at him. She did not say no.

"If you're not here that day," he said, "I'll assume you've made your decision not to see me anymore. Unless I hear differently after that, I'll leave you alone."

Right then, even before she left his company, she was planning a strategy for Monday. Not one bit of the reluctance she claimed to have entered into it.

She gave his hand a quick squeeze and went to the car. She felt nervous suddenly and looked in all directions, as if all the eyes of the community were watching. She saw a motion along the nearest coulee edge, maybe a crow's wing or the black tail of a horse flashing. She drove away, afraid to look in the rear-view.

Tom was wishing Billy was home. He would have been excited to see the expert, Dr. Hemmel, holding a silver bottle up like a priest with his chalice. He'd done something to break its seal and let it fill with air. Tom would have enjoyed explaining it to his son.

Dr. Hemmel was an odd man, all business and rude. He was about five and a half feet tall, with a funny crown of salt-and-pepper hair shaped out to a point in the front. From some angles, he looked like he had a little ship on his head. The scientist had shown scant interest in Tom when Lance Evert had introduced them and kept his hands in his overcoat pockets. Maybe Hemmel thought Tom went around covered in pig shit. Ella wasn't there. She'd gone to town again; her mother had phoned to say Billy wanted her. When the bottle was filled and capped, Hemmel spoke, and Lance Evert wrote something down in a scribbler. Using a fat grease pen, Hemmel wrote #1 on the bottle's silver side.

"We're done here," he said.

"I see you picked a day when it's not stinking," Tom said to the two of them.

"We did not pick the day," said the scientist unpleasantly. "This is the day I could be here."

"I also see the burning pit isn't burning."

The scientist swung a look at Lance Evert.

"It won't be a fair test of anything," Tom said.

"I'll be testing again tomorrow," said Hemmel. "Then I have to return east."

"Jim dandy. Pontius Pilate washed his hands."

"We have a full day of tests. Let's get moving." Hemmel said this to Lance Evert, then went to the truck and let himself in the passenger side.

Tom had been expecting more and he wasn't sure what. Glass globes? Copper pots lit from underneath? Bubbles racing down tubes?

He followed Lance to the truck. "Who ordered this air study?" he asked. "Was it Comstock?"

"I think it was the government. But Aladdin was willing to go along with it."

"I imagine Aladdin had no choice if the government told them to. But I bet Aladdin got to pick the day."

"It's like Dr. Hemmel said. It's the day he could be here. It wouldn't have made any difference if we'd picked it. It's not as if we know what this plant or the weather's going to do one day to the next."

Tom laughed. It was a good answer. Hemmel and Evert had come in a company pickup, and Tom was looking at the rear window, at Hemmel's head inside. Suddenly the scientist jerked sideways and thumped on the truck's horn. Tom's old dog sleeping in a shadow came up barking.

Evert had his hand on the door handle.

"That's not true of the burning pit, is it?" Tom said. "You guys fire that up when you please. Today, you chose not to."

Evert didn't answer, and Tom left it at that. He didn't want to hear the scientist hit the horn again, in case it made him angry enough to jerk open the door and tell the little prick to mind his manners.

Driving home from the Lower Place in the afternoon, Tom saw the Aladdin pickup by the old schoolhouse. Hemmel was holding up another steel bottle. Ahead, Tom could see the black smoke from the plant's burning pit coasting over the rises toward them. He could smell and taste it. He smiled to think of the bottle tasting it too.

It was the Sunday night before her visit with Lance Evert, and Ella was thankful Billy was in town. The smell was the usual one but had a texture, like wads of tissue winding in your nostrils. In the early hours, the plant siren howled for the first time ever, a sound that rose and swooped and did not stop for a long time. The flare was huge and seemed to move in time to the siren.

Donna, who was not the type to cry, was crying. Jeannie called her a baby, and Ella told her older daughter to shut up, words she never used. Tom went outside and came back briefly to say that the first of the sows was about to farrow. He stayed out for more than an hour, until Ella feared he had been knocked out or even killed by gas. She watched out the window until she saw his lantern pick up and move.

Then Tom was in the porch and calling her. He'd left the porch light off because he carried the lantern. Its upward light made him ghost faced.

"What's wrong?"

"It's terrible out there. You and the girls have to go."

"Why doesn't he phone us? Why is nobody telling us what we're supposed to do?"

"Don't wait on them. Just take the girls and go."

"You should go too. It's not like you're any stronger when it comes to gas."

"I have a sow to look after. She's lying down and ready. I want to see her farrow."

"That's stupid!"

He laughed. In the yellow light, his red eyes looked devilish. "This plant makes us stupider every day," he said.

She would have argued more but he left, slamming the door too hard. She did as he said, roused the girls and loaded them into the car.

"What about Dad?" Jeannie said.

"He said he's not coming."

"Why?"

"His sow is farrowing."

Donna was crying again. "Why is this happening?"

They could see across the yard where Tom had set his lantern on the ground outside the pigpen. Jeannie banged the window with her fist. Ella said nothing. She backed the car from its spot and pushed the pedal so hard the back tires spun before they caught. She looked once in the rear-view at Tom's light, then drove. The road and fields were bright but sapped of their real colour. Everything had turned the yellow of sulphur. She told her daughters to hold their breaths as long as they could. Then she gunned it.

In the dawn light, Tom was reaching his pitchfork into the mouth of the pigpen. The sow snorted at him. He fished with the tines beside her pale flank, where the living piglets were hooked to her teats. He drew the fork back and brought another body to the light, turned and tossed it to the top of the dung heap. There were five of them now, sprawled pink, new, and dead on the brown. There was at least one more dead one inside.

He thought last night's disaster merited a visit from Dietz, but the vehicle that came was Evert's. Tom went back to fishing with the pitchfork as the car approached from behind. Its pint-size engine kicked a couple of times and died. He hoped the dog would growl, but he did not even bark. Tom had the last dead pig on his fork, waiting. When he heard Evert's footsteps, he threw it up with the others.

"Half a litter of twelve," Tom said. "That's my profit on the shit pile."

Tom took his flashlight out of his coat pocket and shone the light into the hole, though he was certain he had them all. "I watched them being born. The ones that died took a breath and that was it. They smothered."

"What time?"

"I don't think it matters what time."

"And your family?"

Tom straightened his back. He pushed the tines against the ground, put his gloved hands over the knob end. "You care so much about my family, it took you until now to get here."

"I wasn't on night shift."

Now that Tom was looking at Evert, he saw that he was upset. Grey in the face.

"So what happened?" Tom asked him.

"There was an accident."

"What kind of accident?"

"We lost a man."

"Christ almighty."

Evert's mouth worked but made no words.

"So a man was killed by gas last night and still no one came down here or even phoned. That proves how much you bastards care." Tom poked the fork at the shit pile. "Those could have been kids instead of pigs."

Evert swayed as if his balance was lost. His eyes looked elsewhere when he said, "I do care."

He turned and took a step toward his car. The dog was at his side, nose up, tail whipping.

"I have to check the Gerstens and the Courts," Evert said, seemingly to the dog.

"You going to admit your plant killed these pigs?"

Evert went the rest of the way to his car and opened its door.

Tom leaned over the fence and yelled, "You tell Dietz I want an autopsy on these pigs! You tell him that!"

Ella woke up beside Billy in her parents' guest bed. It was Monday morning, and Ella made everyone's breakfast before the girls went off to school. Then she left Billy with her mother and drove in the direction of home. Two miles from the farm, she turned south, then made one more turn toward Bauers'. This time she parked between the caragana rows. The frost was not yet out of the ground and the old garden plot held her.

Back and forth Ella walked where once there had been rows of potatoes, peas, and beans. Dora had tried corn one year, and it grew tall but the ears would not fill. Ella wished to sing to herself, and the only song that came to mind was "The Tennessee Waltz." "I was waltzing with my darling . . ." After the appointed time had passed, and another hour, she told herself aloud, "Lance is not coming." He had only said what it would mean if Ella chose not to come. Maybe he was busy at work, or maybe it was the same message in reverse:

that he did not want to see her anymore. She waited fifteen more minutes before she circled back around the plant and approached home the usual way.

Tom's truck was not in the yard. She saw the dead piglets on the manure pile, the peculiar colour grabbing at her eyes. She went into the house and waited. When he drove in, Tom didn't come in but went to the pigpens first. Ella had made a pot of coffee.

At the table, Tom and Ella looked in different places and thought their different thoughts. She knew most of the piglets had died. He knew the girls and Billy were in town.

"Did Mr. Dietz come to the house this morning?" Ella asked him after the clock had gone halfway around.

"He did not. Evert did."

She waited.

"He said they'd had an accident. He said a man had died."

"Oh my God. Who?"

"I don't know. I told him I want an autopsy on those pigs."

"And what was his answer?"

"Nothing. He left without answering."

Every minute of that week was strange. She felt like she was living someone else's life. She did not know who at the plant had died—no one in the community knew there had been a death except Tom. She wondered if he'd got it right. She expected every day that there would come a call from Lance; that he would say work, or the accident, had made it impossible for him to meet her. She imagined him apologizing. She imagined telling him that no apology was needed. When she finally got desperate enough to phone the plant and ask for him, the woman who answered said Lance was not there and hung up.

Only then did Ella seriously examine the possibility that Lance did not want to see her again. Maybe he had woken that morning with a picture of her in his head that was different than before: of an older woman, with her husband and children around her. But she could not imagine him being so unkind as to let silence be the messenger.

Alf Dietz came to their house. Dietz knew that four was Tom's time for coffee and a scone, and he timed his arrival to coincide with that. The two men faced each other across the Arborite, and Ella served them.

"I was told you lost a man," said Tom.

"I don't know how you'd know that, but it's true."

"Lance Evert told me," said Tom, and Ella jumped inside herself to hear the name.

"The man who died was a young mechanic. Not from here—from Crowsnest Pass. Name of Andy Flannery. I told those young pups over and over, never open a pipe unless you know what's in it. Flannery tried to change a filter by himself on night shift. It was sour and he didn't know. He was dead a long time before anyone found him. The pipe was open and spewing sour gas—that's why the siren blew. We're lucky we didn't lose half a dozen men."

Tom smoked and Dietz—who had never smoked in their house—reached for the tobacco tin and rolled himself one. Ella filled her sink and slowly washed the dishes.

"It's usually Lance Evert who comes down to talk to us," she said with her face to the window.

Tom said, "I probably scared him. I gave him hell that morning. Did he tell you I want an autopsy on my dead pigs?"

"I don't know anything about that," said Dietz. "Evert is no longer in our employ."

Ella thunked a cup against the wall of the sink.

"That was sudden," said Tom.

"It was," said Dietz.

Dietz violently stubbed his cigarette in Tom's tobacco lid. "What the hell am I doing? Took me twenty years to quit this stuff."

"Any reason Evert's gone?" asked Tom.

"Can't say," said Dietz. "I don't think he's a sour gas man. Not really."

"What about the autopsy, Alf?"

"It won't be me who decides. I'll pass it along."

"I'll have one done myself if you guys won't."

"Keep your shirt on. For a while anyway."

"I'll keep the dead pigs frozen."

Dietz got to his feet, solemnly thanked Ella for the coffee. Stepped into his boots, as usual untied. When he was gone, Tom said to Ella's back, "You've been at those dishes a long time."

She could not answer; was blind with tears. She heard him walk to the porch, the deep rip of his coat zipper, the door.

5

BILL'S CREW BELIEVED that he was always touchy after days off. He had given them this impression deliberately, but it was not true. His happiest workdays came after days off, when the maximum span of work lay ahead. He affected owliness to keep them at bay, while he savoured his return.

Henry came in without knocking.

"What?"

"Dion says he's trying to phone you but your phone's blocked or something. You've left it on call forward. He wants to talk to you."

"What about?"

"Something about Waddens Village. Do you have his number?"

"I have enough Dion Elliott cards to build a house. Why does a PR man need me? Do I look like the public to you?"

Bill asked Henry to close the door on his way out. He did not like to admit how much he wished Dion Elliott would be lured away by some other company. Dion was reed-thin with a pale dandelion coif, but the most disturbing part of him was his mouth: a tiny whipping machine that left simple concepts blurred with froth. He could say things like "inclusive," "stakeholder," and "we must learn from these people" with an entirely still gorge.

What Dion belonged to was the Community Relations Group,

a title he loved. For him, the new moniker was much more than hiding the old bean under a new thimble. It was something they could all shelter under, collectively and inclusively.

Calling Dion a public relations man was mischief on Bill's part, also a strategy by which he hoped to convey that he was not to be trusted with the community, that he was the kind of amber fossil who might call a female operator "honey" or refer to "our Indians" at an open house. This had worked perfectly until two months ago, when Dion came to Bill's office and asked a favour. Before Bill fully understood what was going on, the two of them were across the lake in Waddens Village, parading through the homes of the Natives who lived there. After asking endlessly about everyone's family, Dion issued a bunch of bald-faced pious half-truths about the upgrader, the environment, and the community. He kept turning to Bill to say, "Isn't that so?"—to which Bill weakly nodded.

Bill stood up, did some low squats and circled his desk a few times. The phone glowed with the potential of Dion's call. If Bill let it ring, it was only a matter of time until Dion arrived in person.

Waddens Village was a single crooked street of houses on a shallow rise above the lake. Half the homes were cabins that predated the modern oil sands era. The rest were recent. Marie Calfoux's house was of the modern variety: a rancher on a full basement.

Bill pulled off the centre two-track and drove his grille into a pile of snow. He shut off his engine and sat. The only people he could see were a girl and boy climbing a snowbank that the grader had left in the parking lot of the community centre. Two grey dogs fought nearby.

Behind the kids and dogs, the community centre bestrode the town like a colossus. It had been a gift from New Aladdin and was Dion's baby all the way. From his cultural sensitivity training, Dion had learned that Indians liked circles more than squares, and so the centre was an octagon, the closest design he could find. Two spruce poles flanked the entrance, meeting in a point above—tipi poles.

Since its grand opening, the centre had reminded Bill of the Starship *Enterprise*, as if they'd scraped off the trees and an offspring of the mothership had descended and stayed. On the day Dion hauled him around town on the tea binge, Bill had asked an elder what she thought of it; did they use it much? She lowered her voice so Dion wouldn't hear, said they tried to play cards there the first winter but it was too big, too hard to heat, and everything they said echoed. They'd gone back to taking turns in their houses.

Bill was still in his vehicle, hands on the steering wheel. The engine was off and the cold was stealing in. He watched the two children flying down the gravel-specked snow heap. The dogs were going for the ruffs on each other's necks with wide-open jaws. For all Bill's determination and preparation, Dion had won again.

An hour earlier, Bill had been in his office. He forgot not to answer his phone, and Dion was on the other end. In the middle of Bill's rehearsed speech about why he should not do community work, Dion cut him off with a rudeness Bill did not know he possessed. Dion said he agreed completely; Bill was not someone he wanted doing communication work in the community.

"I tried you that one time because I felt an older person might have rapport with the mostly older population of the village. But you're not suited. You're not positive, and you don't stay on message."

"Then why this call, Dion? To tell me I'm not a team player?"

Dion paused, which was uncharacteristic. "The only reason is that a woman in the community asked to speak to you. Specifically. I believe you know Marie Calfoux."

"I've met her."

"Marie Calfoux does not want to talk to me. She asked to speak to you."

Bill climbed out of his SUV and looked across the hood. Between Marie Calfoux's house and the old cabin next door, he could see the frozen width of Waddens Lake. Across the ice and above the fringe of black spruce, the upgrader raised its hump. Bill reached back into his truck and pulled a sniffer out of the catch-all. He inserted a tube and did a test. A little sulphur dioxide. Woodsmoke was all his nose could detect.

Still, he did not go in. He clung to the still-warm hood. An image of his father rolling a smoke came to him, and he understood how comforting it would be at times like this; to put some distance, however artificial, between yourself and what you had to do. He was also thinking of how he had originally met Marie Calfoux, at a company information session. The upgrader was mostly built at the time, so the meeting was all pretense. *We want to hear what you have to say, but it won't make any difference. A couple of you might get low-level jobs.*

The locals were divided about the plant. By the time Marie got up to speak, Bill had already noted how striking she was. He thought she must be younger than him but she referred to grandchildren—then to a recently arrived great-grandchild. It seemed impossible.

That night, Marie spoke for five or more minutes, more than anyone else from the community. Bill remembered two things she said: that she hoped Waddens Lake construction and upgrader jobs would lure her children back, and that the company was about to scour off the landscape that was her life story. The woods surrounding the lake, their creeks and bogs, were what she had grown up with, where she had gone as a child in the footsteps of her grandparents.

"When the place you grow up in is destroyed, something in you gets destroyed too."

That line hit Bill between the shoulder blades. He was not sure where but he'd heard it before. A long time ago. Close to home.

During the tea-coffee-and-cookies that night, Bill had moseyed around Marie Calfoux. She showed stiff resistance at first, but as they talked, he felt her loosening. He had often replayed this because it was important to know what caused the shift. It was somewhere near the point where she'd asked him what he did at the plant, and he said he turned poisonous gas into sulphur. "A kind of magician, really."

She replied, "But isn't sulphur what they make explosives out of?"

"Only old-fashioned explosives" was his answer, and she laughed at that.

That must have been what improved things: the laughter. When people started leaving the open house, Marie said he should come to her house sometime for tea; see how the Indians lived. He said he would and meant it. What destroyed this good beginning was Dion's using him as the token old person on visiting day. Marie's house, the rancher before him now, was one of the places they had gone. After the dismal fakery of the occasion, he never got the courage to return.

Bill whacked the hood of his truck with both hands. The sudden violence caused one child and both dogs to stop playing and stare. He walked up the swept path. Marie had a horseshoe affixed to her door where city people put their peepholes. The shoe was nailed in the proper manner, open side up to catch the good luck.

When she let him in, the house smelled of meat simmering. Either his nose or his kitbag of Native stereotypes said moose stew. Marie sat him down at the table by the window, exactly where he'd been the last time with Dion. While she finished making the tea and piled muffins on a plate, he half expected her to tease him about waiting so long to come inside. That she didn't reminded him they were not friends. He took his first bite of blueberry muffin, sipped his tea, and admired her figure as she stood with her back to him at the counter.

When she picked up the teacups and pot, he shifted his eyes to the nearest wall, the one covered with family pictures. The photos were arranged by generation, something Dion had insisted she explain in detail.

"So that gentleman is a cousin?" Dion had asked her.

"That gentleman is an ex-husband."

The only very old picture was in the middle: a group photo of Indian kids in uniforms, flanked by nuns, on the steps of a residential school. Marie had talked to Dion and Bill about the damage done to her family by that system. Bill could no longer remember which child was her mother.

Marie set down the cups and the teapot, pointed at a little girl seated on the ground in the front row. "That one. It's the only picture I have of my mother's childhood. I don't have any pictures of her parents."

"That's too bad."

She sat across from him, checked the tea, and poured both cups.

"Tell you the truth, I like it that there aren't any pictures of the old ones. It shows that my grandparents weren't part of a white world. People like Dion talk as if my neighbours and I grew up wearing deer hides. We pretend he's right. But when you come from a time of no pictures"—she blew across her tea and drank a sip—"that's not bullshit. That's true."

The table they sat at had a vintage look, something pulled from another home and time. Otherwise, the furniture, equipment, and decorations that he could see were new. Brushed-steel fridge and stove. Hefty German food processor. Coffee maker like a steel dolphin in the midst of a trick. There was an elaborate workstation on the far side of the living room. Bill recognized the computer suite as a

Mac and new. The printer was a multi-purpose affair, scanner and the rest.

"I get high-speed internet off the satellite. That's how I keep up to date on what goes on around the oil sands."

There. They had arrived.

"What were you wanting to talk about?" he asked.

"I have concerns I want somebody at your plant to hear. That doctor at Fort Chip who they're trying to silence. My friends in that town tell me everything he says is true. Those rare bile duct cancers exist, but he was treated like he made it up. What do you say to that?"

"He got screwed, is my opinion, mainly by his fellow doctors."

"Not by the oil industry?"

"The medical association's report said he went public too soon, something like that. The companies picked out the most damning sentences and spread them around."

She thumped the table with her finger. "I did an internet search on bile duct cancer. That duct is how toxins leave the liver. When it's shown up in the U.S., it's been in places with industrial pollution. Down there, industry uses lawyers to muddy up the connection. You guys use the medical association." She sat back and folded her arms.

"I didn't know that. The part about the bile duct."

"Since there are health concerns downstream of the mines and plants, why is there only one water-monitoring site on the Athabasca River between the strip mines and the delta?"

"Is that so?"

"A scientist at the University of Alberta has been talking about it for years. He says there should be better sampling, but you guys and the province say your system is already adequate—pardon me, 'world class.' One sampling site."

Bill nodded, stared at the remaining half of his muffin. He had no appetite.

"I'm making you uncomfortable," she said.

"I don't like being an information guy. It's Dion's job, his department."

"And you make sulphur. So you told me. But you came. Why?"

"Dion said you asked for me."

She refilled his cup.

"I understand that water doesn't run uphill," she said, "so Fort Chip's problems won't necessarily happen here. But we are on water, and all the water around your plant is connected to us through wetlands, creeks, and lakes. If you guys are putting the same kind of cancer shit in this water, it will come to us. What about that?"

"Our strip mine and plant design is supposed to contain its effluents."

"You mean your tailings pond."

"That's part of the containment system. All the runoff is supposed to be caught so it doesn't get in the groundwater."

"If your tailings pond leaks, then it all comes here. Right here into this lake. Are you going to tell me tailings ponds never leak?"

"I'm not going to tell you that."

"Because they do leak? I've heard plenty about them leaking."

"I'm not aware that ours leaks. I won't say it's impossible."

She sat back again and looked at him quizzically, as if he had played a sleight-of-hand trick she was trying to understand.

"That's pretty good," she said. Then she geared up again—straightening, becoming taller in her chair. "Something else I've researched is tumours in fish. One of my uncles makes his living fishing from Lake Athabasca. I've touched the lumps on those fish with my own hands. A different fisherman, also Native, took a bag of them down to the government office in Fort Mac. They wouldn't even look at them. Let them rot on the steps. Somebody in your business said we're mistaking spawned-out fish for ones with cancers. Do you have any idea how many fish my uncle has handled in his life? Do you think he'd make that mistake?"

"No."

"Then why are they saying that?"

"I don't know."

Marie sat for a time with her arms tightly folded. Then a laugh rolled out of her.

"What?"

"You're not much of a defender of your industry."

"No."

"Then why do you work for them?"

"I take a sour gas stream. I remove sulphur from it. I've done something like that all my working life."

"But if your industry kills lakes and rivers, and people, that doesn't affect you?"

"I think the plants up here are good plants, the ones I know anyway. But the government allowed too many projects, and the companies are building them too fast. Whether they're good plants starts not to matter. Put too many together, on one river, it adds up to pollution. Even if the government made the rules tougher, and we met those rules, there would still be pollution."

"Do you think it will slow down?"

"No."

"Will the government make it slow down?"

"No."

"Why not?"

"Politics. Greed. Pressure."

"You're no spring chicken. You could retire."

"Someone else makes the sulphur. What would that change?"

She smiled at him. "It's nice you came and listened. I appreciate your saying what you've said."

They were done. Though Bill enjoyed looking at Marie Calfoux, he was yearning to go. He picked his cap off the table.

"Thanks for the tea. The muffin was good." At the door, he pulled his boots back on. "Why did you ask to see me? Me in particular?"

She brushed table crumbs into her palm and carried them to the garbage can. "It's not quite right that I asked to see you. Dion phoned and said he wanted to come to my house. I don't like to be rude but I didn't want him here. I said if someone has to come, send Bill, the sulphur man."

"Why me?"

"Dion always brings tobacco, in a cloth bag or sometimes in a brand-new leather pouch. If it's a bag he puts a pretty-coloured ribbon on it. Like it was 1875 and I had never seen a store. It gets on my nerves."

Bill imagined Dion handing over the ribboned tobacco bag. Bowing deeply.

"Bring the Indian tobacco," Marie continued. "It's not *giving* tobacco that means anything, you know, it's *accepting* it. If I take your tobacco, it's like I'm accepting you and your stinking plant. Anyway, I thought you wouldn't bring tobacco and you didn't."

Bill opened the door and the cold leapt in. Behind him, Marie said, "Don't worry. I'm not trying to snag you. My snagging days are over."

"They wouldn't have to be."

"You don't know a thing about it, Mr. Ryder. All the men around here either have money and suddenly think they're special, or else they're like you—sad. Either way, it's not attractive. But there is something I would like to do with you."

"What?"

"Can you snowshoe?"

"Yes."

"I have a few pairs. I'd like you to come and we'll snowshoe around."

"To look for leaks?"

"I want to show you some nice places."

As soon as he had driven his truck the length of main street and was back among the trees, Bill thumped the steering wheel with both hands. He had agreed to go back and snowshoe! To do yet more community work. What was wrong with him?

Bill's plan was to spend every night of his current shift week in the Chateau Borealis. All over the oil sands, faux hotels were popping up, accommodation for the tradesman class that might be the difference between hanging on to a welder and losing him to a project with better exercise machines. When Bill arrived at Waddens, he found out Chateau Borealis had rooms reserved for management and that these were generally unbooked. Local managers regarded the Chateau as a penance, preferring to go home to their overpriced houses in McMurray. Often Bill wanted nowhere near his McMurray home, especially after days off. Borealis was more to his liking.

What he did on his nights at the Chateau was read. He read novels, and he read widely, defined as wide of the mark of himself. He liked novels about nineteenth-century frontier wars. He liked sharp and witty novels written by women in which men unlike him were humorously scourged. He even liked books that broke his heart, except if they broke it by reminding him of the long loser portions of his own biography.

But on the evenings of this week, none of his books could hold him. None had the power to keep him from thinking about Marie Calfoux.

He had several arguments with himself over whether she liked him or just wanted to convey her annoyance. The third obvious possibility was that she wanted to find out inside dope about the upgrader. Rather than ponder and imagine her during these evenings, he could have visited her; she was all of five minutes away. But the notion paralyzed him. He would not see her again until the snowshoe visit. He would not mess with the schedule.

Something he could do in the meantime was investigate her concerns. He had his computer; the Chateau had internet. First, he made a list of what to search for. He wouldn't bother with the medical situation at Chip because he already knew Marie was right on that one. The whistleblower had been fed his whistle as usual.

What she had said about Native fishermen on Lake Athabasca also tallied with what he knew. When the government and the companies got together and sent a team of experts to educate the Indians on fish health and fish disease, he had cringed

What he could research was leakage from tailings ponds. Dion and his boys claimed it didn't happen, but when he typed "Do tailings ponds leak?" in the search bar, a flood of hits said the opposite. One of them was a study commissioned by an oil sands company several years earlier that found that its tailings pond not only leaked but leaked right into the Athabasca River. Of this, the province's environment minister said it was only a small leak relative to the river's volume. In the course of the evening, Bill found a site that claimed a leaking tailings pond had "self-healed." Another company had a moat around its pond to catch leaks. In other words, the answer was yes: tailings ponds leak. So too, probably, would the one at New Aladdin Waddens Lake.

Bill's next query was Athabasca River water sampling. Was it really possible that there was only one sampling site downriver of the strip mines? Like Marie, Bill had heard Dion say that the air and water monitoring effort throughout the oil sands was world-class and a splendid example of industry-government-community co-operation.

Bill was suspicious of things declared world-class, since the oil sands industry, as viewed from within, was a world-class scientific and technical effort to free a world-class resource from nature's stubborn clutches. The industry was bringing a world-class energy product to the world-class appetite of the world-class world.

Skeptical though he was, Bill was occasionally worn down by the propaganda. Hearing the monitoring system praised for so long, he had told himself that surely they could get that much right.

Online, he found an annual report from the industry's own environmental watchdog. It said there were no detectable changes across time in the water resource. He looked up the university scientist Marie had mentioned and found him quoted as saying that the one-downriver-sampling-site system was a joke (a world-class joke, no doubt), designed to find nothing.

Bill shut his computer down and tried to sleep, but he was kept awake by his old nausea. The two sides of these questions were like giant linemen slamming into each other again and again in a game with no end—or until the farmers and environmentalists ran out of bodies or money to pay them.

Bill Ryder wanted to be on *no* side, even as he made his living off one. This had been his dream for as long as he could remember, and Marie Calfoux would not be the first to tell him it was impossible.

The next time Bill saw Johnny Bertram and his nephew, on their ladders with their insulation and tin, he tried to walk by. But Johnny shouted for him to hold on. He zipped down and beckoned Bill to the truck.

"It's me who wants to go for a drive this time."

Behind the wheel, Johnny said, "I've never seen the strip mine in action. With a big boss like you, the security boys won't stop me."

Without guidance, Johnny drove to the dignitaries' viewpoint, a slight rise on the strip mine's edge where the power shovels and mega-trucks could be seen. Visiting dignitaries were brought here because the active part of the mine bordered a played-out section heaped with clean sand from the hot-water separation plant. Left: exploitation. Right: reclamation.

A loaded ore truck roared toward them and swung sharply, flinging black in their direction and yanking a sound from Johnny's throat. You saw these trucks on television whenever the oil sands made the news, but it was different watching something the size of an apartment block bear down on you at speed.

Johnny slapped the steering wheel, laughed. "This could be on IMAX. They could race."

A burly Native banged on the windshield, and Bill showed his ID.

"What about this one?" asked the guard, pointing at Johnny.

"Visiting dignitary," said Bill.

"From where? Anzac?"

"Good one." Johnny gave him a thumbs-up.

When the guard was gone, Johnny said, "Is it true they used to have conveyor belts moving the ore and they broke down all the time? I heard there was a woman VP who told them it would be cheaper to use shovels and trucks?"

"All true."

"And that's when they started making money?"

"That's true also."

"You'd think they'd have statues of her lining Highway 63."

Bill did not answer.

As they re-entered the upgrader, Johnny asked Bill if he was married.

"Twice. Not anymore."

"Kids?"

"Girl and a boy in their twenties. What about you?"

"Celeste and I been married thirty-three years. Four kids. Seven grandkids." After a pause, Johnny asked, "What are you doing about it?"

"About what?"

"Being single."

"Not much. Actually, there is a woman. Sort of."

"Tell me."

"Nothing much to tell. She's interesting, funny, good looking, smart."

"Excellent!"

"But she says I'm sad."

"Meaning what? Sad sack or a sad case? Or just going around looking sad?"

"We didn't get into it. I was only there for tea."

"You mean she's local?"

"She lives in Waddens Village."

"Oh my. I can't wait to tell Shirley."

"Tell Shirley what?"

"That forty years after you were in love with her, you're still chasing Indian women. It'll make her day." Johnny pulled his truck off the service road beside his ladder. "So, *are* you sad?"

"No sadder than most men our age."

"Maybe you don't hide it well enough."

"I should grin more. Tell people to have a nice day."

"Okay, tell me this. Does she want to see you again?"

"She says she wants to go snowshoeing."

"For Pete's sake, Billy! Then there's no problem."

"I think she only wants to show me places the upgrader's going to wreck."

"I'm sure that's right. But still."

As they climbed out of the truck, Johnny favoured Bill with a little song. "Keep on the sunny side, always on the sunny side, keep on the sunny side of life."

At work, Bill tinkered with his corrosion maintenance plan. The idea had been inspired by his long-time boss, Lance Evert—*who he must phone*! About once a day, he thought of the aborted call on his message machine, told himself to phone, and did not do it. An old man now and retired, Lance spent his days combing the Net. Though the two men had not talked in ages, Lance sent him emails whenever he found something exciting. Fourteen months ago, there had been a flurry of emails about refinery accidents in the States, a lot of them involving the hydrotreater.

Lance believed the wave of accidents was caused by hydrogen stress cracking, the old sour gas bugbear he'd fought in the early part of his career. At first, Bill ignored the idea. Processing and refining had moved on, and Lance's idea sounded antique. But it grew on him. Many of the accidents Bill heard about *did* happen in the hydrogen-producing part of the plant, and what Bill was trying to come up with was a way to check potential corrosion sites on hydrogen lines in advance, and without having to shut down the plant. The latter was the unique part, the selling point.

Like a lot of men in charge, Bill's boss lived by best practices handed to him from head office. The idea that his own plant could evolve a new best practice would make Theo Houle laugh. This was the hinterland, the oil sands, thousands of kilometres from the great laboratories of Houston or The Netherlands. It would be like finding a new microparticle with a Christmas chemistry set.

When Bill felt frustrated, he got up and walked around his desk. Either that or go outside. Circling the desk now, Bill saw that the inbox on his desk was stuffed and was unsure how it got that way.

He pulled out the bale and started sorting. Most things went into the trash unopened, but a handful remained. He selected one envelope and shoved back the rest.

The envelope was from a professional association he belonged to. He knifed open the envelope, and, as he thought it might be, it was notice of an upcoming technical meeting in Calgary. He drifted his eyes down the menu: technical papers, panels. There was one called "U.S. Refinery Fires: Should Canadian Processors and Refiners Be Alarmed?"

This might be the answer to Bill's problem. If he went to this meeting and some higher authority suggested the sort of action Bill had in mind, then he could come back here and offer up the corrosion inspection plan to Theo as if it were the idea of another. An expert is a guy from out of town, as the sage said.

He looked at the schedule again, and the meeting date sank in. Thursday. *This* Thursday. Two days from right now.

Bill pitched the letter into the wastebasket, circled his desk, and retrieved it. He would have to leave no later than tomorrow afternoon; would have to drive non-stop to get to Calgary by midnight. His next days-off started Friday anyway, so he could combine the Calgary meeting with a visit to the farm. He pictured himself handing his oldest sister Tom's binder.

Thinking ahead to the meeting, he imagined Lance Evert sitting at a round table, listening avidly. They could sit together at lunch.

He went ahead and registered, and booked a room in the downtown hotel where the meeting would be held. Then his phone rang.

"Bill!" It was Theo. "There's a high-priority tour coming through!"

"Today?"

"Of course today! Two p.m.!"

"Did I miss a memo?"

"We got no notice."

"Who?"

"I can't say. Security on this thing's tight as a button."

"Drum."

"What?"

"Cute as a button, tight as a drum."

"Piss off. I want you at the control room at two. Have your crew ready between two and four in case they want to tour your unit."

Bill set the phone down. The visitor had to be a politician, because only politicians did this: landed in your lap without notice, knowing you could not tell them to fuck off.

Why Waddens Lake was a better question. The older mega-projects, closer to Fort Mac and the airport, were better equipped for political bum shows. More roadside attractions, like buffalo munching on a meadow that used to be a strip mine.

Bill's computer beeped as a message from Dion Elliott arrived. "THIS AFTERNOON, BETWEEN 4 AND 6 PM: OPEN HOUSE AT THE WADDENS VILLAGE COMMUNITY CENTRE!!! YOUR ATTENDANCE IS REQUIRED!!!"

Henry entered without knocking. "The way I hear it, the federal resources minister and some high-up federal American were in Edmonton for an oil sands meeting with the premier. No tour had been asked for, but the American said he couldn't report on what he hadn't seen. He wouldn't settle for a fly-over."

"Why us, though? They never come here."

Henry had a weird facial habit when he descended into deepest thought. His whole face looked like it was extracting a bull sinew from between molars.

"Here's what I think. Our plant is fairly new, and we're not on the Athabasca River. Our strip mine and tailings pond aren't enormous. The community isn't pissed off."

"Yet," Bill and Henry said in unison like a vaudeville team.

The hottest environmental issue of late was water use: how much water withdrawal the Athabasca River could take before it crapped out as a living ecosystem. Even though Waddens Lake drew on Athabasca tributaries for its make-up water, the optics here were better.

"How did you find out it was an American and the rest?" Bill asked.

"Can't reveal," Henry said. "What I can tell you is that Houle has cancelled his golf holiday. Kazcir is flying up on the company jet. Dion's over in Waddens Village bribing locals to come to the open house. He's trying to find a freshly killed moose."

"I suppose he'll show that stupid film again."

"*Beading Our Future*? I don't think so. The American says he wants to meet local people."

Bill was thinking of Marie Calfoux. "I hope a local person takes a strip off them."

Henry did not share this enthusiasm. He was doing the bull sinew thing again. Whatever else the oil sands were, they were Henry's ticket to a good life. Snow-white fishing boat, twin Evinrudes blasting him across Georgia Strait.

"Don't worry, Henry. Even if the Americans wean off our oil, you'll be retired when it happens."

"You too," he said.

"Nope. I'll be dead. There won't be enough organic matter left in me to grow a daisy."

Bill went for a walk around the unit. He was looking for oily rags, safety signs hanging by a corner, wet spots, jokes; places where sweepers had shoved dirt into a shadow. But the unit was pristine.

Back in the control room, he looked over the crew. Whitcomb's shirt was untucked; most of the men hadn't shaved. He went back to his desk and counted out the needed disposable razors. He handed them around. Predictably, Clayton made an unfunny remark about giving one to Marion.

The day was beginning to fall into perspective. Bill's role at Waddens Lake was modest. These tour things were also like football; most things were. Even though the other side seldom ran the ball at the sulphur unit, you still had to have a guy filling the sulphur hole in case they did.

At the last minute, he brushed his teeth and took his sports jacket out of its bag behind the door.

Bill and Henry had a pact; if either one gave signs of falling asleep, the other was to dig him hard with an elbow. Henry had elbowed Bill twice already, though Bill was having no trouble staying awake. It was because Bill wasn't watching the speakers so much as the Waddens Village crowd where Marie sat.

Robert Kazcir was talking, New Aladdin's Canadian CEO. He took turns pitching woo to the Natives and to the table of politicians where the American sat. New Aladdin operations guys like Bill were grouped on the far side of the room, where Kazcir never looked. Bill could see that Theo Houle and the Canadian politicians he was with were listening to Kazcir, but that the American visitor was not. Supporting his chin with one hand, the American made occasional notes on a tablet.

Not long ago—a mere couple of decades—men in Kazcir's and Houle's positions were stout. The American visitor would have been a heavy guy too. Business and political leaders back then packed the bulk that good suits are designed to hide. But Kazcir, Houle, and the American were part of the new breed who did their thinking on a treadmill and bragged of being able to bench-press their weight.

What had not changed was the speaking style. Like their predecessors, they were at home at the podium and masters of the microphone. Their pearly tones were reassuring, even more so if you blurred out the words. As for content, Bill always knew what was coming. He knew when Kazcir would say "team of top professionals" and "safety awards for every unit." "We are meeting or exceeding the toughest environmental standards in the world."

Somewhere ahead there would be a shift from advocacy to humility. Kazcir would note "the concentration of industrial facilities" and "the pressure on the water resource." This would lead to "cumulative effects." Having bravely admitted the most pressing problems, he would swap ends and refute his own charges.

"We understand the challenges better than anyone. I can tell you honestly that we intend to run the best facility, according to the best operating practices and safety procedures, possible on this oil frontier at this time."

It was hard, even for Bill, not to capitulate. It was the brand and style of forthright gravitas the western world had been voting into power for Bill's entire life. Even Native leaders had it nowadays, though they were expected to tell more jokes.

Bill checked Marie again. Her hair was up, caught at the back in a curve of leather. She wore a fitted jacket, floral design on the lapels and cuffs; turquoise pendant at her throat. Her eyes were sparking with indignation, and she probably posed the biggest threat to Kazcir's slick performance—if he had the eyes to see it.

When the CEO was done, he introduced the federal resources minister, a tall, skinny man whose talk was vague and brief. Then came Alberta's resources minister, who managed to sound both uninformed and patronizing.

The final spot on the agenda was the place of honour, and this belonged to the American. He stood at the lectern in silence, surveying the crowd. When he started talking, he was at once more polished and charming than all the rest put together. While the others had directed their talk to the politicians, Natives, and oil bigwigs in about equal measure, the American made eye contact only with the Native audience. He spoke of enduring friendship, not just with Canada and Alberta but with the communities of this region. If Bill were Marie Calfoux, he would have had a sinking sensation. "Enduring friendship" meant status quo. He suspected Marie had come here hoping the American would blister the Canadians about dirty oil, suggesting his president was determined to reduce American reliance on Canadian bitumen. But it wasn't there, not even close.

"While America develops its shale oil resource and makes the transition into the alternate fuels of the future, it is a great comfort to know our best ally is here, to the north of us, with a solid and expanding supply of needed petroleum energy."

For a couple of minutes near the end, the American did address pollution. These issues must be met with better technology and regulation, he said, not just with defensive posturing. But it was an afterthought. The real message was that the world's biggest consumer of oil planned to go on bellying up to Canada's all-you-can-burn buffet for the foreseeable future.

When the Washington man sat down, the business of the evening was over. No showing of *Beading Our Future*, thank God. Dion popped up to thank everyone for coming. He pointed to a crockpot of moose stew and thanked a lady in the front row for providing this fine wholesome local food. She had also baked bannock for the occasion. Tea, coffee, juice, please help yourselves.

Bill went into line quickly and got a small paper bowl of stew, a hunk of buttered bannock, and a Styrofoam cup of black coffee. He carried the grub to the room's far end and put his back in a corner. As he ate, he watched the American giving two-handed handshakes, his perfect teeth gleaming. He was probably a smart guy, well read in philosophy and history; an authority on international oil and free trade agreements. If he were in the next hammock at a beach, he would be charming company. But here, his charisma could not hide that he was a shill. Pumping a message.

From Bill's gunfighter position, he saw Marie approaching. She walked over with the man she'd sat beside during the speeches, a thin, handsome Native in a black leather jacket. She introduced him as James Beaudry. Bill had both hands occupied with the coffee and plate. "No worries," said Beaudry, unsmiling.

"This is the one I've been telling you about," she told James. "He either tells the truth or won't talk. He's quiet most of the time." This made Beaudry laugh.

Bill was flustered, jealous.

"Cat got your tongue?" Marie said. She nodded to where the company brass and the politicians were clustered. "Several cats?"

James said he needed a smoke and headed for the exit.

"Aren't you having anything to eat?" Bill asked Marie.

"That moose stew was frozen solid in Irene's freezer this morning. Hard to get rid of two-year-old stew."

Bill mopped his mouth, put his paper bowl on the nearest table. Marie's eyes were squinted as she looked again at the dignitaries.

"The power of suction in this room. If I only had it to vacuum my house."

They had a good laugh at this. Then Marie said, "By the way, James is my cousin."

"I've been doing research," Bill said. "You're right on all your complaints."

"Which are specifically what?"

"Tailings ponds, lumpfish, water monitoring."

She took a look at him. "If you weren't such an honest guy, I'd think you were shining up to me."

"It's possible I did the research *and* I'm shining up to you."

She smiled across the room.

"What about snowshoeing? You going to have time for that one of these days?"

"I'm going south for the weekend. What about next week?"

"You call me," she said.

That night, Bill lay sleepless in his Chateau king bed. Conversations with Marie Calfoux rattled through his brain but weren't the sort he wanted.

"Why can't the oil sands be slowed down?"

"Because we're the biggest supplier of the biggest consumer on earth."

"I thought the U.S. was finding its own oil. Frack oil."

"That makes governments and companies up here want to go twice as fast. Build pipelines to the west coast. Sell to China."

"Then there's no hope."

"Hope's not my department."

6

BY LATE MARCH, the cows were slow and sway-bellied as they walked among the shrinking drifts and tore at last year's grass. Tom started his final preparations for calving. He bought scour powder, penicillin, and the hormone that prompted cattle to clean their afterbirth. He plugged gaps in the slab fence that the cows and new-born calves would shelter behind. He filled the barn loft with straw bales and the driest box stall with hay.

Calving normally excited him—fresh calf crop, the promise of spring—but this year he was anxious. When he and Ella were first married, when the girls had been babies, he had thought he could deal with calving alone, and lost newborns at an alarming rate. Since then, he'd made sure to have a hired man for the season.

Now it seemed like Kees might be the last of those. Since the Dutchman, there had only been two responses to the ad at the Greyhound stop. First, a guy had come out for one day. He did not even spend the night. Then came a pair of jailbirds in a smoking car. Tom had taken one and sent the other to Johnny Court, who also needed help. After three stinking days, the one who worked for Court drove over to Ryders'. The pair of them told Tom they were going to town for a beer, and they never came back.

Having seen the plant kill the better part of two litters of pigs,

Tom had been worrying about calves. Calves had bigger lungs, but whether that would safeguard them he could not know. Lately, the barbed wire had been breaking along the fence that separated the plant from the farm. When he tried to stretch it, to fix it, it broke again. Gas that could eat wire could probably do most anything to flesh.

At night, over supper, and again at breakfast, Tom would speak about his worries. He did not really expect anyone to listen, but he started to notice that Donna was, and that she did not go to the living room as soon as the others did. The night Tom announced the birth of the first calf, Donna went with him after supper to look at it. She helped him coax two cows with swelling bags into the corral beside the barn. Every night after that, and during the day on weekends, Donna came and helped, without once being asked.

When things picked up, there was no time to consider whether the grislier aspects of calving would be a problem for the girl. That Donna was bombproof was proven on the second weekend. Right after a nice bull calf came the afterbirth and uterus, a shocking sight even to Tom, who had seen it half a dozen times. He sent Donna to the house to phone Doc Moore.

"What do I say?"

"Just tell him prolapse and who you are."

Meanwhile, Tom roped and tied the cow's legs to keep her from getting up. When Donna returned, he was squatted on his haunches against the wall. Donna settled down in the clean straw beside him, staring at the purplish mass on the floor. Tom told her she did not have to stick around. He and the doc could handle this. But Donna said she wanted to see.

Doc Moore sped into the yard and trundled his equipment bag into the barn. He unrolled a rubber sheet and asked that they bring several buckets of water that he could use to clean the uterus.

Then he stuffed it back in. Donna did not flinch, even during the sewing up.

Normally, Tom only set his alarm clock in the night if a cow was close to calving. Now, he set it on any night when there was the smell of gas. He explained his plan to Donna. If a calf was born on one of the bad nights and showed any sign of distress, he would carry it to the truck and drive to clean air.

Donna said she would set her alarm too, so she could share the night work. If a cow was calving or had calved, all she had to do was run to the house and get her dad. Tom agreed, and then Ella insisted on misunderstanding. She would not believe that Donna had asked to do this; she accused Tom of coaxing the girl.

When Tom first noticed that some of the calves were sick, he feared it was from gas, but he was soon relieved to see the familiar sign of scours. The violent diarrhea was far from a joke, and contagious, and it ran wild through the crop of young calves, but it was something he had dealt with often before. Again, whenever she wasn't in school, Donna was with him. Bouncing along in the one-ton, she'd yell, "There's one," pointing at a yellow hind end. He taught her to rope a calf's running legs; how to reach over and grab a rear flank and use her knee to flip it. They forced open the calf's mouth, ladled the purple powder onto the tongue, held and worked the jaws until the medicine was too sticky to spit out.

It was a farmer's dream to have a kid grow up interested in the farm. Tom had assumed he would have to wait until Billy was a teenager to find out if that was going to happen. But here was Donna, as good a hand as he could have foreseen. Far from anxious about the season, he was delighted now. No calves were dying, and he had begun to consider the possibility of a hundred per cent calf crop. He told Donna this, and she became excited too. If they could accomplish it, it would be a victory over the gas plant. They'd have kept the bastards from killing even one.

What Donna reminded Tom of most was Ella in their early days. Back then, before Jeannie was born, they never wanted to be apart and were free to share the entire day. In calving season, when they were chasing scoured calves, Ella could make a loop roll in front of a calf's legs. She had a way of throwing a calf that was all balance and took her no effort at all. He could close his eyes right now and see the smile she flashed when she had him dazzled.

But now she disagreed completely with Donna working so hard with him. Not long ago, she had been criticizing him for being more interested in Billy than he was in the girls; she'd claimed he was just waiting for Billy to mature into a hired man. Now that he was spending part of every day with Donna, he was *too* interested.

Finally, one afternoon when the girls were at school, Ella said, "You're using Donna like a hired man. When she's helping pull a calf, or catching and throwing calves, that's not good for her stomach. That work's too heavy for a girl her age."

"You don't realize how strong she is. She gets stronger every day."

"And I can't believe you let her get up in the night on school days. I've asked you to see about another hired man but you do nothing."

"I can't *get* a hired man! They can work places where there's no stink. It's a waste of time to bring one here."

"So you won't even try!"

He had taken down the ad at the Greyhound. This was what she meant.

All Tom could think to do was leave the house, go to his shop where he'd be left alone.

When most of the calves were on the ground, a wild chinook blew in and ate the snow. The coulees boomed with runoff. The warmth made the calves robust and playful, and on such an optimistic day, Tom was leaning on the sunny side of his truck, smoking and watching Donna coax a calf to bunt her fist.

He asked if she knew what 4-H was. She said she'd heard about it from kids on the bus, the ones who were in the clubs.

"What do you think? Do you want to be in the 4-H beef club?"

"I don't know."

Tom said she could pick the best bull calf in the herd. After they'd weaned in the fall, she would be responsible for feeding and caring for the steer across winter and spring. Come July, there'd be an "Achievement Day" at the auction mart, where ribbons were awarded. That same day the calves would be sold.

"You'd give him to me?" Donna asked. "For free?"

The calf and the feed would be free, he told her. He would help her put the sale money into a Canada Savings Bond. That could be for university or whatever kind of schooling she wanted after high school.

"It's good advertising for the farm. If you beat out calves from local farms and ranches, that would tickle me. But the learning is the most important thing."

"Is that really why?" she asked.

"I couldn't have got through calving half this well without your help. It's a reward."

"What about Jeannie?"

"Jeannie didn't help much."

"She'll still be jealous."

"Well, then she will be."

Tom could not think why Ella would be against a club calf for Donna, but he was certain of it anyway. His instinct was to say nothing, but the longer he delayed, the more likely it was that Ella would hear from Donna, or Donna would brag to Jeannie and Jeannie would tell her mother. So he waited for the afternoon of a school day and declared his plan.

"That's not a good idea."

"Why? Because Jeannie will be jealous?"

Ella took off her apron and threw it on the counter. She was already at the level of anger she'd reached the last time they'd discussed Donna.

"You know I don't agree with Donna helping you so much. It takes her away from her school studies and it's hard on her physically. But I've let it go because I knew calving would end. But now that the end is near, you come up with this. Give her a calf as a pet."

"They're not pets. They teach kids how to care for a steer."

"It just happens it will keep her in the barn, working like a man, until it's time to calve again."

Tom could have let it go—would later wish he had—but his temper had been reached. "Goddamnit, Ella! It's like you don't want my children to be mine!"

"You don't own them!"

This made him boil. Of any father in this community, he was the least disposed to work his children hard. Ella knew that because her own parents had worked her like a slave, an only child who had to be her father's and her mother's helper, both.

He took a step back and, in the widest corner of his vision, he saw Billy. All through this bitter exchange, the raising of voices, the boy had been in the shadow beyond the kitchen door.

Tom fled into open air. The 4-H calf for Donna must stand. A deal with one of your children is no less of a deal.

Looking for something useful to do on a hot day in early April, Ella took the feather ticks off all the beds and carried them outside one at a time. She had seen people hang rugs and quilts over the clothes-line and go at them with a broom, but the cloth of these feather ticks was old and almost rotten. The best she could do was hang each one over chairs on the lawn, flip it gently in the breeze.

Billy was outside with her. He was happy to be out but annoyed that she'd made him wear a coat. The anemia made him prone to colds.

Often these days, she seemed to be arguing with someone in her head. If forced to picture her antagonist, it was always Tom. She had thought a lot about this and knew it had something to do with love. When people are in love, they give lists of reasons why, but even when Ella was in her teen years listening to her girlfriends talk about the men they'd picked to marry, she never believed in recited virtues as the cause of love. Love didn't happen because a man was smart, strong, or handsome; it was simply there, like this sunny day.

It had taken the last year of her marriage to learn that the opposite could also be true. When love was gone, it was also like weather. Endless cloud; occasional storm.

The hottest point of difference these days was Donna. A year ago, Donna had seemed barely to notice her father, but now she stood by him in everything, fiercely. If it wasn't Tom coming in the house to brag of Donna's cleverness or strength, it was Donna praising her dad for a farming trick or, recently, for his "colourful language." Where she got "colourful language" Ella didn't know, probably out of a book at school. Donna was so proud of her father's cursing she'd taken to copying it, as any fool could predict.

The day before, Donna had come racing into the house, full of giggles.

"The sprockle-face took a kick at Dad. He called her a cross-eyed whore and said she'd drive Christ off the cross!"

"That's not funny, Donna."

"Oh, Mom! It is too."

"I suspect Jesus doesn't find it amusing."

"Jesus shouldn't be thinking about Dad. He should be thinking about the atom bomb."

"That's hardly for you to say."

In bed that night, she told Tom he had to stop using words like whore in front of his daughter. He was silent. Ella knew he thought that made him the more reasonable one. Since he was choosing not to speak, she decided to give vent to other frustrations.

"As for 4-H, you should let the subject drop until fall. Chances are Donna will have moved on to some other interest by then. If you keep pushing, she'll feel trapped into it, whether she has any interest left or not."

"I'm not worried about that," he said, "I'm worried about the plant. I'm not sure a club calf will do well in this yard."

"I am so sick of the plant," she said. "This barely feels like home anymore."

"Does that mean you'd consider leaving?"

"I didn't say that."

Now, tired of flipping the feather tick, she pulled a chair out from under it and sat. The sunlight was hottest here, on the south side of the house. The sun's rays reached her both directly and reflected off the wall. Billy was crawling around the peony chasing a cat.

"Billy, don't. You'll get ants on you."

For months now, Ella had been evaluating her days by how much or how little she thought about Lance. She was always thinking about him to some degree. However rude he'd been to leave the way he had, she could not be angry with him, not really.

She supposed, if she forced herself, she could remember times when she'd been angry at Lance Evert, when he'd stared at her at the meeting, and later when his plant had made her children sick. But absence had sainted him. She pictured his clean-shaven face, his perfect nose, the softness of his cheeks and lips. It made her smile, even if, at the same time, she was swept with pain.

She did not know what to call the thing that had happened. It wasn't an affair. But if she couldn't name it, she was fairly sure why it had happened. Lance was just old enough to find older women interesting and she was just young enough that her face contained the prettiness of her younger self. When she crossed the yard carrying buckets of swill, she imagined Lance then too; imagined him looking at her, astonished. "Oh yes," she told him. "This is me too."

When she was thinking of Lance, she hated the intrusion of Tom or thoughts of Tom. She did not want to think of when or why things with Tom had soured, or even if there had been very little wrong except that the marriage had cooled. The plant had come and made every disagreement abrasive. Ironically, the plant had also provided the one thing that made things better.

But Lance Evert was gone, and with no farewell. He had been replaced by an older man who was not nice at all. On her angriest days—and this was fast becoming one—Ella believed Tom might have driven Lance away. It was a fact that six newborn pigs had died during the night before she was supposed to meet Lance that second time. Lance had come to the farm that morning. Tom bragged that he had sent him packing, but maybe it wasn't just a saying. Maybe he knew something, or had put two and two together, and there'd been a fight.

Old King came running across the south field. He came to her wet with sweat and with his tongue out, forced his muzzle under her hand. The vehicle she had heard passing must have been Tom. In a minute the old truck would rumble into the yard. Four o'clock.

A week into April. A school morning.

The night before, Donna and Tom had come back from the

barn in high spirits. The last cow had given birth—to twins! The living twins meant they had a hundred per cent calf crop; only the second time this had happened since Tom and Ella were married.

"If you count the twins," said Jeannie, "it's more than one hundred per cent."

"I'll be damned," said Tom. "Jeannie's right. It *is* a record, then."

It was almost fate that a happy time would rouse the plant's ire. The volume of sound seemed to double in the night. The gas seeped in and woke them. Ella got up and wet some towels. She put the big ones across the bottoms of the two doors that led outside, smaller ones across the window ledges where the old putty was letting in night air.

This morning was a school morning. Jeannie was in the bathroom curling her eyelashes. Donna had gone to the barn with her father to see how the twins were doing. As bus time approached, Ella went to the door and looked toward the barn. You could not yell across that distance. With five minutes to go, she instructed Jeannie to go to the road and ask Mr. Snow to wait. Jeannie snapped back some contrary thing but Ella was already running down the path in her dress and gumboots. It made her so angry when Tom and Donna did this, forced her to pry Donna away—as if the only person responsible for Donna's schooling was Ella.

As soon as she passed the coal shed, she saw them come out of the barn, and knew something was wrong. Donna liked to run around her slow-walking father, punching and picking at him, but there was none of that this morning. As they came closer, Donna started running. Ella called to her but the girl shook her head and passed by.

"Did one of them die?" she asked Tom when he reached her.

"Both."

"What?"

"Sonofabitching plant killed both of them."

Ella went to the barn to see for herself. In the dim light, she saw two barn cats tearing at the afterbirth. Tom had set a sheet of plywood to close off the far corner of the room, and behind it was where she found the calves, side by side on the straw. Their front hooves were touching and the eyes, the two she could see, were open and sightless.

She didn't hear Tom enter. When he spoke, she jumped.

"Christ," he said. "It's me."

"Should I call the plant?"

"I will," he said. "Or I won't. Bastards don't do anything."

"I wish you didn't have to curse everything."

"We've got dead calves, and you're correcting my language."

She wanted away from him. He did not touch her but stood in her way.

"We've got to talk about this," he said. "It's one thing for new-born pigs to die. They're like—"

"Canaries in a coal mine. You don't have to tell me everything a dozen times."

"But a calf has lungs the size of a child's."

Ella could not stop the rush of tears. "Let me go. I've got to go to Billy."

"It doesn't matter a damn anymore that you were born on this farm. We have to get the hell out of here."

"All right. Now, please, get out of my way."

"I know what you're thinking . . ."

"You do not know what I'm thinking!"

She shoved his chest and he stepped back. He said something else but she did not listen or care.

Late that night, Tom sat at the kitchen table trying to write. Against a heavy drift of fatigue, he tried over and over to explain their problems on paper to Ormond Cardwell. The failures lay in little balls around him on the floor.

When Ormond had offered his assistance at Kresge's lunch counter, Tom had appreciated it but thought he didn't need him. If Tom had a beef, he'd talk to his own MLA. But writing to Ormond tonight had to do with their childhoods. He needed someone who knew who he was.

"We have been losing half our pig litters. The piglets are barely born and smother. Last night it was stinking and two calves died, twins." When he read it back, it sounded like a child's writing.

He wanted Ormond to know, not just about the dead animals, but about how sick Billy got on those nights. How he puked until he was as bent and stiff as a hay hook. How it exhausted him. How his blood was no good.

"A calf's lungs are the same size as a boy's lungs."

Tom's hand shook as he wrote it. He had begun to fear his son would die.

Things were not getting better. That's what he had to get across to Ormond. All spring, the smell had been hellish. Every damn thing was worse.

Tom set the pen down. He combed the fingers of both hands back through his hair. There was something else on his mind, something he could not tell Ormond or anyone. A few weeks back, he had gone to the Lower Place to fence. When he was driving home after dark, vehicle lights popped on and off ahead of him at the school. In the flashes he recognized Hughie McGrady's Ford.

Hughie was an old cowboy from Wyoming who had arrived in the country half a century ago with a wife and brother. Now he was over seventy and alone. Tom stopped and got out. The two men leaned against the fender of Hughie's truck and smoked. Hughie asked how things were. Tom knew there must be some pressing reason the old fellow had flagged him, but such were Hughie's manners he had to hear Tom out first. It was not long after the two litters of pigs had died, so Tom told him that, then about Billy's illness.

"How is it with you, Hughie? The gas must be bad at your place too."

The bit of orange light from Hughie's pipe lit his face and the underside of his floppy hat brim. Tom saw the old fellow's lips draw back, the teeth clench hard on the pipestem.

"That slough west of my house? I checked that one morning and seen some woollies lying by the dugout. I come closer and by God they were dead—three ewes. I started down and got dizzy as hell. I figured it was gas so I ran back up. My legs turned to punk and I fell down. I was out cold but maybe the wind blew it off. I woke up anyway."

"Did you phone the plant?"

"Nah. I phoned that buzzard Dietz a couple of times early on. All he ever did was offer to visit. I told him I wasn't looking for company."

Tom had begun to understand that the story about the sheep dying was not why Hughie was here waiting.

"You got something on your mind, Hughie?"

"I do, Tom, and it ain't easy."

"Go on."

"You know I rented some Bauer land for pasture?"

"I do."

"I was riding there, to see if there was enough grass for my woollies. It was afternoon, and I saw your car parked where Bauer's house used to be. I thought that was strange so I come closer."

Hughie stopped. Tom told him to keep going.

"I'da said sooner but I couldn't make up my mind. I saw you go by earlier, and I thought, I got to tell him. Thing is, Tommy, I saw your wife and she was with that young fella works with Dietz at the plant. It was probably nothing."

"What were they doing?"

"They were standing. They had hold of each other. I turned my horse and got the hell out. I don't want to cause trouble, but it didn't feel right not to say."

Tom's cigarette was dead. He plucked it from the corner of his mouth and laid it in the can lid. He pulled another sheet of paper forward, picked up the pen and dipped it.

"What's hard is how it gets to everybody. It's family that pays. Besides my son being sick, no one in this family gets along like they used to. Not my daughters. Not me and my wife. I don't even get along with myself. Don't even recognize myself. I thought I was a good farmer, good trader, good husband, not a bad father. I counted on respect and had it. I don't know what I've got now. Some days it doesn't feel like much."

Tom stared at these words and panic took him. He scrunched the sheet, squeezed it into a hard ball. He gathered everything from the floor, lifted the trash burner lid, and dropped the papers in. He stirred the coals until a flame appeared and the paper balls caught.

In a whisper, he said to Ella, "I do know what you're thinking."

7

Waddens Lake

BILL BOLTED OUT OF BED at Chateau Borealis, skipped breakfast, and drove to the plant. He was working out the details of his trip to Calgary when Henry opened the door.

"Houle wants to see you."

"When?"

"Now."

"Why?"

"He didn't say."

"Who else is going to be there?"

"Just you, big guy."

"I can't phone him?"

"In his office first thing is what he said."

Bill put his winter gear back on and walked fast through the plant. He could have called someone to drive him, in a quad or truck, but preferred, for the sake of wakefulness, to walk in the cold. He sucked the icy breaths in deep.

It was a poor time to run into Johnny Bertram—but, around a blind corner, there he was: he and Elmo flopping insulation bales off the truck.

"Johnny."

"Hey, Billy-boy. Where you off to so early?"

"Called on the carpet by my boss."

"Been screwing the pooch?"

Houle's secretary was a stylish, sarcastic Native named Paula. In his crossings through this antechamber, Bill had learned to like her even though she reliably did not remember his name. Now she twisted her torso toward him while leaving her eyes glued to the computer screen. It looked like a yoga pose. She offered him a coffee and he accepted.

"Bill Ryder, correct?"

"Correct."

"I don't know why I can't remember. Maybe you don't look like your name."

"You can call me Mr. Walker if that helps."

"Okay, Mr. Walker. You can go in."

Bill entered Houle's sanctum. All the other working spaces at the project looked temporary, like trailers, but Houle's was a reasonable facsimile of a Calgary executive office. Giant desk. Corner windows that framed a few trees.

Theo spun a coaster under Bill's lowering cup.

"'Lo, Bill. How are you this morning?"

"Didn't sleep. Fine otherwise."

"You stayed in camp, didn't you? What did you find to do all night?"

"Usual mid-week bunga-bunga party."

It wasn't a good sign that Houle smirked. Ordinarily he was a hearty laugher.

"I'll cut to the chase here, Bill. I'm sure we're both busy. I heard something last night at the open house. It was a woman telling a man that you never lie to them. Bill the sulphur man never lies to us, she said. They were Native people."

"Did I miss a memo? Are we supposed to lie to them?"

"I'm kind of serious here, Bill. It reminded me of something else I heard from a community woman." Houle picked a sheet off his desk and shot it into a tray. "Something about you saying our tailings pond leaks."

"That's not what I said."

"So you remember saying something. By the way, I'm being less than transparent. It wasn't two women. It was the same woman twice. Mrs. Calfoux."

"Right."

"So when Mrs. Calfoux suggested our pond might leak, you said?"

"Oh, hell, I don't know. Something like that it wasn't impossible."

Houle flipped his hands over, a pair of puppies exposing their bellies. "So you did suggest to her that our pond leaks."

"Theo, look. This happened because Dion told me I should go talk to the woman. I tell Dion whenever he asks that I don't like talking to locals. I'd rather be left out of that side of things."

"You appeared to enjoy yourself last night."

"I went to a corner to eat. Marie Calfoux came to talk."

"Yes, the woman in question came to talk. Our pond doesn't leak."

"When she said tailings ponds, she meant all tailings ponds, not just ours. If the context matters."

"And you know for a fact that other ponds leak, do you?"

"Come off it, Theo. One project has a moat around their pond to catch leaks and put them back."

"They do that so the pond doesn't leak. Obviously."

Bill sat back and folded his arms.

"It seems to me a matter of loyalty," said Houle, "to our company and our industry."

"You know, Theo, I don't like being told what to say and not say. I don't like being told who I can talk to either." He realized he was angry, but it was impossible not to be. Houle was being an asshole.

"If you're working up to telling me I'm fired, let's go there. You have the power, get on with it."

"I thought you liked your job."

"I do, and you know it."

"It sounds like you're ready to walk."

"A long time ago, someone told me never make a deal unless you're willing to walk away."

"This isn't a deal—it's a job. And a damn good one."

"A job is a deal of sorts."

Something in Houle's demeanour changed. "Let's not get carried away," he said. "I'm not questioning your ability. All I want is for you to be more circumspect about what you say to the people you talk to around here."

"That sounds like what I said I don't like."

"Is it my job, really, to give you everything you like?"

"My job is running your sulphur plant. Why don't I go do that?"

"You're pretty cocky today."

"How would you like me to be?"

The frozen air soon cooled him off and left him feeling stupid. Marie was relaying to his boss things that he said. It probably meant she had no interest in him beyond that; she'd been playing him like a harp. It was also true that she had told him she wasn't trying to snag him, and had called him sad and unattractive. If he kept on thinking she was romantically interested, who was to blame?

Bill forgot to avoid the place where Johnny Bertram was working. Johnny downed his tools.

"You don't look so good, Billy. They didn't fire you, did they?"

Bill groped for a witty remark. Johnny grew more serious.

"Jump in the truck." Inside the cab, he fiddled with the dials on his dash, made heat pour. "Did I make a bad joke?"

"Pretty good one, actually. I think I came pretty close to being on the job market."

"What did you do? Your plant hasn't blown up. You haven't killed any neighbours. I doubt you steal." He thumped the dash with his big mitt. "Poontang! Has to be poontang."

The antique word made Bill laugh. "Sort of correct," he said. "Though, for the record, no sex was asked for or received."

"That's good. I'd hate to think anyone got laid up here."

They sat for another minute.

"Harassment would fit," Johnny said philosophically. "No result. But you can still get fired for it."

"I didn't get fired."

"Maybe that's why you look so sad. Just about had the big severance package in your hands, and they said you have to stay."

"Thanks for the warm-up."

"It's something about the woman in the village, isn't it? You can hire Indians, just not sleep with them. Pretty good rule, actually."

"See you later, Johnny."

Back in his office, he realized he hadn't told Houle he was going to Calgary. Fuck him. Bill got his crew sorted and left.

Between Fort Mac and Edmonton, clouds hung low, and the snow kept moving out of the trees and across the lanes. Semis ripped the drifts into whiteouts. Patches of black ice felt like the earth opening. Still the maniacs sped. If Bill needed further intimations of mortality, there were plenty in the ditches. White crosses stuck out of the snow, some hung with plastic wreaths. Stuffed animals, booze bottles.

It wasn't the best time for thinking, but he did anyway. A woman gives him tea twice, they share a few laughs, and what? And nothing. It was a simple enough thing. He should be able to stuff it in his bulging live-and-learn file and move on. But here he was, full of boyish sorrow—and humiliation. It had been so easy for her to get him to talk about the plant, to say things that she could then quote back to his boss—and anyone else she pleased. What kind of simpleton had he become?

On a two-lane section, a truck coming from the south swerved into his lane. He hit his brakes and started to slide. Then the truck was past him and in the ditch.

Bill drove onto the shoulder, clicked on his flashers, walked back. The truck was mired in the snow at the edge of a little patch of spruce trees, but it was right side up. The door swung and the driver jumped out. He did not limp or appear to bleed as he walked to his truck's front end, where a tree had pushed a dent in his hood. The guy flailed his arms, kicked the tree; his shouts pared down by wind sounded like a bee in a can. The absence of gratitude made Bill want to deliver the blow that fate had spared him. But the guy was large and the hurt would be on Bill. He went back to his truck and kept driving.

It fell dark where the boreal started changing to farmland. Enough sky cleared for the moon to light the snow in the fields, the cross-hatch of animal tracks. His thoughts were finally off Marie, but they'd gone to the equally sad topic of whether Houle meant to fire him. Story was that many engineers had been laid off in Alberta during the economic disaster a few years back, and that they were shipping their resumés by the bushel to places like Waddens. Maybe old Theo was sending feelers back to see if any of these young geniuses wanted to be a sulphur boss.

Retire was something Bill had sworn never to do. No pension or fat severance. No boiling palm-tree town in an American swamp or desert. When he thought retirement, he saw fleets of bellied geezers lining the mahogany at a faux-tropical bar, turning like birds each time the buxom barmaid passed. Endless casinos.

At a 24-hour truckstop in Edmonton, the waitress called him Junior, served him over-easy instead of sunny side up, white toast instead of brown. Off again down the QEII. Three hours to Calgary.

North of Red Deer, a ranting blizzard hit. Ice balled the wipers and built on the windshield. Pythons of white sped by his doors and across the black gloss. Cars hit the ditch like toys with dead batteries. When he crept into Red Deer, he'd had enough. So many had given up before him that hotel after hotel down Gaetz Avenue had the *No* above *Vacancy* lit. Ceasing to look for comfort, he sought comfort's opposite, and the strategy led him to Sonny's Motor Inn. The room had it all: curtains that did not meet; the ghosts of ten thousand cigars; TV remote in three pieces; dripping shower head; iron-stained toilet; bed in the shape of a ruined back.

Before sleep, Bill thought to phone the Calgary hotel and tell them he was weathered in. A silky voice told him that, because of the deep discount he was receiving and the lateness of the hour, they would not be able to re-credit his credit card.

For some reason, giving up the money without a fight put him in the mood to phone Jeannie.

"Bill!" Her enthusiasm shook him. So genuinely glad to hear his voice he almost cried. She filled him in on the Hatfield Corners weather: two inches of fresh snow, minus eighteen by the thermometer out the kitchen window.

"Did you get the box? Dad's binder?"

"Got it. Thanks."

"Thanks, I bet. I knew you were mad when you didn't answer my calls."

"Me and telephones."

"Soon, you can communicate with me in a less personal way. I'm getting internet."

"On the farm?"

"It's expensive. Satellite. But I don't want to get bushed."

He told her where he was and about the meeting; about his days off.

"Are you saying you're coming down?"

"It's up to you. If you want company."

"Course I want company. When will you be here?"

"I don't know exactly. Tomorrow night?"

"For supper?"

"I guess so. Sure. What time?"

"Whenever you get here, we'll eat."

In the morning, the highway south was closed. Ploughing and sanding in progress. By the time the highway opened, the panel on corrosion was about to start. At best, Bill was ninety minutes away.

By quarter to eleven, he made it to the Calgary hotel. He entered the hallway outside the conference room and saw black-tie waiters setting up the second coffee service. After a muffled blast of applause inside, double doors flew open and men and women streamed out: a mixture of city suits and vinyl-looking leather that Bill found familiar—or did until he realized he was only recognizing types.

He joined the line for coffee and pastries. Conversation circles were forming down the hall. He wandered the alley between them. It had been three years since he'd last attended one of these, but the interval was apparently crucial, overlapping the retirement or death of the world of engineers he had known. He didn't see a soul he knew.

He was walking in the direction of the parkade elevator when he saw something different: a lone circle of old men. Leading with his coffee cup, Bill parted his way among them, and a hearty welcome burst forth. A round of handshakes and backslaps.

Surveying the faces, Bill felt sad and damp. The pinkness of them. The white-tonsured shiny baldness. The odd bandage over what was probably skin cancer. They loved that he was with them, and it had to do with his relative youth. He would forever be Billy, a hard-charging youngster when they had been the powerful ones: the silverbacks of the oil jungle.

Now, they took turns reminding him to think about retirement.

"Don't wait till your health goes."

"Quit while you can get it up."

When he asked what they were doing, they looked down or away. Someone mentioned golf. Sol and Hugo, standing together with the railroad map of southern Britain printed on their noses, were living posters for what they'd found to do in their retirement years.

A guy Bill only vaguely remembered started into a story about how he and two buddies were buying propane from little prairie plants and trucking it to remote spots beyond the natural gas lines. They'd even scored some federal recession money to hire kids to do the driving. The story embarrassed the others. Work was not supposed to be a nostalgic hobby. When retirement came, you were supposed to fuck off to the golf course where you belonged.

In the wake of the propane story, Bill asked if Lance Evert was around. This was met with silence. Don Giotto put a meaty hand on Bill's shoulder and steered him away.

"Hate to be the one to tell you, Billy, but Lance has cancer. You know how he is—soon as he got the diagnosis, he researched it, started eating broccoli by the yard." Don pretended to laugh, took a handkerchief out of his back pocket and dabbed at his red-veined eyes. "But he's not going to beat it, Billy. You should go see him. He likes company. And Judy could use the break."

Don patted him on the back and departed. The crowd was moving into the meeting room again. Bill tried to remember the agenda, what came next. He took a few steps and stopped.

In the underground parkade, he sat in his truck. In the exit's golden mouth, a hooker strolled back and forth: fishnet stockings under a puffy faux fur. As he emerged onto the avenue, Bill was trying to tell himself that he was on his way to Lance and Judy's house in Brentwood. When he passed the city limits going west, he knew he wasn't going to Jeannie's either.

8

Ryder Farm, 1961

TOM HAD BEEN SOWING OATS all day in the meadow northeast of the house. A near-windless day and pleasant until the gas moved in after lunch and hung in the bowl where he drove the tractor back and forth. The rest of the day was spent getting dizzy and clearing his head, arguing with himself whether he should quit or finish. He thought of Hughie McGrady's dead ewes and how Hughie almost died along with them. It could happen so easily. It might be happening now.

The field was small, a one-day job, and he stuck with it until he was finished. For the last while, he was squinting into little pools of tractor light, looking for the lines. Back at the house, he found the girls and Billy sitting at the table. There was nothing on it but his dinner on a plate, his knife and fork. The kids, all three, were scowling at him.

"What's going on? Where's your mother?"

Donna looked at Jeannie, and Jeannie spoke. "She told us we had to sit here and wait for you. She's got something she wants to tell us."

Donna said, "Mom's been crying all night."

Billy looked like he had been crying too. He looked frightened.

Tom went through the arch and knocked on the door of their bedroom. "Ella, I'm here."

He heard nothing back so he went to the table and sat, picked up his knife and fork, and cut into a slice of cold roast beef. "Wait with me a minute, all right?" he said to the kids.

Then Ella came. Her face and eyes were red. It came to him that someone must have died. Probably her father, who hadn't been well for years. Still, it was an odd thing to do: to not tell the children, to make them wait.

"What's going on?" Tom asked her.

She had a handkerchief in her hand. She lifted it and pushed it against her eyes.

"I've made a decision," she said. "You're right. We have to go." She ran back into the bedroom. The door slammed.

"Right about what? Go where?" Jeannie glared in the direction her mother had gone.

Donna said, "She means leave the farm, right, Dad?"

"That's what she means. She means we should move."

Jeannie was standing. Her arms were rigid and her fists clenched. "That's not what she means. It can't be. Mom would never."

"She has to," said Donna. "She just said it."

"Oh, shut up! You don't know what you're talking about!"

"Jeannie, slow down. I'll talk to your mother, but I'm sure that's what she means. That's why she's upset."

"You're making her."

"The hell I am. It's her farm—her parents' farm. Her decision. But it's the right decision. We can't stay here being sick. We'll wind up like the pigs and calves."

Now Billy was bawling.

"Come here, Billy. You can sit on my knee while I eat."

Billy shook his head. He slid off his chair and ran into the dark. They could hear him banging on the bedroom door until his mother let him in.

"This is a damn nuthouse!" Jeannie stomped out of the room, then loudly up the stairs.

"You can go too if you like," Tom said to Donna.

Her face was stern at first but then she smiled. "I'm glad we're going."

She stayed sitting with him until his plate was empty.

9

Casino

BILL SAT ON THE EDGE of the bed. He had changed out of his suit and into casual clothes. All that remained was to go downstairs, find a cash machine, and walk the rows of VLTs until he spotted one that had a look of promise.

He pulled his cell phone from his shirt pocket and stared at it. He had hoped there would be no reception here by the mountains, but there was. He poked out the number. Jeannie answered. He pictured her in the farm kitchen, holding the black receiver to her ear. He told her he would not be coming to the farm. Not tonight. Not this weekend.

"Shit, Bill."

"I'm sorry."

He pocketed the phone, got to his feet, and went to the door.

PART TWO

In the school library, the boy found the book. It had a black cloth cover and was full of drawings of tools and machines.

The first picture was a bolt and nut. The bolt stood straight with the nut next to it. There was nothing else on the page. The grooves—threads, his father called them—rose up the bolt but were not straight across. If the bolt was huge and you were tiny, you could walk around in the grooves and get to the top.

Over two days, the boy drew a copy of the nut and bolt. When he was done, he folded it and slid it into the snap wallet chained to his belt. At home, when supper was over and his mother and sisters finished dishes and went to the living room, he unfolded the picture in front of his father. After looking in silence, his father beckoned. They put their winter coats on.

In the shop, his father pulled the string that lit the yellow bulb. He drew a flat box out of a drawer and unhooked the lid. Inside were bright steel circles, each a different size. Beside the circles was a bar with handgrips and a hole in the middle.

His father stepped outside and found a foot of iron rod in his junk pile. He tightened it into his vise so it stood up straight. He picked a steel circle from the box and pressed it into the hole in the bar. He squirted oil on the rod, balanced the bar on top, pushed down, and turned.

After a few turns, peels of curly steel came out the bottom. After many more turns, the rod rose out the top—only it wasn't a rod anymore. It was a bolt with threads!

The father released the vise, brushed the threads with sandpaper; rummaged in a drawer and found a nut the right size. He turned the nut onto the bolt and placed it in the boy's hand.

1

Ryder Farm, 1961

TOM DID NOT ANTICIPATE difficulty selling the farm. Aladdin would be glad to see them go. When he was ready to talk, he went to the plant to see Alf Dietz.

Dietz came in with his hard hat tipped back on his balding head. Sweat beads stood out on his long forehead. He had a grease smear across his nose. He stripped off a glove and gave Tom a sweaty hand to shake.

The office secretary brought coffee and the two men faced each other across the desk. Tom told Dietz he and Ella wanted to sell. When pigs and cattle die, that's your profit gone. You're farming for the hell of it. He did not speak of the risk to his family. He wasn't going to beg. Dietz told him the Court family was leaving too, and it was the first Tom had heard of it. How could your neighbours plan to leave without your knowing?

But Alf Dietz couldn't help him with selling the farm. All he could do was let Clint Comstock know. Tom said he'd rather deal with Dietz. Dietz shook his head and said it couldn't happen that way. He was sorry but it couldn't.

Two weeks passed before Tom heard more, and then it was just Dietz stopping by to tell them Comstock was going to send Tom and Ella a letter. He'd be coming north to check on the plant in the fall. He'd visit then. This bewildered Tom—you say you want to sell and get away, and it's treated like a matter of no urgency. Maybe he should have said his family was in danger. Probably Johnny Court had said he wanted to move because their daughter was sick, and so his deal was done—quietly, as if it was something shameful.

By then, it was the beginning of July and school was out. Jeannie came to Tom while he was greasing the mower and said she wanted to work in town for the summer. It was hard to keep back anger. Here they were heading into haying season without a hired man, and his oldest daughter wanted to work away.

He said he would talk to Ella, and Jeannie stormed off. By that, he understood that Ella had already turned her down. When Tom went in for his afternoon coffee, he brought it up, and Ella said Jeannie's plan had nothing to do with work or wanting to make money; it was all because of her boyfriend. Tom felt like a fool; he did not know there was a boyfriend. Ella not only knew one existed but who he was. He was the son of the new engineer at the plant, Bert Traynor, the man who had replaced Lance Evert. Now that it was summer holidays, the boyfriend was working at the plant too.

None of this made sense to Tom. How could wanting to work in town be about a boyfriend if the boyfriend was going to be working out here? It was also a good question why Ella knew about this boyfriend but had not told him. She no doubt assumed he would blow his stack over the boy's being the plant engineer's kid. Even he was surprised at how little this affected him. It seemed inevitable. You couldn't expect girls to marry local farmers like they used to.

What he did say to Ella was that Jeannie shouldn't count on having the car. Because of the plant, Ella needed it. You never knew these days when she would have to grab Billy and run for it.

That didn't matter, she said, because Jeannie's intention was to board in town.

"The hell she will!"

Jeannie was outside, lying on a blanket in her swimsuit. Tom told her flatly it was out of the question. She was too young to live away from home.

"Your mother tells me that boyfriend of yours, who you never told me about, works at the plant for his father. He can come here and visit you after work. I imagine your mother will give him lunch now and then."

Jeannie picked up a little bottle and poured oil in her hand. She sat there with it cupped on her palm. "You don't like Gerry because Mr. Traynor's at the plant," she said.

"I just said he could come for lunch and visit after work. Does that sound like I'm against him? Anyway, how would I know if I like him? I don't know him. That's your choice, not mine."

Jeannie never did bring the boyfriend for lunch, and their visits amounted to her walking up the road in the late afternoon when his shift was done and the two of them sitting in his car for an hour. "Listening to the radio," she called it.

Tom started knocking down the alfalfa, and when some of it was ready, he taught Donna how to rake. The side rake was the easiest implement on the farm, an array of spoked wheels that whipped the mown hay into a swath; just the thing for training a kid to tractor work. Later, when she'd raked everything and he needed to run the baler, he taught her the side mower. The mower was trickier to operate and frustrating in heavy hay, but she picked it up quickly. A few times, when he wasn't using the baler, and Donna was mowing, Tom put Jeannie on the rake.

When everyone was out in the field at once, maybe gathered around a lunch that Ella and Billy had brought, Tom tried to feel good about the family pitching in together. But it was never a happy work bee. If it wasn't Jeannie making it known she'd rather be in town, it was Donna and Jeannie exchanging barbs. Ella was sour too. She hardly ever had a smile for him.

While Tom was baling the last field, a stretch of the Lower Place close to the river, it started to stink. A ridge of high hills separated the field from the plant, and the smell was usually less there. He was trying to figure out why it it was different today when his breath caught in his chest. He stopped the tractor. As he was standing down from it, the world turned black and he hit the ground. His lungs were like boards, each breath a labour. He told himself to get up and run, to climb the nearest hill, get his head into higher air, but his legs would not answer. His head would not come away from the ground. He wondered if this was it, then. He thought of Ella, Donna, Billy, Jeannie; Ella again.

The day had been sultry, a near absence of wind. As hope and sense were leaving him, a few gusts combed down through the uncut hay. The next breath was less hard to pull in. When he had enough air to think, he thought the gas must be coming out of the river valley and the cleaner air from the west. His lungs softened enough so he could stand, though he swayed like a flag. As he began making stumbling steps, his head screamed in pain and he threw up into the hay stubble.

He had no idea how long it took him to walk from the tractor to the truck. Sometimes he had to crawl. On some higher ground in the middle, he slept in the dirt and woke up retching. He took a piss, and it came dark orange.

Going home, he passed Ella in her garden. She must have noticed he was driving like a drunk, for she met him in the yard and guided him into the house, onto their bed. She placed a bucket near his head, mopped sick sweat off his forehead with a wet face cloth.

"Leave the tractor and the baler where they are," he commanded. "Don't go near them. That gas came from the river."

Ella left the room, and Billy, who must have been outside the door, slipped in. He looked at his father in amazement.

"Never saw me on a bed with clothes on, did you, buddy?"

Billy was shy, as if it might not be his father at all.

"Give me an hour, young fella. I'll be better then."

The boy came and rested his hand on Tom's hairy arm below the rolled sleeve. Billy seemed to know how much good it did his father to have his hand there.

Day after day Tom stayed in bed. He could not remember any time like it. Even in the coal mine when a poorly set charge blew him against a rock wall and broke four ribs, he had been on his feet sooner than this. But every dawn when he snapped awake and tried to rise, an anvil bore him down.

Over and over, he came out of his doze worrying aloud that Donna was trying to finish the baling. Before he was gassed, she had asked if she could run the baler, and he'd said no. Those old round balers were dangerous. They had powerful twin rollers that snapped in the hay, and if they plugged and you forgot to disconnect the power takeoff, your whole arm could be sucked in.

Ella cut him off. "You're not listening, Tom. I told you that Vic finished the baling."

"Right, right," he said, but it would not prevent him from forgetting again.

Throughout the day and night, he would wake in panic. A milk cow dead with her head in the milking stanchion. Ella and Billy collapsed between potato rows. Donna crawling and coughing. How had his and Ella's failings combined to keep them here so long?

After a week, Ella took him to the doctor, though he protested against it. The doctor listened, a little too patiently, as Tom explained what had happened. The doctor put sticky pads attached to wires all over his bared chest. When he wanted to know what it was, the doc said, "ECG."

"But that's for the heart."

"Middle-aged man falls down in a faint, I check his heart."

"It wasn't a faint. I told you, I was gassed."

The doctor kept on with the electrocardiogram.

"He didn't believe me," Tom grumbled on the way home. "Bugger thinks I made it up."

After two weeks in the house, Tom went back to work. His neighbours had most of their bales piled already. Usually he would have gone out with the tractor and hayrack, but that was impossible. He would never be able to throw bales that high. He and Donna took the pickup and put on small loads. But they were hardly making a dint.

After they'd finished the smallest field, Ella suggested they stop. She had remembered a time before her father retired when he had been in the same predicament—sick and with hay bales in the field that he could not stack. Knowing that hay kept well in round bales, her father left them on the ground. Each day of winter, he picked up enough to feed his cows.

At first Tom fought the idea. He did not like how it would look, the weakness of it as seen by his neighbours. But when September came and the girls were in school, he had no choice.

There was not a lot of grain to harvest, just enough oats and barley for the feedlot. Tom did the tractor work, and Ella drove the grain truck. Tom never admitted to his family how weak he felt, how often a clammy sweat forced him to stop and sit, or even to lie on the ground. After such a moment, he would always think of the upcoming meeting with Clint Comstock: what he would say when it was time to deal.

During the weeks after Tom was gassed, the house had a supernatural feel to it. Ella was conscious every moment of the man in the bed in the bedroom, the one whom she had never seen in a weakened state of any kind. But there he was unmoving on the bed as daylight shifted through the rooms.

At times, when Tom was fully asleep, she would creep in and sit on the side of the bed, studying his face. He had a specific look when he slept, and sometimes too when he was awake, that reminded her of their courtship. When he had arrived to visit her, after riding miles through the hills in the evening, he always wore traces of what he had been thinking. What she saw wasn't just affection but also how alarmed he was to have lost command of his emotional state. It made him resent and fear her at the same time as he tumbled into love.

Now, when he could barely lift a water glass, he was like that again. He did not enjoy being helpless and dependent, but at the same time was grateful. He knew she was being kind and patient with him. She was giving him the food and water that would allow him to get up and return to independence.

When he did finally have the strength to leave the house, it was like watching a soldier put on armour for a return to war. He assembled his anger, clapped on his hardness, covered it with an air of being the only one who could protect them against the plant. Last of all came the distance that had existed before, to which she responded with distance of her own.

But the time between, from the gassing to the return of distance, had taught her something she hadn't known. Able to feel her old love for Tom—and she did feel it in the time of his helplessness—she was able to measure it against what she felt for Lance. She found that the love for Tom was greater, maybe not stronger but greater. When she and Tom returned to their distant poles, she went back to thinking of Lance fondly. But she would never forget which love weighed more.

Weaning was always done in the inner yard of the feedlot. The slab enclosure was much smaller than the three-acre outer yard: just a set of walls anchored by a grain box and a roofed bed ground, two feed troughs down the middle. Only here could they hold the desperate calves and their mothers separate, the flaw being that it was fifty yards from the well.

The whole family was needed to haul water by bucket up the slope. They emptied the water into barrels roped to the inside of the gate, and the frantic thirst of the milk-deprived calves drained the barrels again and again.

The sound of hoarse cows and the shrill calves was composite, nearly solid. It dropped a pall of sadness over everyone as they worked. The world of the cows and calves was coming to an end, and it would have taken a heart of stone not to feel it. Donna was the only one who smiled, and that was from enjoyment in showing off how many more times she could carry two full buckets of water up the slope than her sister. Jeannie had no desire to win. She stopped often to rest, checking her fingernails for damage.

Billy took the work seriously. He had insisted on bringing a small bucket they used for tempting the horses with oats and went back and forth at a run.

What Ella noticed, as they did this work, was how little stamina Tom had, and how hard he tried to hide it. He was a terrible colour and sweating badly. Every time he came to the well end of the journey, he stripped off his glove and made a cup of his hand under the water's pour.

"Don't make yourself sick," she said, but he didn't reply or stop.

From the feedlot, Ella saw the mail lady's car at the school corner. Wanting a break anyway, she drove down there. The letter from Comstock was in the roll. When she got back, Tom was sitting on the edge of the tank, heaving for breath. He had his cap off and his hair was a tangle of wet strings. She opened the letter and held it to the light so both of them could read.

"So he'll be in Alberta a month from now," Tom said when he was finished. "'We can discuss the matter of your farm then. Please have two independent appraisals done.' Christ!" He put his hat back on.

"You should rest more."

"I've been buying, selling, and trading things since I was fifteen. Can you imagine if I asked Joey Lemaire, when he comes to trade a horse, would you mind having an independent appraisal done?"

"It's just a different way of doing things."

"Oh no. It's not just that. It's mockery. Aladdin bought Bauers' and they bought Courts'. That gives them two prices. They could average them and offer us that. But no. He wants me to jump fences first."

Donna stood there, puffing but fresh. "Dad, are we going to bring my calf home tonight?"

"Not tonight, no. Give him another day of weaning with the others. Then we'll run him into the small corral. I'll have to get the stock racks on."

"Can I stay home from school to help?"

"No," said Ella.

While they waited for their day with Comstock, Ella took Billy and looked at farms for sale. Nothing made her feel as black as this: walking through a stranger's house, around a foreign yard. Every nook and cranny made her see the equivalent in her own home, garden, barn. There was no emotion or memory in anything she saw, and she feared there never would be.

She got the idea that living near Dora Bauer might be a path out of emptiness, but the only place anywhere close to them was one that had been on the market for years. A bachelor lived there, and the house was unimaginably dirty. Cobwebs, stacks of yellowed newspaper, mouse dirt. When they left, Billy solemnly said, "Don't make us move there, Mom," and for some reason, that made them both laugh. Other places, not so easily dismissed, made Ella cry on the drive home.

As the time for meeting Comstock drew closer, Ella feared that too. What she was afraid of was Tom being too prepared. Too muscled up, as he might say. Tom had said more than once that it was her farm and no deal would be struck without her say-so. But he did not tell her his strategy. That was the horse-trading part, and he guarded it jealously.

Tom felt that Comstock had got the better of him, and, for that, he wanted revenge. Ella worried that Clint Comstock would know how to draw that anger and use it to trip Tom again.

When the assistant piloted the big white car into the yard, Tom was waiting beside his own truck in the turn-around. It was a cold day, a dip into winter, and, stepping out of the car, Comstock wasn't dressed for it. After their handshake, the Texan tried to pass Tom to the house, but Tom blocked him.

"There are things I want to show you before we talk."

Comstock looked at his watch.

"You know, Tom . . ."

"You made me wait months. I guess you can spare me an hour to look at what I'm offering to sell you."

Tom told the assistant to go inside and have coffee. He wanted

Comstock by himself. He drove them to the Lower Place. Bouncing across the hayfield there, Tom explained the work that had gone into this part of the farm, since they had acquired it ten years before. Tom had traded his original family farm for this land. That brought the two halves of the farm closer and made the whole easier to operate. This had added value to their holdings.

At the river escarpment, Tom stopped the truck and asked Comstock to get out.

The breeze rising up from the river was cold. Tom stood looking into the valley, letting Comstock shiver in his city overcoat. Then he said, "Right on this spot is where I got gassed last summer."

Ella had found out from people who lived in the river-bottom that a well test had been done that day, on the only well drilled into a valley bench. Tom studied Comstock's face for signs of his knowing this. He spared no details about how it had been, how he had crawled and stumbled to his truck; the retching, the blackouts, the burnt-orange piss.

Before they left the field, Tom described the course of his sickness, the fatigue that had kept him in bed for weeks. Two weeks of work lost in the heart of summer, and no hired man. "A neighbour had to come do my baling. Ella and the girls worked like navvies."

Close to their driveway, Tom stopped again. "Something else to show you."

"Tom, I do not have time."

"This is the last one."

He led Comstock across the ditch. At the fenceline, Tom grabbed the top wire and broke it with his hands.

"You just broke your own wire. Is that a good business practice?"

"I'm no Hercules. Wire I can break with my hands won't hold a cow. You can't even fix this corroded crap. Breaks if you stretch it."

"I was told we had given you replacement wire."

"What I was given replaced three hundred yards. Including cross fences, there's three miles of ruined wire on this half section alone."

Inside the house, they sat at the table. The assistant was in Tom's place, and Tom told him to move. Ella poured them tea.

"So what do you offer us for our place?"

Comstock laughed at him.

"You have a curious way of dealing. You spend an hour running down the asset, then ask me to name a price."

"I'm guessing you came with a figure in mind. I want to hear it."

"I asked for two independent appraisals. Can I see them?"

"We don't do that here. I know what it's worth."

"Then you tell me."

"The first time I talked to you, you said your company was willing to buy us out, like you bought out Bauers. You've since bought Courts. I think you know exactly what you mean to offer."

"I really don't have time for this."

"Then hurry up and tell me, and we'll both get back to work."

Comstock said a number.

"That's twenty dollars an acre less than what you paid Bauers," Tom told him. "Being close together, their land and ours has to be comparable."

"The Bauer land was needed for our plant site," Comstock replied. "We paid a premium for that. Your place doesn't even have wells on it."

"I just showed you thousands of dollars of damage, and that's only the beginning of what your plant has done to this farm and to us. There should be a premium for that too."

"Fine, then," said Comstock. He upped the price ten dollars an acre. "You've got all my wiggle room. That's it."

The amount was enough to buy a decent farm somewhere else.

It would not be as nice a farm, but theirs was not as nice a farm as it used to be. He looked at Ella. She gave a shallow nod.

Tom swallowed hard. He told Comstock he considered the price low but was going to accept it because it was important, for safety reasons, to get the family out of here before another winter.

Comstock said, "You understand my offer is for this half section, the land closest to our plant. It's not for the whole farm. We are not interested in that part by the river."

Tom's face burned. "That's not how you sell a farm, or buy one. We want out of this stink. I just told you I was gassed on the Lower Place. I was in bed two weeks."

"You can do what you want with that land. If you don't want it, sell it. Our only interest is in buying the half section closest to the plant."

Tom knew he was red-faced. His first thought was that Comstock was punishing him for acting as though he could control the negotiation, for taking him on the tour. But likely that wasn't true. The man probably came here to say exactly what he'd said.

"I'd appreciate it if you told your company that my wife and I will accept an offer of seventy dollars per acre for the entire farm."

"I *am* the company, Mr. Ryder. I'm refusing that deal."

"My wife and I *are* this farm. You are not your company."

—

Dear Tom,

I apologize for the delay. There were things I had to wait for, so as to have anything more than sympathy to offer you.

In the first year of the Hatfield plant's operation, there were many complaints from down your way. We told Aladdin

Oil and Gas to get an independent report on how the plant was working. Mr. Onge, our health minister, suggested they get Dr. Hemmel. You know that part because one of his tests was in your yard.

That report took a long time to get to us. We regarded some of what was in it as serious. The worst reading for sulphur dioxide was in your closest neighbour's yard. The highest reading for hydrogen sulphide was downwind of your house and feedlot.

After we got those results, we went back over things with Aladdin. They said they had fixed a lot of their early problems, and that the expansion plant was constructed differently to counter those problems. They also claimed there were mistakes in Dr. Hemmel's testing that made it seem worse than it was. We're not listening to that part.

Our decision is that the company and our government should co-operate on a health study around the Aladdin Hatfield plant. This will happen over the next year. Mr. Comstock said a health study at your farm was not necessary because you were planning to sell. I bet it's not easy for you and Ella to walk away. But maybe it's for the best. I'll regard this matter as settled unless I hear from you otherwise.

Yours truly,
Ormond Cardwell, MLA

Dear Ormond,

Clint Comstock and I could not agree to terms for our farm. I accepted their price per acre, but then he said he only wanted the home half. That kind of deal would leave us in a fix forever. If he thinks our troubles with this plant are restricted to the home half, he's not listening. This summer, on my Lower Place (the part he doesn't want to buy), I got gassed so bad I lost two weeks' work. He knew that.

As a farmer yourself, you'll understand it makes no sense to sell a farm to get away from a problem you don't get away from. You'll understand too that if I sell half my farm, buyers will fleece me on the other half.

If there's a health study in the works, my family wants to be part of it. We need a proper study because people around here don't believe what we say. People in Haultain, including the doctors, think we're complainers. The store owners in town like the money that comes with the plant and don't give a hoot about us anymore.

Ella and I are tired of fighting this plant and would sell if they took the whole thing. Otherwise, there's no deal. I appreciate your going to bat for us.

Yours truly,
Tom Ryder

2

AFTER TWO DAYS in the casino, Bill stepped into a blast of light. He found his sunglasses in his coat pocket and put them on so he could see the ash-coloured flat surrounding him. Beyond the fenced lot, a file of painted horses walked away, their long tails dusting out their tracks in a thin coating of snow.

When he stepped clear of the building, a hard wind cut his face. His truck stood alone under a light standard. He threw his suitcase in and was soon eastbound on the Trans-Canada.

Half the cars and vans coming from the other direction had skis on top, and he felt a brief temptation to cross an overpass and join them. At one time, he had skied every resort from here to Vancouver, had been known as a good powder skier. For some reason, no reason, he had quit. When he added up the years, he was surprised to find that he hadn't skied once in the last ten. There had been no popped ACL, no series of concussions. He did not even have arthritis except in the immediate locale of once-broken bones. If anyone asked, he'd say, "I used to ski a lot at one time."

He imagined saying that to Marie Calfoux. She would come back with something perceptive and pointy. "Sounds like you had a great life, *at one time*."

After half an hour on the four-lane, he turned north onto a

secondary highway, a narrow strip of blacktop made dangerous by logging trucks. People with farms and ranches along the forest reserve were selling off whole quarters for clear-cutting: a one-shot approach to retirement and agricultural debt that left the country looking like a plucked chicken.

He was trying not to think of the weekend's gambling but it was there in his head anyway. He regretted an argument with an American guy at the next machine, who took issue with Bill's refusal to celebrate jackpots.

"You just won a thousand dollars, man! Whoop it up. Holler. Something, for fuck sakes."

Bill had pointed to another line of machines, to a couple sitting thigh to thigh before one screen. "Those two kiss every time they make five bucks. There's a chair open beside them."

Which caused things to get heated. In a better mood, he would have made peace, offered the man a beer instead of insults. As for the issue of celebration, he could have explained.

"It's a drug. Self-medication. You don't cheer when you take Valium. Most people don't even cheer a line of cocaine."

If the American had been really patient, Bill could have told him the whole story, how he had started out on a machine in a rural saloon—not far from where he was driving right now. He had seen others poking away at the VLTs in the corner and found himself envying their intensity and absorption: how they never had to stare at the bearded buffalo on the wall or the rodeo saddles over the rafters while drinking alone.

So he started betting a few bucks, playing blackjack because he knew the rules. He bet the lowest amount. When he saw that the other gamblers preferred the spinning-reel games, he switched to those and his wagers climbed. Soon he was betting five lines, like everyone else.

Some days he broke even; most days he lost. Then, one day, he won three hundred dollars. There wasn't a soul in the saloon at the time, except Mitch the bartender. When he cashed his ticket, he told Mitch it was the first time he'd won anything significant, to which the barman twitched up his moustache ends and said, "Trouble doesn't start until you win."

At the time, Bill was working at a plant near the mountains and rented a single-wide trailer on a country acreage west of the saloon. He was in a relationship with a younger woman that was inching its way to an inevitable end. He soon discovered that the pain of the faltering romance stopped when he played. This only worked as long as you kept the twenties flowing, kept your mind busy with the spinning reels, but that could be hours if you chose to afford the losses.

After the relationship was over, VLT gambling stayed with him. He was by then well addicted, but the habit left him able to remember the phone numbers of his children, and he still got to work on time. As far as Bill could tell, gambling did not show on him—no needle tracks, no splash of ruptured veins on the face. It was a vice unlikely to get him fired.

The worst side effects were sleepless nights, disgust with himself, and half-serious considerations of suicide. That and the eyestrain he could stand. It seemed right that relief should have its cost.

A truck stacked with chained logs passed Bill and wrapped him tight in a swirl of snow. When he could see again, he was a quarter-mile from the turnoff to the village he'd been thinking about. The saloon, Mitch; the VLTs he had trained on. Farther up that road was the acreage and the trailer.

Like most things of the sort, the relationship with the young woman had started well. An adventure in the woods. She told him she liked to ride, so, as a surprise, he'd bought a pretty sorrel mare. The stuff about riding turned out to be mostly untrue. She had ridden twice, at stables, and had a theory she'd like riding if she did it more. The mare, who Bill named Dingbat, had a robust personality, not all positive. The girlfriend was afraid of her. In the end, it was Bill who rode Dingbat. If the girl felt anything for the horse it was jealousy.

Another hour of driving and Bill entered a familiar town. He was passing its hospital when, seemingly without instruction, his vehicle bent to the curb and stopped. At once, he was imagining his way around inside the one-storey building. Its polished hallways. The sickly antiseptic smell of the rooms. The fluorescent brightness that vanquished all shadows.

"Farm kid?" the doctor had asked him as the gurney approached the rubber doors of the surgery. Bill thought it was an odd thing to ask at this point but said yes.

"Heavy lifting when young," the doctor declared, as though denoting a sinful pastime. "Prolapsed hemorrhoids. In a farm community like this one, I could make my entire living off this one operation."

A few days later, when Bill was rousing from his daily morphine dream, he saw his sisters, like a pair of roosting angels at the foot of his bed. All it meant was that his girlfriend had picked up the ringing phone at the trailer. Poor woman was caught in the act of packing up to leave him, but she told Jeannie where he was and why.

"Why didn't you tell us?" were Jeannie's first words. Before he could reply, Donna suggested he was embarrassed at the nature of his problem. She told him how stupid that was in a grown man. He agreed with her; it would be stupid if that was his reason for not calling. In fact, he had doubted they would be interested. He neglected people and expected them to neglect him back.

When he was finally deprived of his morphine and evicted from the hospital, he had returned to the trailer, to its frightening, propane-smelling emptiness. He found he owned very little now that his girlfriend's effects were removed, and he decided he would move too. He would leave his job at the sour gas plant by the mountains and look for something up north. There was a boom gathering in the Alberta oil sands, which some were calling the last megadeposit of petroleum on earth. Bill decided to go there, to be one more luck-starved Klondiker.

Dingbat got antsy when the first boxes appeared. Given Bill's condition, riding her seemed out of the question. He lacked a horse trailer in which to move her, and the boreal forest was an unlikely place to find horse pasture. Dingbat would hate forty-below.

He decided to give the mare to his landlady, or, really, to her horsey granddaughter, a strapping blonde who knew how to keep a horse civilized. The whole time Bill packed and loaded his truck, Dingbat leaned over the fence and gave him shit.

"I used to ride quite a lot at one time."

By the halfway mark between Red Deer and Edmonton, Bill was sick of the trip and exceeding the speed limit. His wallet was so fat with profit it was giving him a sore back. He threw it on the dash. He had another roll of twenties inside a sock in his suitcase.

The American was far from the first person to be affronted by Bill's lack of enthusiasm in a casino. It made him unpopular with casino workers too. The bosses and staff wanted players to hoot and holler, kiss their partners and lovingly polish the machines with their sleeves—all crucial to making the gambling public run to the cash machines with their debit cards.

Instead of feeling happy about the money, Bill's body surged with unpleasant after-effects. His lungs seemed too large, felt as if they were crawling up his throat. He'd been yearning in the direction of every VLT lounge in every town he passed. In his trailer days, he'd played them all. The only way to stop feeling disgusted over the waste was to gamble more.

His job was the only thing that could reliably stop a binge. In this way, work and gambling were essential to each other. The balance between them had to be maintained if he himself was not to crumble. Part of his legend in the oil sands was that he was the only unit boss who came back from holidays early, claiming to have had an intuition that something at his plant was going wrong.

Covered in shame after a binge, Bill would send cash to his children. "Here's for nothing," he'd scribble on a note folded around the bills. He used to send money to ex-wives and girlfriends too, until he realized it insulted them and made them hate him even more.

By the time Bill had passed Edmonton and was back on Suicide 63, his thoughts had shifted again, to his only serious attempt at curing himself. It happened in Mac in 2008, in the months before the Wall Street collapse. Still in the boom, dozens of companies were digging new mines and pumping steam into in-situ fields. New upgraders were a-building, and companies clambered over each other for machines and men. To keep him from jumping ship, Bill received a lavish pre-emptive raise. The next weekend, in less than two hours, he lost four thousand on his lucky VLT.

The nausea that usually waited until next morning came at him like a tight pattern of darts. He was still in the casino, still at the losing machine and intent on losing more. That's when he looked up at the "When It's No Longer a Game" sign and memorized the help-line number. It felt so important that he broke his rule of silence and told the woman beside him what he was planning to do. She wanted to know how much he'd lost, and when he told her, she laughed at him. She said she'd lost three times that much in one day. She pointed at the sign Bill had been looking at.

"I'll tell you, my darling," she said, "it's never been a game for me. It's damn hard work."

Like everything in the world, getting help hadn't been as neat and simple as he'd imagined. He'd thought it would be like the emergency surgery on his hemorrhoids: the person at the help number would hear his problem, and he would soon be on a shrink's couch. But after he had stated his predicament to the woman on the help-line, she offered a placement in a therapy group in Edmonton. He took down the information while knowing he would never go.

Instead, Bill figured out where the McMurray psychologists were clustered. They were in the same building and shared a phone number. Their receptionist asked him a long list of questions, and, next thing, he had an appointment.

When he got to the office, the waiting room was nearly full, but it was not long before his name was called. He was directed into a small room. Three chairs, a low table, a tissue box. The psychologist entered and sat in the chair opposite. He was a younger, chubbier man than Bill was expecting, and he lost faith accordingly. He could not imagine this fellow understanding his problems.

The psychologist looked no more pleased with Bill.

"When you called our receptionist, she listed some categories. You said your problem was addiction. Is it a drug problem?"

"I'm not a crackhead."

"Why don't you tell me what you are, then?"

"My problem is gambling."

The psychologist sat forward with his pen poised over a writing pad on the table.

"And alcohol," Bill added.

"How often do you drink?"

"Couple of times a week. My days off."

"A twenty-six per sitting? Or more?"

"A bottle or two of wine usually. A twenty-six of anything hard would make me sick."

"Let's look at the gambling. Do you lose a thousand a week?"

Bill calculated.

"Let me rephrase that. You look like you have a professional job. Does more than forty per cent of your net income go to gambling every month?"

"Maybe a thousand a week if I'm gambling. But I don't gamble every week."

The psychologist set his pen down. He pushed his chair back from the table and let his chubby hands hang down between his knees.

"Are you suicidal?"

"I think about it. I assume everyone over thirty-five does from time to time."

"How often do you think about it?"

When he saw Bill struggling with the question, the psychologist thumped back in his chair. "How often did you think about suicide last week?"

"Couple of times. It was a bad week."

"And what made it bad?"

"I blew four thousand dollars on a VLT in one session."

"How about in the month before that week? I'm still talking about suicide, not your wins or losses."

"Hardly at all except for last week."

The psychologist bent forward and picked up the pen, clicked the point back into the body, clipped it in his shirt pocket.

"I'm going to level with you. There are not nearly enough psychologists in this town. To say we're overloaded is a hilarious understatement. You got in because you used a phrase that is a red flag for potential suicide."

He paused to see if Bill would comment, then went on. "I treat meth addicts, crackheads, alcoholics who beat their wives and children so badly ambulances have to be called. Guys going home to their wives in Newfoundland carrying STIs from camp whores. Pedophiles who work in daycares. A woman who cooks in a camp and has fantasies of mass murder. There are many rapes in this town, and sometimes the rapists and their victims both come to me as patients. A lot of people who come here kill themselves anyway."

Bill slapped his hands down on his knees and rose. "You've been a great help."

"I don't need your sarcasm."

"Do you generally send people away feeling worse than when they came in?"

"I'm asking you to leave. I have a button under my desk. If I push it, a cop comes. I'm serious. Go right now, or you'll wind up with a criminal record. As for your problem, if you feel it's that serious, call the 'When It's Not A Game' helpline. There are therapy groups and counsellors who deal with your type of problem."

3

Ryder Farm, 1962

COMSTOCK'S REFUSAL to buy the farm hit Tom and Ella hard. For Ella it was like the Bible story where God asks for a sacrifice. After she had suffered over the decision and agreed to it, God changed His mind. She could have been relieved except for the way it left her: vulnerable and full of guilt.

The effect on Tom was hard to gauge except that it drove him even further away. The refusal caused something like a blind to draw partway down behind Tom's eyes. Week by week, it dropped the rest of the way. Together in the house or car, they spoke so little it was barely human.

"The milk cow is drying up."

"Billy needs bigger shoes."

"Some of the hay bales are frozen to the ground."

In the house Tom did not volunteer anything but would answer any question from Billy or Donna. Billy's were the scattershot questions of an inquisitive child. Donna's were mostly about her club calf. Jeannie had no questions for Tom, nor he for her. But there was something about Tom's look that made Ella think he was no longer comfortable with himself. Everyone left the kitchen after dinner, children first, then Ella, leaving Tom alone at the table. That was not new. But when Ella passed through the kitchen, Tom never seemed to be doing anything. His Christmas books sat closed beside him, the newspapers were by the radio, his pencil and scrap paper were in a drawer. All he did was stare at the table or scratch at it with his fingernails—and smoke; he always smoked.

The look on his face was not anger or worry, but something less, she thought, something like embarrassment or confusion. Whatever it was, he hung on it, like a sack from a hook. She longed for the days when they had sniped at each other. At least there'd been life in that.

Ella had thought the club calf a stupid project, but now she felt relief when Tom and Donna went to look at the animal. The steer's shed had previously been used for young calves, a place to warm them during a blizzard. In the summer, Tom had cut the door larger and strengthened the fence, lashed in a water barrel. When Donna lured him down there, he would lean over the fence while she fooled with the calf. She led the steer around on a halter, in circles and figure eights, and this brought a wan smile to her father's face. She brushed the steer until he shone.

When neighbours dropped by, Tom held up his end of the conversation. As Vic Sebald and he drank coffee one day, Tom let slip something he had not told Ella. Vic asked how the 4-H calf was coming along, and Tom said with sudden anger, "It's no damn good. It was the best one in the bunch as a calf, but it should be a third bigger by now."

"Why would that be?" Vic asked.

Ella turned so she could see. Tom said nothing, only jutted his chin at the window, at the plant.

Ella felt for Donna. She did not want her girl to be humiliated by the judges in front of the other kids and parents, come July. But she was pleased to see Tom's brief fury.

During that winter, Ella felt lonelier than at any time in her adult life, an echo of the loneliness she'd felt when she was a girl and an only child. She still missed Lance, but now she missed Tom too. Her girls were mostly lost to her: Jeannie with her boyfriend and Donna with her preference for her father. Ella could have visited Dora Bauer or picked up the phone any time, but she didn't, because the things that bothered her could not be said. Instead, she spent her time imagining what went on in Tom's head. Was he blaming her for their situation? Thinking they could have been gone on the heels of the Bauers, except for her feelings about home?

She found herself arguing back. What about your stupid horse-trading? That was why Comstock had punished them. If Tom hadn't been so determined to get the better of the deal, there might have been a deal today.

At times, when she was feeling angry, she imagined Tom that way too. She imagined them roaring in each other's faces like bears. In reality, the only thing she found to do with her emotions was to go to her sewing room and cry. When the sobbing stopped, stone-cold thoughts remained like gravel on a floor. There is no court, she said to herself, no judge. There is just Tom and Ella trapped in silence.

As that winter deepened, Ella's thoughts became more refined. Comstock's refusal to buy them out, Tom's and her rejection of the half-deal, meant they had chosen to stay. It was a choice to go on imperilling their children. That was what they could not say to one another, and any conversation lacking that statement was not worth having.

They were waiting, and the only thing they could be waiting for was disaster.

Billy took to arithmetic. He had started school in September, and by February was adding and subtracting like nobody's business. He never had enough work from school to satisfy him and was always plaguing his mother to write down more problems. "No, Mom. Harder."

Lately, he was drawing pictures too, and it was both happiness and heartbreak to see him hunched over the paper with his pencil clutched.

At the end of February, the health study started. A government man brought a wooden box twice the size of a dog house into their yard. Billy was beside himself. He spent that day standing in front of it in his hooded parka and scarf, staring through its one glass side at the coloured pens that drew lines on a circle of cardboard.

"It's a clock, Mom."

"No, Billy. The man said it was a Titrilog."

"It's still a clock."

"He's right," said Tom, who had wandered up. "The cardboard circle is geared to a clock."

"Fine," she said. "It's a clock." And left.

No matter how many times she came to pull Billy away from the Titrilog, to get him to come in to eat or sleep, he would unfailingly tell her, "Blue is hydrogen sulphide. Red is sulphur dioxide."

How could something moving so slowly excite a boy? To please him, or try to, she bent over and looked at the two lines creeping and jiggling along.

Another crew from the plant put a "birdhouse" on one of their fence posts. People called them birdhouses because they were about that size and had louvred sides that let the wind through. Again Billy watched the installation and came back to the house knowing everything. It wasn't a birdhouse; it was a Stevenson Screen, he told them. There were two jars inside, wrapped in two cloths, each dipped in different stuff.

"They turn a colour if gas gets on them. One's for hydrogen sulphide, the other's for sulphur dioxide—just like the Titrilog." It did amaze her how much he could learn and how precisely he could repeat it all.

In mid-March, a government air pollution trailer arrived. They set it down in a field fifty yards west of the house. While a couple of men worked at setting it up, Billy stood outside the door peppering them with questions. That night he sat across from his father and drew a picture of a wind-speed gauge, putting curves like eyebrows beside the cups to show that they were twirling.

Then came a Saturday when Tom and the girls were in town. Tom had offered to take Billy too, but the boy said he couldn't go. He considered watching the Titrilog his duty. Because the rotten-egg smell had been bad all night and was still awful when Ella went out to milk that morning, she kept Billy in the house until they'd had lunch. The smell was still bad then, but he was desperate to go. He ran to the Titrilog and came straight back, running even harder.

"Billy, what on earth?"

He yanked on her dress. "It's the Titrilog, Mom! It's broken!"

As Billy ran ahead and Ella walked behind, she felt as if she was parting invisible clouds of stink. How typical, she thought, that the machine would break when most needed.

"We have to do something, Mom!"

The boy's face was greenish. She felt woozy herself. It was warm but there was almost no wind and the sun was brilliant on the wet snow. It was hard to see into the Titrilog's window. But finally she saw what Billy was telling her. Both pens had drifted off the edge of the cardboard circle. They sat there jerking, like dying insects.

"The cardboard is still going around," Billy said. "That's why the pens aren't at the end of the lines they made to the edge."

"What do you think it means, Billy?"

"Something bad," he said. "The lines go out if there's more gas. If they go right off, that's really bad."

"Could it be broken? Could the clock have come unwound?"

"I just told you," he said, "the clock's still going."

Fear rose through her. She was dizzy and had to grab the box to steady herself.

"Billy, we have to go."

"We have to tell the plant."

"That's what we'll do. Get your pyjamas, your toothbrush, and two pairs of underpants, really quick! We'll go to the plant and then to town."

Tom was in the Co-op warehouse when Billy came running and wrapped himself around his leg. The warehouse was an old grain elevator. Pallets of bagged fertilizer, weed killer, and seed rose into the darkness. Billy was chattering about the Titrilog. He loved saying the word and always punched the "tit" part.

"So what's wrong with the Titrilog, Billy?"

"It went right off the cardboard! Both pens!"

The image settled into Tom's neck.

"We told the plant. Mom and me."

Ella was there now. She nodded.

"Did you talk to Dietz?" Tom asked her.

"He wasn't there. I spoke to Bert Traynor."

Traynor had told her the technician who looked after the Titrilog worked out of Calgary. They shouldn't expect anything to happen today, nor tomorrow since it was Sunday.

"That sonofabitch," Tom muttered. Ella turned away and looked into shadow. But, really, who was Traynor to talk as if the Titrilog belonged to the Ryders? As if fixing it was a favour to them?

Tom had told the girls to meet him at the drugstore at two. It was almost that time now. Ella told him she had brought overnight things for the girls and Billy—and herself; she thought she should stay too. They did not need to say that Tom would go back and look after the animals. That was understood.

When they got to the drugstore, only Donna was there. As soon as she heard her mother's plan, she said she would not stay in town. She had her calf to look after.

Tom could see that Ella wanted his help. "You better stay," he told her.

Donna turned her hard look on him. "I'm going with."

Tom shrugged, and Ella's face grew darker. He could not think of what else he was supposed to do. "We'll be careful," he said, but could not tell if Ella was listening.

When Tom and Donna were in the truck, ready to leave for the farm, Billy ran out of the house. He was crying. Tom told Donna to roll down her window.

"I want to go too!" the boy yelled.

"Titrilog's locked tight, Billy. There's nothing you can do but look at it."

"That's what I want! I want to look at it!"

"Sorry, buddy. Step back now. You're staying here."

The boy crumpled to his knees. He was punching his fists into an old snowbank as they drove away.

Tom and Donna were quiet during the drive. They talked when they were at ease, kept quiet when they had things to think about. He remembered the look she had given him when he said she should stay in town. He supposed she felt betrayed; that the two of them should be more of a team.

"I'm going to halter my calf and lead him around. Give him lots of water," she said when they were closer to home.

"Why?"

"If something makes you sick, you should move around. Drink lots. Wash it out."

"Why are you sure he's sick?"

"When I fed him this morning, he didn't want to eat. He didn't want to be scratched."

At the farm, Donna did not come in to change her clothes. She put on gumboots and ran for the corrals. Tom went into the bedroom to change and was still there when he heard her. It was a strange sound. A scream. A yell. She smacked the porch door open.

He met her in the kitchen. Floods of tears were pouring down her scarlet face.

"What the hell, Donna?"

"Goddamn fucking sonofabitch is dead!"

"Hey, now. Sit down. Sit here." He pointed to her seat at the table. She threw herself onto it, buried her face in her folded arms.

Tom went and looked at the steer. It had bloated so high its legs jutted out. Back at the house, Donna was not in the kitchen. She had gone upstairs.

He phoned Doc Moore's office but no one answered. He tried him at home and got him. When Tom had explained things, Doc asked if he had phoned the plant. Or maybe they should try to get the government vet to come.

"I don't want a company man or a government man on the place," Tom said. "I'll pay you to cut the animal open."

Doc tried again to make the point that, without a company or government witness, an autopsy wouldn't be official.

"I don't care if it counts with them. I want to know for myself."

Tom and Donna were back at the calf pen when Doc flew into the yard. He came with his heavy canvas bag.

"You better go to the house now," Tom told Donna.

Her tears had dried to salt on her cheeks. She would not meet her father's eyes. She wasn't going anywhere.

Doc went to work. First he stabbed the bloat with a nail, stood back while the rank gas blew out. From the first slice through the hide, and right on down to when he was cutting out and removing the lungs, Donna stood stiff as a statue. She did not take her eyes off the bloody blade as it danced in the black-purple of the calf. When Doc hauled out a length of intestine, slit a length of it, and washed away the stinking contents, she was with him then too.

Once in a while, Doc set down his knife and signalled them closer, pointed his flashlight at something. He remarked on the swelling of tissues in the lungs. He shifted the light into the stomach and asked what the calf had been drinking.

"Water from our well," said Tom. "Same as we drink."

"No," said Donna, the first time she'd spoken. "I've been taking him to the field. I let him drink at the coulee."

Doc pointed the flashlight into the calf's gut. "I expected the lungs to be like they are. Inflamed, full of fluid. Pulmonary edema. It's probably what killed him. But the gut and intestines are inflamed too, like he was getting poisoned at the same time. Where does that runoff come from?"

"Coulee starts just below the plant." Tom swept his arm along the coulee's path.

"Christ, man. That goes right to your feedlot."

"Feedlot's fenced out. Calves drink from a well."

Donna walked away, stiffly. When she got through the gates, she started to run, a careless, flinging gait as if her body had forgotten how.

Doc Moore sighed. "Now I've done it. She thinks she killed it."

"She's tough," Tom said, more in hope than certainty. "She'll get over it."

Tom did not get into bed but sat on the edge of the mattress. He must be cold, Ella thought, staring at his back, but he did not move for the longest time.

Tom had phoned her at her parents', told her about the calf but also that the stink had passed and they could come home. When they entered the house, Tom was in the kitchen. He started explaining what Doc Moore's autopsy had shown, but Ella ran past him. She found poor Donna upstairs, under the covers, staring at the wall. Ella assumed she wouldn't talk but might accept some comfort at least. She reached and rubbed her back.

Donna bolted upright and started chattering. She let her mother hug her and stroke her hair as she described over and over what the calf looked like when she found it, what the autopsy had been like, how Tom had asked Doc Moore to write down what he had found in the innards.

Ella kept thinking that her daughter was released. Something had been holding her. Now she was free of it.

"Why did you ask Doc Moore to write everything down?" Ella asked Tom now, while he continued to sit on the edge of the bed in the deepening cold. "Are you going to show it to the company?"

Without turning, he said, "I will show it to no one at that company. I don't trust them. I don't trust the government either."

"What's it for then?"

"That's what I'm thinking about."

Given their talking habits of late, Ella assumed he was finished. She rolled away and into her own thoughts. But Tom stood up and began pacing the little distance from the night table to the dresser.

"I told Doc that Donna would get over it. It's true. She will. We all will. If we just let everything be, it will all go away. The kids will go away. You and me will go away. We'll disperse is what we'll do, like Alf says gas does. Go away from each other and pretend we're people who never had this in our lives."

"Is that what should happen?" she asked.

"Some might say so. I don't think so."

"But how can you prevent it?"

"That's what I'm thinking about. I'm thinking there has to be a way. They can't come in here and wreck our farm and our family. I have to find a way to stop them and make them pay."

"Do you think there might be something in the health study?"

"That'll be the day, Ella," he said, and the back of her head prickled at the rare sound of her name. "There will be nothing in that study that does us any good. But we can't be the only ones. Everywhere these plants are, there must be people like us. I'm going to find them and I'm going to talk to them. *That's* who I'm going to show Doc Moore's autopsy to. I'm going to show it to them."

4

Waddens Lake

BILL SAT OUTSIDE THEO'S OFFICE, pretending to read an industry magazine. Paula hammered away at her computer. He had tried to restart the Ryder-Walker joke, but she would not bite. A bad sign. You don't make jokes with the condemned.

While he waited, he rehearsed. First, he would say he was sorry about Dennis Whitcomb. After that, the apologizing must stop. "The rule for days off is to be reachable by phone," he would say. "I was."

When Dennis had his accident, Henry Shields was at home with the flu. Clayton Brock was shift boss and he phoned Bill's cell. It must have been when Bill was in the casino. He hadn't heard the ring or felt the buzz. Instead of trying to phone later, Clayton texted Bill twice, then gave up.

"I didn't know my phone did texts," Bill planned to tell Houle. It was a questionable tactic—an engineer pleading ignorance of technology to save his job—but Bill had gone over the alternatives, and it was the only one that might not lead to further questioning of his whereabouts.

Dennis Whitcomb had been knocked down by gas in the sulphur unit on Saturday night. In the days before, a maintenance crew had opened and closed a sour pipe. Any crew rebuttoning a pipe connection had strict rules to follow about how tight to cinch the nuts, and because the wrenches showed the pounds of torque, it was hard to screw up. Despite all these rules and precautions, maintenance had managed to leave a couple of nuts loose enough to leak.

During Dennis's rounds, he'd smelled sour gas. Everything he did beyond that point was wrong. He was supposed to leave the area; he didn't. He was supposed to get help; he didn't. Acting on a potential gas leak without backup, he had also failed to mask up. He went sniffing around the vessels and pipes like a dog, until he finally arrived at the leaking bolts. The hydrogen sulphide nailed him.

In Bill's forty-year career, he had never seen anyone go to so much trouble to get his little bell rung. Dennis had breathed in just enough to make himself fall over, to have to crawl for his life out of the building. The Waddens Lake sulphur unit's perfect record for lost-time accidents was kaput.

The rest of the crew were furious with Whitcomb, whom they had long ago renamed Menace Fuckwit. They had been proud of their safety record, to the point of arrogance, and the ones Bill had talked to so far wanted Dennis fired. No one seemed to blame Bill—or rather, no one except Theo Houle.

The wait in Theo's anteroom continued. The fact that even Paula was ignoring him made him think his getting canned was a real possibility this time.

Paula's phone buzzed. She picked up, listened, redocked the handset, and looked at him sorrowfully.

"Mr. Houle will see you now."

Theo was sitting with closed fists on his desk calendar. Bill imagined a knife and fork sticking out of them.

"First off, Theo, I'm sorry about Dennis Whitcomb. I'm sorry he got hurt. I'm glad he's okay. But the rule about days off—"

Theo lifted his fists and thumped them down. Bill shut up.

"That's not what I want to talk to you about. I've seen the accident report. I'd fire the stupid prick, but I can't. Head office has told me to hang on to everyone. They think there's going to be another manpower panic."

"A firing freeze?"

On any other day, Houle might have laughed. Since he had no response, Bill said, "I'll talk to our safety man, Gid Couture, and have him do some refresher training. I don't know what to do about the idiots who under-torqued the nuts."

"Bill, I'm not going to beat around the bush. There were New Aladdin people at the technical meeting in Calgary. Not one remembers seeing you. Apparently you never picked up your welcome package or name tag. The main desk says you never asked for the key to your room."

"I don't wear name tags."

"And you don't sleep in your room?"

"I can explain this if I have to. I was at the conference."

They stared at each other. It was Houle's turn but he wasn't speaking; he waited for more from Bill.

"So some young puppy who doesn't know me says I wasn't there. I don't give a fuck what your spies say. I'm telling you I was there. I expect to be believed."

"They're hardly my spies."

"You make them that when you ask them to spy on me."

"You should calm down."

"Do I get to explain, or is this a straight-up lynching?"

Houle sat back and stared at him.

Bill explained about the snowstorm and having to overnight in Red Deer. "By the time I got to the hotel, the panel I wanted to attend was over."

"Apparently you didn't go to anything else."

"At coffee break, one of the old guys told me Lance Evert was dying of cancer."

"If I'm supposed to know who that is, I don't."

"He was my mentor in gas processing. When I heard he was sick, I left the meeting."

"So instead of attending the technical meeting, you went to see your friend. Is that what you're telling me?"

"I didn't go see him."

Houle looked embarrassed. He did not want these confidences. They had taken some of the edge off him, and he resented it. "What you did or didn't do about your friend is not for me to judge. But taking a day off to attend a technical meeting that you don't attend is a piss-poor example."

"I was there."

"For a coffee break? Even if the rest of the meeting wasn't of interest to you, you were there on behalf of New Aladdin and the Waddens Lake Project, on company time. You could have found things out that guys in our other units need to know. More and more, I get the sense that you're a solo player here. A free agent."

Houle had been rehearsing too.

"That last part is probably true. Is that it, then? I'm out?"

"You're doing it again. Talking like you don't give a shit if you're here or gone."

"I do care, but I won't beg for my job."

"I'm not asking you to beg. I'm not firing you either. I just want you to act like a New Aladdin unit manager. Ducking out of a technical meeting is kid stuff. I'm not telling you to love the company, but there's a code of conduct, isn't there?"

"I don't know what you're saying. I should *pretend* to love the company?"

"Damn it, Bill, that's exactly what I'm saying. If I left New Aladdin for a better offer across the street, I'd be one hundred per cent loyal to this company until I walked out that door, and I'd be one hundred per cent loyal to the other company the minute I sat down. That's part of any management job. It should go without saying."

"Okay, I've got it. Are we done?"

There were three messages on his office phone, all from Marie Calfoux. In the first one, she asked him to give her a call. In the second, she asked about snowshoeing and what he was doing Friday. The final one said, "You better be away, because if you're not, and you don't call me soon, I'm chucking your number."

Then he phoned Dennis Whitcomb at his apartment in McMurray. Dennis didn't have the sense to turn down the blaring television before he answered. A golf announcer in Arizona said Henrik Stenson was leading by three strokes heading into the final nine.

"So what do you think, Dennis? Will Stenson win it?"

"I wasn't really watching."

"You can watch what you like. But could you turn it down while we talk?"

The volume came down and Dennis returned. "You're phoning to fire me, right?"

"I can see why you'd think so, but you've lucked out. I'm phoning to ask how you're feeling."

"I'm not fired? Wow. Then I guess I feel pretty good."

"Good enough to come back to work tomorrow?"

"You bet. I'll be there."

Bill worked late that night, then drove home to McMurray. He had calls to make and didn't want to use his office phone. If Houle really didn't trust him anymore, it was possible that the office was bugged. Being a post-9/11 facility, Waddens Lake had that kind of equipment.

In his condo, Bill opened a bottle of wine and threw a dozen frozen wings in the oven. At nine o'clock, he was sitting in front of a plate of bones and realized he'd been staring at the phone for an hour.

From the sheet of phone numbers in front of him, he finally dialed Lance Evert in Calgary. He was assuming Judy would answer. He was prepared for her to put the receiver to her chest and yell, "Lance! You'll never guess!" But it was Lance himself who picked up. When Lance tried to speak, his voice came apart. He covered the phone and coughed.

"Sorry," he said when he came back. "Now who is this?"

"It's Bill Ryder. Should I call you back?"

"Believe it or not, this is a good time. I'll probably have to stop now and then, but we can talk. It's good to hear your voice, Billy."

"I ran into Don Giotto at a meeting."

"And he told you what I've got."

"Not in detail."

"Detail. I don't think it matters where it started or where it went, or even what it is. It's an opportunistic disease. As someone interested in science, I half admire it."

"Don said you were battling it hard."

"Donny hasn't been in touch for a while. I'm not battling anything. You have to know when you're beat. Fighting's just a waste of time."

"I'm sorry, Lance."

"Me too. But how are you, Billy? You're up north, right? Oil sands?"

"I work for New Aladdin, at the Waddens Lake upgrader. Sulphur unit."

"Right, right. Is New Aladdin like our old Aladdin at all? Texans and that?"

"Not much, no. Different money. You know corporations nowadays."

"Yeah. Same face on them all. Owned by people all over the planet. We used to think they had personalities, didn't we? I doubt it was ever true. And you run their sulphur plant?"

Bill talked sulphur lingo for a while—modified Claus plant, closed-loop system, analyzers, scrubbers.

Lance had another coughing spell.

Coming out of it, he said, "You're not married now?"

"No. Second marriage went the way of the first. I should stay single."

"Ah, well. And Martha and Will?"

"Good. You must hear about them from Ginny."

"We do. Good kids."

"Maybe I should go, Lance. I'll call again."

"Always good to hear from you, Billy. You were always a good engineer. I often think that."

"That was long ago."

"You still have a good reputation."

"You know what that means."

"What?"

"I haven't killed a village or poisoned a major river."

Lance laughed, coughed. "Just a minute," he said. He finished coughing and came back exhausted. "Oh, never mind. The thing I was going to say was stupid."

"Go ahead."

"I'm so foggy with drugs, I almost asked how your mother was. Sorry. I guess I should have kept that to myself."

"That's okay. It's kind of nice somebody was thinking of Ella as alive."

"A fine woman, Billy. Your dad was a lucky man."

———

After the conversation with Lance, Bill could not imagine talking to anyone else. He took a pill, went to bed, and waited for the drug to take command.

"I am stuck," he said to himself.

5

Ryder Farm, 1962

CALVING SEASON SEEMED TO COME out of nowhere that year, and when it did, Tom knew he would have no family helper. So suddenly and cleanly had the death of the calf severed the bond of work between Donna and himself, Tom sometimes felt it had never existed. Ella had put up a new ad for a hired man in the Greyhound station, and Tom barely had time to say it was a waste of time before the phone rang. Like a crusty angel, Hercules Bernier drove into the yard in a wartime truck and proceeded to work for the Ryders for exactly the length of calving season. Hercules was old and not particularly strong, so Tom did not require him to get up in the night. They did all right anyway. A couple of calves died that more night-watching would not have saved. One of those deaths was on a bad gas night, and Tom wrote it in the diary that he and Ella still kept.

Hercules drew his pay and left the day the last calf was born. He had given no reason for coming and gave no reason when he left. He drove off in a glower of black smoke.

Only then was Tom able to turn his thoughts to finding other communities and farmers whose lives were affected by sour gas plants. The first thing he discovered was that he wouldn't find them in Haultain's public library. The embarrassed librarian explained that her budget did not stretch to regional newspaper subscriptions. He would have to go to Lethbridge.

Tom made a plan to go the following Saturday and to take Donna with him. The girl had been keeping away since the death of her calf. She almost never spoke to him unless he pushed her. It did not seem fair that the calf's death should stick to Tom, that she should avoid her father as part of shedding her pain. Emotions weren't about fairness; he also knew that.

He went ahead and asked her anyway. Donna had her school-work spread on the table. He could tell her instinct was to say no, before examining what it was she was refusing.

"I need to go to their library," Tom told her.

The word sparked her but she remained cagey. She asked what he would be doing there.

"I want to look at newspapers to see if there's anything about people in other communities with sulphur plant problems."

"Can I go to the library if I don't help you?"

"Of course," he said brightly, quickly, though his wish had been exactly that.

This was in May, in the spring of Jeannie's final year of high school, and Tom considered asking his oldest girl along as well. But at the exact moment he would have asked, an argument erupted between Jeannie and her mother over whether Jeannie could stay in Haultain on Friday after school and spend the whole weekend there. Ella was saying she couldn't stay over Friday, but that Gerry could come early Saturday to pick her up.

Billy got wind of Lethbridge and was determined to go too. Men had come and taken his Titrilog the month before, right after that the government trailer was removed. Only the Stevenson Screen, the birdhouse, remained after the health study ended. Billy had been weirdly attached to the Titrilog and weather trailer, and their loss created a desire to go farther afield in search of wonders like them. A big building full of books held the right kind of promise. Before the boy started crying, Tom said he could come.

He should have asked Ella too—that is, he should have asked her first. Tom had his doubts if Ella would have gone to Lethbridge in any case, but, having been asked last, she coldly refused. More grit between their edges.

Tom took Billy to the children's section and found some books of the kind he wanted. Then he got stern with him.

"Now, buddy, I've got things to do here, so after you finish with those, you look at the shelf and find more yourself."

A passing librarian said, "Don't worry. I'll help him."

A different librarian in charge of newspapers listened to Tom's request and suggested he go at it one town at a time. It was a tedious business, looking through newspapers, and he was finding nothing. Half his time was suddenly gone. Seeing his frustration, the librarian led him to a map on the wall. It came from the government and showed Alberta's petroleum resources and facilities. Staple-shaped marks were wells. A red dot was a gas plant. A black dot was an oil refinery.

In southern Alberta there were lots of staples but not many dots. Tom showed the librarian where Aladdin Hatfield was. It was easy to see which plants were closest. She went off and returned with an article in a recent *Lethbridge Herald* about a gas plant and community controversy in Dry Fork. Tom knew Dry Fork. It was not a town but a community, about two hours' drive from Haultain.

The librarian left the newspaper, and he read the article twice. Hot prickling spread across his face and scalp. This was it. A couple of farmers were quoted about problems with their plant that were exactly the same as at home: newborn pigs dying, reduced rate of gain in beef animals. It was a different oil company, not Aladdin.

One of the farmers, John Darby, referred to a government health study, clearly the same study that had put the Titrilog and weather trailer at Ryders'. The farmer said he didn't know when the results would come but had been told it would be soon.

There was even a mention of Tom's plant. "A government representative admits there have been complaints from other communities. Pressed for an example, he named the Aladdin Hatfield plant near the town of Haultain."

The only things Tom had written down were "Dry Fork" and the names of the two farmers. He believed it was enough.

On the ride home, Billy chattered non-stop. "I found a book about kinds of machines that build roads." "I found a book about how birds fly." "I found a book with pictures somebody drew of the insides of houses."

Tom leaned sideways and asked Donna what she had found. She said she'd looked at books about tropical islands and European castles. He wished she would ask what he'd found but she did not. He told her about Dry Fork anyway. He said he would look for someone local who knew people down there, then he'd arrange a visit.

"Does that interest you at all? Would you be interested in going there, if I made the trip on a weekend?"

"I'm busy with school, Dad. I got behind. I want to do well."

"That's okay. Good to get school under control."

"I'll go, Dad," Billy yelled from the back.

"I'm sorry," Donna said, staring out the side window.

"Nothing to be sorry for."

"I'll go, Dad! I'll go!"

"Okay, Billy. I hear you."

A week after Tom's trip to the Lethbridge library, Ella told him she had to go to Lethbridge too. She invented a story about needing a kind of pill, woman trouble, that could not be had in Haultain. She hinted it would be better if she went without Billy, but Tom said she would have to take the boy. His plan for the day was to take apart the old baler, which involved heavy parts put up on jacks. He couldn't work under there and keep an eye on Billy too.

For an entire year, Ella had been carrying around the sin of Lance Evert, the coveting of him while married to Tom. She had not taken communion since then, because that would be an even greater sin than what had happened. Luckily, Tom was a convert to Catholicism and casual about religion. A born Catholic would have wondered what she'd done that made her go from taking communion regularly to never taking it at all. Ella was sure the neighbours had noticed, but not Tom.

Catholicism affected Tom mainly in the stomach. He took communion because he felt it was part of the deal, but hated the fasting beforehand. Worse were meatless Fridays. "A bunch of men who never worked a day in their lives deciding that working men have to go without meat."

Ella was not going to confess to Father Frustig at St. Bruno's. She needed to find a church where she was not known, a priest she had not met. Luckily, Billy did not yet understand communion or confession, or religion at all. He accepted it calmly when she left him in a pew of the Lethbridge church and went to the back. "I'll just be a minute. Stay right here."

When the priest slid the panel back and asked her to confess, she could only see a trace of his profile. She guessed by his voice that he was old, and this increased her anxiety.

She made herself say the words in a straightforward way. There was no sense being vague with God. But His representative, the priest, was either genuinely confused or an old snoop.

"Now, wait a minute, child, are you saying you had sexual relations with this man who was not your husband?"

"I did not."

"Was there anything of a sexual nature?"

"I wouldn't say so, no."

"But there was touching by the sounds of it. Please be clear."

"We hugged. I kissed him."

"And no one else was present? No one saw?"

"No one else was present."

"On the cheek or on the mouth?"

"On the mouth."

"How many times?"

"Twice or three times."

"Either it was twice or three times."

"Three times."

"And all on the mouth?"

"Yes."

"My, my. Is this ongoing?"

"No. It is not."

"You and the man had a falling out. Did you tell him to go away and leave you alone?"

"He moved away. There was no discussion."

"Was there a farewell? More kissing?"

"There was no farewell."

"Do you give yourself sexual gratification while thinking of this man?"

"Oh, for heaven's sake. No, I do not!"

"Don't be cross with me. You know this is a very serious matter in a Catholic marriage. These are questions I must ask."

"I understand the seriousness, Father. That's why I'm confessing to you."

"And you are truly sorry for your sins?"

"I am."

"And how are relations with your husband now?"

"They are better."

"Are there sexual relations with your husband?"

"No."

"Hmm. That is part of a marriage, you know."

"I know, Father."

Finally, finally, the priest moved on to absolution.

Billy was on his knees on the bench looking backward when she returned. She sat beside him and said she was sorry she had taken so long.

"You're all red."

"It was hot in there."

"Let's go."

"I have to say some prayers now. I have to kneel."

"Do I have to kneel too?"

"No, you can sit. But you mustn't interrupt."

It felt wonderful the following Sunday to take communion, to feel at peace with the Lord after the stormy year. That she continued to argue against Tom's interest in the community of Dry Fork was another sin, she supposed, but not one that demanded immediate confession. She could confess the sin of her impatience to the local priest.

Ella did not quite understand herself when it came to Dry Fork. Tom's point when he spoke about it—and he spoke a lot—was that teaming up with another community might make their own community strong enough to go after the oil companies.

"Go after them? What does that mean?"

"We've lost livestock and land value. If someone took bales out of our field, we could get the courts involved. Why should this be different?"

"Go to court?"

"I don't know if we'd go to court. That's the sort of thing I want to find out at Dry Fork."

Why be so against this? Why could she not see it as hope for their safety, for getting money back that they had lost?

"Why not wait for the health study results? Maybe the government will do what you're hoping the courts would do?"

She could see him fighting down his temper, the desire, almost a need, to curse and denounce the government and her idea of waiting. To contain it, he rolled a cigarette and went outside to smoke.

All Tom was asking from her at this stage was to talk on the phone to people she knew, to see if any of them had acquaintances in Dry Fork. She thought this an old-fashioned way of doing things. She was sure you could ask the telephone operator and be connected to the farmers he wanted to meet. She did not say so, because she didn't want Tom to make these connections at all.

After going to confession, truly and finally putting Lance away, Ella immediately began to fear that she had lost Tom too, or might do so soon. Even though he didn't know about Lance, there was such a thing as balance. She found herself considering him as another woman might, or as she had long ago when he came courting. He'd always had strength, not just brawn but strength of character. What made that more attractive was a bit of uncertainty, a trace that kept him from being just another overly certain man, a type Ella had seen too many of. And he was nice looking, Tom, nicely proportioned. Light brown eyes that could speak both kindness and anger.

As to the many flaws she had seen in him over the past year, she wondered if she had been seeing them clearly. He was certainly angry, but he had a lot to be angry about, with a sick boy and dying farm animals, the whole destiny of the farm wrenched from his control. But she had hated to look at it, and the more she felt for Lance the more hateful Tom's tirades and anger became. Wasn't that natural too, to see nothing but flaws in a man who stands between you and the one you think you love?

The question was: what if he had given up on her? If so, what had happened to Ella could happen to him. He could meet a woman, in Dry Fork, whose anger against the oil companies was as strongly felt as his.

Not long ago, such ideas would only have irritated Ella. Go, then! she might have said. Now she felt sad and afraid. She wanted to go toward Tom slowly. She wanted them to knit back together, without any spoken recognition that they had ever been asunder.

Tom found his connection to Dry Fork without Ella's help. Though he usually approached the telephone as if it was a rattlesnake on the wall, he phoned two ranching families he had worked for in his youth. The second call was to an elderly ranch woman, widowed and boarding in town. Ella could tell the old woman was delighted to hear from Tom by how long it took him to ask his question.

After he'd hung up, he said, "Mrs. Turner has a younger brother who married a woman with a ranch at Dry Fork." Mrs. Turner phoned back when Tom was out and told Ella that her brother, Donald, and sister-in-law, Abigail, were looking forward to meeting Tom. He should go down in person, because Donald was hard of hearing and would not get a hearing aid. Talking to him on the phone was hopeless. Abigail was shy and he would have to encourage her or she wouldn't speak.

"But they'll be so happy to have his company. Come see me sometime, Ella, and bring Tommy. He's such a nice fellow."

Tom's trip to meet these people worried Ella, but she refused when he asked her to go along.

"I have to look after Billy," she reminded him.

"No, you don't," the boy said. "Take me, Dad."

The drive was enjoyable. He'd left Billy at home and so was free to study the country. He was fairly sure he had gone through this area during the Depression. But he had been in a boxcar then, hoping to find work in a coal mine near Medicine Hat.

The directions were good and he found Smith-Archibald's ranch without having to backtrack or ask around. A fine old spread of slightly rolling native grass, never ploughed. The buildings were near a shallow lake covered in ducks. The visit began slowly, as Donald and Abigail both took a lot of time to listen, hear, understand, and respond. The house smelled of old wood and varnish, not unlike Mrs. Turner's home in the Hatfield hills, where Tom had worked. It had the same kind of big oak table and glass chandelier above. A black bottle of port on a sideboard.

During the tea ritual, he got across that he was interested in the Dry Fork sulphur plant.

"We're upwind!" Donald shouted at him.

"We've had no difficulties," said Abigail in a whisper.

Tom asked about Darby and Arsenault, and the old couple knew them and were more than happy to put Tom in touch. It was clear, though, that they wanted no further involvement themselves.

Donald yelled, "They're just wasting their money trying to fight an oil company!"

"It's not for us to say," said Abigail.

"There are two Arsenaults, but it must be Eddy if it's the plant!"

Donald gave good directions, and Tom found the Darby farm within a half-hour. He passed the gas plant just before he got there, and it was like seeing their own plant with the mountains peeled off the horizon.

Joan Darby was expecting Tom. They drove together to where John was shovelling chop over a canvas into his feedlot bin. There was an extra shovel, and Tom helped him finish. To the west Tom could see the plant stack and smell it too. They went back to the house, and John Darby offered a shot of rye whisky that Tom accepted.

Over the drink, Tom laid out his plant problems. He did not want to take a lot of their time, so it was a quick litany. "I've been thinking I need to get out and talk to other people who are going through the same thing."

Tom had brought the pages Ella and he had written, what Donna called the Stink Diary. He read a few entries, and the Darbys laughed. Joan got a scribbler down from above the fridge and read some things that were close to identical.

"The worst," said Joan, "is our daughter Edna has asthma. We don't know if it's caused by the plant, but the gas certainly makes it worse. She's in high school now and boards in town. It feels like we've lost her." She dabbed her eyes with the tail of her apron.

Tom told them about Billy's troubles with anemia. Same thing: a person couldn't know for sure if the plant caused it, but no one in their family had ever had it before.

"Have you thought of leaving?" Tom asked them, and wished he hadn't. The expression on their faces was different enough to suggest a disagreement. But they were a jolly pair, and the cloud passed quickly.

"I'll tell you," said John, "I hate to let them win. Drive us all away. We were here first, don't you think?"

What a pleasure all this was for Tom, to talk to people who knew what he meant and what he'd experienced. When they talked about pigs, Tom knew right away that their community was ahead of his own, more organized by far.

"We're out of pigs now, all of us," John said. "On the downwind side of the plant, you won't find a pig for fifteen miles. We all lost litters, and what's the sense of keeping on?"

When it came to how the plant treated them, it sounded worse than Tom and Ella's experience with Dietz, but there was a man from head office in Darbys' story who sounded much like Comstock. "We're enemies is what we are," Joan said. "As soon as we told them we were thinking of talking to a lawyer, they cut us dead."

"You've started your lawsuit?" asked Tom.

"We have," said John. "It's taken time and some doing. Lot of folks were scared of the cost, and you can't blame anybody for that. We talked about it for months, and then we had phone calls with the lawyer. But it was the health study that turned the key. Two weeks ago when we heard the news on it, we had a meeting. That's when we phoned the lawyer and said we'd go with him."

"I'm not getting this," said Tom. "You know the results of the health study?"

"You bet. Over two weeks ago. Government said there were no significant problems. No danger to the people living here. I heard that and I said to Joan, 'That's it, then. We gotta take this thing into our own hands.' She agreed with me."

Tom felt like a fool. How could the health study results be out, and no one in his own community knew? He also felt a surge of anger toward the *Haultain Herald*. He read it every week, front to back, and the only thing they'd ever said about the study was a mention when it started. Nor did their ignoring the news make sense. Like the town's businessmen, the newspaper was all in favour of the plant and the money it brought. If the health study said there were no problems, no basis to the farmers' complaints, you'd think the paper would want to carry the story.

Joan leaned toward Tom. "I take it your community isn't the same? Not as committed?"

"No," Tom said. "Some are too cheap. Some are scared. Some hope their sons'll get jobs at the plant. There's two of us who are trying hard, and a couple more we might convince." Only half the community had signed the letter they sent to the government. A few of those wouldn't talk about it any more once the health study was announced.

It was getting late and, since the whisky had kept pouring, Tom was in a bind. He didn't feel he could drive home. He also wanted to meet the Arsenaults. The Darbys said they had a guest room all made up and would be happy to have him stay. He asked to make a phone call. Ella answered, and he told her he was staying. Their cows were out on grass now and didn't need him. If she could give the pigs some water and chop, that would take care of things until tomorrow evening.

She asked if he'd been drinking, and he said he had. She said something about Jeannie, some problem, but he said they could talk when he was home.

When Tom came back to the table, John Darby said, "Since nobody's driving . . ." and poured more whisky.

Next morning, with an aching head, Tom went to the Arsenaults'. They were fine people too, ranchers who'd had a couple of cows abort when the sulphur gas was strong. They were very interested in Tom's story of the club calf. They read Doc Moore's autopsy notes several times.

"Too bad you don't live down here," said Kelly, the wife. "We could use your help."

Tom was wishing it too: that he lived here and was part of their fight. He really did want what the Arsenaults and Darbys had. The pride in what they were doing; the confidence that they would get it done.

What was needed at home was a leader, and Tom realized he had to go home and be that leader.

Ella was annoyed that Tom had brushed off Jeannie's problem over the phone. The day he had left for Dry Fork was the day of Gerry Traynor's high school prom. Jeannie's grad event at the Catholic school had been the Friday before, but Gerry's school, being much bigger, had more money to spend. There was going to be a popular band all the way from Lethbridge. Jeannie had bought a bright lemon-yellow dress.

The night before Gerry's prom, Jeannie stayed with her friend Eleanor in town, so she could get to the hairdresser early on Saturday. But Saturday afternoon, Ella got a phone call from her mother. Jeannie had turned up there and wanted Ella to come and get her.

It could only mean that she had decided not to go to Gerry's prom. Ella had enough to do without making a trip into town, and she tried to get her mother to put Jeannie on the phone. She said Jeannie was in bed and didn't want to talk. Ella pushed for more information, but all her mother would say was something about hair, and that Ella should come right away.

Ella left Billy with Donna. On the drive in, she felt angry. She thought the problem must be that Jeannie did not like her hair. Ella did not have time for such nonsense.

When she swung into her parents' driveway, Jeannie was waiting outside. She jumped in the back seat and said they had to stop at Eleanor's to get her suitcase. When they got there, Jeannie asked Ella to go in. She didn't want Eleanor or Eleanor's mom to see her.

Of course, by then, Ella had noticed Jeannie's hair. Alice had given her an updo, a real tower with ringlets hanging down. The hair was still more or less all right on one side but was all pulled down on the other.

Ella put the suitcase in the trunk and got back behind the wheel. She looked at Jeannie in the rear-view and asked if Gerry had done it, meaning the hair. Jeannie said no. Ella drove them home without pressing for more.

Next day, while Jeannie was having a bath, Ella took Donna aside and asked her if she knew what was going on. The sisters hardly spoke but did share a room; it seemed possible Donna would know. Donna's guess was that Jeannie and Gerry had broken up. Why else would she cry all night?

Ella phoned the hairdresser and asked how Jeannie had seemed when she was getting her hair done.

"Kind of sad," said Alice. "Or I guess I should say she *got* sad. She was happy as a lark when she came."

"What caused the change?"

"You know she's in the paper this week, don't you?"

"No, I don't know. We don't get the paper until Tuesday."

"Front-page story is about the health study at your plant. I showed it to Jeannie while she was in the chair, because she's quoted. I thought she'd be pleased to be a celebrity, but she got all upset."

"Did she do anything to wreck her hair?"

"Something happened to her hair?"

"Oh, never mind." Ella could hear the tub draining.

"I did her hair real pretty."

"Of course you did, Alice."

The newspaper article was another mystery. If Jeannie had been interviewed, why would she have kept it secret? Everyone in the house would read the paper eventually. And what could have been so shocking about seeing in print what she'd told a reporter?

After her bath, Jeannie went and sat on the outside porch. She took a magazine with her, but Ella could see through the kitchen window that she never looked at it. She stared across at the mountains and was stone still. She had washed out all trace of the prom hairdo, and her long hair hung wet.

"Are you warm enough?" Ella called out to her.

"Yes."

Nothing had changed by the time Tom got back from Dry Fork. Ella went to his truck as he was pulling in, so she could talk to him before he saw Jeannie. He was puffed up and right away started to tell her about his adventure. She said with emphasis that he needed to know what was happening here first.

"Something's up between Jeannie and Gerry, and she's awfully blue." Ella quickly said the rest: about the health study article in which their daughter was quoted.

"That's what they said down at Dry Fork, that the results are out. But why would Jeannie be quoted?"

"Newspaper will come in a couple of days. I guess we'll find out then."

On Tuesday, when Ella saw the mail woman's car stop at their box by the old school, she went to where Jeannie was sunning in the yard and asked her to drive down and get it. Jeannie was soon back and dropped the bundle on the kitchen table.

Ella asked, "Did you look at the newspaper? Someone said you're in it."

"I've seen it," Jeannie said, and went back outside.

Ella pulled the newspaper from the pile.

GAS PLANT HEALTH STUDY FINDS NOTHING

Though Alice had told her, it was still a shock to see that: the blunt headline. All that time that the Titrilog had sat in their yard, and it had found "nothing"—even when the gas killed an animal the size of Donna's steer a hundred yards away. She remembered the two pens bumping off the edge of the Titrilog's disc. One of the worst days, and because it was so bad it broke the machine there would be nothing in the study results about it. It was a week before someone had come to fix it, and the air had stunk the whole time.

Ella went through the article carefully, then read the part about Jeannie a second time. "Jeannie Ryder, a teenage girl living on a farm close to the Aladdin Hatfield gas plant, said her family had often been sick from the gas fumes. They suffered nosebleeds, headaches, and sore eyes on many occasions. Some of their farm animals had died, supposedly from the gas. Miss Ryder, who was visiting friends in a popular Haultain restaurant, also said that she supposed the plant was progress. The smell was 'the smell of money.'"

There was a small paragraph at the head of the column, set with different print than the rest. It said the piece was a reprint from Edmonton's newspaper. So that made sense. When the reporter had told Jeannie he was from an Edmonton paper, she might have assumed no one down here would ever see it. That would explain her dismay, once she realized everyone, town and country, would soon read what she had said.

Jeannie was sitting on the porch. Ella stepped outside and perched on the railing beside her. Her daughter's eyes were full of tears.

"I never said it was the smell of money, Mom. Stupid Gerry said that. Now everybody will think I'm awful."

"You told the truth about the sickness and the animals," Ella said.

"That's what I mean about everybody. The people in town too."

"So you and Gerry had a fight about it?"

"Bette asked Gerry to bring me to their house so she could see my hair. Bert was on days off and was there too."

"Had he seen the paper?"

"Oh yeah. He had it on his lap. Bette asked me to sit down and have a lemonade. Then Bert said I was no expert on sickness and pigs. He called us complainers. I got mad and told him we're just as good as him."

"I don't suppose you broke up with Gerry because his father's mean."

"I left the house and Gerry came after me. He tried to smooth it over. Said his father'd had some drinks and he'd forget about it in a day or two. He said his dad was mad because he'd been the one who recommended the reporter talk to me at Mah's. He thought I wouldn't talk like that about the plant, that I'd have more sense and be loyal. That's when I blew up."

Jeannie laughed, and Ella knew the rest. She pictured her daughter sticking a hand into her tower of hair, yanking it down. She got up and hugged Jeannie around the shoulders.

Ella noticed there was an opened envelope on Jeannie's lap.

"What's that?"

Jeannie fished a page out and handed it to Ella. It was a letter from Notre Dame University, in Nelson. They had accepted her into their teaching program.

"You didn't tell me you'd applied."

"I didn't want to tell you until I was sure. I guess there's nothing stopping me now."

"Quite a mail day," said Ella.

"Did you see the one for you?"

"What?"

"In the mail. There's a letter for you."

Ella went back to the kitchen and brushed through the envelopes. It was the strangest thing to see her name, just hers, printed on a letter. She picked it open and a blush rose to her face.

Dear Ella,

I'm sorry that I left suddenly with no goodbye. The friend I shared a house with, Andy Flannery, was killed by gas. Maybe you heard this from Alf Dietz. I don't suppose it was in the paper. I had a difference of opinion with Dietz and then the company over Andy's death and how the plant was operating. I went to Calgary that day and resigned.

I'm at another sour gas plant now. The gas that comes into this plant is about the same as at Aladdin Hatfield but everything else is different. This place is like a laboratory and our goal is to get as close to 100% recovery of sulphur as we can. The scientist in charge thinks 100% is possible, and that would mean there would be no hydrogen sulphide or sulphur dioxide going into the atmosphere at all. If we can achieve that, and the government makes it the rule for all sour gas plants, that would be the end of problems like yours.

I didn't write this to gloat about landing on my feet. I wanted to apologize that I was unable to improve the situation that you are living with. I keep in touch with two men at your plant, and they tell me that there have been some positive changes. The burning pit that was a big source of hydrogen sulphide should be retired by now. The hydrogen cracking in the steel is better controlled. But your plant has a long way to go to be safe. I'm not convinced the company is determined to solve things.

I hope you and your family are well. If you feel like writing to me, I will always be happy to hear from you.

Your friend,

Lance

Ella blushed again at how the letter ended. Before she had any chance to think about what this meant to her, she heard a sound at the window and, looking up, saw Jeannie's face on the other side of the screen. For the first time since coming home, Jeannie was grinning.

"Who's it from?" she asked.

"Lance Evert. Do you remember him?"

"Of course. The engineer before Gerry's dad. He used to come here for coffee."

"He's at another plant now. He wanted to tell us how much better it is there."

Jeannie still looked amused.

Ella pushed the letter into the envelope. "I'll show it to your dad tonight," she said, realizing that now she must.

Once in a blue moon, Tom would come back to the house after a day of work and feel that everything had changed in his absence. This was such a night.

He had spent the day in the hayfields trying to decide what to cut first. As soon as he sat down to supper, Jeannie told him she was going to B.C. for university, to Nelson, a town in the West Kootenays. She also showed him the *Haultain Herald* delivered that day, with the front-page story about the health study—the one Ella had told him about. Jeannie said she was quoted incorrectly; she had not said anything about progress or the smell of money. Gerry, the ex-boyfriend, had said those things.

As he ate his dinner, Tom found himself looking at Donna, expecting some bombshell from her too, but Donna was where she always was these days: a place far away. The next piece of unexpected news came from Ella. She went out of the room and returned with a letter. She set the page on the table beside his plate, smoothed it, and put the envelope, addressed to her, beside it. She stood and waited for him to read it.

Though short, the letter managed to say several important things. Ella's showing it to him said still more. He read it twice. *Dear Ella. Your friend, Lance.* Lance would be happy if she wrote back. Tom made himself concentrate on the gas plant information. By doing that, he came up with something to say.

"The burning pit is still going."

"Maybe he means it's going to stop but hasn't yet," Ella answered.

"I have trouble believing there will be plants with nothing coming out but hot air."

"They might get closer, though."

"I suppose."

He did not know what to say beyond this. He glanced at Ella to see if she was going to speak, and it seemed not. She was just showing the letter and showing herself showing it. Only Jeannie paid attention. The other two were straining to get away.

"You can go, you two," Tom said to Billy and Donna. They did so quickly.

"Are you going to answer the letter, Mom?" Jeannie asked, and a flicker of heat passed across Ella's face.

"No," she said. "Your father can if he likes."

Tom felt heat rising in him as well, and he decided it was rude to carry on about this letter when there was Jeannie's news to talk about. He had only glanced at the newspaper piece but now he read it closely. When she guessed he was reading the smell of money part, Jeannie said again that it was Gerry who'd said that.

Tom laughed.

"What's funny?" she asked.

"It's the smell of money for us too. The smell of money leaving."

Jeannie laughed with him. Ella was still standing and had not picked up the letter.

"You going to take your letter?" he asked her.

"It's not mine. You can do with it what you like."

After a slice of silence, Ella went to the sink and ran water.

"I'll put it in the binder," he said to her back, then folded it and shoved it in its envelope. He pushed his chair back and reached for his tobacco can.

"Nelson," he said. "That's not too far away."

"That's what I was thinking," Jeannie said, and he was struck by how completely he had her attention in this moment.

"I don't think I knew you wanted to be a schoolteacher. Was that me not listening?"

"I didn't know for a while either. Gerry wanted me to go where he's going. He wants to be an engineer and applied to Calgary and Edmonton."

"Is it over, then? With him?"

"It's over. That article was just the final . . ."

"Straw."

"Straw. I won't marry someone who pushes me around. It makes you feel small all the time."

"I'm glad you decided what you did, then."

They talked about money. Jeannie had looked into student loans and thought she would live in residence. The amount was considerable, but Tom figured he and Ella could dig that much out of their savings and make it up again. Suddenly, he was thinking of Jeannie in the world: a tall girl with lots of energy. Pretty. He liked the idea of her in a residence, living with a bunch of young people. She made friends easily. If she lived alone, she would get lonesome and have another serious boyfriend too soon. This way, she might have some not too serious ones first, get to know better what she liked. He was amazed at how many thoughts he had on this subject now that it had arisen and his opinion was asked for.

Ella still had her back to them washing the dishes. Maybe you shouldn't try to read someone by their back, but he thought hers looked put out. Jeannie suddenly said, "Mom! You should have waited. I would have helped you."

"That's okay. You're having a good talk with your dad."

He doubted Ella felt that, but it was respectful to say it, in the way that the letter was not respectful. While he talked with Jeannie, he could not help but think of the hundred per cent business, one hundred per cent recovery of sulphur. What was possible would be important if it came to a lawsuit. If the company was doing less than it *could*, that reflected on both Aladdin and the government: one for not trying and the other for not insisting.

Jeannie helped put dishes away, wiped down the counter. Tom went and put the letter in the binder. *Dear Ella. Your friend, Lance.* Jeannie going off to become a teacher. He could not think clearly. He was like a magpie jumping from branch to branch.

A few nights later, over supper, Tom said he didn't know how he was going to get the haying done without a hired man. Jeannie said she would do the raking. Donna said she would run the mower. Ella said she and Billy would help on the stack.

It happened exactly that way. They did every bit of haying themselves. In the hottest part of each afternoon, the kids went for a swim. They jumped into the old pickup and Jeannie drove them to the swimming hole on the Callaghan. Billy complained at first about sharp rocks in the river, so Ella cut the toes out of an old pair of runners.

By the time Ella and Jeannie were packing her boxes for Nelson, the kids were friends in a way they had never been before. Ella could not stop herself from crying when they had Jeannie's boxes and suit-cases in the car. Donna and Billy were close to tears as well. Jeannie told them all to cheer up.

"B.C.'s not the end of the world, you know."

Billy, who'd been practising his sarcasm, said, "Not quite," and was rewarded with a cuff on the head.

6

A KNOCK CAME on the office door. Clayton entered. "Marion, Huge, and me were wondering if you'd come to The Pit for a beer tonight."

Clayton had his chest stuck out and his bottom lip pushed over the top one. The suggested group was strange. Bill was never asked for drinks unless Henry Shields was involved. Henry would be working tomorrow so would not be drinking tonight. As for Marion, she was never invited to The Pit if Clayton was going, as Clayton disapproved of drinking with women. He preferred them naked and wrapped around a pole.

"You want to talk to me about something. And that something would be Dennis."

Clayton's brass neck fell loose. Bill enjoyed the response.

"We're really pissed about him," Clayton said.

"I know that. And what are you wanting me to do?"

"Fire him."

"First off, I won't be coming to The Pit. That's not the place to discuss Dennis. I'll discuss him with you right now."

"All of us agree it's unsafe to work with Dennis. It's not right to expose us to a guy that's screwing up all the time. He could get us killed."

"Dennis isn't going to get fired. Theo Houle and I have already talked about it. In my opinion, Dennis is no more likely to cause a four-alarm catastrophe than anyone else, including you."

"That's complete bullshit!"

"Fact is, Dennis probably became a much better operator when he hit the deck the other day. You also don't get to pick who you work with, in this business or in any other, unless you own it. If you see him do something questionable, I suggest you tell him. He can learn. We all can."

"You're pretty holier-than-thou for someone I couldn't get ahold of when Fuckwit had his accident."

"You're right. I should have been easier to contact."

"You say I cause problems just like Dennis. Name one thing I've done wrong."

"It's what you might do that concerns me."

"I'm not satisfied with this. Not one bit."

"Okay by me. I don't really care if you get so hot you catch fire. Could you ask Marion to come in when you leave?"

Marion stuck to her guns for a while, until Bill pointed out she was only being asked to The Pit to up the numbers trying to get Dennis fired. At that, she wilted.

"You earn respect by doing a good job," he told her, "which you already do. As for Dennis, he knows he's getting a break. He'll repeat his safety training. He'll be listening this time."

When Huge came in, Bill gave him the same spiel. The big man seemed incapable of reply. It was possible he longed to say it wasn't his idea, that Clayton had bullied him, but he did the dignified thing and stayed quiet.

Why not head for Edmonton? That casino on the north side? Remember that machine? The one with the Irish jig music? You had those lepre-chauns dancing.

All the way to Fort Mac, the Voice droned on. Bill knew a mighty tussle lay ahead.

At the other end, in the condo, he did as he had promised himself. He put a steak in the microwave to thaw. He opened a GSM from the Barossa Valley, swished the black wine around the bell of the glass; sipped. He remembered the forest of lights over the casino entrance as he had passed it. The Voice was at its most incessant then. But he had made it by; he had made it home. Now he was settled in and drinking. He got up and put some music on: the big rumbling piano of Chucho Valdés.

The only problem with alcohol was that between the first drink and oblivion came actual drunkenness. While drunk, the part of Bill that fought the Voice lost power. It could get mushy and uncertain—or, worse yet, playful. Next thing, Bill would be inside Mr. Khalid's sweet-smelling taxi with the Muslim prayer beads swinging from the rear-view, the ninety-nine names of Allah. One look at Bill, the shape he was in, and Mr. Khalid would start for the casino without being told.

Talk as much as you like, he challenged the Voice. You prattle, and I'll make a nice dinner and watch some hockey. After that I'll read a book. The Voice stayed silent, saving its energy.

Bill took his time with everything. He made a marinade and got the thawed meat into it. He drew out his biggest cutting board and sliced and chopped vegetables until they were several little hills around the wood. He pretended that the ball of desire building and rubberizing in his chest was not there. More wine.

In what seemed like no time, the cooking and eating were done. The dishes were in the sink. He carried the wine's sad remnant to the living room, set the bottle and glass on coasters. It was the second intermission of the hockey game. His success at watching it was such that he did not know the score.

Sitting here by yourself? Drinking alone? Is that any kind of answer?

I like my own company.

Tell me another one. You need decibels, man. Lights. I give you one more hour before you're thinking about the Native woman and your ex-wives. Whimpering about your kids and your dad.

If Bill could work one thirty-day stretch, spending all his nights in the Chateau Borealis, he was pretty sure he could beat this thing, but that was not a discussion Theo Houle would entertain. Back when Bill was new and had asked to spend nights in camp, Theo had argued against it. Why on earth would he want to, when he had a nice condo in Fort Mac? Bill said he didn't enjoy the drive. Next, Theo argued that the company was cracking down on expenses and would find Bill's stays in camp unacceptable. New Aladdin had just accepted delivery of a vessel from an Ontario fabricator, two months late and a million over budget. Bill had allowed himself to laugh.

But he did understand Theo's objection. It was not the expense but that Bill was turning down relative luxury. If the oil sands made sense at all, it was the sense of money and economic privilege. If someone did not obey those laws, the whole thing swayed in the muskeg.

"I'm single" was what Bill told Houle finally. "Besides, isn't it a benefit to have an engineer in camp at night? Five minutes away as opposed to an hour and a half?"

Bill won that round, but a thirty-day shift in camp would still be out of the question. It was the sort of thing that would pop up like the devil's prick in an accident investigation: Bill's weird love of endless work could void their insurance.

He drank off the wine, checked his watch. It was not yet nine. He got his computer out of his briefcase, booted up, and induced a gambling-addiction site to appear.

"If you stop gambling, that is of course a wonderful sign. *Terrific progress! Good for you!* But if the problem gambler feels he or she has conquered the addiction, look out! Real lasting progress can seldom be made alone. Progress begins with the admission that you are an addict and always will be."

Bill went to the extra bedroom. Every wall except the one with the bed against it was lined with books. He searched and searched for something to read, but found nothing that would hold his attention tonight. He got a bottle of single malt from the cupboard and sloshed some amber into his wine glass. But alcohol would also not be enough.

He thought of the binder. It was in his truck, where he'd left it after the failed attempt to go to Jeannie's. He went to his storage cupboard and rooted in the boxes, came back to the living room with a few photo albums. He needed to look at Ella. She had always given him, not strength exactly, but a modest backbone. Loving but unfooled was the look he remembered, a look with the power of a crutch. It held him up but never let him forget he was crippled.

Ella was not in the first two-thirds of the childhood album because she was the one taking pictures. Gangly Jeannie curled around baby Billy on a blanket in the yard. Billy and his sisters squinting into the crazy noonday sun. Jeannie and Donna modelling white dresses: Jeannie's confirmation and Donna's First Communion. He flipped the pages quickly, and he and his siblings grew like animated rhubarb. Fattening, thinning, pimpling; acquiring and losing period hairdos.

When Jeannie mastered the Brownie, Ella appeared. Bill's favourite was a picture of himself at six. His mother stood behind him, her dark summer forearms on either side of his head and her hands flat down his chest. He could still feel her hands if he tried hard.

As he leafed through, he was trying not to see his father. If pictures of Ella beefed him up, pictures of Tom sapped him. Though camera shy, Tom had not totally avoided being photographed. In the picture of Billy and Ella, Tom was on the edge, cut in half, grinning with his missing tooth on display.

Bill closed the album and stared at the wall, still unsatisfied, still squeezed. He turned to the first of the newer albums, and was soon looking at himself standing next to Ginny, his tall, thrillingly beautiful first wife. Their children appeared and sprouted.

The pictures of Martha and Will always hurt him—more even than the last image of Tom before he died, or the pictures to come of Ella as she got old and ill. To look at himself holding a tiny bundle of baby, then leaning down to lead his children by their gummy hands. Though the children didn't know it and he didn't either, he was about to leave them. The pictures after the leaving hurt him too, the barbs set at different angles. Always a fair woman, Ginny sent him photos of the birthday parties he missed, and the Christmas he spent in a blinding desert in Kuwait. While he'd worked in that open-air plant, dizzy with heat, he'd chanted a mantra about money: the stupid sum the American company was paying him to be there. The sun blazed off the steel, and his loneliness made a sound like warping tin.

He kept at it for a long time, staring at each picture and sipping whisky. He finally closed the album on a page of his children as teenagers and pushed the stack to the couch's end. He considered what the Voice was saying about good old-fashioned revolving oblivion. How good the casino would feel right now, or at least how not-bad.

But, unlike other nights, he continued to fight. He sat and stared; de-focused his eyes and chanted.

He startled awake. He touched his face and found the couch's nubby surface printed there. There was a ringing sound but it wasn't either of his telephones. He understood finally that it was the buzzer for the lobby door.

Light was spraying through the plastic blinds. He got up, took a step, and fell. One leg was asleep. Bill was certain the buzzer wasn't for him but pressed the button anyway, just to make it stop. It was a surprise a couple of minutes later when his doorbell rang. Through the peephole, all he could see was a gooey substance crossing his eye. He jerked the door open and there was Donna.

She had on a parka bigger than herself. Her bare head sat in a ring of fur.

"Stop staring and invite me in. What have you done to your face? You look like that guy in *Moby Dick*. The one with the tattoos."

"Queequeg."

"That one."

She pushed past him. He tried to hug her on the way by. "Get off. Wait until I'm out of my coat."

Bill looked at the clock on the stove. One p.m.

"You must have left Calgary in the middle of the night," he said. "Or did you stay in Edmonton?"

"It's Elmer. He's been sick. I have to have a cat sitter. One thing about the great lesbian sisterhood, you can always get a cat sitter. Anyway, I had to leave early and can't stay long."

"That doesn't seem worth it."

"You're worth it, Sunshine. Unless you mean I'm not worth it in which case you can F-O."

He mumbled an apology.

"Oh stop it. Go make coffee while I chance your bachelor bathroom."

Bill ground beans and loaded up the coffee maker. He was getting down cups when he heard the plastic blinds clatter in the living room.

"This looks bad in here, Billy," Donna called. "Like some demented drunk surrounded himself with photo albums, drank a bottle of whisky, and passed out."

"I was trying to stay in."

"That's a mortal struggle? What else is there to do? Singles' night at the Legion?"

He came with the coffee. "Among other things, I was looking at pictures of you."

"Ugh. You had anemia but I *looked* like I did." She swept up the album, found the right page, and looked at herself. "See? I look sick. I look worried."

"I guess there were reasons."

"The local shadow of death?" She turned the album around so he could see one of himself, grinning toothlessly. "Why don't you look worried, then?"

"Too young. Too dumb."

"Let's have our coffee in the kitchen. It's creepy in here."

They sat across the table.

"What made you decide to come?"

"This is called a visit, Bill. The idea is for you to be glad."

"I am glad."

"Okay, here's what I want to do in the next twenty-four hours. All you ever read about in the papers these days is the tar sands— and Fort McMurray. I want a tour."

"Mac's pretty ordinary."

"Except for nine cars per household."

"Are you planning to stay here?"

"Of course. What a question."

"I'll have to tell the Newfies to find somewhere else to sleep."

"Okay. That's good. Not great, but it's a start."

Bill had a shower. They went for lunch, then crossed the bridge and drove north on 63. The first stop Bill made was at the oil sands' tourist attraction: the buffalo paddock. The buffalo were fairly close to the fence, where they had been fed. Used to visitors, they kept grazing the green path.

"I read about this. This is a reclaimed strip mine or something."

"An old retaining pond, I think. I actually don't know."

"An official viewing place anyway."

"Right."

"Something nicer to look at than the rest."

"They leave trees here and there, to mask the strip mines from the highway."

"Thoughtful."

When they were driving again, Donna said, "Be honest with me, Billy. Can this really be reclaimed?"

"All the strip-mined areas used to be boreal forest. Wetlands and bogs. You can't make a boreal forest in under a thousand years."

"Will they kill the river?"

"If all the land currently leased is developed, they'll kill the river."

"Jesus Christ."

"A friend of mine told me there's only one water sampling site between the strip mines and Lake Athabasca. It's true—I looked it up. I think they're going with the principle that you can't find what you don't look for."

"You sound greener than I remember."

"Guess I've been paying more attention."

"Why?"

"Personal reasons."

"That's the stuff you're supposed to tell your sister. Will it make you quit?"

"I doubt it. I need to work."

"You must have lots of money by now."

"I go through it pretty fast."

Donna wanted to see Bill's plant, and the question was if he could get her inside. He phoned ahead and talked to a few people. It was touchy because they only allowed official tours. Finally, he had to phone Houle, who made somewhat of a big deal out of consenting. He was told to go straight to his own control room and office and straight out again.

"She'll have to wear visitor ID—and a hard hat."

"She'll love the hard hat. Thanks."

"She's not a reporter or anything?"

"She runs a travel agency."

Henry's crew, staring at Donna, were like yokels at a fair, like she had horns. When he introduced her as his sister, it got worse. He never talked about a family so they'd assumed he didn't have one. He saved Henry Shields for last, after the others had gone back to work.

"Henry's from our way," he told her.

"What's your job, Henry?"

"Make the big guy here look good."

"Best of luck with that."

In Bill's office, Donna let out a happy yell. She had found the framed photos on the desk. "Jeannie and me on the farm! And your kids! You're so much more human than we think."

Back on the road, Donna wanted to know about the village across the lake. Bill explained: Native town that happened to be where the geologists found an oil sands deposit shallow enough to mine.

"That sounds a little familiar."

"It's not as bad as when we were kids. These plants are better."

"Still, big ugly plant across the lake. They can't be happy. Can we go there?"

On the main street, Bill listened to himself describing the village. He sounded defensive and promotional.

"Standard of living here is okay. Most of the people are old but some of their kids and grandkids are in the industry. A few of the houses are nice, like that one." He pointed at Marie's.

"What the frig is that?" Donna was looking at the community centre.

He parked in the centre's lot and explained Dion's gift. Donna laughed at Bill's Starship *Enterprise* comparison. While they were talking, Marie Calfoux came out of her house and started shovelling snow. Bill made a U-turn, buzzed down his window, and stopped beside her.

"Hey, Marie."

"Mr. Ryder. Thought the tar sands had swallowed you."

"This is my sister, Donna. Donna, Marie Calfoux."

Marie bent low so she could see Donna. She reached her arm in and they touched mitts. "Your brother's showing good manners today."

"He used to have manners. I can't speak for now."

Bill said they had to go before all the restaurants in Mac were full. When they were out of the village, Donna punched him hard on the shoulder.

"You're a madman. That woman is seriously nice—and good looking—and you were barely civil."

They agreed not to change clothes when they got to Mac. After a fifteen-minute wait, they were seated in Bill's favourite steakhouse. Donna was chilled and kept her parka on, zipped to the neck.

"Did I mention you look like a severed head on a fur platter?"

"The point is to be warm. I'm not concerned what I look like in Fort McMurray."

The waiter came, his hands extended toward Donna.

"I don't want you to hang up my coat. But I want a hot rum toddy very badly."

Bill ordered a beer. There was a silence after the waiter left.

"You're making me feel unwelcome again."

When the drinks came, Donna unzipped her coat halfway. "Jeannie thinks there's a woman in your life."

"Jeannie's wrong."

"She says you're doing the sort of things you do when there is."

Bill ignored her and poured his beer.

Donna persisted. "Not even in the relatively recent past?"

"I guess there was."

"You guess? There was someone and what? You broke up? It never got started?"

"Both."

Donna reached across the booth and swatted at him. "You nut! It can't be both."

Bill stared into the kitchen, where smoke had burst from the grill.

"There used to be a woman but there never was a woman," said Donna. "Okay, it's a riddle." She climbed out of her parka but kept it behind her on the bench. "You were interested, but you blew it before anything could happen."

"That's pretty good."

"Let's toast, Billy." They clinked glasses.

"So let me flesh this out. You used to call her. You went out a few times."

"No."

"Which part?"

"Didn't go out."

"Phone calls?"

"Some."

"Sometimes you called? Sometimes she called?"

"Mostly she did."

"Really? Then what? She stopped calling?"

The waiter returned, and Bill ordered a bottle of wine.

"How's the travel business?"

"Our survival depends on old couples who haven't figured computers out."

"You should sell to your partners."

"I've suggested it. I went about it like Dad. Told them it's no good then offered to sell it to them."

When the waiter came back for orders, Donna wanted steak. "What's a baseball steak?"

The waiter explained the shape. A special feature of their restaurant was a super-hot prong that cooked them from the inside. "Thousand degrees. We can do it Chicago style."

"Say what?"

"Charred on the outside but medium-rare inside."

"Okay, I'm having it."

"Have anything but the baseball steak," said Bill. "It'll be raw in the middle."

"Don't listen to him."

"I'm not listening. I'm having it."

The wine arrived. Bill passed the tasting glass to Donna. She admitted it was good.

"You were about to tell me something," she said to Bill. "About the phone calls."

"C'mon, Donna. Let's not talk about this all night."

"You c'mon. Tell me."

"She called me a couple of times. I didn't call back."

"Why not?"

"It's complicated."

"She's got a drug habit? She's a stalker? She's fourteen and her father's a Muslim camp cook? A hooker?"

"Donna, stop."

"Tell me if I'm hot or cold."

"Stone cold."

"You like her and there is no obstacle."

"There's an obstacle."

"She's married."

"Divorced, but that's not it."

Bill picked up a cardboard coaster and bounced the edge while Donna thought.

"I've got it. She's an environmentalist."

Bill tried to keep his face expressionless. Donna waggled her finger at him. "That's it, isn't it?"

"No."

"But I'm warm."

The food came. The baseball steak was raw in the middle. Donna sent it back. It returned a few minutes later, still raw.

Donna looked at the disgraced waiter. "That's not the hottest prong in the west," she said.

Finally, the steak made it to medium-rare.

"Okay, you've made your smug little point, Billy. Shut up and eat. I'm having fun, by the way. I'm glad I came."

"Jeannie sent you, didn't she?"

"Jeannie doesn't send me. I'm not twelve."

"But you two discussed me and concluded I needed a visit."

"Of course we discuss you. There are three Ryders, not ten."

"Jeannie thinks I'm a mess."

Donna raised her eyebrows, chewed some steak.

"What?" Bill asked.

"I'm remembering your apartment."

"I wasn't expecting company."

"So, whenever you're not expecting company, you get shit-faced and sleep on the couch?"

"I told you, I was trying to spend a night at home. I go out too much on days off."

They ate their steaks. When their plates were taken away, Donna wanted coffee and brandies.

"I'll have to call Mr. Khalid."

"Who?"

"Cab driver."

The brandies arrived. Donna lifted hers off the stirrup and sniffed deeply.

"But let's not get sidetracked. You still haven't explained why you're not answering the woman's calls."

"Donna. No more."

"What did she do to make you so rude?"

"It's not like I hang up on her. She leaves messages. I don't answer them."

"That's worse!"

"We met a couple of times at open houses. We had a few laughs and I got my hopes up." He shrugged and took a drink.

Donna jumped in her seat. "I've got it! It's the woman in the village!"

Bill signalled the waiter for the check.

"I'm right, aren't I?"

"You're right."

Donna let out a low moan. "Oh boy, this is serious. She's even your age. And available?"

"Seems so."

"You say you got your hopes up, but she's the one who's phoning. And she seemed glad to see you today. So that makes no sense."

"Couple of things have happened that suggest she just wants information about the plant. I'm more candid than our PR guys, so she wants to talk to me."

"You're not that much of a company man, are you, Billy?"

"I don't know what you mean."

"That you'd write off a promising woman because she doesn't like your stupid plant?"

"I'm not that much of a company man."

"What, then?"

"I told you. Her interest in me is she wants plant information. It's not going anywhere."

"What if you're wrong?"

Bill picked up the coaster again. Donna swiped it out of his hand.

"Is it not possible?" She paused, considered. "Is it not possible that a woman could like a man and see him as a source of information too? I can imagine that."

"So can I."

"So you did pick the company over her!"

"I don't think so."

"Then answer the woman's calls."

"Ah, Donna. It's lots of things. I'm not good at relationships. Baggage. Bad habits."

"So wash more. Quit the nose picking."

Bill laughed. He reached for his cell phone. Donna lifted off the bench to stop his hand.

"I want to be serious for one minute. Then you can phone Mr. Farouk." She composed herself. "I'm addressing you as your big sister. You're too young to give up on the romantic side of life, since that's pretty much like giving up on life itself."

Her face drew down. Her eyes filled.

"I would be so happy if someone I liked phoned and left a message. And don't—please—for the love of Mary—now or ever—say one consoling word."

———

In the condo, Bill turned up the heat. He got the space heater from his office and pointed it at Donna's feet. She was sitting on the couch in her parka, shivering. In the billows of her down lap was the binder. She had asked Mr. Khalid to stop at Bill's truck so she could get her extra pair of mitts. She'd found the binder on the back seat.

"I'm making a comeback," she said to Bill. "Let's have another bottle of wine. Nothing good, just some routine plonk that we can drink or not."

Bill got a bottle out of the wine fridge.

Donna patted the binder. "I'm going to open it."

"Donna, don't. Please."

"Why not? Did you already?"

"I'm not interested in it."

"But you remember it."

"Of course I remember. It's the stuff from Dad's lawsuit."

"Right. The suit that wouldn't float."

"It'll only be depressing."

"You've had decades to get over it."

"I'll go to bed. You can look at it to your heart's content."

"I promise—if it's depressing us, I'll close it again." She jerked the zipper and the rusted fob came off.

"Nice one."

"Shut up." She pushed the zipper down with her fingernail.

The stuffed binder flipped open. Envelopes fell. On top were a few loose sheets. She held up the top one and shook it. "Billy! The Stink Diary!" She dug in her purse for reading glasses.

"'April 10. Serious air . . . pollution for five days. Lost six pigs from a . . .'"

"Litter."

"'Litter of twelve.' Thought you hadn't read it?"

"What else do you lose six pigs from?"

"'Balance of litter did not do well. When shipped they were con . . . condemned as arthritic. April 19.' Now it's Mom's writing. 'Trim paint on buildings damaged by gas fumes.' Back to Dad. 'May 23. Air pollution very bad. Wife and children quite ill. Hired man left. Unable to stand odour. Hired another man. Worked one day. Quit same reason. July 10. Lost eight pigs from litter of thirteen. Gas very bad at this time. Pigs appeared to smother.'"

"You said if it was depressing you'd stop. It's depressing."

"Are you serious?"

"Yes."

"It's our life story, kiddo. It's interesting."

"I shouldn't have to justify what I find depressing."

"Okay." She looked at the mess around her. "I'll never get all this back in." She folded the binder over its contents, pushed it away from her. "More wine, please."

Bill poured some, left his own glass empty.

"You *are* depressed," she said.

"I'll get over it, like you say."

"Maybe you should talk about it if it bothers you so much."

"You missed your calling. The world of psychiatry lost a genius."

"None of this makes sense. For entertainment, you pull out old albums and drunkenly pore over them. Then when I want to look in the binder—"

"Don't tell me what to do with my time. Don't tell me what to get over and what not to get over."

"Whoa."

"I asked you not to open the frigging thing."

"You can cap up the wine, brother. Off to bed I go."

———

They stood in a funnel of light from an overhead lamp. Donna's car engine was beating itself to life, as Bill scraped hard frost off the windows.

"You should get in your car," he told her.

"It's got seat warmers. I'm waiting for a warm seat."

She signalled him to stop scraping and give back the brush. She opened her arms and they hugged.

"What's her name again?"

"Marie."

"Phone Marie."

"I'll think about it."

"Don't think. Phone."

"I'm sorry about last night."

As she sat down into her car, the parka puffed upward. She was rummaging for something in her pocket.

"You look like your airbag's deployed."

"Shut up. I found this on the floor in the spare bedroom." She handed a piece of paper through the window. A VLT ticket. A winner. "I don't know the local customs, but where I come from, we cash these."

7

Dry Fork, 1967

TOM AND BILLY were in the pickup, going south, parting the summer hills. The destination was Dry Fork. John Darby had invited Tom to meet their lawyer. It was five years since his first trip to meet the Darbys, and he had gone down about once a year since then.

Billy was twelve, and there was not much conversation in the cab. Tom assumed the boy would rather have spent the day in town with his friends. A swimming pool had just opened, a present from the oil companies in the region. Or maybe Billy would have gone somewhere with Donna, who had been his pal since Jeannie left for B.C. The only reason Tom had asked his son along was that Ella had urged him to.

After miles of farms, they crossed a long ridge that had never known a plough. Tom nudged Billy, pointed at two mule deer in the scrub higher up.

It was a summer like any other except that their family was smaller. Jeannie had phoned to say she wouldn't be returning to the farm this summer. She had been teaching for a couple of years and had a new beau. She planned to live in the West Kootenay town where he and his parents lived.

More unexpected was Donna's plan to quit school. A couple of weeks back, at the end of grade eleven, she had announced she wasn't going to bother with grade twelve. She was moving to Calgary to work for a travel agency.

Ella and Tom had taken turns arguing with her, pushing her to stay and complete high school. "After that, you can head for the city and train for whatever you want."

Donna's answer was that she had been training for years. All those books she had read from the Department of Extension, about countries all over the world. She had written to travel agencies in Calgary, and two had invited her to come and talk.

Tom looked across at Billy, who was staring out the side window. He did not look resentful so much as blank, a look he had perfected recently. Tom thought of himself at Billy's age. By that standard, the boy should be thinking of girls, baseball, fighting, horses, or scrambling up mountains. At Billy's age, Tom's father had told him how to figure out what sex a gopher was. All the ones you see running across roads, or flattened on roads, were males, in search of females in other colonies. It was almost time for Billy to be off and running.

"What do you think about Donna quitting school?"

Billy turned his head a bit. "She's got a plan, I guess," he said.

"That's a plan? To quit high school?"

"She'll finish. She says there's night schools in the city."

"That sounds like something somebody would say but not do."

Billy shrugged.

"What about the meeting we're going to?" Tom asked.

"Don't know anything about it."

"We'll meet the lawyer the Dry Fork farmers hired, to bring a lawsuit against their oil company."

"Oh yeah."

"You've never met a lawyer, have you?"

"Nope." The boy glazed over. Made himself into wax.

As they got closer to Dry Fork, Tom was wondering why Ella had wanted Billy to go with him. It was not the first time she had pushed the boy in his direction lately. Other suggestions were fishing, camping, and shooting gophers.

This was against Ella's own best interests, for she loved having Billy around. They always had things to say, when they worked in the garden or drove around. They made each other laugh. They even milked cows together. Ella had taught him, and he was almost as good as she was.

Whatever the answer, it probably had more to do with Tom and Ella than with Billy. That Ella wanted Tom to be closer to their son had a whiff of sacrifice. Maybe it had to do with Donna having worked with him and then not. Or it could be the other thing, the engineer.

Whichever, it was probably a bid for peace, not love. Tom had long ago accepted that things for them wouldn't ever be the way they had been early on. That was long ago and gone.

On the phone, Joan Darby had said the meeting would be just Darbys, Arsenaults, a bachelor rancher named Larry Erickson, and the lawyer. Once there, Tom introduced Billy around, and a fuss was made over the boy—except by Erickson, who stuck his chin at them and said, "I told the others I don't think it's a good idea you and your boy being here today. I don't beat around the bush. I don't think Geoff will like it."

John Darby jumped in. "Hell, Larry, Tom just wants to get his lawsuit going. He needs to meet Geoff."

Erickson folded his arms and stared at the wall.

Geoff Purcell drove into the yard in a small foreign car. Joan went to fetch him in, and when the lawyer entered, Tom was surprised at how tall he was and how young he looked. His hair was longer than farmers wore theirs. He had an innocence that was at odds with how forcefully he took charge.

"I see we have a newcomer," he said, rubbing his hands together as he came near Tom. The look he gave was not unfriendly but had a question in it.

Tom introduced himself and Billy. He found himself awkward in explaining why they were present. John Darby took over.

"Tom lives downwind of the Hatfield plant. I invited him because he's interested in starting a suit."

Joan asked Geoff if he would like tea or coffee. He asked for a pop or a juice, and Joan apologized that she had neither. They were childless, and adults didn't drink pop here unless they were Mormon. Tom wondered if Purcell was of that religion.

"Water's fine," he said.

The lawyer turned to Tom and shook his hand. He reached and shook Billy's too. Billy was leaning against the wall.

"I'm glad to meet you both, but I should explain that confidentiality is an issue for us. The company must never know what we know or don't know. As we build our case, we'll acquire more evidence. Meanwhile, we're like the animal in the forest that puffs up to look bigger than he is."

"I get that," said Tom.

Geoff asked if the others had the diaries he had asked for, meaning the ones that kept track of bad odour days, sickness, and livestock problems. Geoff had asked them to make copies, and Kelly Arsenault brought a stack of paper to the table.

"Wonderful!" said Geoff, thumping the pile with his open hand. "I've got my office assistant collecting everything available about sour gas, while I research other pollution lawsuits."

Geoff started talking about the smelter at Trail, B.C. Tom knew of it but was surprised to hear it had been there since the nineteenth century. The sulphurous smoke had killed the nearby forests and farmers' crops. There were legal proceedings and settlements way back in the 1920s.

"In my opinion things might have stopped right there, except it was an international problem. Smoke from Trail poured into the United States and did damage there too. The smelting company built a four-hundred-foot stack, and that actually made things worse. The smoke went all the way to the Columbia Valley. Scientists tried to get the company's sulphur emissions down, and money was paid to farmers again in the 1930s.

"Who knows where it would have gone from there had there not been a war. The smelter was important to the war effort, so the two governments were protective of it. The final settlement during that period was small. But the key thing"—Purcell thumped the pile of diary pages again—"is that a precedent was set. The polluting company was legally responsible. That's what we have to build on."

John wanted to get the whisky out, but Purcell said he needed to get back as far as Calgary tonight. He had business there first thing in the morning. The Darbys coaxed Tom to stay longer, but he said Billy had school in the morning.

The truth was, Tom wanted to get Geoff Purcell alone. "Sorry I had to be a little heavy-handed with you fellows at the start," Geoff said when the three of them were outside. "I'm sure you understand we can't risk having our information get to the other side. They'll have a lot of legal muscle."

Tom assured him again.

"Are you serious about a lawsuit at Haultain?" Geoff asked.

"Sure am."

"Is your wife okay with it?"

The question was unexpected. Whatever Tom's face did made Geoff Purcell laugh. "I won't pry. But what about the community? Have you got solid support?"

Tom said he did, even as an image floated before his eye of Bertha Kenhardt, Hughie McGrady, and Vic and Pearl Sebald, as if seated for a photograph.

"I hope you stick with it, Tom. Farmers have got to be the ones to push this thing. The government isn't going to help. You've probably figured that out already. Oil and gas have pulled this province out of the Depression. Some Albertans are richer now than they ever imagined possible. What we've got going for us is that we're right. The companies damaged you folks and you deserve compensation. Do you have pigs?"

"Did have."

"You lost a bunch of young ones and got out of it, I bet."

"We lost cattle too. My neighbour Hughie lost sheep."

"You lost full-grown cows?"

"Two calves and a ten-month-old steer."

"Ten months. That's a big animal. And you're sure it was gas?"

"I had a vet do an autopsy. He wrote me a report that shows it was edema of the lungs, and maybe poisoning from water that ran down from the plant." Tom saw the lawyer's eyes pop and felt proud.

"Sounds like you're on your way." The lawyer gave Billy's shoulder a pinch. "This one here might turn out to be your best asset. Young people understand things we don't."

They were both excited on the drive home. Tom had liked Geoff Purcell; so had Billy.

"Think we should do it? The lawsuit?"

"Guess so. Sure."

"Take a lot of time. Dry Fork started with Geoff Purcell five years ago and they still haven't made it to court. That must cost quite a bit."

"Did you ask him if he'd help us?"

Billy knew Tom hadn't. "There's no *us* to work for yet. I'm sure he understood I'd be calling him when I get a group together."

"Will it be like *Perry Mason*?"

Tom had bought a television in the spring. *Perry Mason* was Billy's favourite show.

"These things either settle out of court or have to be decided in a court. If it goes to court, it might look like *Perry Mason*."

They went silent for half an hour as Tom drove through the dark. Finally, Tom asked, "You want to be a lawyer like Perry Mason?"

"Don't think so."

"A farmer?"

"Yeah, sure. Maybe."

"But you'll go to university first."

"Yeah."

"What will you study there?"

"I like math. Or something about machines."

"Engineering, then."

"I don't know what that is."

8

THE YEARS AFTER the girls left home seemed both to drag and speed by. Time dragged when Ella was waiting for things, usually for one of her girls to say she was coming home to visit. Those times were spaced further and further apart. If she complained, they said she could come and visit, and, on occasion, she did. But both girls lived in tiny studio apartments, one bed and no couch. There was nowhere to put Ella but beside them. Jeannie was not a good sleeper to begin with, and besides, Ella felt she might be supplanting her boyfriend, Hal. At Donna's, it was more or less the same, except for the boyfriend, which she did not have. Donna liked to go to a bar where her women friends gathered, and Ella found she could not hear a thing in those places. This made her feel stupid, a lump, Donna's old mom.

What made time speed was the sight of Billy. He had grown past his father's height, to six foot tall. His weight had not kept pace, so he looked stretched. She could not look at her son without seeing him gone. She knew how that would happen, all in a tumble. Suddenly it would be time, and there would be a flurry of preparations, and he would be her friend at home no longer. What stood beyond that point was something she was desperate not to think about.

With two sisters and a mother in the house, Billy had grown up with a naturalness around women that she supposed would mean girlfriends galore as soon as he understood it. He had trailed around after Jeannie like a dog, begging her to throw a ball. He and Donna became conspirators and jokers after Jeannie was gone. And now Ella and he talked easily about many things: Donna and Jeannie, and what he himself would do after high school.

They had also had a few odd honest talks about the plant, mostly about how it had changed things. These were conversations about a destroyed future, a cutting off of past from present, that might leave this place empty someday: a community of rotting houses. They pretended to be talking about other families when in fact they were talking about themselves.

Ella did not know how Billy could think such thoughts and still go with his father to the meetings at Dry Fork, but he did. Somehow, he was able to hold the two thoughts in his head at once.

Ella had given her son the first push toward Tom and his everlasting lawsuit. She felt she owed Tom that much. Now her husband loved to talk about how Billy could understand pollution documents that befuddled the rest of them.

In their evenings, Tom withdrew to his office (her sewing room with the tiny desk he had inherited from his father) and sat there in the feeble yellow light typing on Donna's portable that she had left at home. He typed letters and kept carbon copies: to the government, to Aladdin, to the Dry Fork people, to Dry Fork's lawyer in Edmonton—even to newspapers. That was how confident he had become: that he would write letters to the editor.

She burned then to tell him it was a waste of time. He would never arouse their neighbours, especially now that the worst of times with the plant were over. The plant stank and was no doubt dangerous but was nowhere near the dragon it had been. The truth was that awful Bert Traynor was better than Dietz or Lance at wrestling the plant into balance.

When Tom did his rounds of the neighbours, that was what he heard back. Things were not so bad now. What about all their losses, he would say, all the illness they had endured, the death of livestock, the rotten fence wire, the steel gone from their cultivator shovels? But they would put him off. Only recently, when Tom had persuaded Dry Fork's lawyer to come down from Edmonton to see them, had their curiosity picked up.

What it would not change, lawyer or no lawyer, were Ella's feelings about it all. If they had asked her, she could have told them their future, Tom's and Billy's, and it was a much different future than they were assuming. There would be no lawsuit. Even if the neighbours thought at times they would go along with it, ultimately they would not. And Billy would never be a farmer.

Ella counted twenty-three people in the room. Without the addition to the house completed last year, this meeting would not have been possible, but everyone fit easily in the extended living room.

It was a proud day for Tom. Of all the time he'd spent pushing neighbours to consider legal action, this was the biggest outcome by far. The lawyer from Edmonton stood talking at the far end of the room, framed by the picture window.

Ella had not seen Geoff Purcell before and was surprised how tall he was. It was hard to tell his age because he had a gangliness that didn't last long in farmers. When he wound himself up—as he was doing now—he reminded her of American preachers on Sunday morning television. He had their kind of passion and need to convince. But what religion was it in his case? Something to do with justice and nature—a desire to safeguard rivers and air, animals and people, from things like sulphur plants.

When Ella had realized how much interest people had in seeing the lawyer, she had asked the other women to bring extra folding chairs and card tables. Bertha had brought puffed wheat cake and Tilda Mueller had brought macaroons, which along with Ella's sandwiches would be enough when they broke for coffee and lunch at the end.

The meeting had been under way an hour, and most people were still holding their copies of the book. It had caused a stir when the lawyer arrived, twenty minutes late, carrying a heavy cardboard box. He'd set it on one of the card tables, ripped the tape off, and started handing out new copies of a book called *Silent Spring*. Ever fearful of expense, Kurt Mueller had asked how much.

"It's something you should read if you're going up against oil companies," Purcell said. "It's a gift."

That was when everyone noticed the lawyer had not come alone. Following behind was a much younger man, introduced as Ross Beattie, another lawyer. He would get around to Ross later, Purcell said, whatever that meant.

Geoff Purcell had started his talk with *Silent Spring*. The book had turned his world upside down, he said; had shown him the path his legal career would take. Up until its publication, there had been a lot of individual stories about pollution, stories like theirs. What Rachel Carson did was gather them together and put a scientific foundation under them. She showed how industrial chemicals were not just hurting individual lives but were tearing huge holes in the very fabric of nature.

To illustrate, he told a story about DDT. The pesticide had been widely used in the fifties—everyone in the room nodded. The chemical was so greatly admired that its inventor had been given a Nobel Prize for science. Then they started to figure out that DDT was causing birds like eagles and falcons to lay eggs that had no hardness to their shells. Many of these birds—even the bald eagle, symbol of America—were headed for extinction.

The people in this room had handled thousands of eggs in their lives. The idea of shells too soft to incubate sickened them. He had their attention.

When he was finished talking about the book, Mr. Purcell started in about Dry Fork—how that community had the same problem with their gas plant as people here did with Aladdin Hatfield. They had been part of the same government study, and when the government claimed to have proven there was no health risk, that was when the people of Dry Fork phoned Purcell and said they wanted to go ahead.

Ella leaned forward in her chair so she could see Tom. His forehead was knotted as he surveyed the room. He would be thinking about all the time his own community had wasted while Dry Fork went ahead.

Purcell looped back in his story and talked about how he had been raised, a city childhood with many trips into the mountains for hiking and fishing. He mentioned a few trips to Europe and Mexico when he was a university student, as if that was a common thing to do. Ella wondered what he would think if he knew that most of them had never been outside this province, except over the border to Montana for a different kind of chocolate bar.

Still, he seemed an earnest man and had them listening—even though some would not look at him. This was a thing Ella did not like about her community: the need to tell people from outside, "We are not impressed by you. Don't think you're any better."

"Where we're at now with the Dry Fork suit is very close to what's called examination for discovery. Discovery is a court process before a judge. It's not a trial. Both sides can ask questions of witnesses under oath, so you get to see the opposing side's evidence.

The judge determines if there's need for a trial or if the two sides might settle out of court."

Purcell raised his hand and brought the tips of the pointer finger and thumb close together. He squinted one eye. "We're about this close to going to discovery. I'll tell you, it was a long shot we'd ever get this far."

He asked if they could keep a secret. Heads nodded.

"I'm going to tell you our biggest challenge at Dry Fork. Even after all our years of work, we have a relatively poor understanding of the plant process. That's pretty basic to getting at how these plants make pollution. The only people who know this stuff work in the industry, and there's no way any of them are going to explain it to farmers or lawyers trying to sue. I tell you that because, if you're going for a lawsuit for yourselves, you should spy on your company and its people every chance you get. Write down every little thing you find out. But I would appreciate if you kept this part to yourselves.

"The better news is that, while the oil industry has been stonewalling us, society itself, in the U.S. and Canada, and in Europe too, has been moving in our direction."

As proof of this, he mentioned two couples from Dry Fork who had been on Peter Gzowski's *This Country in the Morning*—something Tom had heard and talked about frequently at home.

"Canadians all across this nation heard that show," said Geoff. "News exposure like that, and everything else I've told you here tonight, amounts to spadework you people won't have to do. *Now*"—he slapped *Silent Spring* across his open palm, making everyone jump—"I want to hear what *you* have to say."

After a shy silence, Joe Graff asked, "How much has it cost those families down at Dry Fork? So far."

"I can't give out their confidential information, but I can say it's not much considering how long ago we started. It's a new area of law, and it's slow. I'm not asking more than costs at this stage. I can tell you folks, I'm not getting rich at this."

Some laughed; others didn't. Looking at her neighbours, Ella knew which ones would never back the lawsuit. Ones too tight with money; others who would never say a negative word about anyone in power. It was an old-country thing, a fear of soldiers coming in the night and setting fire to your house and barn. Coming to this meeting was about all they could bear. Going to court, being mentioned in the newspapers—not a chance.

But, in this look around the room, she saw something else that caused a cold prickling on her skin. After all these years of believing Tom was chasing his tail, she was suddenly not sure. Several faces in the room had a helpless look, the look you get when you are dragged off your moorings and set afloat. Husbands and wives were facing each other, having silent arguments.

Out of the eleven couples, five seemed to be in that condition. If ten people went for it, plus Bertha and Tom, that would be enough. It sent Ella scrambling in her own mind to think what she would do, how she would think and act—whether or not she really wanted to punish the company.

And money. Whatever Geoff Purcell said about money, the idea that the suit might happen gave Ella a worried feeling. A sum like a thousand dollars might not be much to Purcell, but it was a fortune to them. And she knew Tom would be willing to spend more than she was.

Purcell talked on, something now about a killer fog in Belgium in 1930. Ella started to hear the creaking of folding chairs. She tried to get Tom's attention, but he was riveted to the lawyer, listening to every word.

It was Billy, finally, who saw her waving. She mimed drinking coffee and pointed at his dad. Billy pulled Tom's sleeve and whispered, and Ella started for the kitchen. But when Tom stood up, interrupting Purcell to thank him, Purcell interrupted back, said he had one more thing to say.

"Thing is, folks, though Tom Ryder has suggested you might do me the honour of asking me to represent you if you go up against Aladdin Oil—"

Tom and Bertha clapped. Purcell signalled them to stop.

"No, no, please. The thing is, friends, there is no possibility of that. Frankly," he chuckled, "I can't afford another pollution suit like Dry Fork."

Ella came back and stood behind the chairs. There was a terrible silence in the room. The couples that Ella had seen coming around were sour faced now. Tom had a red stripe across his cheekbones.

"I'm sorry if that's unwelcome news. But something more promising is that Ross Beattie is here tonight. Ross is a brilliant young lawyer. His marks out of law school are some of the highest I've ever seen. Ross was admitted to the bar a couple of years ago, and he has a very strong interest in pollution law. I asked Ross to come with me tonight and speak to you."

The young man stood up and talked. Everyone listened, but it meant nothing, Ella knew. It was not their way to invest money in a man this young. The true sign of what a failure the evening had been was that half the people did not stay for coffee. Some even left the free copies of *Silent Spring* on their chairs.

Tom was not a calm man but sleep usually came to him quickly. It was odd to hear him silent. Maybe she was imagining it, but she thought she could feel tension and anger pulsing out of him.

"You awake, Ella?" he asked after a long time, maybe an hour.

"I'm sorry, Tom. I know you had your hopes up," she said.

But in an excited voice, he said, "I've been thinking about tonight.

Remember Geoff saying the hardest part was knowing how the sulphur plant worked?"

Ella felt a grab of irritation that Tom called him Geoff. Pathetic to assume that he and the lawyer were friends—after Purcell had turned him down flat in front of their neighbours.

"I was thinking about that letter you got from the engineer," Tom said.

"What are you talking about?"

"That letter Lance Evert wrote you. He said things about how our plant worked. About the problems they had while he was here, and how things were done better where he went afterwards." Tom rolled over. She felt his breath on her face.

She wanted to knock this thing out of the air before Tom could say more.

"What if you were to write Evert back and ask him questions? Things about sulphur plants. Get him to go into detail. The kinds of things Geoff wants to know and can't find out."

"Mr. Purcell said he wouldn't help us. That wasn't about information. That was about money. He can't afford us, is what he said. A letter from Lance Evert would serve no purpose."

Tom moved again. He'd lifted himself onto an elbow.

"It would, though. Geoff is close to going to court but doesn't have an expert. If he had an expert, the folks down at Dry Fork could win. What if I was to say to him, we might be able to help you with your expert, if you change your mind about representing us? It would be a trade."

"No," she said.

"No to what?"

"To all of this. To your horse-trading foolishness. Just because Lance wrote us a letter years ago doesn't mean he'd go to court against a sulphur plant."

"Let's get something straight, once and for all. Lance Evert didn't write *us* a letter. He wrote *you* a letter. I think he might go to court for Dry Fork, and for us, if you asked him. Even if he wasn't willing to speak for us in court, we would still have any letters he wrote to you. Inside information."

"That's dishonest."

"There's not much fair or honest in this situation, is there?"

"I can't do what you're asking."

"You mean you won't."

"Who's us, anyway? Dry Fork? Where we don't even live?"

"No. It's your husband and family. Help us. Be loyal to us."

She was suddenly as angry as she'd ever been. "I *am* loyal! If I wasn't, I wouldn't be here."

She turned her back, clung to the bed's edge. She heard nothing but the pulse in her temple tacking against the hard pillow.

PART THREE

Carbon steel mistakenly chosen for repair. Sulphidic corrosion in heat exchanger outlet. Explosion and fire.

Force of gas dislodged particulates. Leak in finned tube. Explosion.

Flammable-gas detectors not used at time of maintenance. Red glow observed in darkness. Flames rippled through catalyst bed. Burn victim.

Outlet piping in hydrogen-treating furnace corroded. Explosion and fire.

Gas valve leak in hydrotreater. Explosion.

Pipe rupture caused hydrogen sulphide release. Explosion and fire.

Carbon steel elbow in hydrogen line fails. Explosion.

Fire in residual hydrotreater. Hydrogen sulphide escaping. Vapour cloud explosion. Four of five deceased were contractors.

1

Waddens Lake

BILL STAYED IN the Chateau Borealis for the first three nights after Donna's visit. In the middle of the third night, he was awakened by a heavy thud. The metal hangers in his closet jangled. The clock read 1:04 a.m. There were shouts in the hallway.

"What the fuck?"

"Earthquake, man!"

Bill had been in Chiapas in 1976 when, across the border, an earthquake destroyed Guatemala City. The hotel bed under him had bobbed and danced like a boat in a wild sea. This was no earthquake.

He got up and stood listening. Cold needles from the electrical outlet sprayed against his bare ankles. He threw on his full winter battle gear, was twisting open the lock on his door when, behind him, his cell phone vibrated on the dresser.

"I just got a call from the plant." Theo Houle.

"I'm at Borealis. It woke me up."

"I'm in Calgary, waiting for a driver to take me to the airport."

"What did they tell you?"

"Don Kruger says the hydrotreater blew up. That doesn't sound right. It must have been a leak. Vapour cloud, maybe."

"Was anyone in the unit?"

Houle blew on his phone. "Somebody outside was knocked off a catwalk. Broke his shoulder. An insulation maintenance crew was scheduled in the hydrotreater unit. It's too dangerous to go in and see. You'll be there soon, right?"

"Leaving now."

"Kruger's in the control room. Guide him through."

Bill dropped the cell into his pocket. In the passage to the front door, crazy exchanges ricocheted off walls. Men as white as mushrooms stood outside their doors. Tattoos, fancy gaunchies.

Insulating maintenance, Bill thought. Johnny Bertram.

Beside the road to the upgrader, the haloed lights of Waddens Village bounced across the lake ice. A slight wind shifted snow snakes on the road. Ahead, the treetops were visible against a nimbus of yellow.

At the main gate, he could see the thrashing flames. Vehicles with emergency flashers bore down on him, and he pulled to the side to wait. First came a fire truck, then an RCMP cruiser, its LEDs stabbing. By their extra light, he saw men lining the outside of the fence. Somebody was marching past them with a clipboard in his mitts. Bill couldn't hear above the sirens but imagined the guy yelling names. Something about the gate was strange. Only half of it was standing. The other half lay twisted in the ditch.

Someone in a snowsuit and traffic vest crossed the road to him. A flashlight beam bored through the windshield into his eyes. Bill buzzed down the window and held up his ID card. Inside the hood was a woman's face. She looked angry, but when her flashlight hit the card, her expression melted.

"How's it going?" he asked.

"Pretty bad."

"There's a guy hurt, right?"

"Knocked off a scaffold. Ambulance took him to Mac."

"Anything about an insulating crew?"

"That, I don't know."

"I better get parked."

"Your unit and parking lot are off limits." She pointed to some vehicles with their grilles to the chain-link. "I'll meet you there."

Bill parked at the end of the line, groped on the floor for his hard hat.

"Don't put it on yet," she said. He'd opened the door and she was standing there, waggling an air mask.

Bill got out of the truck and waited while she straightened the straps.

"Is evacuation complete?"

"I don't think so," she said. "It's a mess. Only the upgrader personnel were supposed to evacuate but some of the contract bosses told their crews to go. Everybody came to the gate at once, and I was supposed to stop them. I got a call from my boss to take down names and check inside."

"Contraband check? You're kidding."

"That's what they asked for. I did it while the other guy took names and swung the gate. Everybody was so pissed off. One guy got out of his truck and yelled right in my face. I told him to get back in. He called me a cunt. He was the one who drove the gate down. Bunch of trucks went through after him."

"Sort of screws your count. Is Don Kruger still in the control room?"

"Follow the ribbons."

The lens of his mask was gletzed, as if a kid had played truck with it in a sandbox. He walked toward the flashing lights. The fire truck was hooking into a hydrant. A flat hose started to fill. Water python. When the spray hit the end and launched, the men holding the nozzle fell backward. The climbing water churned geysers of steam and smoke. Wherever water hit the cement, it turned instantly to ice. Scattered around were bits of insulation, burned back to glass. He pictured Johnny Bertram. Elmo, Shirley's skinny son.

He kept moving toward the control room, aiming for a convergence of yellow fluorescent tape. Gid Couture, festooned with masks, appeared out of one drape of smoke and disappeared into another.

A fresh explosion whacked Bill's ears and the murk became total. Solid flecks were hitting his mask.

A flashlight came burrowing. Another big man, not Gid, pushed Bill in the chest, blocked him backward. The light bored in through the lens.

"Ah shit. Sorry, Mr. Ryder." Bill felt himself being turned around, then a guiding push. The control room door appeared. Bill imagined bodies on the checkerboard tiles, faces mashed into keyboards.

In the bright room, men sat before the banks of computer screens and others stood behind them. Marion was also there, taking sniffer readings in the corners. When Bill pulled his mask off, Henry Shields was looking at him. Bill took a step toward Don Kruger. Kruger's skin was lumpy with old acne. He regarded Bill coldly. Most screens were solid blue. A couple had messages in capital letters explaining that nothing means nothing. The hydrotreater screen was dead.

On his own unit's readout, some lines wiggled faintly, dying sperm under a microscope. Everything to do with sulphur, H_2S, and hydrogen was sending distress messages. NO FEED.

He looked at Henry.

"I got most of it," he said.

Bill rolled up a chair and poked some keys. Most of the upgrader was down, the rest shutting down. Henry had done their unit except for small things that Bill pulled the pin on now. He tried to remember who else was working. He saw Clayton, stabbing keys on his smartphone.

"Don't text me, Clayton. I'm here."

Bill caught Kruger's eye. "Have the government guys arrived yet?"

"Two. They've given us a stop-work order. I think we could keep one train going but they're not interested."

"What about the insulation crew in the unit?"

The change on Kruger's face was slight, a sort of drawing room response, as though Bill were forcing him toward an indelicacy.

"No way to know," he said. "Camera in the hydrotreater unit kakked when it blew. I'm not sending anyone in there till it cools. Government guys can go in if they want."

"How big an explosion?"

"Blew off the walls if that tells you something. The guy who got hurt was outside on a catwalk. Big sheet came flying. Smashed up his shoulder when he landed. Paramedics took him. Something else blew a minute ago. I'm trying to find out what."

"Did the insulation crew sign in at the gate?"

"There was a fuck-up. Gate guy was sleeping. Something was written in his book while he was dozing but nobody can read it. Suggests someone's in here and we don't know who. Could be the insulation guys."

"There must have been a permit."

"Well, of course. It was left at the gate and it isn't there anymore."

Gid came in. He ripped off his mask and took huge gulps of air. He looked on the verge of cardiac arrest. Bill caught his arm, pulled him aside.

"Do you know who the insulation team is? Is it Johnny Bertram?"

"Bertram and his nephew were scheduled. I don't mean they're in there. I mean they were the ones who got the call."

"So nobody saw them before the explosion?"

"Nobody I talked to has been near the hydrotreater in three hours. The insulation guys could be there or not. There was a screw-up at the—"

"I heard. I also saw somebody mowed down the outside gate."

"Right. If Bertram was in and left with that crowd, we wouldn't know either. I tried his cell. It doesn't ring."

Bill and Gid were near the control room window. There were two hoses now, and they could see them arcing water. Gid tried to pull away; Bill held on.

"What's the wind direction?"

"Hardly any," Gid said.

"But what?"

"Southwest, zero to three."

"That's straight for the village. Has anyone checked it?"

Gid flared. "What do you think, Bill? Friggin' thing blew a half-hour ago."

"If the wind speed is three or less, and the lake's two kilometres, and a half-hour's gone, you could still get there before the gas."

"What gas?"

"Fuck off. The eighty per cent H_2s that must have blown out of the hydrotreater."

"I'm not sending anybody until things are sorted here."

"Then I'll go."

Gid's shoulders dropped. "I don't think you have to."

"Who's the contact there? For evacuation?"

"I don't remember. Woman. Her name's in my office."

"Marie Calfoux?"

"Yeah, that one."

"I want you to phone her and tell her to get the village ready to go."

"I don't have her number."

Bill took out his cell phone, found Marie's number, wrote it on Gid's parka sleeve. Next, he went to Kruger and asked what his plans were. Kruger stared out the window and said nothing.

"Theo told me to back you up. That's why I'm asking."

Kruger rattled off some standard procedure. The only gap was the village. Bill told him he was going there now to evacuate it.

"The fuck you are! Theo didn't order that."

"*I'm* ordering it."

"That'll make this a bigger fuck-up. Public fuck-up."

"You can't assume H_2S isn't moving that way. Wind direction says it is."

"You think you know something, I guess."

"My assessment is that there's a reasonable doubt about safety over there."

"Fuck!" Kruger turned away again. His phone rang and he grabbed it.

While Kruger was talking on the phone, Bill got out. Back in the smoke and steam, he ran for the parking area. His mask was off and that was stupid. When he got where he could see, there was a crew bus among the trucks and cars along the fence. There was nobody inside. The door was unlocked; keys in the ignition. It was still warm when Bill climbed in. The engine started easily. At the gate, the woman he had talked to earlier held up her arm. He cranked open the door and told her he needed the bus to evacuate Waddens Village.

The bus was huge on the ploughed main street. All the house lights were on. The community centre was lit up inside. Bill parked there and left it running.

The main hall was white-lit from a bank of hanging fluorescents. Marie came from the back, arms full of air masks. She had on a purple parka.

"Thought it might be you," she said.

She told him she'd ordered the town's younger people to wake the old ones.

"We're going to be short of cars."

"I brought a crew bus."

He tried to take some of the masks but she shrugged him off.

"There's a bin back there. Bring the tanks."

The lid of the bin was open. Marie had tossed things out to get at what she needed. In the swath of stuff on the floor, he spotted sniffer boxes, and stuffed some in his pockets.

Back outside, Bill armed one of the sniffers and carried it down an outhouse path. Standing in a drift, he broke the tip and aimed the tube at the plant. After the tube took its breath, he held his pen flashlight over it, and felt relief and disappointment in equal measure. The tube was reading clean. No evidence that what he was doing was necessary.

By the time he got back, Marie was guiding the last elder up the bus steps. All the masks were distributed. The trucks and vans had already left. Someone had turned on the interior lights, and Bill counted eight heads, all old folks.

"That everybody?" he asked Marie.

She was looking at a list. "All accounted for."

"Where are we going?" He sat in the driver's seat.

Marie was standing on the steps. "The evacuation plan that Dion gave me says McKay but everyone here has relatives closer," she said.

"Where, then?"

"Six of these people want to go to St. Bernadette. Two have relatives in the bush near there." She came the rest of the way in and sat. "I'll help you find it."

An old lady the size of a child was worrying about her cat. Marie ran to her house and got it: a hissing, scratching evil until the old woman hushed it like a baby.

"Turn the light out," said the only man. Marie snapped a toggle above Bill's head.

The village of St. Bernadette was not far. Marie had phoned ahead to the families of the six who wanted to be dropped there. The rendezvous was a wooden church, and the hand-off went smoothly. The last two were on a bush road just outside. The old man was first. He got out and followed a curved path to a door with a light over it. The last was the woman with the cat. A lady wearing a ski jacket over her nightie stood in the doorway as Bill helped the woman up the shovelled path. At the door, the cat leapt and raked Bill's hand, skittered through the door. The old lady shrugged. "Can't do anything with her. She doesn't like white people."

Then it was Marie and Bill in the hollow bus.

"Where do you want to go?" he asked her.

"You tested at the village before we left? What did it say?"

"Clean. It might not be now."

"Let's go see."

They did not talk on the trip back. Marie sat on the first bench seat, leaned toward the windshield, probably worried that he'd hit a moose.

Bill had lots of sniffer tubes, so he tested the last two kilometres into Waddens. He tested again near Marie's house. That tube showed sulphur dioxide. No hydrogen sulphide. They continued on to Marie's path.

"You haven't told me what happened," she said.

"Didn't Gid tell you when he phoned?"

"Whoever phoned said there was a possibility of poisonous gas and someone was coming to help us evacuate—as a precaution."

"There was an explosion, in the unit called the hydrotreater. Hydrogen gas is reactive. If it gets loose, it often explodes."

"And it's poisonous?"

"Not hydrogen. It was hydrogen sulphide that I was worried about. A couple of lines in the unit would have been full of H_2S. The fire was still burning when I left."

"Why do you think the gas didn't get here?"

"The fire was hot. With not much wind, maybe the H_2S converted to sulphur dioxide in the fire. Or maybe it went somewhere else."

"Will you know for sure when you get back?"

"It's not possible to know that."

They continued to sit in the bus, the engine drumming. Bill pulled out his cell and pressed the power button.

Marie laughed. "It was off?"

"Wouldn't have made much difference. Looks like the battery's dead."

She held out her own cell. He poked the number for the control room. Kruger answered, and Bill asked for Houle.

"He's gone. Back to Mac."

"Does that mean the fire's out?"

"Contained."

"What about the insulation crew?"

"John Bertram phoned at three to say his truck broke down."

"Whew. That's a relief. So who signed in at the gate?"

"Some prick fessed up he'd done it as a joke. He saw the gate guard sleeping, so he took the work permit off his desk and scribbled something unreadable in the book."

"Good news all around, then."

"Not really. Did you get your village moved to safety?" Kruger changed voice for the last part. Singsong. Fruity.

"We did."

"You planning on returning the crew bus? Some men would like to go home."

"Shortly."

"Something else. Houle wants you to phone him first thing. Phone him at home at seven, is what he said. He's pissed."

Bill looked at his watch. It was nearly six a.m. "What's his problem?"

"What do you think?"

"Any further instructions?"

"Just the crew bus. No, wait. Mr. Houle said you're not to talk to reporters."

Bill looked for the off button. Marie reached and took the phone.

"It sounds like it's safe for you to stay here," Bill told her. "Fire's under control. Nobody died."

"What are you going to do?"

"Return the bus, then phone my annoyed boss at seven. Guess I'll go to the camp and try to sleep for an hour."

"You can come back here. I'll make breakfast."

"That would be great."

They didn't eat. They went to bed. She was beautiful and smooth, and moved with grace. She rolled on top of him and rode him to the end of both of them. They were lying together under the warm duvet when Bill bounced up and cursed.

"What's wrong?"

"I forgot to phone Houle."

She felt for her phone on the bedside table and gave it to him. When he got through, Houle was mad about the lateness of the call—and everything else. He didn't specifically mention the evacuation of the village. He said he was coming back to the plant and wanted Bill in his office at two sharp.

"What was that about?"

"Not sure. Boss wants me in his office at ten."

"That's hours from now," she said and drew him down to her.

Bill was still feeling dazzled when he entered the anteroom of Houle's office.

"Someone looks happy," said Paula, and he adjusted his face before going in.

A half-hour later, when he returned to the icy, smoke-smelling morning, he was dazzled in a different way. He was unemployed.

In the control room, he told Henry that he was in charge until further notice. He went to his office to collect some things. He had to come out and ask for a box. When Henry gave him one, he happened to look up and see Clayton's thyroid eyes boring at him.

The picture of his sisters. The picture of his kids. They could keep his consolation golf trophy and the mail in his inbox. He zipped the computer and its cords into the travel bag. What was left on his desk was the corrosion maintenance plan. Fuck it. He put his keys and ID on top of it. There was a knock on his door. The SS-looking security man was waiting.

"Do you need your keys, Mr. Ryder?"

"They're on my desk."

"I'm thinking I should take your computer."

"You're a little ahead of yourself, Hansen."

In his car, he phoned Marie.

"Leave with pay until further notice," he said.

"What does that mean?"

"I think it means they're on their way to firing me. I'll tell you more later."

"Why not come now? Sounds like you have the time."

"I'd be poor company."

"I can live with a bit of that."

———

Marie was making the breakfast they hadn't had earlier. She was dressed formally, which he did not understand.

"Thought they couldn't do without you," she said from the stove.

"Apparently, they think they can."

"Who's taking your place?"

"Guy named Henry Shields. My junior engineer."

"Caesar is dead; long live Caesar?"

"Henry's a good guy."

"Really?"

"They're not all assholes."

"What reason did they give for putting you on leave?" she asked.

"Evacuating the village."

Marie looked surprised. He hadn't told her before that he was the one who called it.

He told her the rest of the story, starting with Houle on the phone telling him he was to guide Kruger. But when Bill had sat down with Houle, they'd immediately argued about what "guiding Kruger" meant.

"I did not give you carte blanche. You know that."

"Since when do we need permission to keep communities from getting gassed?"

"That assessment of risk is your opinion. Shared by no one."

"There was lots of H_2s in those lines. You don't know what left that area when it exploded."

"Neither do you."

Back and forth. There was no wind. There was a bit of wind. It was blowing in the direction of the village. It probably missed the village. Somewhere in the middle it got nasty. Houle said Bill was taking sides against the company, *as usual*. Bill called him gutless.

"I'm not going to argue with someone who's lost his temper—
and his objectivity," Houle said after that.

"You're objective? Don't make me laugh."

In the story, as told to Marie, Bill left a part out: where Houle
had said, "I can hardly ignore that the same woman's name comes up
every time we have this discussion about company loyalty."

Houle had noticed—or someone had—that Bill's phone call to
the plant after the evacuation was made from Marie's phone.

"I did not choose Marie Calfoux to be the emergency contact at
the village."

That was when Houle told Bill he was on leave, effective immediately. He paused before adding, "With pay," so Bill would know
what a thin string he was dangling from.

"And if I don't accept?"

"We'll dismiss you for cause."

"They're trying to keep you quiet," Marie said when he finished.

"That's the plan."

"And will you?"

"I'm not giving a good demonstration right now."

She laughed. "Will you go to the media, though?"

"I don't even know if they'd be interested. But I won't take the
company's money and talk to the press too."

She might have been disappointed. In any case, she let the subject drop. They ate the big breakfast she had prepared: fried eggs,
thick bacon, toast and honey.

When they were finished eating, she asked, "Is it likely to happen again? That explosion?"

"I don't know. My opinion, for what it's worth, is that they need to
do a kind of maintenance they're not doing now. A continuous search
for changes at possible corrosion points. Hydrogen got out of the pipes

somewhere and caused an explosion. That's a fact. They have to investigate how."

"So is it safe for me to live here or not?"

"A week ago, I'd have said it was. Now, not so much."

She checked her watch. "I have to be somewhere at one-thirty. I job-share as a teacher at an elementary school in McKay. It's someone else's day but she has a dental appointment this afternoon."

"I didn't even know you had a job."

"Thought I was a shiftless Indian, I guess."

"I don't know what I thought."

"I have a few jobs. I do a newsletter." She nodded at the bank of computer equipment.

"What sort of newsletter?"

She laughed. "Think you've been under surveillance? Don't worry. It's for an association of Native-owned companies in the oil sands. They're so pro-industry, it's sickening."

Bill was finding it impossible to be here, to even keep it in his mind that they had made love all morning. He attempted an apology.

"I'm guessing you're not used to being fired. How about you come out again for dinner on Friday. You can phone me if you don't feel like it. I'm hoping we have lots of time."

She got up and gathered the dishes. When she came back, she ran her hand through his hair.

"I like you, Bill Ryder." She hurried to the bathroom. Yelled back, "Go now, okay?"

On Highway 63, he could not breathe to the bottom of his lungs. When Marie appeared in his mind, he shook his head to dislodge her. She's fine, she's lovely. He wanted to be in her bed again—but not now. Something unidentified was pouring down his throat, fanning to his fingers.

By the time he crossed the bridge into the city, it was like an iron loop was being pulled out of his chest. Late afternoon, still daylight. A spot in the casino parking lot stood waiting.

2

AT THE END OF AUGUST, Ella and Tom drove Billy to Calgary to begin university. Billy spent the trip pointlessly arguing with his father about the pickup truck. Since he would be living in residence, Tom said he didn't need it. They could talk about it again at Christmas.

The sight of the residence room that Billy would be sharing with a stranger made Ella cry. So small and odd smelling. Once they had all his things inside, Billy kept looking out the window and out the door; it was clear he wanted them to go. The drive back to the farm in the dark was silent and eternal. Nothing but the highway lines and the two funnels of yellow beating back the darkness. Ella was faint with hunger but let the service stations loom up and slide by.

After twenty-five years of children, the emptiness in the house became worse as the weeks crept by. A cat's yowl, a sudden wind gust—things like that grabbed Ella by the shoulders and twisted like God. Work was a blessing, but when the work stopped, the problems in the house quivered and strained, and the lack of conversation had no excuse. She crocheted, knitted, quilted, bought patterns and made the girls and herself dresses. The Singer electric sizzled miles of seams until it was too hot to touch. Hearing from Billy in a phone call that other students were wearing macramé belts, she found out what macramé was and knotted three of them, with embedded beads and dangly ends. It would go well with his Lauren Bacall hair. "Why three?" he'd asked her over the phone when he got them in the mail. "You can wear one," she told him, "and sell the other two."

Ella preferred not to sit at the table with Tom as he rolled and smoked his cigarettes, read a page of his Christmas book and shut it again; doodled on the back of a Co-op flyer. She had come to detest the smell of cigarette smoke. Surely there was enough infor-mation nowadays about tobacco and cancer that she should not have to argue.

Tom seldom talked to her about the plant. He behaved as if she had forbidden the topic. Things still came in the mail from Purcell, and Tom would write back immediately. If she asked him what was going on, as he typed or licked an envelope shut, he would say Dry Fork was close to its settlement. They had been close for years, and Ella doubted it would happen. Tom's own lawsuit had died the night Purcell announced he would not work for them. What Tom had done since was help Dry Fork.

Everything missing from their marriage seemed to reside in the letters Tom had wanted and that Ella had refused to write. It had begun to sicken her to be touched by him, even when he rolled toward her in the night and his heavy arm fell against her hip. The rare times when he tried to kiss her neck while she worked at the sink or counter, she always moved away. In those moments of revul-sion, Lance's image would flash.

When she wrote to or phoned her children, these were the things she did not say. Donna and Billy were oblivious anyway. Donna was involved in her job and travels. She would ask about her father the way you'd ask about a dog. How's Dad's lawsuit? Does King still chase cars? Billy seemed to believe the purpose of a phone call home was to give a report: how school was going; what he did with his time. When she told her son about the farm work his father was doing, or his worsening smoker's cough, Billy had no comment. If she were to say, "Dad and I had a nasty bout of cholera last week," he might reply, "Oh yeah? And how was that?"

But it was a good thing Billy and Donna were so interested in their lives—that they had lives to be interested in! Ella was happy for them and didn't want the state of things at home to dampen their pleasure.

Jeannie was not so easy to deceive. She taught school in a B.C. town. She was still engaged to Hal. Though they'd been in the same teaching program at university, Hal had found more lucrative work with the Department of Forestry. It was Hal's hometown Jeannie taught in, and the family she boarded with were close friends of his parents. Jeannie might as well be married, except that she wasn't and was in no hurry to be. The length of the engagement was already a topic of gossip, and not just in B.C. Concern about it had spread to Tom and Ella's community.

Sometimes Jeannie's calls to Ella were only small talk, but when she called from the pay phone outside the hockey arena, that meant she was miserable. During those calls, she always cried. "It's like my life is already over," she would sob, and Ella would say, "The reason you're having an engagement is so you can decide these things. You don't have to marry Hal." That would prompt Jeannie to list Hal's good qualities. "It's not his fault, Mom. It's not him." And Ella would say, "You have a life too. It's just starting and it's just as important as his. Don't throw it away."

The new rotary phone in the Ryders' house was on the wall beside the kitchen table, where Tom stayed sitting after supper. The hockey arena calls always came in the late evening, and Tom could not help but hear. After Ella hung up, she saw her husband's ears flame. "I don't know why you'd tell her that," he said once.

In Tom's estimation, Hal was the perfect husband for Jeannie: dependable, conservative, sturdily built. He had a good job that would make for a stable future. Hal was the kind of old-before-his-time hard worker that Tom's generation of men could not help but admire.

Ella said, "If we had a private phone, you wouldn't know what I say to my daughter."

"Since it's a party line," he replied, "the neighbours know too."

Even more difficult was the fact that Jeannie, because of her own pain, was attuned to Ella's.

"Something's wrong between you and Dad, isn't it?"

"Dad's fine." If Jeannie kept pressing, Ella would say, "Dad's right here. Why don't you talk to him?"

As that Christmas approached, neither Donna nor Billy would confirm they were coming home. Finally, at the last minute, Donna phoned to say they were. They arrived in Donna's Volkswagen on Christmas Eve. Jeannie and Hal went to midnight mass in B.C. before driving to Alberta on Christmas morning.

The Ryders didn't open their presents until late afternoon, after Jeannie and Hal had arrived and after Tom and Billy had fed the cattle. Then came the turkey dinner that the women worked on together. Even Donna, who claimed not to cook, had peeled and chopped.

A smooth, nostalgic event, marred only by Hal's repeating that the plant smell made his food taste like rotten eggs. He then apologized at length. "It's just I know what a good cook you are, Ella. I feel I'm missing out."

On Boxing Day, Hal wanted to leave early so they could make the whole trip in daylight. Tom said that was good sense. Jeannie announced she wasn't going back. Though Hal had to start work right away, she did not have to teach until after New Year's. She'd like to spend a few days at home, she said.

"I don't get it," said Hal. "You want me to come back and get you?"

"No," Jeannie said. "Mom can drive me."

That caused a look to shoot from Tom to Hal. They suspected a women's plot.

Tom started objecting on the basis of safety.

Finally Ella said, "Have you forgotten Jeannie and I can drive?"

"If you have to put chains on . . ."

"We'll get somebody to help us."

"What about coming back? You'll be alone."

"If there's bad weather, I'll stay longer."

The two men were on the couch, staring at the women. The similarity in their expressions made Ella and Jeannie laugh.

Hal went back on Boxing Day. Next morning, Donna said it was time for them to go too. When she and Billy were ready, Tom suddenly said Billy could take the pickup truck.

That left only Jeannie, who sat in the living room for two whole days, staring out the south window at the mountains. On the third day, Tom asked her if she would feed cows with him. She put on some old clothes and went. Ella worried that Tom would use the time to force the issue of Hal and break whatever peace Jeannie was finding. But when they came back, both looked happy. Tom was always pleased to have one of his children along when he worked. Jeannie was delighted by the crazy-eyed eagerness of the cows she'd dragged bales through. "They pressed in so close!" It was a detail she had forgotten.

On New Year's Eve, Tom asked if they would like to go to the dance at Hatfield Corners, but both women said no. Tom, who had always complained about the ritual of the New Year's dance, looked disappointed. They watched New Year's Eve on TV, each with a drink in hand. Though all three were yawning before midnight, they stuck it out. Ella's and Tom's New Year's kiss, forced on them by Jeannie's presence, was awkward. Ella had to steel herself not to shift away.

The instant that Ella and Jeannie were alone in the car, Jeannie began to confide. Teaching in Hal's hometown had made her beloved by practically everyone. To the children of the town, she was beautiful Miss Ryder who was going to marry the top scorer on the hockey team. The little girls all wanted to be Jeannie; the little boys loved her.

Hardly anyone in town could see Jeannie without sentiment turning their faces to pudding. God, how she hated it! She wanted to curse like a sailor, to tell them she was joining a commune in the Slocan where clothing was optional. Whether Hal was a good man or a bad man had become beside the point. She needed to go as far away as she could imagine.

Ella had not intended to talk about her own problems, but, later that night, something about sharing her daughter's bed caused it to begin. After she'd admitted she was not happy at all with her marriage with Tom, Jeannie said she had guessed some of it over the years.

"But it seemed like you were getting on better. Back when Dad was building onto the house?"

"It was better then," she admitted.

"Is it about the plant?" Jeannie asked.

Ella stayed silent for a moment, to make sure she knew the answer.

"I'm not sure it will make sense to you, but it *is* about the plant, even though your dad seldom talks to me about that. It keeps going on and on inside him. He fiddles with the Dry Fork lawsuit, though it can't do us any good. He won't let it go, and he blames everybody for the fact that he has no lawsuit himself."

"He blames you?"

"Yes."

"Why you?"

Ella found she could not say it. "He blames everyone. I just happen to be the one who lives there."

"Does he get mad at you?"

"No. But he's always mad about it in some way. Cursing away to himself."

The plant had changed him, she said, had made him lose faith in himself. The lawsuit was his attempt to get his dignity back. When he couldn't start a suit, he'd become worse. As she explained it to Jeannie, Ella felt a sympathy for Tom she had not felt in a long time. She also felt guilt, for not telling what else lay behind it, the part that was her doing.

"What are you going to do? Will you leave Dad?"

"I don't see how I can go on. But I don't think I'll leave right away."

Saying that made Ella shudder. She imagined Tom standing on a street corner with a suitcase. Where on earth would he go? Where would he live? He wasn't even a drinker, and what did single men do at night if they didn't go to a tavern?

The thought came back to her that Tom, handsome for his age, would attract a woman. At that moment, her only thought was that she hoped he would find someone nice.

"You don't have to decide everything this minute, Mom," Jeannie said, squeezing her hand.

"Maybe I won't go anywhere," said Ella.

Jeannie turned on the light and took a tissue out of the box on the night table. She held it out to Ella and pulled another to wipe her own eyes.

"Look at the two of us," Ella said.

"Maybe I'll tell Hal I can't stand to be without my mother," said Jeannie, with a wet smile. "We'll move in together, you and me. Dad can come for supper."

"He'd like that," said Ella, and they laughed hard at the sad absurdity of it all.

3

Fort McMurray

THE PHONE IN HIS CONDO was ringing when he entered. He wanted to let it go but feared it could be trouble: his sisters, his children, Marie. He was too sick to talk after so many hours on the machines, but he picked up anyway.

"You cared, Billy."

"What?"

"You cared that I might be dead. Burned to a cinder."

He recognized Johnny's voice.

"Yes, I did."

"I'm touched. I really am. And you got canned."

Bill tried to reply and nothing came out.

"It's big news, Billy. Thousands come and go in the tar sands but it's still news when a big boss gets the frozen boot."

"They're calling it leave with pay."

"That's a nice way of putting it. Caring and gentle."

"You phoned to cheer me up. I appreciate it. But I don't think it's possible right now."

"Okay, Billy. You've got my number."

It felt like three in the morning but was nine at night. Six hours in the casino proved Einstein's theory. Time could bend. In a casino, it almost ran backward.

"What can I do now?" he asked himself, and the options spun and made an electric sizzle as they rolled to a halt.

TV. I don't think so.

They rolled again.

Book. He was sure he could not make his eyes do that. It would look like there were ceiling fans spinning between his head and the page.

Eat. Something else he could not do.

Alcohol. He splashed some whisky in a glass and sucked it through his teeth.

A Pollyanna in his brain was advocating that he call Marie. That would be lovely.

Why do you sound like that?

Like what?

Like your teeth are chattering? Like you have malaria. Like a zombie is eating your head.

The phone rang again. He picked it up and said hello a couple of times. There was nothing there but breathing. He was about to hang up when a grinding cough blasted his ear. More coughing followed, but the sound was muffled.

Lance Evert asked, "Were you there when it blew?"

"Close. Arrived half an hour after."

"Paper said. Only one man hurt. That true?"

"I believe so. Fellow was knocked off a catwalk and broke his shoulder. How are *you*?"

"Let's not talk. About that." Lance cleared a strangle. "Been doing research. Refinery accidents."

The voice sounded like the creaking of an old saddle. Bill tried to understand the rhythm.

"You on oxygen?"

"You want to hear?"

"Yeah, sure. Go ahead."

"Found twenty. Accidents. On the internet. Fires and explosions. Usually the. Hydrotreater. I've got to rest. Don't hang up."

The line was quiet. The sound of air sucking in, wheezing out.

"Billy?"

"I'm here."

"Two safety guys. In the States. Call it an epidemic. The oil's worse now. Heavy and sour. Using H_2S. To make hydrogen. Call it hydrogen attack."

The long string of talk had to be paid for with coughing. Then came not silence or breathing but something like surf in a bathtub.

"I'll send it. Sorry." The line went dead.

Bill made coffee, and thought in blurts like Lance's speech.

He was glad Lance had hung up before he had to tell him about losing his job. But he was sorry not to have told him how right he'd been about hydrotreaters; right to warn Bill and to get their organization to spread the word. Amazing that he could do this when half dead.

Bill fell down on the couch. He shifted around so the back of his head was on an armrest. He had a sudden chill and dragged the old afghan over his legs and up to his chin. He began to shake all over.

"What in God's name am I doing to myself? Why can't I stop this?"

He longed for anyone, even the Voice, to answer. But the Voice was never interested in him afterwards. Seduction, not pillow talk.

While he whimpered and simpered, and wished himself dead, the self he would be tomorrow did not sympathize either. He wanted to be that person now, but many shitty hours had to be weathered first. Hours like this one that bent the other way, the seconds snapping off like matchsticks with time shivering in between.

Somehow sleep found him, put him away for a few rounds of the clock. He woke in the night as he usually did after a gambling binge, wakefulness caused as if by stock prod, a four-alarm fire, a gas plant exploding. He walked the apartment in the dark, fast and crashing into things, talking to himself. Even at this stage he saw that he was better than before.

When it was finally morning, the phone rang again. It was Jeannie. He'd been asleep on the couch and had to stop himself from asking her the date and time.

"Did you tell your kids?"

"What? That I've been fired?"

"You've been fired?"

"Oh. You don't know."

"You can tell me, but first I want to know if you've phoned your kids and told them you didn't die in the explosion."

"Isn't that a bit like phoning to say I haven't frozen to death over winter?"

"It is *not* the same. The accident is all over the news."

"What?"

"Your plant blew up. A village had to be evacuated. I saw it on the CBC national news."

"Holy hell. What did they say?"

"There were pictures of the plant, from a distance. You couldn't see much. A government guy said it was all shut down pending investigation. They interviewed people from the Native village. The announcer said the company had been contacted but refused an interview."

"Do you remember who they interviewed in the village?"

"There were two. An old man who said he was taken away in a bus, and a nice-looking woman."

"What did the woman say?"

"That someone came to evacuate the village after the explosion because he thought hydrogen sulphide might reach there. She said someone else came later and said there was no danger."

"Did she name me?"

"She didn't name anyone. Which one were you?"

"I decided they should evacuate and took a bus over."

"You got fired for that?"

"The evacuation wasn't authorized by anyone but me. Boss didn't like it, so I'm on leave with pay."

"Those assholes. You said you were fired. Is that what leave with pay means?"

"Leave with pay is to keep me quiet. I'll be fired later."

"I don't know what to think of that, but you have to phone your kids."

"Okay."

"You won't do it, will you?"

"I'll do it."

"Are you on a binge or something?"

"Sort of."

"You're not twenty-five, you know. You could damage yourself. Donna said you'd met a woman. Are you in touch with her?"

"No."

"Why not?"

"I can't talk about it right now."

He made a pot of coffee and drank cup after cup. He slammed his eyes and tried to see black. What rose instead were the spinning wheels. Stars, cherries, peaches, plums, cartoon dogs, rhinos, six-guns, leprechauns, rockets, wildebeest, sports cars, harps, cartoon fish, cowboy boots, musical notes, sevens, sheriff's stars, birds, wine glasses, camels, mansions, tigers, hookahs, snakes, palm trees, surfers, bowler hats, crowns, knives, cannons, roasts of beef, pirate trunks spilling gold.

He looked at his watch. It was nearing ten. The casino would be open soon. He saw himself there. He would go out for breakfast first. Maybe read about himself in the paper over his bacon and eggs.

He thought about Marie talking to reporters. He thought about his old ideas of her. The Mata Hari, milking him for info. That she was talking to national news reporters had to make his job situation worse—if it could be worse. But was that her problem? He thought not.

He groped around for some kind of emotional response. Hurt. Anger. Love. There was nothing there but the desire to get back in front of a machine, pumping twenties, changing lines, hitting and hitting and hitting. Pigeon and disc.

Another casino day, another bad night in which his gambler's alarm went off at five. This was the hour of no defence, when his mind chopped excuses like Jackie Chan did bricks.

He got up and, without thinking, fetched the binder from the storage closet, where he had put it after Donna left. He sat on the couch in his bathrobe, with the thing heavy on his knees.

"I will not open it," he said to the shadow-filled air, to the frost on the balcony door. "I don't need to."

He didn't need to because he could see it all in his head. He might even be able to recite some of it, especially episodes of the Stink Diary. There were letters received and carbons of letters sent, to and from the lawyer mostly. And mimeographs of research papers on sulphur pollution, wind plumes, weather inversions—and the long-term effects of sulphur dioxide on lungs and heart. These he knew doubly: from when he had been Dry Fork's secret helper and later after Tom died and he was back living on the farm by himself.

"I don't need to read any of it," he said again to the air, to Donna in absentia. "I don't need to, and I don't have to. And I will not."

It had to be near the weekend but he did not know the day. He'd come back from the casino after spending ten hours to break even.

Maybe a hundred dollars lost but that was all. He had eaten a casino steak somewhere along the line. Wolfed it in fear that someone would take his machine.

"What do I need?" he asked, now thoroughly used to talking to himself out loud. He was still trying to answer when the doorbell rang. It wasn't the buzzer from the lobby but his actual doorbell. For a second he had the notion it was Donna.

He could only see the back of a coat, a fur collar. The person turned, and it was Marie. Friday. He was supposed to be at her place for dinner. He snapped back the locks and pulled open the door.

"Marie, I'm sorry. I should have phoned."

He stopped when he saw her cheeks were wet. He stood aside and let her in.

"Do you want to sit in the living room?"

"I don't want to sit. I have something to say and I want to be quick."

She stayed standing in the front hall. Purple coat. White scarf. She brushed her eyes and cheeks with a handkerchief.

"You and me," she said. "I was enjoying it. But now I have to stop it. Neither of us has been honest. I don't even mind that, it's probably natural, but one of the things you didn't tell me is something I can't . . . I do have to sit down. This is making me sick."

She passed him and sat on the couch. He leaned against the wall.

"Yesterday, James Beaudry came to my house. You met James at the community hall. I told a lie about him then. I said he was my cousin. He's my ex-husband and friend. He told me he saw you in the casino every day this week, ever since you left my place. James is a gambling addict. He knows one when he sees one.

"I've had two husbands. James is the second and my favourite. He was very nice to me. When he started gambling, I worried but I let it go. I figured he'd see the stupidity and waste of it and stop. But he kept on. It went out of control. We had a house in McMurray. I'd paid my half but it was in his name. More than half the mortgage was paid off when he took that deal where you borrow cash against home equity. Before I figured it out, he'd lost it all. That house was where all our savings were.

"I left him. I had to. I had kids at home. It's taken me ten years of working two jobs to get back to where I was before James took it away."

She stood up and rewrapped her scarf.

"I'll never go through that again. I'm thankful you're not talking, giving me reasons or making light of it. And no promises. It doesn't matter to me what you feel or how you rationalize this thing to yourself."

She walked past him and out the door. He closed it behind her.

4

Ryder Farm, 1973

WINTER WAS FINALLY SURRENDERING its hold. When Tom awoke in Billy's bed, he could hear Ella in the kitchen downstairs, shaking down the ashes, making a new fire in the trash burner. He got up and peeled his combinations down to the waist. In the dresser mirror, he posed like a weightlifter on the back of an old comic.

"You are not old," he whispered. "Whatever you are, old's not it."

On his way out to his morning chores, he passed through Ella's kitchen quickly. He said good morning but tried not to see her. Outside, he went behind the woodshed and had a piss. He could smell the plant right through the urine. It had started stinking again, not surprising considering the relic it had become. He tried never to talk about the plant to Ella, but she had stated an opinion recently. She believed it stank because Bert Traynor had retired. Unpleasant though he was, he'd had some magic that was missing since. But, though the plant smelled, Tom could not remember the last time it had made him dizzy or sick.

He got on with his chores, shovelling chop into buckets, pumping water, carrying buckets. The work spread a paste of calm through him that was as good as the first smoke of the day. In recent years, when farmers had bought tractors with enclosed cabs, Tom saw them in their fields behind plastic windows and knew he would never own such a thing. He wanted the wind and the sun burning through his shirt. He even took pleasure in the bite of cold.

When Ella called him for breakfast, tension clamped in his chest right away. He'd been thinking of quitting tobacco, but he stood and rolled a smoke. He needed this one before he went in and probably another after he ate. Mealtimes were hard. Ella's conversation was often about him digging at his shoulders and neck, rubbing his chest. She wanted him to tell her what it felt like, why he was doing it. He told her he was only working out some tightness, and he never said the discomfort came from how things stood. Whatever the feeling was, it was not anger. His anger was spent.

When Ella and Jeannie had left for B.C. on New Year's Day, Tom had stood in the yard, watching the car's rear bumper with blurred eyes.

"I have lost her," he had said aloud, perhaps the first time he'd understood it was true.

The attentive dog had pressed harder against his knee. For some time, Tom didn't move, quiet on the outside but full of commotion. The arguments he'd had with Ella, the ones about the plant and Lance Evert, blew out of him. His craving for a lawsuit ran around inside his chest looking for an exit too. All kinds of things struggled out of him that day, and a hollow formed that felt bigger than the rest of him.

After Ella had phoned to extend her time at Jeannie's, Tom started writing letters to her. The first attempts were long-winded, heavy on explanation. Gradually they worked their way down to simpler pleadings.

Dear Ella,

I know you're thinking about ending our marriage. I have
thought of it as hopeless too. If we could go back where we were
before the plant came, it was not perfect but it was good. There
was love for sure. I don't know where it went or why but I would
like to try again. I have been hard to live with. I'm sorry I asked
you for that letter.

Sometimes, if he managed to convince himself that Ella and he
could make a fresh start, the writing excited him. Later, when he saw
the words on paper, the hollow inside him said the time for that was
past. He'd thought "blood running cold" was just a saying, but each
time his hopes crashed, that was what he felt: a cascade of cold falling through him.

Every written word went into the trash burner before bed.

By the time Ella drove into the yard, Tom had cleaned the house
as best he could. There was no letter and no plan to say anything. He
would change his actions and that would be enough—or it wouldn't
be enough. He had filled the kettle with water, and as soon as he
heard the car, he turned on the burner. Thawed scones were on the
table, on a plate inside a plastic bag.

He hurried outside and took Ella's suitcase as she was lifting it
from the trunk. He was going to carry it to their bedroom, but she
took it from him. When she returned to the kitchen, she had a work
dress on. She reached her apron down from its hook, put it over her
head. By now, Tom understood that all the writing, thinking, and
planning were not going to change what was coming. While she
made tea, he sat at the table, smoked and waited.

Ella set the teapot on its mat, then turned her chair to face him.
Her hands were fists in her lap. She said she could not go on the way

things had been. She had not made up her mind what to do, but, while she was figuring it out, she would feel better and rest easier if Tom would sleep in Billy's room.

The weather changed, warmed, but the hills stayed brown. It was the windy time that pushes real spring ahead of itself. The upstairs-downstairs agreement continued, was routine, but a deadline approached. Though Billy had muttered all winter about not wanting to work at home this summer, he had called on his final day of classes to say he would be back in three weeks. Tom would have to clear out of Billy's bedroom—and not just across the hall into the girls' room. Things would have to be explained, and to explain anything to Billy, they had to know the answers themselves.

Every day closer to their son's return, the knots in Tom's guts and chest pulled tighter. He could barely stand to be in the house and worked later and later outside. He ran out of things to repair, grease, and sharpen, and at times just stood at his shop bench staring at the split window. Other times, he sat on the cracked saddle he had not ridden or oiled for years, where it hung over the iron seat of a pedal grindstone. Sometimes the smell of dirt, weeds, and oil irritated him. Other times, he cherished the stink as something he might lose.

With only days to go, Ella went to town for a long list of supplies. When her car was out of the yard, Tom went back inside. As he'd done when Ella was in B.C., he sat at the table and tried to write. There was a tradition of old bachelor farmers and ranchers going to town and living in the highest, cheapest rooms of the King George Hotel. Doing that was the only thing he could think of—not as a final destination but somewhere to go until he had a better sense of the future. He would not put that in the note because the idea of the decrepit upper floors of the George would make Ella angry: a bed of nails he'd chosen to lie on so she would pity him.

All he wrote was that he thought it was time to go, and that he would live in town and come out to do his farm work each day.

When the phone rang, he thought it would be Ella, needing him to check the supply of something in the pantry. But it was not Ella. He waited for the other person to speak. Whoever was on the other end was doing the same. Silence gaped.

"Is this the Ryders'?"

Tom could not say how he knew, but he knew it was Lance Evert.

"You're looking for Ella?"

Evert tried a couple of times to speak but bungled it. Finally he told Tom his name. He was phoning to tell them he'd come back to the old plant. He was the engineer in charge. He'd arrived a few days ago.

"I remember you," Tom said.

"I was wondering if I could come down and have coffee, with you and Ella. Remake your acquaintance."

"Why not today?"

"Sure, if you folks have the time."

"Ella's in town but she said she'd be back by three thirty. Turns out I have to go in there myself. Meet a guy about a piece of haying machinery."

"I'll come another day, then."

"Sounds like you were ready to come today. Ella would be very pleased to see you. Come at three thirty. It'll be a nice surprise."

Tom hung up quickly. He tore the note he'd written into pieces and dug the bits into the ashes under the trash burner. He wrote a new note that said Lance Evert was back at the plant and was going to visit at three thirty today. Below that he added that he needed to go to town and would not be home before six. He left it on the table, between the salt and the pepper, where they always left their notes.

Tom had heard Ella tell a friend on the phone that there was a new florist in town, next to the undertakers. When he got into Haultain, that was where he went. The woman apologized for how few blooms she had; there'd been a funeral. He looked at the few flowers she had in a glass case and saw something blue. Ella liked blue flowers. After paying, he asked the woman if he could leave them in her cooler until it was time to go home.

He went to the machinery dealer at the station and bought a part, something he didn't need but might before summer's end. Not much time had passed, so he entered the yeasty gloom of the beer parlour and slowly drank two glasses of draught.

At a quarter after six, Tom was back home. He entered the farmhouse. Ella was not there. He checked the basement, and her milk bucket was not on its nail. He cut the ends off the stems and put the flowers in water; saw two teacups and saucers in the drying rack by the sink. Outside, he did his own chores. When he saw Ella carrying her milk pail to the house, he checked his watch and told himself to stay out another twenty minutes. Before that time was up, she came outside and called him for supper.

The flowers had been put in a nicer vase. It sat on the back half of the table. The front half was set for supper. He tried to act like he normally did—except for not smoking. He would do his smoking outside from now on.

They were eating supper when Ella mentioned the visitor. Lance Evert was back to run the old plant. "Of course you knew that. It was in your note."

"That's all I know. That he's back."

"It's strange. What he said sounded like he'd done very well in his career. But here he is running our old thing."

"He didn't say why?"

"Not really."

She said Lance must be serious about staying because he had bought a house in Haultain. He and his fiancée were going to live there after they got married in the fall. Her name was Judy and she was a Calgary girl who worked for an oil company in the city as a secretary. Then Ella thanked Tom for the flowers and asked if he'd like some dessert. She'd found a jar of his favourite canned peaches in the basement.

Two days later, Tom came inside after chopping barley. He'd beaten the dust out of his shirt and pants outside, but still needed to change to get away from the itch. Ella stopped him on his way to the stairs.

"Your clothes are down here," she said.

The bedroom felt strange. The smell that used to be a mix of them was Ella now. He was taking off the dusty clothes when he saw that the near side of the bed was turned down. His cufflink and tie-tack boxes were on the bedside table.

Ella had decided she was going to call Billy *Will* from now on. Bill was a plain name, she thought, and as a professional engineer, her son would need a city name, more of a man's name. A lot of thought had gone into this, and she was poised to start the moment he arrived.

In fact, he was very late getting in. About the time Ella was going to give up on him and go to bed, he drove into the yard. In the house, he smelled strongly of beer. He was in a surly mood.

She had a cold plate of supper saved for him. He sat and ate it, and made a show of his disappointment at being back at the farm. Ella felt like clouting him, but his father acted as if nothing was wrong. Tom told a story about the Depression and how he was having a good time riding the rods and living in hobo jungles when somebody from home got word to him that his father was sick and his mother needed him.

"It was hard to come back," the story ended.

The only sign that Tom did not feel entirely at ease was the way his hand kept rising to the bulge of makings in his shirt pocket. He had stopped smoking in the house. Tonight, she could almost feel his need in her own chest.

The Depression story softened Will's mood. He had always liked his dad's stories about the thirties, playing hide-and-seek with railway bulls and those who would have put him in a relief camp. The Huck Finn part of his life.

"You know," Tom said, after a silence, "I'm not sure you have to work here this summer. If you'd help on weekends, I think we could make out. Leave time for another job."

Will was eating the last thing on the plate, a cookie. He sat there with his mouth open and a ball of dough on his tongue. Ella was stunned too. "Job where, though?" Will said.

"At the plant," Tom answered without hesitation. "They shut down every summer to do maintenance. Call it turnaround. There'd be lots of overtime but it wouldn't last long. If I were you, I'd go talk to the engineer in charge. It's a guy who was here at the beginning. He's come back to run it. Lance Evert. Tell him you're in engineering and he'll be interested."

The next morning, Will was back from the plant in an hour, whooping. Lance had given him a job, and not just on turnaround. He would be a summer student, replacing well switchers in the field as one by one they went on holidays.

In the week after that, Ella saw her son as happy as he'd ever been. He ate breakfast in a rush, grabbed the lunch pail she'd filled for him, and sprayed gravel behind his pickup as he tore away. Every day, he returned bursting with news, the things he was learning about gas wells and how you regulated the supply from the field. There was also a little compressor plant in the hills that pushed the condensate to the big plant. It was his job to take readings and to soak up the oil the compressors leaked with rags from a box.

Ella realized the decision to let Will work elsewhere suggested Tom had given up the idea of their son taking over the farm. At the very least it meant he wanted him to experience other work so he could make an informed choice. She believed it was no contest and never had been. Will loved machines, and the plant simply had bigger, more interesting machines than the farm.

"How long have you been thinking about letting Will work at the plant?" she asked, when various hints had failed to produce.

He laughed every time she called their son Will. He said it made him think of Shakespeare.

"I've been thinking about it for a month. Seemed like a good compromise."

As summer went on, it did prove to be good. Will was happy in his job and plunged into the farm work after shifts and on weekends. Ella assumed his old school friends must be after him to go drinking, but he only went on Saturday nights and would work again on Sunday.

Of course the situation with Will and Tom was not the only thing different about the summer. Ella had her own feelings, shared with no one. Lance was a much different man now, heavier in the shoulders. He was even a little plump in the waist, something she would never have thought possible when he was young and thin as a greyhound. He still had the beautiful face, beautiful lips.

The fact that he was about to marry was the final and fitting end to Ella's worry and her episodes of yearning. She had always been too old for him, but now she looked it, with her greying hair and engraved lines fanning out from her mouth and eyes. When they met after his return, alone at the house, he'd said she looked wonderful, but it did not mean the same thing as it would have a dozen years ago. On a weekend in June, Lance brought his Judy to the farm to meet them—to meet Ella, really—and it felt unflatteringly like a nephew introducing his fiancée to a favourite aunt.

Once and for all, that left Tom, and that was strange too. Over the years she had assumed Tom wasn't even aware of many of the obstacles between them, but he proved otherwise by taking them all away. After Ella was certain the changes were firm, not just short-lived acts of contrition, she phoned Jeannie.

"Wow, Mom. That seems unbelievable."

"It is hard to believe but it has happened."

"He doesn't even curse?"

"Not around me. And he's trying to quit smoking. He won't succeed, which is sad, but he doesn't smoke in the house."

"Is that going to be enough for you?" She didn't mean smoking or cursing; she meant the marriage, which of course was a much tougher question to answer.

Not long after, Jeannie phoned to say she had handed in her notice to the school. Right after that, she had told Hal she was leaving him. Ella asked if Jeannie wanted her to tell Tom.

"Will he flip his lid?"

"My guess is not."

"You might as well tell him, then."

Ella gave Tom the news over breakfast. She told him about the teaching job first. She let that soak in. Then added, "She's given Hal notice too."

Tom cocked his head. "Does she know what she'll do?"

"She's saved quite a bit of money. Donna is helping her make travel plans."

"Where?"

"She thinks Australia. She wants to teach there, maybe at an Aboriginal school."

"I always thought I'd like to go to Australia," he said.

As Tom was finishing his coffee, and beginning to show his nervous need to get outside and smoke, he said, "I know she'll think I'm on Hal's side. I'm not. I want her to be happy. Would you tell her that?"

The days and weeks of that summer passed quickly. There were no frosts, so the succession of wildflowers was uninterrupted. Every time Ella looked up, it seemed, more of the farm work was done than seemed possible. By the end of July, every hayfield was cut and baled. By the middle of August, all the bales were in the pile.

At the beginning of that month, Tom had asked Ella if she would mind if he sold the cattle and rented out half the land. Of course her answer was yes. It was something she had wanted for years. He also asked whether, with the cattle gone, they should stay on the farm or go. Lance claimed he was going to fix the plant, modernize it, reduce its pollution, he said, but, if Ella wanted to move, Tom was willing.

The surprising man had been working it all out in money terms: what the cattle and the land would bring, what they had in savings, what a small house in town would cost. In the better grain years, they had saved money for the children's education. Jeannie's program hadn't been long. Donna had gone straight to work. Billy was receiving scholarships. All in all, if they were frugal, which was the only way they had ever lived, they could retire.

Ella surprised herself by saying she was content to stay on the farm, for now at least. Maybe they could think of moving to town when they needed to.

Tom brightened. She thought he was just glad not to have to uproot himself, but there was something else.

"If we stay, I think I'll keep a few cows, maybe twenty."

"What for?"

"A show herd. People ask me what I did all these years, I'll point at them and say, I did that."

Twenty head would hold them down almost as securely as a hundred and twenty. They would still have to be fed and looked after. But before the thought could get out of her mouth, she understood how lost he would be without any work to do, and said nothing.

Tom asked Billy to help him choose the cows he was going to keep. The boy reacted as if it was an unreasonable favour, something outside their contract.

"I don't have time."

To agree to evenings of stacking hay and yet balk at leaning over a fence to say "That cow's better than this one" made no sense, but Tom let it be.

After he'd thought about it more, he decided Billy's reluctance to help choose the show herd was similar to his own reluctance to listen to his son talk about the plant. For years, Tom's greatest wish had been to have someone, anyone, tell him how a sour gas plant worked. Now he had a son champing at the bit to tell him, and he could barely make himself listen. He really did not give a damn anymore what they cooked and served up there. His thoughts were on cows: whether to keep the Simmental crosses or to concentrate on the old breeds; how much hay land he should keep out of the rental contract for summer grazing and winter feed.

Then one Saturday, Ella came back from a supply trip to town with the Lethbridge paper. A big headline on page one said Dry Fork had won a settlement. Tom understood what it meant before he read the article. It was a settlement out of court, something the companies would never have dreamt they'd have to pay. As Purcell had said, society was moving against corporations on air pollution. Alberta's new government had brought in tougher air pollution rules. So the company wanted to put an end to things. The families, Arsenaults, Darbys, took the money. It was more than they believed they'd ever see.

As he read the article, he could feel Ella watching him closely. He recognized her fear that the news would bring him to a boil. And it did crank some old starter in his chest, to see his friends at Dry Fork victorious when he had never won a thing. It also touched the old fury to know that the settlement meant nothing was proven against the plant. The sour gas companies had not admitted a thing. Not one gassed farmer, not one dead pig, was laid at their door.

Geoff Purcell was quoted. "If in future anyone takes on an oil company for a complaint such as this, it will be less difficult than it has been for us. It's like climbing stairs. The next person starts on the highest step the last person reached." Tom did not even know if it was true but could imagine Geoff needing to say and believe it.

He closed the paper and pushed it away. "Good for them." He did not know what else to say.

As the summer drew to its end, Billy's desire to talk about the plant waned. When he and Tom were together, they settled into a routine of talking about the farm, about cows mostly. Whatever had made Billy not want any part in choosing the show herd was gone. In the cool of evening, they often walked among the cattle, reminiscing.

"Remember that old girl? The spring her calf was born dead? I wanted to get rid of her, but you talked me into giving her a second chance."

"I remember."

The day the cattle liner came to haul the Ryder cows to the auction mart, Billy took the morning off. Ella came out to watch, but was crying so hard after the first dozen cows boarded that she returned to the house and stayed there. Tom could not have explained why he was in a good mood, but he was. He felt young that day, had a real hop in his step. While Billy and the trucker hazed the cattle into the chute, Tom hung over the side and watched them go, recognizing each and every one. When a cow stopped, usually to shy at the blackness inside the truck, Tom would give her a nudge. If that didn't work, he'd twist her tail and launch her through.

When the inner doors were closed and they were down to the last fifteen, they were dealing with the hard cases: stubborn, wily old girls. One of these went halfway up and stopped. The trucker yelled and gave her a boot in the muscle of her hip. She lay down, filling the chute.

Tom watched the cursing trucker head for his cab and knew he was after his stock prod. On the way back, he zapped it against a post to make sure it was working. By then, Tom had hopped over the wall and stood at the base of the chute, between the trucker and the cow.

"Nope," he said. "No one's ever used one of those on these girls, and no one ever will—not on this farm anyway."

The trucker cursed more and threw his prod back in the cab. He came back and stood with his thumbs in his belt loops. "I got another load to pick up today," he said.

"Tell you what," said Tom, reaching for his shirt pocket. "Let's have a smoke. My guess is, by the time we light up, that old girl will be sick of lying there."

Tom was licking his cigarette closed when the cow rose and walked aboard.

Tom followed the truck to Haultain Station. He wanted to see as much of the cows as possible before they were gone. In the corrals at the auction mart, he was standing by the fence looking into their pen when the part-owner of the mart came over and shook his hand.

"End of an era," Herb said with a sadness he did not feel.

"My era," said Tom.

"They're lovely animals. Since you listed them, I've been telling everyone I could. A lot of guys said they'd be in for the sale. See if they could pick up some Tom Ryder cows."

"They're Ella Ryder cows too. Every one carries blood from her parents' herd."

"Your son's not interested?"

"He's going to be an engineer."

"Too bad these young fellas aren't much for ranching these days."

"Not too bad for them."

"That may be a good way to think about it."

At home, Ella was angry.

"Billy's gone to Waterton with Lance Evert to have a meal at the Prince of Wales. On his last night home! I have a nice roast in the oven."

"That's too bad."

"I'm not blaming Billy. He felt bad about it. But what's Lance Evert thinking? Has he not had enough of Billy's time?"

They ate the roast themselves. Tom complimented Ella on it. She laughed at him. It was the same kind of roast, cooked the same way, as they'd had every second Sunday forever. It was only then he realized it was Friday.

"The Pope might mind," said Ella, "but I doubt God cares."

Tom was down in the corral with a flashlight, checking on his remaining cows, when a car came over the hill and entered the yard. The night was clouded and black. A solitary frog called from the slough across the fence. The car sat running. Tom imagined Billy and Lance Evert in the front seat, saying their farewells.

After the car drove off, the gate hinge creaked. Billy came walking.

"Enjoy your meal?"

"All right. Rather have eaten at home."

"Last time I spoke to Evert, he was pretty high on you. 'That Billy's smart as a whip.'"

"I heard that about six times tonight. Lance got kind of plastered. He hardly drinks usually."

"Sounds like he had something to tell you."

Billy hesitated, then said, "Yeah. He's quitting here. He thought he could get this plant modernized, but his bosses won't spend the money. He's got another job to go to. Better plant. He offered me a job there, for next summer."

"Where is it?"

"A few hours north."

Tom had the flashlight on an old sprockle-face. Her jaw revolved as she chewed her cud. "Remember this one?"

"Oh yeah. I was surprised you kept her."

"She's the only one in the bunch that shows the Shorthorn. Cochrane Ranch paid a thousand guineas for a Bates Shorthorn from England. Record price for a cow at that time."

"Tomorrow's the big day," said Billy.

"You'll be heading back."

"I meant the cow sale."

Tom moved the flashlight to another cow, a younger Simmental-Hereford. She spooked to her feet.

"Ah, hell. I should leave these girls rest."

He snapped off the flashlight. It was coal dark until their eyes changed. A cat came and twined around his legs.

"I'm fine with it, you know," he said. "I imagine Ella thinks I should retire completely. Can't imagine hitting a little ball around a field, though."

"There's probably other things to do," said Billy.

"Guess so. Guess I'll find out what they are."

The next two summers, Billy worked for Lance Evert at Sulphur Falls. The plant was new and enormous, set a long way back in the bush south of Jasper. During his second summer there, Lance asked Billy if he would join their company full-time, after he finished his degree. Because of all the experience he would have by then, he could start as junior plant engineer. Of course Billy said yes. It would put him years ahead of the usual trajectory for an engineer in his field. A dream job.

Once, Billy had stood outside Lance's office door and listened to him brag up his protégé on the phone: "Billy Ryder will be no average BEng when he graduates. He's already a member of our professional organization and has delivered his first paper at a technical meeting."

The paper compared analyzer performance in complex CO_2 and H_2S gas streams, and even though Lance had coached him through it, it was ground-breaking stuff. Billy had received whiz-kid accolades, and it all seemed easy.

In his last year of university, Billy became engaged to Ginny Maier, Lance and Judy's favourite niece. They planned to get married after he graduated. Beyond the wedding and honeymoon, their destination would be High Brazeau, the town closest to Sulphur Falls. They would live in a wood-frame house Billy had bought for a song and renovated during his evenings.

Brazeau was a rough little town left over from a coal frontier, and Billy knew it was not a place Ginny would like. He hoped that wouldn't matter. They wouldn't be downing pitchers at the local tavern or watching the street fights on Friday night. More likely they'd spend their evenings with Lance and Judy, who lived there too. Billy liked being in the bush where there were no farmers and ranchers, just a few squatters living out antique lives in the woods. He would never have to deal with smell complaints and sickness.

Ginny was an industrial lab tech, and there was no immediate job for her at Sulphur Falls. A capable Chinese guy ran the lab, and it would be hard to convince him he needed more help. Lance had to be careful too how he brought his niece onto the payroll, now that Billy was almost family. Nothing was perfect, the two men reasoned, but it would sort itself out in time.

The work was what Billy liked. The field at Sulphur Falls was enormous, and the hydrogen sulphide content was double what it had been at Aladdin Hatfield. They were making mountains of sulphur, mostly for Japan, and they were doing it right. Outside their specialized world, few wanted to hear the details; few could even understand them. Even Ginny, whose background was in oil and gas, glazed over. But it was interesting to Billy. He knew exactly what he was doing and why.

As for Tom and Ella, Billy did not see them much. They were still on the farm. Aladdin Hatfield was still choking down gas across the road, but it wasn't the same situation. There had always been two fields at Hatfield, one more sour and higher pressure than the other.

After Lance left, the company sold the more sour field to another plant better equipped to deal with it.

In their phone calls, Ella said the plant still smelled but the dangerous days were few. When she put him on the phone, Tom said it was a shame Aladdin hadn't sold that field twenty years ago. But that's all he would say about it.

Tom had his cows still, and, in the summer, put up a bit of hay. He sold the calves in the early fall, and his feedlot stood empty. Ella gardened still but on a reduced scale. For recreation, they took drives together along oil exploration roads into the mountains; nothing too adventurous, never overnight. They liked home was how Ella put it.

On a weekend off, Billy took Ginny south to introduce her. It was the expected success. Ginny had low-key ways, an infectious laugh. Ella and she did the instant-bonding thing women do. By the second day, Tom took Ginny out in his cigarette-butt-strewn pickup and showed her the sights. Ginny loved Tom: the jokes, the languorous stories, his old-fashioned chivalry.

"He's so handsome and funny," she said as they drove away. "So calm."

"Do you think I'm like him?"

"You might *get* like him."

When he finished his degree and went to work full-time at Sulphur Falls, Billy lived in the High Brazeau house and counted the days until he and Ginny were married and living together. Even with the loneliness, he would have told anyone his life was great, almost perfect—until one night when the phone rang quite late, and it was Ella.

"Billy. I'm sorry to tell you but your dad is dead. Tom is dead."

The line bristled. A million mites were crawling up the wire.

"He came in from the cattle. We had supper. I was carrying our dishes to the sink. I heard something, and he was on the floor. I didn't have time to do anything. He was dead."

She was not crying, but her voice was pulled tight.

"Is he there?"

"What? Oh, you mean his body. No. I called the priest but he didn't come until after the ambulance had taken Tom away. He said he would go into town and give him the last rites there."

Then she cried. He heard a clatter. He pictured the receiver swinging from its cord. Far away, she blew her nose sharply.

"This is what I want you to do. Donna is waiting for you at her place. The two of you come down together. There's no reason to hurry. Do you understand that?"

Billy said he did.

"I'll phone Jeannie now." She hung up with the faintest click.

Donna and he were silent in the car. Somewhere near High River, she said she could hardly believe it. Billy felt the same, but his thoughts were on times when Tom had noted discomfort: tightness in his lungs, a pinch in his ribs. There was his rumbling smoker's cough, and the fatigue Ella mentioned. Why had it not been obvious?

As quickly, Billy knew why. Even carved down as Tom was by everything, he was still the family's leader, its strong man. If Tom did not declare himself to be in a dangerous state of health—and he never had—none of his children could move past that to any other conclusion.

This was the first thought that seemed worth saying to Donna, but many more miles passed before he did. They were crossing over the Porcupine Hills by then, and in the east, a half moon had risen high enough to stare at them through the trees.

"I let him think I was so interested in the farm. The cattle," she said.

"You *were* interested."

"I was interested in *him*. I wanted Dad to love me more than he did anyone else."

"He did love you more."

"And then after the club calf died, I dumped him."

She was crying, and Billy let her be. His car rose and fell through the shadowed landscape. He knew what came beyond every hilltop and curve. On the flat, he could see each living home, each deserted shack. He felt where the creeks narrowed into culverts beneath the highway. Billy slowed when the road wove through a break in the ridge. A buck stood on the shoulder, grazed by the headlights.

Donna kept on sobbing and Billy saw in her state what it was going to be like from now on. Each Ryder would believe she or he had caused Tom's death. Each of them would insist on it, would see his or her line toward this night as the bold one. Billy did not have to think why he was the cause. He had always known.

After the funeral, Jeannie decided Ella should not stay at the farm. Jeannie omitted the word "alone" but Billy knew that was what she meant; alone even while her son was in the house and looking after the farm.

Prayers, Mass for the Dead, ceremony at the graveside, lunch at the house: through every stage of the community's farewell to Tom, Billy answered each question he was asked, responded to each comment that wanted response, but an inappropriate hostility roved inside him that he could not hide. Donna poked him in the ribs; Jeannie rebuked him in an upstairs bedroom; still he could not do other than what he was doing.

Ginny seemed to understand better, or at least made no criticism of him. She had a nice way of talking about Tom, whom she'd only met once, of consoling Ella and Billy's sisters. She did well too at representing the silent man onto whose arm she held tightly. Lance and Judy had brought her down, and Billy suggested she return with them. He explained he had to stay and look after the livestock, which was true but not his motive. Ginny knew he didn't want her there. She accepted with grace his choice to go it alone.

On the night of the funeral, after the last car pulled out of the yard, Jeannie's car with Ella aboard, Billy found a bottle of blended Scotch in the saved-paper-bag cupboard and started to drink. He drank out of the mineral-encrusted water glass from the porch. He was mad at everything that came into his mind. All he could commend himself on was that he had kept this anger bottled until now. Fear of not being able to was why he did not want Ginny here. It was the same reason he did not want Lance and Judy around.

Whatever Lance thought about his goodwill toward the Ryder family, Bill saw it as bullshit now. He recalled the man's words about wanting to modernize Aladdin Hatfield, but he was hearing them tonight as Tom must have, as self-aggrandizing and less than true.

And the job of turning Billy Ryder into a crackerjack engineer, wasn't that also bullshit? Something to soothe Lance's conscience about the plant his industry had dropped in the Ryders' lap? Lance had come and gone, then had come and gone again. There were always greener pastures for Lance Evert.

At the funeral, Billy had watched with a fire in his head as Lance bowed before Ella and took her hand. He saw a pain in his mother's face that was different from what the other condolences were causing her. If Billy had let himself loose in that moment, he might have hit Lance, might have thrown him out of their house and harried him into his car. This: to Lance and Judy, who had done so much for him, who had treated him like family.

When Lance, Judy, and Ginny did leave, Ginny had looked back at Billy out the back window of the car as long as she could. Just before the dust rose, Billy saw the sun glint off the tears in her beautiful eyes. He was being unfair to her, she who had never done him any wrong, who contained almost no capacity for harm. Choosing him to love was her only crime.

While Billy was drunk—and he got deeply and lastingly drunk that night—he clung to the neck of a gallon bottle of sweet sherry and stood on top of the driveway hill. A hard wind blew in his face, and the old plant's flare jigged in the wind.

"You fucking killed him!" he yelled at it as loud as he could. "You cross-eyed son of a whore!"

Later still, he staggered around the power pole, in the circle of yard-light. What drove him was electric and jagged and centred in his heart. His course around the driveway circle made him so dizzy he fell and mashed his cheek into the gravel. "Hundred per cent fucking idiot," he told the cold grey rocks. He went to lift the jug and found it light. Nothing left on his finger but the glass loop.

When he got to his feet, he returned to the house and opened the porch cupboards until he found his father's lantern. He walked to the barnyard and let himself through the gate. He moved the cone of light in search of cows. The evening of his death, Tom had brought two into the home corral, one with a swollen hoof and another about to calve. The pregnant one was lying down and did not seem to find him strange; likely she could see nothing but light and assumed the human behind it was Tom. In the curve between her back leg and belly, he saw the white-haired udder round with milk, the teats pink and inflated. His insides zoomed with pleasure. A calf to deliver; to watch grow.

——

Bill had been on the farm two months. He did not buy newspapers or watch TV, and estimated the date by what wildflowers were blooming. During the day, he went out to the pasture and walked among Tom's show herd. Sometimes he lay down in the grass and slept. In the evenings, he spun playing cards into an inverted cowboy hat. He turned down all invitations from neighbours to come for meals. He went to town when he was out of food and beer, and otherwise stayed home.

His sisters called to scold him. They'd heard reports from neighbours of emptied whisky bottles strewn on the lawn, of Billy wandering the roads in sock feet. He told them it was untrue. In fact he kept himself and his clothes neat and clean. After the first week of excess, he drank only beer. Between rounds of card-tossing, he did push-ups and sit-ups.

When Lance called, he would ask about Ella, her health, her mental state, before he asked about Billy. He would tell him about the plant, and at the end of the conversation, would urge Billy to come back to work sooner rather than later. Its junior engineer was not something a plant could do without. Lance was covering the gap by bringing in old friends, retirees, but that could not go on much longer.

When it was Ginny on the phone, Billy would say he was not ready to come back. He had to wait for Ella's return. They would decide together what to do.

Ginny would start out soft with him, but, when she heard him saying the same things, chapter and verse, she would begin to cry. She said she was not sure how much longer she could stand this.

The timing of Ella's phone calls could not be predicted. Somehow she knew he would never answer anyone else's call if he knew which ones were hers. She understood many things others did not. She was often harsh with him, telling him how foolish he was to gamble Ginny and his career. There was no reason he couldn't leave the farm right now. Half a dozen neighbours were willing to look after Tom's cows. Nor was there much hay to cut. It could be contracted out.

Bill tried to get her to come home.

"I'm taking good care of things. I can cook, you know. You can rest all you like."

"I'll come home when I'm ready," she said.

Looking out the kitchen window on a hot morning, Bill saw Ginny drive into the yard. Before she stepped from the car, he knew she had come to leave him. "Fine, then," he said. "The hell with you." But when she was inside and speaking her piece, he wept and begged her not to do this. He would change; he really would. He was not sure why he was like he was, but it wouldn't last; it couldn't. When it was over, they could go on with the plans they'd had before.

Sad, and now defeated on top of it, Ginny got back in the car and drove away. She would wait, she'd told him, but not much longer.

Then Ella did return. She was not there to live with him, as he had hoped. She had rented a basement suite in town and would live there for the time being. She had come to tell Bill that she had listed Tom's cows for sale. Starting today, she wanted him to prepare for that sale and for an equipment auction. She was not sure yet what to do with the farmhouse and land, sell it or keep it. She would call a family meeting later in the summer.

"I have to hay," Bill said.

"I've sold the hay crop to Vic Sebald."

Ella was thin and older looking, but brisk and certain.

"What should I do?" he asked her.

She was sitting at the table, in Tom's place. She looked him in the eye and there was no softness there.

"You should get on with your life. If you intend to marry Virginia, do so. If you want to work in gas plants, phone Lance and tell him which day you'll be back."

Ella looked around her house, at the dishes in the drying rack, at the hatful of cards on a chair.

"Each of us treated Tom worse than he deserved at some time or another. It does him no good to throw your life away now."

5

Fort McMurray

"HELLO, JUDY? It's Bill Ryder."

"Billy. We were just talking about you."

An image of Lance and Judy in the kitchen nook: Lance with his nose tubes.

"Good things, I hope."

No reply.

"Look, Judy, can Lance talk? I have a business question."

Judy made a strange sound, a laugh and a cry both at once. "I don't think you'll get an answer, Billy. Lance died."

The line sang. Judy covered the mouthpiece and said something to whoever was there. When she was back, Bill said he was sorry. "When you said you were talking about me, I thought you meant you and Lance."

"It's funny. I'm with Ginny. We were talking about how I couldn't find you. I phoned and left messages. I phoned your plant and they acted like they'd never heard of you."

"You were calling to tell me about Lance."

"Well that, and about the funeral. He wanted you to be a pallbearer."

"I'd be proud to."

Another pause. "Lance and I had a lot of time to plan this. I had the funeral right away. It was three days ago."

"Oh."

"He wanted the young fellows he'd trained to carry him. Lance thought so highly of you, Billy. You were the first. That's what he always said: 'Billy was the first.' And then there's this letter."

"I'm sorry, a letter?"

"Lance wrote you a letter. I was wanting to be sure of the address before I mailed it. I don't know what's in it but Lance was concerned that you get it soon after he died."

Bill gave her his address.

"And you, Judy? Are you okay?"

"Oh. I don't know. The kids were here. Ginny's staying with me. Would you like to talk her?"

Ginny's voice came on. "How are you, Bill?"

His eyes blurted tears. "I'm okay. And you?"

"Fine. Have you talked to the kids?"

"No, I haven't. Are they okay?"

She laughed her slow laugh. "Martha's fine. I don't get to talk to Will long enough to know. He's always busy. But you must be sad. I know how much Lance meant to you."

"I'm okay. It's nice to hear your voice."

He sat in front of a VLT. Its theme was Australian. He imagined whiz kids in California inventing it with the help of Google and Wikipedia. *Is a wallaby a kangaroo or that thing that lives in a tree?*

The casino was packed. The Australian machine was the only one available. He had played it before and did not like it. He remembered that a didgeridoo played when you won a certain amount, or was it when three Aborigines appeared on the same line? He hadn't put money in, just sat there watching the display.

He flipped through the information screens, found out how the special worked. Something about cane toads on a highway. He could not seem to concentrate. He had come here in flight from dead Lance, from lost Marie, from his lost job. There were a lot of things he needed not to think about, but his arms flopped on his thighs like sandbags.

He looked up and checked James Beaudry. They had seen each other when Bill came in. Bill had been trying to remember if he'd seen him here before. Nights here were not for remembering.

What did not matter was that Beaudry had ratted on him. Except for the probability of misunderstanding, he'd go right now and tell him that. But Marie's ex-husband was in a headlock with his machine. If tapped on the shoulder, he might not feel it, or might yell and jump a foot. His body was as tightly wound as a bridge cable. He jerked every time he hit Play and lost. When he got a small win, he would gulp a breath, reach up and grip his neck. If he got something bigger, he paused to work his shoulders and roll his head around the stem of his neck. Bill watched to see if he was putting in bills or playing down credits. It was the latter: grinding away his winnings, bearing down on zero.

"You going to play that machine?"

A woman was standing close, almost touching him. She had a dirty white purse over one shoulder and a fistful of twenties resting where the purse clasped. Between the open sides of a puffy jacket, her belly pressed out like a harvest pumpkin.

"Well?"

Bill took out a twenty and slid it up the neon slope, heard the machine swallow. He felt along the dashboard for the Play button. No didgeridoo, but some Australian beast briefly yelped.

"That was stupid. You bet one credit on the middle line. You had four kangaroos on the diagonal."

Bill didn't look at the screen but at the woman. She wore a sea creature on a silver wire around her neck. He pushed the button again.

"Three surfboards, and you didn't get that either."

Bill pushed the button.

"I could make money on that machine. What a waste." She turned away but didn't go anywhere.

Bill finally looked at the screen. On his only pay line, three crocodiles sat in a row, their jaws munching. Crocodiles were worth more than other symbols, and he was money ahead. It gave him an idea how to treat this night. He would bet five lines, close his eyes, and spin. Wake up every ten minutes and see how he was doing. Let the machine tell him by going dead under his finger when he'd hit zero. It was no stupider than anything else that happened here.

Down the line a couple were fighting.

"I'm not giving you any more. You always lose on that one but you keep playing it. Here's a ten. Now go away. Leave me alone. I'm doing good here."

Bill closed his eyes and his mind floated.

"Sir? Sir?"

A short brown man was standing where the pregnant woman had been. He wore the green vest of an employee. His face was tight and his eyes dog-sad.

"We're very full tonight, sir. If you're not feeling like playing, I wonder if you would kindly cash out."

It was true. Bill wasn't playing. He had been imagining it without doing it. "You'd like me to leave."

"Perhaps you might care for a bite to eat, or maybe a drink in our lounge. We have a fine entertainer. Miss Sally Lee Rivers of Nashville, Tennessee."

"I'm fine here."

"It's just you haven't been playing, sir, and some people who don't have VLTs are complaining. If we weren't so busy, there would be no problem."

Bill pressed Cash Out.

"Are the tables full?" he asked the man. "Blackjack or roulette?"

"I'm afraid so, sir. The oil price went up today. And a new project has opened its hiring office."

Bill was stiff in the back when he stood. His knees and hips felt in need of replacement.

"Thank you, sir. You are a gentleman."

The woman sprang into the emptied chair, slid her twenties in one after another, as fast as the machine could swallow.

"Hello, Johnny."

"Billy? How the hell are ya?"

"Wondering what you're up to."

"I bet you're wanting me to come watch you drink. I'd love to, but I'm seven hours away."

"Working?"

"I did a stupid thing. Decided to sell heat tapes. The kind that run along pipes and keep them from freezing?"

"So where are you?"

"On the prairie somewhere. I'm looking for a mini gas plant that's plugged end to end with hydrates because my heat tapes didn't work."

"That's too bad. I'll let you go, then."

"Billy, hold on. I don't like how you sound. What you gotta do right now is head for family. Family has to take you. That's the rule. You do that, okay?"

Donna lived in an old community north of Calgary's river, in a brick townhouse with a white porch. She had purchased it with a woman named Adele and then bought out Adele's share when they split.

Bill stood on the porch now, watching the last crust of snow melt through the cracks. The wood was black with mould and he imagined replacing it. Beyond the steps, generations of cats had patterned the grass with their potent pee.

He rang the bell again. It was morning but not so early that she would be asleep. Her peephole had a metal eye patch, and he heard it *snick*. The door jerked open and Donna walked away down the hall: blue bathrobe, flapping slippers.

He went in and kicked off his boots, left them on the entry rug beside a row of his sister's footwear. The closet was full so he flopped his coat over the half wall.

The kitchen was at the back. Morning light pooled there. Donna sat with her back to him at a table she'd rescued from the farm. It was cluttered with books and bills, and a half-eaten plate of ravioli. The ancient tomcat rose from its pillow on the far-side chair and stretched its back round.

There was a third chair but Bill could not make up his mind to remove the stack of newspapers and sit. Donna hadn't said a word. It seemed possible to turn and go.

"I suppose Jeannie sent you. To look after your depressed sister."

"No."

"I don't believe you."

"I could use a drink," Bill said.

"It's morning."

"Germans drink in the morning. We're half-German."

"That logic's airtight."

He found a couple of glasses and reached for a pull above the fridge.

"If you think the booze is there, it means you haven't been here for three years."

"Where, then?"

"Cabinet in the living room."

He found it and, in its interior, felt familiar square shoulders. "Gin all right?"

"Perfect."

In the kitchen again, he decided Donna did not want mix or ice and poured her a splash. She took the glass, drank, and shuddered.

"Adele has cancer," she said. "She's dying."

Bill absorbed the news. "Did she call you?" He knew they were not normally in touch.

"A friend did." Donna downed the gin and held the glass out for more. "Adele doesn't want anything from me. She has all the love and support she needs, apparently."

Bill moved the newspapers and sat.

"What does it mean," Donna said, "if after that many years with somebody, she doesn't want to see you, even in her dying days?"

She looked at him across the rim of her glass. The emotion in her eyes was frightening. "I'm in no mood for advice, sympathy, or any happy shit, okay? The only thing I want to hear is cold, hard truth. If you can't deliver that, you should go."

He sat quietly for a bit, then said, "I lost my job."

"Jeannie told me. She said leave with pay."

"They'll fire me as soon as the story goes quiet."

"What else is shining up your life?"

"Marie and I started something and it stopped."

"Why? Because you're unemployed?"

"Because I'm a gambling addict."

"I thought maybe. Can't you quit?"

"I might have already. If I tell her that, she won't believe me. I wouldn't either."

"But you think you have?"

"Addicts always think that."

"This is pretty good, Billy. I don't usually believe you, but I'm believing you now. Got more?"

"Lance Evert is dead."

"Oh shit."

"Lance was a good guy."

"In states of drunkenness, you've said otherwise."

"I was full of shit. He was always a good guy."

Donna stood up and took the ravioli to the garbage. She cleared off the rest of the table. The cat convulsed suddenly and threw up. It went on the newspapers, on the pillow and the floor. Donna began to cry, great gulping sobs.

"Fuck!" she yelled. When she caught her breath, she removed the cat to his basket. She gathered up the dirtied newspapers. The smell was terrible.

With the newspaper, she gestured toward the cat. "Elmer has cancer too. He's scheduled to be put down next week. Everyone has cancer. I'm expecting mine any time."

Bill stood to make room for the clean-up. She came into his wheelhouse and he put his arms around her. She cried against his chest.

"Somewhere in this hug is a lot of cat puke," she said.

He held on until she pushed him away. She brushed at his sweater but there was nothing on it. She went out the back door to the trash can and came back smiling.

"Willbilly," she said, "I have an idea and I won't be denied. We need to go see Jeannie. You, me, and Elmer in his box. He always loved a road trip."

Bill thought he was good to go but was hit by fatigue while Donna got ready. He said he had to sleep and took to the living room couch. The cat, no longer nauseated, snailed in his crotch.

He'd said he needed an hour, but Donna left him to it. By the time they were free of the city and had begun to weave through the high foothills, it was Charles Marion Russell time, pink, blue, and threads of amethyst. When the sun was dropping into mountain cloud, they were well past the mansions, the thoroughbreds in New Zealand blankets. Ordinary horses and cows stood behind the wire of down-at-heel farms.

"You all right?" Donna asked, after he had been silent a long time.

"I'm fine," he said and believed he was. Distracted and numb but fine. "You?"

"Elmer's still sleeping," she said.

It was a stretch of highway they had pounded since youth. At times, Bill felt he was in his '64 Chev half-ton, with its cow dents and fenders rubbed raw. Shards of the invulnerability that had been normal for him then zipped through him now. He had hit many things with that truck, but the cab always held its shape, protective as a hockey helmet.

Donna turned on the overhead light and opened the console, flicked through his discs. "What strange taste you have."

"Whatever was at the gas station when I felt desperate."

"Here's *Bob Dylan's Greatest Hits, Volume II*. We're saved."

They listened awhile. "Do you ever wonder?" Donna said and stopped. The light was less by the time she spoke again. "If the three of us got wrecked?"

He gummed this but had no answer.

"That maybe we were wrecked before we left home? Even before puberty?" she added.

He waited longer. A song ended; another began.

"If you mean we were headed somewhere, and then the plant came, and we never got there, I think that every day."

They reached the farm in the dark. A chinook was blowing seventy. The flare stack at the gas plant was belching fire. The door to the porch was unlocked, and when they entered the blackness, cat claws panicked on the linoleum. For the first time since Calgary, Elmer woke in his box and yowled. Then the kitchen light came on and Jeannie stood in front of them in a flannel nightgown. She was holding her cat, and both of them stared with big eyes.

"Go to bed, both of you. I have work to do in the morning."

Donna and Bill climbed the stairs, giggling, joking about how inhumanly steep the steps were. Bill was glad to be back under the old roof, having traced his sadness to its source.

Jeannie was behind a closed door doing mysterious internet work. Donna was lying on the couch staring at the ceiling. Both declined Bill's invitation to walk.

In gumboots, he started up the rise behind the barn. The morning air was soft and still. Beads of dew in last year's grass wet his jeans at the knee. After going up and coming down, he entered the coulee, jumped the creek, and walked a cow path across its cut face. The stream sluiced along below him, brown with its burdens.

The grass had not been grazed over winter. By the look of it, there hadn't been much cow action in the fall either. When they'd had over a hundred head, this field was always overgrazed, a sacrifice zone near the corrals and barn. Now it was restored, like only prairie can do.

He walked to Tom's feedlot. The disaster of time had struck it flat. Silver slabs blown off their nails lay rotting on the ground. Only a few leaning posts and the well shack remained. The one-lung pump engine was still in its shack and giving off a smell of ancient oil.

Back at the house, Jeannie had made lunch. Sitting down to the table, Bill noticed, as if for the first time, how the pattern was worn off the Arborite in five places. His hair rose to see these ghosts. They were sitting at their childhood places, and, seeing this, Jeannie said, "Stupid," and shifted to Ella's chair at the end.

The lunch was exactly as Ella would have done: two slices of cold roast beef on each plate, with a few refried potatoes and a slice of raw tomato. From a Brown Betty, Jeannie poured tea of shocking blackness.

Donna and Bill awaited a pronouncement.

"Okay," said Jeannie. "This is what we're going to do."

Jeannie held down the wire so Donna could crouch through. There was a No Trespassing sign hung on the fence, and Jeannie gave it a slap with the back of her hand. "There's no security," she said, in the same way one might say, *Our enemy is weak.*

They were on the land that Bauers had sold to Aladdin. The current owner was trying to start a different kind of plant, fed by gas from the old one. Jeannie and some neighbours had organized against it.

They walked across a broad dip and came to some plastic flags. Each marked a corner of the proposed building. Farther on, Jeannie pointed into a low spot that was to become the runoff capture.

"When they had the first MD meeting, the company said the runoff would never go into our coulee," Jeannie said. "It looks designed to go there." She added, "I don't think they thought anyone would care enough to object."

"That's what most projects are based on," Bill said.

"That people don't care?"

"They care but they don't think they know enough to challenge the industry or the government. No matter how many screw-ups happen, they still trust industry's professionalism and government's duty to protect."

"Do industry and government have those values?" Jeannie asked.

"Sort of. But protecting people isn't concern number one."

As they poked around, Bill wondered whether Jeannie and her friends had a hope. When a Cree trapping family comes up against an eight-billion-dollar oil sands project, nobody bets on the trapper. Maybe down here, on a small project, it could be different.

A silence from his sisters caught his attention. They were staring at him.

Jeannie said, "I've got the papers the company filed with the MD at the house. Would you look at them?"

"Sure."

Next stop was St. Bruno's. They drove up the hill and parked by the concrete steps of the church. The door wasn't locked, and his sisters went inside. Bill walked to the graveyard and let himself through the gate. Tom and Ella's grave looked nice. Jeannie had been looking after it. The dirt surface was smooth, ready for flowers.

Bill felt a child's kind of shame. Here he was with his addiction and all the failings that came before. If things were to change, what better place than here and now?

"I will do better," he said aloud. Cleared his throat and said it again.

There came a rush of pride, awe, grief, all messed together.

His sisters were walking from the church, heads inclined together, hands gesturing. The wind combed the hair back from their high foreheads. Love, he thought. That's what this was.

Come evening, they split up. Donna had discovered a school friend who was back living in Haultain; she was going there for dinner. Jeannie had a meeting in town with the group that opposed the new plant. It was a momentary glitch of goodwill when she asked Bill to come with her, and he said no. To compensate, he spent an hour with the documents the company had filed.

He was relieved to see how childish the process drawings were, and the few lumpen equations, stuff that anyone could come up with using a search engine and a database. In the written part were claims of proprietary technology: company secrets. This was a usual justification for saying nothing.

Bill imagined facing an appeal board. Besides calling the drawings generic, he would note the absence of a material balance. How can you assess a proposal if it doesn't account for what goes in and what comes out? They claimed there would be no emissions, and that would be another mistake. Bill would turn it into a joke. "That's quite a plant you've got there. You're going to do what no industrial facility in history has done."

He told Jeannie some of this and wrote a few things down before she left. She couldn't wait to pass it on.

Donna insisted on taking Elmer to town because she did not believe Bill would stay home. He said he would; imagined himself walking around the farmhouse, poking his nose in places where he had played and hidden as a child. If that got tired, he had novels to read.

After two hours of listening to the house groan and tick, the good feeling of the past two days was frayed. Without Donna and Jeannie, the house was a shell, empty of everything but memories he'd rather not have. He got in his truck and drove.

Jeannie had told him about a new restaurant at Hatfield Corners, on the site of the old service station. She said the food was good and you could get a drink. Once there, he did not feel like eating. He sat up to a tall bar that divided the kitchen from the tables and ordered a beer. As he drank and watched sports, he took occasional glances at the others in the room. He thought he didn't recognize anyone but gradually understood that he did. A stiff-backed cowboy had the face of a kid he'd ridden with on the school bus. A pretty young woman turned out to be the daughter of the woman he thought she was. People came and went wearing the DNA signatures of families he'd grown up near. He introduced himself to a few, and when they told him about their lives and families, it pleased him beyond measure.

By the time he left, he should not have been driving, even on the lonesome back road he nursed his truck along. He stopped to pee in the amazing stillness. After that, he stopped two more times just to look into the dark and listen to the coyotes sing.

He was thinking of Marie, had been all night. He imagined she would have liked the café and the people. She would like this too: the Milky Way unobstructed by upgrader light. He pulled out his cell phone, rolled to her number, and poked it.

When she answered he did not say who it was. Said only, "Hi."

"Oh," she said.

"I'm down at my sister's place. At the farm. I'm staying here. I went out tonight."

"Gambling?"

"Drinking. Visiting with locals."

He was wishing by now that he hadn't called.

"You should see the stars here. There's almost no light pollution."

He could tell she was arguing with herself. Let him talk or hang up.

"Coyotes are singing."

"How drunk are you?"

"A little."

"Stars are pretty good here too. With the upgrader shut down."

"That's good. I'm glad it's still down. They won't be calling me."

"It's kind of late, Bill."

"I'm sorry."

"I'm not. But I've got to go. Take care of yourself."

The wind started up in the night and blew fiercely. Morning arrived with a bend in it. On days like this along the mountain flanks, things blew down and things blew up. School buses fell over sideways. Roofs de-shingled themselves like a card trick. Sometimes people went crazy and did things they would never have done otherwise.

Bill came downstairs conscious that his mind was not the sweet thing it had been the night before. The idea of telling his sisters about it—the people in the café, the drive home—was torn by a conviction that the message could not pass from him to them intact. Donna and Jeannie sat in their own rings of mood. The three made and ate their breakfasts separately and without comment.

Even though the wind would rip him lengthwise, Bill needed to be outside. He drove the two miles east to the Lower Place. He left his truck by a wired gate and started down. The wind wrapped his trousers tight to his legs, and his windward ear hurt. At the bottom of the slope, the renter's cattle were lying in the shelter of a cutbank. Closer up, he saw them chewing their cuds, many with their eyes closed. They would have paid more attention to a tumbleweed.

When he returned to the house, the kitchen was full of the rich, sweaty smell of chicken: a Hutterite meat bird in the oven. Jeannie and Donna had cracked beers, and he pulled another from the fridge, twisted the cap off, and sat.

"Where have you been?" Jeannie asked.

"Lower Place. River bottom."

"Vic Sebald's been telling people a grizzly denned there last winter."

"I didn't see anything. Couple of deer."

The conversation bumped along. Jeannie and Bill had a second beer. Donna opened wine.

The silent drinking continued until Donna said, "The harshness and inexplicable strangeness of life."

"What?"

"That's what Hermann Hesse said we need alcohol for."

Bill carved the chicken, and, after they filled their plates and took the first bites, Jeannie said impatiently, "Why don't you two just move here? Move into your old rooms and be done with it. We're old enough to retire. There's not going to be anywhere cheaper. Life could be easy, like it's meant to be."

"Life's meant to be easy?" Donna said. "Why didn't anyone tell me?"

"Bill's and my kids are grown up. None of us has a partner who needs to be involved. What's not easy about it?"

The moment was confounding. Bill couldn't imagine them all living in this house, but it was true they could live somewhere down here; in something like peace, perhaps.

Donna pointed at the chicken. "No offence, Jeannie, but until this big guy started roasting, I was thinking how much the plant still stinks. You're probably used to it and maybe I could be again, but I'm not sure I want to be."

"And Calgary's what? A posy?"

Everybody shut up and ate.

"Another reason," Jeannie started up again, "is because we could make a difference down here. Bill, you told me a couple of times that the oil sands are out of control. I think you said 'out of anyone's control.' Down here, the oil industry isn't that strong anymore. Power is proportional to money, and the oil companies here are cheaping out. They're losing control. Seriously, things could be done. I want to see that old plant gone. The land reclaimed. No new plant in its place."

Donna said, "Can I fight from the city? From somewhere with good coffee?"

"First my house stinks, now my coffee's no good."

"Joke. Sort of."

"Okay. Donna has spoken. She can't live here because it stinks and the coffee's no good. What's your excuse, Bill?"

"I'm at a crossroads. Don't know much more than that."

"Well, get on with it. Life is short."

This idea clubbed them silent for a while.

"What's *your* plan, Jeannie?" Bill asked. "If you can stop the new plant, you stay. But if they build it, will you go?"

"I'll probably stay either way. I'll probably die here."

"That reminds me, Jeannie, did Willbilly tell you Lance Evert died?"

Jeannie went blank.

"Jeannie, c'mon. Lance Evert. Ginny's uncle. The guy who used to work at the plant before your boyfriend's father? Same one who liked Ella and turned Billy into a boring engineer."

"Yeah, yeah. Bert Traynor came right after him. You're right, he did like Ella. I remember when he sent her a letter."

Donna said, "Was that when Mom was thinking of leaving Dad?"

Bill startled. "What?"

"Wow," said Jeannie. "I thought we all knew that."

"Billy was probably drawing a machine at the time."

"Is that true? Ella wanted to leave?"

Jeannie turned to him. "When I was trying to get out of my engagement with Hal, Mom came to B.C. with me. We had some heart-to-hearts. She really wanted to go."

Bill tried to think where he'd been in his own life. University. The year Tom suggested he work at the plant.

"I lived here that summer. I worked at the plant. They seemed fine."

"I know," said Jeannie. "I came to visit before I left for Australia. They *were* fine. I could hardly believe it."

"It's weird, in my opinion," Donna said. "Lance comes back, and Mom and Dad make up?"

"But what did Ella say, Jeannie?" Bill asked. "What didn't she like about Dad?"

"His obsession with the plant. The stupid lawsuit. The way he wouldn't give up when it was obvious it wouldn't happen. But Dad was really different that summer. You must have noticed."

"Yeah, and I didn't like it. I was wishing he'd blow his stack so things would feel more normal."

"Dad wasn't my favourite when he was grouchy," said Donna. "Talking big. Saying he was going to do some drastic thing that he never did."

"It was the plant."

"Uh-oh. Billy lost the thread."

"No. It *was* the plant. The plant made Tom look bad. He wanted to do something about it and couldn't. Think about it. If there had been no plant, what would he have looked like to you? Strong. Capable. We would have admired him."

Next morning, they were hurting from the previous night's excess. But the wind was down. The phone rang.

"Wow, I'd forgotten that thing was connected," said Donna.

Jeannie answered it. She looked puzzled and handed the receiver to Bill. The voice on the line said, "You have your cell phone turned off."

"It ran out of charge. How'd you get the number here?"

"I pried it out of the guy who's taken over your office. Henry. I hate small talk so I'm going to get to the point. I've been feeling bad about how I ended things. I've also been missing you. I realized that when you phoned last night."

Jeannie and Donna had figured it out. Jeannie was rolling her hands as if to say, "Get on with it." Donna had her fists against her temples, as if to say, "Don't fuck it up."

"I've missed you too."

"I'm hoping we can see each other again."

"I'd like that."

"You might not when you hear my conditions."

"Fire away."

"I want you to see a counsellor about the gambling."

"I'd do that. I tried once in Mac but couldn't get the guy to talk to me."

"I'm hoping you'll try again. This is what I've done. I phoned a psychologist in Fort Mac and told him who I was and where I live. I said I had someone close to me who works in the oil sands and has a serious gambling addiction. Sorry about the next part. I said I thought the person might be suicidal. He said the person should come in."

"The psychologist will think I'm Native."

"That's the idea. If you're white, you won't get in. They're too busy. But if you're Native and you work in the oil sands, chances are much better. Suicidal clinches it."

"He sees me, then what?"

"I never said anything about your being an Indian. If he says, 'You're white, go away,' you can go to Human Rights and complain."

Marie gave Bill a name and number. "Since I turned it into an emergency, you'll have to go quick. But maybe now that you know my conditions, you've changed your mind."

6

Fort McMurray

IT WAS THE SAME social services building he had gone to before. After a long sit in the crowded waiting room, they moved him into a small room and offered coffee. Three chairs at a round table; tissue box. He was thinking how exactly the same everything was when the psychologist walked in, the same one as before. He stopped abruptly.

"So the friend who called on your behalf is Native but you aren't. And we didn't ask."

"Guess so."

"Joke's on us."

"On me too. I didn't know it would be you."

They studied each other.

Bill said, "Bad idea all round. I'll go."

"No. Please." He was holding out his hand. "Joe Fistric."

Bill shook his hand. "Listen, Dr. Fistric, I've got the same puny gambling addiction and intermittent reliance on alcohol as before. I haven't become more interesting."

"I'm not a doctor, not a medical one. Your friend mentioned suicide."

"I told you back then, I've thought about it but not seriously."

"Listen, Bill, I can't stop you going, free world and all that, but you must have needed counselling to come here."

"Yes."

"After you were here the first time, I felt like crap. I've never been farther below professional conduct than I was that day. I wanted to apologize, but by the time I put that thought into action, our secretary had deleted your name and number."

"Don't worry about it. Let's call it square and I'll hit the road."

"I have another suggestion. This clinic still has more clients than we can deal with. If I took on a non-violent, non-suicidal client, my partners here would freak. What I'd like to suggest is a kind of friendship."

"I have no idea what you mean."

"We could meet for dinner or walks, or drinks. You'd tell me whatever you came here to tell someone. No fee involved."

"What's in it for you?"

"I'm assuming I'd talk too. That's why I'm saying friendship."

"I'm an engineer, Mr. Fistric. We're not known for our insights into human nature."

Fistric laughed. "It's a compromise. If I could see you in the normal way, or think of someone to send you to, I would. What I'm suggesting is on my own time. Nobody else's business."

To get to the appointment on time, Bill had gone straight from the highway to Fistric's office. On the way to his condo afterwards, he remembered that Lance Evert's letter would be waiting. He pulled to the curb and watched a go-cup bob in a melt lake beside him. The sign for the corresponding coffee shop leaned into the road ahead. He drove there and parked.

He drank two cups of coffee, ate a doughnut, and finally considered the question of why Lance's letter was scaring him so. Why, when faced with the prospect of reading it, was he catapulted into the condition he'd been in before he left for Donna's?

At his building, the mailbox was empty. When he got to his apartment, the door pushed against something that turned out to be a pile of envelopes and fliers. On top was a note from the care-taker: "When you don't empty your mailbox, the mailman shoves it in. It goes all over my floor!"

He nudged the pile apart with his foot. The envelope from Lance was there. He had printed *CONFIDENTIAL* on both sides.

Bill made coffee and took the letter to the table. What he should be feeling about this letter was sorrow, but he felt mainly fear. The room was stuffy, and he got up to open the balcony door. The track was jammed, and he shook it hard until the ice broke. A burst of birdsong entered.

He propped the letter against his salt and pepper shakers. He reached for a pen and a flier with a blank side. Wrote: "After the farm, I came back to Mac. I saw a psychologist. On the way home, I felt afraid. When I saw the letter from Lance, it got worse. I had my hopes up. I had started to feel better with my sisters. Then Marie said that we might try things again. But the letter set me back. When I go back, it's never just a step. I go all the way. Maybe Donna's right and I got wrecked when I was just a kid on the farm. Maybe that's what I go back to."

They were in a restaurant, and Bill had given Joe Fistric the note he'd written.

"So what did the letter say?" he asked.

The place was Fistric's favourite, called Peking Surprise. It was bugging the hell out of Bill. If they were in a bar, full of cranky addicted people, he might have a chance of telling this guy his story. In this chamber of lucky colours, with parents teaching their chil-dren how to use chopsticks, it was no go.

"I really can't talk here."

Fistric looked around in search of the problem. That he was unable to understand was not helping Bill's confidence.

"Could we go to a bar?"

When they were standing outside, Joe Fistric suggested they look for a place without gambling machines.

"We might as well go home, then."

Piggy's, the cavernous sports bar Bill chose, had lots of gambling machines as well as parimutuel horse betting in a back parlour. But it was a dark night in the NHL and the place had more echoes than people. As they walked through, Bill counted three couples in the dining area, all bleary with drink. Through an arch, five elderly punters were hitting themselves with racing forms.

Bill led Joe to the far side of the horseshoe bar. The fake plank was empty and gleaming. They mounted barstools.

"That feels better," Bill said.

Joe frowned. "I find this place depressing."

The bartender swirled a damp rag over the clean bar, leaving greasy circles. Said what'll it be. Fistric wanted beer but could not think of a brand. It was like he'd immigrated yesterday, from Tehran. Bill asked for an IPA, and Fistric said likewise.

"Do you know what IPA means?" Bill asked when the bartender moved away.

"No idea."

"You don't come to places like this much."

"Too likely to see clients. Clients don't like it if they see you where they drink. They want you to be above all that."

The beers arrived.

"Where do you want to start?" Joe asked. "And cheers, by the way."

They clinked their pints. Bill tried to think of a starting point. The thoughts that came were mostly things he'd prefer not to talk about.

"India Pale Ale," he said.

"How about we start with the letter?" Fistric suggested.

"I don't think we'll get far with that."

"Why not?"

"I haven't read it."

"I'm confused then. At the restaurant, I asked how you were, and you said, 'Not so hot.' You gave me the note that you'd written referring to a setback caused by a letter from a friend."

"The man who wrote the letter is dead. I can't face what it might say so I haven't read it."

"Okay. You realize you're going to have to tell me who this guy was. And why a letter he wrote before he died could make you feel so bad you can't read it."

Bill took a deep drink, then said that Lance was the man who had trained him to be a gas plant engineer; that Bill had married Lance's niece. He said a few other things.

When he stopped, Fistric said, "I think you must've skipped the part that made you unable to open the letter. Unless that's your response to grief over his death."

"That's not it. What I left out is that I disappointed Lance in important ways. He was a great engineer and a great teacher. I tried to be as good as he was. Then some things happened, and afterwards I was content to be average. I also left his niece and our children."

"I guess you should tell me about the things that happened."

"Maybe it's only one thing. My father died."

Fistric left a gap. He took a tiny sip of beer. Drummed his fingers on the bar.

"We should talk about that," he said. Then he looked alarmed. "You okay?"

Bill did not want to think whether he was okay or not okay. The moment had raced up; he was suddenly there. He felt he had to say it quickly or he might lose courage and never get this close again.

Everything collided on his tongue. When it started to come out, it did so in tangles, out of order. He couldn't imagine he was making sense, but Joe Fistric listened steadily, intensely. His fingers had stopped drumming.

"So, you're talking about loyalty," he said when Bill ran out. Fistric's face had become gentle, thoughtful.

"Betrayal," said Bill.

"But what's betrayal? A failure of loyalty, I think. But there's something I'm not getting. You said your father was okay with your going into the oil industry. With this Lance. So what made it a betrayal?"

Something rose in Bill. He turned on the stool and hung forward. The feeling was big and swarming. When the force of it ebbed, he said, "Sorry."

"Don't be. This is all good. But you look pale. Why don't you take a walk around the room, or go outside? After that, if you feel like stopping, we will. If you want to go on, we can do that too."

In the deserted bathroom, Bill washed his face over and over. He would wash it with cold water, dry it with a paper tower, then long for the cool water and start again. After drying off the last time, he stared at himself in the mirror. There was something in his expression he didn't think he'd seen before. Exhaustion wasn't the right word but in the ballpark. He was often told he looked young for his age. This was not a young face.

He returned to his barstool and said he wanted to continue.

"Do you want to talk about your father? Or about Lance?"

"About Tom. My father."

"It upset you when I said your father was okay with your becoming an engineer. It wasn't like that? He wasn't okay?"

"When I came home that spring, I was expecting to work on the farm, like I had every summer. When I got there, Tom said I should check for work at the plant. Lance gave me a job. The plant was a messed up sour gas plant, and my father had fought it for as long as I could remember. Even after it was obvious he'd never get anywhere, he kept fighting. He was trying to launch a lawsuit against them. Then his only son goes to work for them, and he's fine with it?

"That summer I went to work for Lance, Tom was suddenly different. Really different. He didn't talk about the lawsuit at all. I was willing to tell him everything he wanted to know about the plant, but he had no interest. He accepted things that used to make him crazy."

"Are you saying he had a temper?"

"Legendary. Then, poof, it was gone."

"You sound disappointed that he changed."

"I thought it was fake. I even thought he was putting it on to make me feel bad."

"And it did make you feel bad?"

"He was so mild it was making me sick. It was like he was saying, 'If this is what everybody wants, I give up.' He sold most of his cows that summer. I don't know what to call that."

"Prostration?"

"You've got it. He was prostrate."

"Did other people in your family see it that way?"

"Ella, my mother, said I was making this stuff up because I felt guilty."

"Do you think your mother was right? In hindsight?"

"I did feel guilty. But what I saw with Tom wasn't something I'd invented. I had to be the cause of it, at least partly."

"Later on, when your father died, did you feel that again? That you'd caused it?"

Bill felt bashed again. He stared at a scrunch of napkin. It floated above the black floor like a lily. He wanted to wash his face again.

"He died young, I take it," Fistric said.

"He was the same age I am now."

"You know, don't you, that a lot of people feel responsible when a parent dies, especially if the parent dies young?"

"I know that. My sisters felt responsible too."

"How many sisters?"

"Two. Both older."

"What do you think? Do you want to call it an evening, or do you want to talk about Lance? Why the letter is a problem."

Bill was about to say he wanted to go on but realized he could not.

Later, in bed, he thought about Marie. He wanted badly to call her, but what could he say? *I saw the therapist in a sports bar. We're calling it a friendship. Gambling didn't come up.*

"How about the letter? Are we going to get around to it tonight?"

Fistric was sawing through a steak in Bill's usual restaurant.

"Guaranteed," Bill replied.

"Why so confident?"

"I read it before I left home."

"And?"

"Let's finish eating."

"Okay, sure."

"You can talk if you want."

After suggesting he wanted these sessions to be mutual, Fistric had proven reluctant. He'd been divorced in the last year, and, if he tried to talk about it, he got tongue-tied and glum. He did so again for a minute or two now, then shrugged.

"Let's keep going with you. It's more promising."

By the time they finished their meal, the adjacent lounge had emptied. They moved across and settled into a pair of chocolate armchairs. Bill pulled Lance's letter out of his shirt pocket, shook out the folds. He had marked certain passages. He read the first one to Joe.

"'When I worked at Aladdin Hatfield, I found your mother very attractive. When I first saw her, she was with your father and you. You were a little boy. It was a meeting at Hatfield Corners hall. I don't know what else to say but that I fell instantly in love with her. I also felt that Ella knew this right away. I was a nuisance around your home after that, dropping in for tea. I should mention I wasn't in the habit of dreaming about older married women.'"

Bill stopped reading.

Fistric said, "Wow. And you never knew? That he was interested in your mother?"

"My sisters said something recently, that Lance had a crush on Ella. I can't say I ever saw it. This is the first I've heard about it from him. I worked with Lance for years. I kept in touch with him afterwards. The only thing that connects to this is that, whenever my mother came up, he'd say the same thing: 'Ella was a fine woman.'"

"Was he single, Lance?"

"He was single when he worked at the plant the first time. He married Judy after the first summer I worked for him."

"Did he have any expressed opinion about your father?"

"He said a few times that Tom was a lucky man. I always took that to mean he didn't like Tom and felt he didn't deserve Ella. Otherwise, why call it luck?"

"Is there more?" asked Joe, pointing at the letter.

"There's not a lot here that I didn't know before. When I worked for him he often talked about how he'd quit our plant the first time because he had a difference of opinion with his boss about how to run it. It came to a head when a worker was killed. Lance went to a better plant, learned how to do things properly, became a great engineer and all that. Now, here in the letter, he says his quitting had something to do with my family."

"About his being in love with your mother?"

"The guy who got killed was his closest friend at the plant. He was gassed. After the death, Lance went to our place for fear we'd been gassed too. We were okay, but a litter of pigs had died, and Tom was angry. Here's the interesting part.

"'Your father demanded an autopsy be done. What's shameful to me, still to this day, is that I wouldn't even agree that the plant had killed his pigs, which of course it had. As for his wanting an autopsy, I didn't even reply. When I got back to the plant, I felt gutless. I started saying the things I should have said to Tom. That is, I said them to Alf Dietz, my boss. He said I was sympathizing with the community and should figure out which side I was on. It escalated and I claimed to Dietz that I was the one who wanted the autopsy done on the pigs, that I had already promised this to your father. Dietz said I had no right and implied that he'd fire me if I tried it. I drove to Calgary and they told me the same thing there. So I quit.'"

Bill set the letter down. "Lance says this kept bothering him for years. He felt he'd betrayed Ella and our family. He wrote Ella a letter to tell her about the better plant he worked for after ours, and how they were developing systems that would improve the whole industry. She never wrote back. Finally, that was why he came back, why he took a job running our old plant. He thought if he modernized the plant, that would solve his conscience problem. Here, I'll read that part.

"'When I came back to Aladdin Hatfield, I did so for your mother. In my mind, fixing your plant would be my gift to her, the only meaningful thing I could still give her. Judy was already in my life. We were engaged, and I never told her about Ella. I am about to die without telling her. I don't have any problems with that. I loved Ella and I love Judy. That's just the way it was.

"'Something else I don't think you know is that your father came to the plant to see me, just after I moved back. I couldn't imagine what he wanted. I thought he might know about my feelings for Ella and had come to let me have it.

"'What he asked was if there was summer work for you at the plant. I said there might be. At the end of our conversation, he asked me to keep the meeting secret, from you and Ella both. I've kept that promise until now. Once you were working for me, you became the focus of my trying to make things up to your family. I wanted to do what I could to make sure you were a really good engineer, and, in that, I succeeded.

"'Another failure of course was that I could not fix your plant. It would have taken a lot of money, and the company simply would not pay, given its age. But you know all that.'"

Bill refolded the letter and put it in his shirt pocket.

"Is that all?"

"I want to keep the rest to myself. What I need to talk to you about now is gambling. I have to know if I can stop. If I can't, there's a woman I love who I'm going to have to leave alone."

—

That's pretty well it, Billy. I'm running out of gas, and there's no more to buy. I hope you don't mind that I had to write this to square things. My opinion is that you've looked up to me too much and to your father too little. I was a company man when I started my career. The little good I did early on was because

I was in love with Ella. If I became a better engineer later, I owe some of that to Ella, and some to your father.

As for repaying my debt to them through you, I know I went too far. It caused you problems when your father died so young. If not for me, your life might have been simpler and better. I also know it's silly to think I know—just because I'm dying—what effects I've had on anyone.

Lance

—

Bill tried to phone Donna in Calgary. There was no answer. It was a weeknight, late, and the phone ringing in her house panicked him. He hung up on the answering machine and phoned Jeannie. Donna answered.

"Billy! It's you! We were just talking about you. We're drinking."

"You're still down there."

"Again, not still. I went home, Elmer died. I came back."

"I'm sorry."

"No, no. It was good. Jeannie drove me back to Calgary, and that very night, he died. He died in his bed instead of at a vet's office. So I brought him here to the farm, and we gave him the nicest burial. Do you remember where we buried King?"

"Of course I remember. King was my dog."

"King was not your dog. But anyway, Elmer's buried right beside him now. It was sweet. I made Jeannie sing 'Comes a Time.' We cried like babies. So tell me, how's it with you? How's the shrink? Are you in love? Are you heartbroken? Gambling like an idiot? Back at work?"

"The psychologist is good. He and I go for dinner. We're calling it a friendship."

"God! You're not having *sex* with the man, are you?"

"No sex. The dinner thing is the only way he can take on a non-suicidal client."

"Okay. Just a minute, Jeannie's shrieking in my ear. She demands to know what's going on with you and the woman."

"I haven't seen Marie yet."

"But you're talking on the phone, right?"

"Actually, no."

"Oh boy. Jeannie! He hasn't even phoned her yet. Wait. Jeannie tells me to tell you you're a friggin' nutcase."

"The psychologist and I haven't talked about gambling yet. I didn't think I should talk to Marie until we had."

"Of course you've been talking about gambling! Whatever you talk about, Dad, Mom, Lance, Ginny, your kids, Marie, your job—*it's all about the gambling*!"

"I hadn't thought of that."

"Anyone with ordinary movie IQ would know that."

"So what are you saying? I should just phone her?"

"Yes!"

Bill was planning his phone call to Marie when the phone rang. He assumed it would be her. But it was Henry Shields.

"Bill, I hope you don't mind, I read that corrosion maintenance plan you left on your desk."

"That's good. It's probably the last thing I'll ever do in my career. Be a shame if nobody read it."

"It's great. I wanted to tell you."

"You don't have to shore up my ego, Henry. I'm fine."

"I'm phoning because Houle wants us to do a unit corrosion check. He's asking all the unit managers. It's plant-wide. Thing is, what he's asking for is almost exactly what you've done—only yours is better because it doesn't require shutdowns."

"If you're asking can you use it, be my guest."

"That's not it. What I want, with your permission, is to show Houle your plan. I'll say it was on your desk, I read it, and so on."

"I don't see the difference."

"What I want to suggest to Houle is that he ask you to come back and supervise the corrosion check, for the whole plant. Who better than the man with the plan?"

"Houle wouldn't have me on the place."

"I'm going to make a guess. I bet you haven't been watching the news much since you left."

"No."

"All hell's been breaking loose. University of Alberta released a study that proves more pollution is getting into the river than anybody ever admitted, a lot of it through snowmelt. The premier has publicly accepted the study as fact. There's talk of a federal-provincial action plan to revamp the river monitoring system."

"That's good. That's the right thing for once. But I don't see what it has to do with me."

"Suddenly everybody up here wants to look busy on the environment file. All Waddens Lake has done recently is blow up its hydrotreater and put the guy who evacuated the nearest Indian village on leave. That made the national news, by the way."

"Which is why Houle won't want me back."

"The opposite, big guy! If you and I were running New Aladdin, we'd be thinking, 'We had one guy who showed he cared about local Indians—and we put him on leave?' We'd be thinking, 'How can we beg this guy to come back?'"

"What do you want to do?"

"With your permission, I show Houle the corrosion maintenance plan. I tell him you'd be the right guy to put it in action plant-wide. If he doubts you'd be willing, I'll offer to run it by you."

"I'm not sure I would be willing."

"What would you want? Big raise? Public apology?"

"Why don't you ask him if he wants to try the corrosion plan first?"

He phoned Marie and asked her if she would go for dinner with him. She said she wouldn't come to the city because she was teaching in the morning, but he could drive out. Conditions were, he must bring no wine and leave by nine.

He phoned Joe Fistric and got the receptionist. When Joe came to the phone, he was annoyed.

"This is not within the rules."

"We have rules?"

"I have somebody coming in in about one minute. Get talking."

Bill said there was a possibility of his being asked to go back to work and that he was going to Marie Calfoux's for dinner. Did Joe have any advice about either?

"Keep a cool tool."

"What?"

"I'm joking. You're on your own."

While Marie grilled steaks, Bill went down the hall and looked out the back-facing window. The upgrader sulked above the treeline, a breathless dragon. He had no feelings for it now. He could take it; he could leave it—the ideal conditions for a horse trade, according to his father.

When they sat down at the table, they had a good long stare at each other. She had her hair tied back, her sweet ears showing. She was all pretty, this woman. He was full of fondness.

"You cleaned up good tonight," she told him.

"You look nice too."

"Your steak's getting cold."

They ate for a time in silence.

"You're happier than before," she said.

"I think so."

"Why?"

"I'm happy I called you. Happy you invited me out."

"There's other reasons, though."

"I had a good time with my sisters down south. They want to meet you."

"And what else?"

"The therapy's going well. I have no interest in gambling. Not a single urge."

After they put the dishes in the dishwasher, she decided a beer couldn't hurt and got a couple from the basement. The bottle she gave Bill was moist and chilly. They sat on the couch and touched the long-necks together.

Marie slid closer and put her head into the cup of his neck and shoulder. "I still don't think you told me *all* the reasons you're happy."

He told her about the plant, about Henry's phone call; what Henry was intending to do, with Bill's permission.

"After this beer, let's go for a walk," she said, "in the midnight sun."

They went along the lakeside trail, same one they had used when they went on snowshoes. Where the trees blocked the last of the houses from view, Marie stopped.

"So, do you think your boss will call?"

"Henry seems pretty sure. I'm not as certain."

"Do you want to go back to work there?"

"I'd want concessions. No more telling me what I can do and say around you. I'd have to be in charge of the corrosion plan. They'd have to give me the resources to do it right."

"Is that it?"

"It would have to be okay with you."

"Can you ask them to collect up all the copies of *Beading Our Future* and burn them?"

"Done."

She laughed and hooked her arm through his. They kept on along the squishing path.

7

Waddens Lake

WHEN HENRY ENTERED Theo Houle's office and sat, Theo did not speak. He finished reading a page and shot it into a basket on his desk.

"Henry."

"Yes."

"I've read the plan you gave me. We might be able to use some of it."

"That's great."

"Then there's Bill Ryder." Houle leaned forward until his chest touched the desk's edge. He placed his hands one on top of the other. "Henry, what you need to learn to go forward in your career is loyalty. You'll say to me you know what loyalty is, and that's why you're here. That's why you're recommending this plan and Bill Ryder to run it. You've done the two things because you're loyal to Bill."

"Well . . ."

"You can talk when I'm finished. If Bill Ryder is not loyal to this project or this company, then you are not loyal to this project or this company when you come here out of loyalty to Bill. It's an iron-clad fact that Bill Ryder will never set foot in this plant again. I will tell him so tomorrow morning. That is more than I should confide in you, because it is my unpleasant duty to inform you that this is your last day at Waddens Lake as well—your last hour of working for New Aladdin. When you leave my office, Mr. Hansen from security will go with you to your office so you can collect your effects. Then he'll escort you to your car, take your office keys, your ID, your gate pass, and your computer.

"What I regret in all this is that you are a top-notch young engineer. Except for this business with Bill Ryder, you would have been named as his replacement. Now that promotion will go to someone else. I wish you luck with your career, Henry. I suggest you get a lawyer who can talk to our lawyer about the conditions of your severance. I'm not willing to argue any of this with you, now or ever, but if you have questions relating to how we go forward, I'll put you in contact with an HR person in Calgary."

8

Highway 63

ON BILL'S DRIVE back to Fort McMurray, the sun was lowering into the forest. The final rays touched the tree horizon and gold splashed across the oil sands, making the strip mines, upgraders, and tailings ponds disappear. The land was reclaimed by light.

Bill was thinking of Marie and all the promise that now existed between them. He thought too of Tom and Ella, and his sisters, and of himself when he'd been Billy—of all the people, animals, and things whose fate it is to be born too close to the fire.

The shaking house, the creatures born dying, the rivers running discoloured to the sea.

ACKNOWLEDGEMENTS

Who By Fire brings together strands of experience from my personal life and my freelance writing life. In both these compartments, there are people I could thank for help with this novel—but I will not name them, partly because I'm not sure they would want to be thanked, and because many are not around to ask.

This novel is not autobiography even though I did live many experiences described in the story. Tom and Ella Ryder are not based on my father and mother, though I borrowed a trait or biographical element here or there. Likewise, the sisters are not my sisters, and the neighbours are not our neighbours. For one thing, I wanted to write a story less satisfying to live than my own family's. My parents were part of an air pollution lawsuit in the 1960s and '70s that resulted in a settlement. This came as a great surprise, for it was regarded as impossible for a few farmers to push oil companies hard enough to make them settle out of court. There were many sour gas plants in Alberta at the time with many rural neighbours who simply suffered the consequences, without feeling recognized or repaid. That is the reality I wanted to express.

I have dedicated this novel to my parents and sisters, and I thank them again now: my parents for their example of courage, and my sisters for their demonstration that we are still people who will put up a fight if things become unjust.

I do want to name and thank the late William Geddes, who during his career as an Edmonton lawyer helped translate civil law and government regulations into real obligations for industries that harmed their neighbours.

I owe a different kind of thanks to the people in the oil and gas industry who hired me over the years not just to celebrate their industry but to tell the truth about how it developed, disasters included. My portrayal of Lance Evert as an idealistic oil and gas industry engineer comes from many people I have known. Industry-community relations have always had an adversarial side, but it was not for lack of determination by individuals inside the industry to improve things like sulphur recovery from sour gas. That said, the petroleum industry is in a destructive phase now, and governments have never been more averse to doing an honest job of regulation.

I thank environmentalists and scientists for their work on behalf of the planet—specifically David Suzuki and friends Andrew Nikiforuk and Sid Marty.

For the making of this book, I would like to thank, first of all, my great editor Martha Kanya-Forstner, whose guidance as I fought my way through various thickets of this story was always professional. I thank her too for never saying this book was good until she felt it was. My thanks to Kristin Cochrane and Doubleday Canada for another great experience. I thank my fine agent Anne McDermid.

At home, my wife Pamela Banting provides an atmosphere that is cheerful, literary, and engaged in the world every day. I benefit from this in countless ways and am always grateful. When we were not talking about this novel, we often were.

I have always been lucky to have a circle of friends and family who, collectively, keep me convinced of the value of literature and the value of writing. My thanks to Chris Fisher, Marina Endicott, Jack Parr, Greg Axelson, Merna Summers, Don Domanski, Caroline Adderson, Wade Bell, Curtis Gillespie, Gordon Pengilly, Kate Stenson, and Ted Stenson.